Transition

The Final Journey

Stella McMillan

Transition – *The Final Journey*
Stella McMillan
Copyright © 2019 Beverly Bree
Brisbane, Australia

ISBN: 0-9578813-7-1
ISBN 13: 978-0-9578813-7-2

Publisher: Beverly Bree
stellamcmillan.com
stellamcmillan.com.au

Cataloguing in publication data:

1. Metaphysical/Spiritual/Past Lives
2. Fiction

Contents

Transition – *The Final Journey* consists of four small books. Book Two, Book Three and Book Four are unrelated to the story of the Transition of Mary in Book One. The final section is: ***Guidelines to Self-Healing.***

Book Four – Page 185

Timelessness

Creeping away on the winds of the plain
blow the sands of time.
Curling away on the foam of the wave
blow the sands of time.
Thus, the Timelessness of everlasting life.

Coming to Earth for yet another life,
our Golden Age babes, fresh and alive;
our hope for the New Age yet revived.
With them, humanity's enlightenment arrives,
blown along on the sands of time.

Aquarius' dawn forever glowing a'bright.
The end is in sight; the end is in sight!
For ALL, 'tis time to soar – to take flight!
Another Age arrives and a Master alights,
blown along on the sands of time.

Alleluia! God Be Praised.

Stella McMillan

Transition

The Final Journey

Book One

Transition – *The Final Journey*

Chapter One
The Transition of Mary

Peace, silence and stillness permeated the room. The single bed in this private hospital room was surrounded by Mary's immediate family. Mary, with her eyes closed, was concentrating on her breathing as she willed her body to take one more breath. At what hour will my body give up the fight and accept its final fate, Mary wondered. There was no pain. There was no fear. All that she was experiencing in this now-moment was acceptance.

After all these years, how could it possibly have come to this, she queried, as the thoughts rolled on, with one following on directly from the previous thought. She had consciousness at present and she had hearing. Hearing was the last of the five physical senses to leave as the soul departed the physical body. She had read that observation somewhere.

Now, Mary was observing something else. She could see her family clearly. Her eldest daughter was seated by the side of the bed with her husband of three months standing as a statue would and directly behind her. He had his two hands resting on Karen's shoulders. Darren's comfort, support and love would be needed desperately in the weeks and months ahead, because Karen would need time to come to terms with her mother's passing.

Lucy was sitting in a chair beside Karen and she was holding Karen's hand. These two sisters had been inseparable always and, in age, there were only two years separating them. Mary had been thirty years of age when Karen was born. At the time, she had been married to her first husband, Tony, who had asked permission to be present today. Mary had refused. She did not want his overbearing nature and his disruptive energy to disturb her peaceful transition.

Tony had been a powerful and possessive influence in her life for twenty years. If she needed to describe him, it would be as the belligerent bully whose own needs superseded the needs of everyone else. Why had she been so weak that she had allowed him to dominate her for all of those wasted years, Mary questioned herself. She hoped that Karen would be stronger where Darren was concerned. He was twenty-eight years old and Mary had witnessed many traits in him that were reminiscent of ones, which Tony possessed. She hoped that Karen would be a little more forceful than her mother had been in this regard.

Lucy was holding the hand of her grandmother, also, and all four members of her first family were sitting on the left side of the bed. They would support one another through this family tragedy, Mary knew, because her departure would leave a gap in their lives. Gran, as Mary's mother was known affectionately, had celebrated her eightieth birthday some months earlier and Mary had chosen to withhold her own devastating news from her family until after that wonderful milestone had been celebrated in style.

There was a tight grip on Mary's left hand as Karen clutched her mother more firmly as though she wished to hold onto her forever and to never let her go. Mary turned her attention to the right side of the bed. There were three members of her immediate family sitting there. Peter, her second husband, had tears streaming unashamedly from his eyes. Seated on either side of Peter were their two children. Alana was fifteen years now while Ben was fourteen years old. Both were clinging to their father, with their arms wound through his arms as they sat rigid in the chairs. All seven closest members of her family were present and they were in deep shock. She loved them all so dearly and she did not want to be parted from them for one, single minute. Yet, today, it appeared that she would be doing so and this parting would be permanent, presumably.

Outside the hospital window, she could see the traffic streaming along the busy road. She could see people moving from the cars in the hospital car park and walking towards the main entrance to the hospital. Everyone outside of this room was going about these normal activities in their lives on a day that was normal no longer, from Mary's perspective.

Fifty-five years ago, she had come while tumbling into this world many weeks ahead of schedule. Now, she was leaving this physical reality and many years ahead of schedule as far as she was concerned, because she had much that she wished to accomplish. There was no time. Time was something that was being denied to her. And, why, she did not know.

Her mother, Maria, who was stunned obviously by what was occurring with her youngest daughter today, had witnessed the passing of many friends and other family members before now. She had not expected to be saying farewell to one of her own children who was leaving ahead of her.

Mary surveyed them all – one-by-one – before turning her attention to the peacefully-sleeping form in the bed as she floated above it. It was in this moment that she asked the obvious question of herself. How was it possible to be viewing all of her family members so clearly and to be feeling their pain so acutely when her own eyes were closed?

To this question, Mary did not have an answer.

Chapter Two

Glancing around the room, Mary realised that there were many people present to witness her transition. Most of those who had appeared from nowhere seemingly were family members and friends who had made the great transition ahead of her. She recognised some of them instantly from family photograph albums and she was somewhat surprised.

Amongst the welcoming party, there were at least two males who had declared forcefully to her on separate occasions that there was no life after death, because everything just faded to black. Yet, here they were before her and along with everyone who was present this day, they were sporting wide grins or beaming smiles of welcome.

She studied two other males and two females who were unknown to her. They were dressed in long, flowing white gowns and they were standing to one side as though waiting their turn to welcome her home. Suddenly, two women who had been her aunts in this physical life grasped her hands and they whisked her out through the doorway.

Once outside the hospital room, Mary was surprised by her unusual surroundings. She was in an area that resembled a massive aircraft hanger while immediately ahead, there was a line of approximately twelve travelators and all were moving in the same direction.

Many groups of people stepped onto these moving tracks. Everyone was laughing and joking together. There were one or two people who appeared to be making the transition alone, but for the most part, the returning travellers were greeted by family and friends, with the reunions being joyous events for all of those concerned.

Mary's group proceeded slowly along to the nearest travelator and stepped aboard. She noticed that the four strangers, who were wearing long, white robes tagged along at the back of Mary's entourage. Puzzled, she questioned one of her aunts regarding the identity of these people and the reason that they were accompanying her group. Her aunt explained that these were Mary's own special Spirit Guides whom she knew well. They greeted her always on her return after every transition.

Surprised by the explanation, Mary turned to survey them as she wondered at the statement regarding every transition. Surely, this was the first time that she had passed through the veil of physical death? How could it be otherwise? She had been taught from birth that we had but one-life-only to become perfect in God's Eyes. The reincarnation theory was nothing more than a smoke-screen to lead unsuspecting recruits on a wild-goose-chase and away from the one True Religion, to which Mary had belonged for all of her life. There was no doubt on that score.

As she stepped from the travelator, Mary found herself facing two escalators – one ascending and one descending – while to her right, she observed a set of double doors. At the base of the escalators, there were two males who were dressed in white shirts and white trousers, with knee-high black boots and who were standing guard there, obviously.

One man who was travelling alone stepped from the travelator. He appeared to be a business man, because he was dressed in a dark grey suit while sporting a dark grey tie over a white shirt. He appeared to be approximately fifty years of age and, as with everyone else, he approached one of the escalators.

Immediately, one of the guards stepped in front of him. The guard raised the implement in his hand and the rod began to glow brightly. With it, he directed this new arrival to the set of double doors. The implement that he was holding resembled a laser rod as depicted in science fiction movies.

Mary witnessed the surprised glance that the gentleman gave to the guard before he followed the directive and walked slowly towards the doors, which opened automatically as he approached. The doors had a black line painted down the centre and this was jagged as it resembled a lightning streak. The colours depicted on either side of the lightning streak were bright red on one side and bright orange on the other side.

When the doors separated, Mary observed a large reception room, with a desk in the centre and another guard stood behind the desk. He raised his arm and, without speaking, he directed the new arrival towards a curved staircase to the left of the desk or front counter. The area reminded Mary of a hotel lobby. The staircase was bright orange in colour, with its carpeted area being a burnt orange shade. There were only two steps up to the next level.

As the gentleman moved from the steps, he was facing another travelator, which disappeared down a long, dark corridor. Mary surveyed him until he disappeared from her view. To the right of the desk, there was another single door and its surrounds were glowing in a bright red colour. There was a glass section in the centre of the door. Through the glass, Mary noticed that there was another travelator visible. This apparatus disappeared down another long, dark corridor, also.

Slowly, the double-doors closed and that area was removed from her vision. Her merry group of travellers pulled Mary to the left side and away from the two escalators. The guards who were standing there were laughing and joking with everyone and the whole atmosphere was one of frivolity and laughter.

The other section of this aircraft hangar where they were approaching now seemed to be a large cafeteria, which stretched for the full length of the building. It was well-patronised this day and there were tables and chairs everywhere. There were few vacant tables, she noted. Along the long wall, there were counters where drinks could be procured although Mary did not see any food being eaten or displayed here.

Somewhat nonplussed, she continued to swivel her head as she studied the whole area. It all seemed very familiar. She knew that she had visited this place previously, but she could not recall the occasion. One of her group located an empty table while another left to procure refreshments for everyone. There did not appear to be any form of trade or barter and no money was exchanged.

Everyone settled at the table and awaited the return of the young lady who was attending to the refreshments. Another older lady took a hold of Mary's hand and she squeezed it gently.

"Where am I?" Mary asked, with a deep frown on her forehead. "What is happening here?"

"Don't be concerned, dear. It is always something of a shock when we return here as we try to understand what is occurring. It is especially so for those who have been conditioned to believe that there is only a heaven or a hell awaiting them, with nothing in-between. As you have probably realised, this is merely the first stage of your own transition. Don't be afraid. There is only love here while hell is nothing more than an earthly illusion," she stated softly and matter-of-factly.

"I don't understand," Mary murmured. "Why has no one explained anything to me before now? And, who are those men and women standing by the table and wearing long white gowns?"

"They are your Guides, as I mentioned earlier. They will take you to a place of healing shortly. You need much healing before you can begin to come to terms with what has happened. After all, you have spent many decades on Earth in physical form. Your physical body has been discarded now and it is in the throes of disintegration. You have returned to your on-going permanent life and some period of adjustment is necessary."

"But, I am alive still! Why are you the only one to speak to me? I have been visiting here for what seems like ages. What is your name?"

"I am known as *Elizabeth* and I was your aunt when you were back there in that other realm. You probably don't remember me, as I passed over when you were a small child. When you accept that your physical life was a temporary experience while the wondrous place where you are going now is your permanent home or reality, all of this will make sense to you. After that, acceptance will come."

"But, I must return to my family. They are all in shock and, especially my children. How will they cope without me? I must return. I need to see them . . . please."

Elizabeth smiled at Mary and nodded her head slowly.

"Yes, of course, you wish to see them. That is a normal and natural reaction. We all experience it . . . some to a lesser degree than others, mind you. You have free will and you can return there at any time. Bear in mind though that while you can see them, they will not see you or know of your presence in their midst, so you will not be able to intervene in any way whatsoever. Their grief and sorrow will be raw. You can place your arms around them in comfort, but they will not know you are with them. Such is the tragedy of Earth, as the consciousness of those who are incarnate there was altered many centuries earlier and death in that realm is regarded as a permanent parting now, unfortunately."

Mary remained still as she absorbed Elizabeth's words that were contrary to her own beliefs. She had an urgent need to be with her own family. All else must wait.

Chapter Three

Together, they sipped the beverages and Mary noted that the liquid tasted of a combination of pineapple and orange. This was more of a sensation that she was experiencing rather than an actual taste, she realised. She did not understand anything that was happening to her currently.

Without communicating again, they stood to leave. As they did so, Elizabeth took Mary's hand. She led her gently and slowly to where the four people who were dressed in white gowns were waiting patiently. Mary, Elizabeth and the Spirit Guides walked towards the escalators, with the other members of Mary's entourage following closely behind them. Unlike the incident with the businessman, the guards smiled as they allowed them to pass. Her party ascended to the next level and, as she stepped from the moving staircase, Mary surveyed her immediate surroundings.

Directly in front of her, she observed an opening, which was bathed in a bright golden-white light that was blinding and, which almost obscured the set of white double doors there. She turned to her right and noticed two elevator doors that were closed. On her left were two more closed elevator doors.

Surprisingly, every door was a different colour, with these ranging from green to blue to purple. The fifth door was yellow in colour. The purple one was shimmering as though it were a brilliant amethyst on display there.

"These are the colours of our chakras or energy centres," Elizabeth stated, and she seemed to be speaking almost in a whisper.

The door to the green elevator slid open and their whole party stepped inside, Mary included. After the doors closed, there was silence for a few short moments before the doors opened again. Elizabeth and Mary, along with the four

Spirit Guides, moved from the ascending vehicle. The remainder of the party continued on while giving a brief wave as the green door closed.

They were standing now in a large reception room that was completely white. Everything was white, including the desk, chairs and sofas that were scattered around the room. Several doors that led to other rooms stood open and Elizabeth guided Mary towards one of these rooms. Inside, there was a healing bed, which was referred to sometimes as a massage table in Mary's former world. Mary, at Elizabeth's suggestion, settled onto the bed while Elizabeth placed a white pillow beneath her head before covering her with a white blanket.

"I will remain with you for a short time as your Guides take over from here," Elizabeth stated. "Just relax as you enjoy this wonderful healing experience. Close your eyes and concentrate on the brilliant white light that you can see there."

One of the female Guides moved to Mary's head and placed her hands there. The other female stood with her hands on Mary's heart centre while the male Guides stood close by them. Elizabeth took a hold of her feet as Mary succumbed to the peace and silence surrounding her. Elizabeth closed her eyes.

Mesmerised, Mary watched as brilliant shafts of white light shot from the heart centres of all those who were surrounding her now. Mary closed her eyes as the sound of lilting voices that were raised in song, began swirling around her. The surreal sound had an immediate effect on Mary. She felt as though she was floating on air. Then, a brilliant white light appeared, as Elizabeth had predicted. Imperceptibly, a feeling of weightlessness overwhelmed Mary as she felt herself being submerged in light. Her consciousness appeared to be suspended as no thoughts came into her mind. She felt intoxicated by the waves of energy that were flowing over, in and around her. The feeling could be described only as one of sheer bliss.

The bed began to move very slowly and in a clockwise motion. Consciousness left her.

Chapter Four

Almost imperceptibly, Mary became aware of another reality. She had flipped back in time and she felt as though she was watching a video clip. She was in a schoolyard. She was seven years old again and playing with her group of special friends. Another little girl approached their group of five children and she asked to play with them. Mary was the ring-leader and she made the immediate decision that this was not acceptable. She refused permission without consulting with anyone else in her group. She ordered the newcomer to go away.

She observed the distraught expression on the girl's face and she appeared as though she was about to burst into tears. As the little girl walked slowly away, Mary was overwhelmed by a sense of power. Then, she noticed the loneliness that was permeating the child's aura. She was horrified at her own actions back then and devastated that there was no way of redressing the situation all of these decades on from that event, brief though it was. How could she have been as cruel and as callous as that at such a young age, she queried of herself.

While she was contemplating the situation, another vision presented itself to her. This incident had occurred at a period in her life when she was fourteen years of age. One after another, the visions kept coming to her. These incidents from her life were viewed from the perspective of the casual observer, but these were fragments of Mary's life that were being replayed before her stunned gaze. The visions came in a series of eight segments, with every segment depicting approximately a seven-year period. With her fifty-sixth birthday on the horizon for her at the time of her physical demise, these dramatic segments were showing to Mary the life that she had endured and enjoyed from birth to death.

As with a video clip, when the segments concluded, the recording appeared to be placed in a file, which she knew consisted of all of the other video clips from her other incarnations in physical form on Planet Earth. She felt that one of her Spirit Guides completed this task of filing away the history of her ongoing, eternal life.

What an amazing – as well as a startling – revelation for Mary!

She rose slowly from the bed. When she walked away from the healing room, many thoughts were racing one after another through her somewhat-confused mind. Her Spirit Guides, including Elizabeth, remained in the room.

Once outside, she was joined by another Spirit Guide who was a stranger to her. He introduced himself to her. His name was Gabriel and he asked Mary if she had any questions that she wished to ask of him. She stared at him in stunned silence for some moments before nodding her head furiously and in the affirmative. Then, Gabriel walked beside her. He led her into a common room that was deserted at present.

At his direction, she sat down on an armchair, which was positioned in such a way that she had an uninterrupted view of an obviously lovingly-tended garden. This peaceful setting brought serenity to her as she watched Gabriel who made himself comfortable on the blue couch that was positioned opposite her. He stated that he would endeavour to answer all of her questions as succinctly as possible. There were so many questions buzzing around in her mind that she asked the most obvious and the simplest one first.

"The drink I consumed in the cafeteria earlier . . . how was that possible if I've really died and I possess a physical body no longer?"

"The exercise was simply to make you feel more comfortable in your new surroundings, so that you would not go into fear over your separation from your physical form.

After all, it has been your current vehicle for fifty-five years of Earth-time. The permanent parting from the body can be a frightening experience for some people. The liquid that you drank simply dissipated and transformed into Light once it reached your mouth," Gabriel explained.

"That's amazing!"

"No, it is just a normal and natural sequence of events."

"What do you mean by Light?"

"I refer to Divine Light."

"I see," she replied, although she did not understand at all. "So, what happens with me from here?"

"When you have exhausted your questions, I will escort you to a transitional area. Once there, you can consult with your Guides and you can come to a decision on your future. You will have the choice to return immediately to another physical form, if you so choose."

"As a baby, you mean?"

"Precisely!" he replied. "However, that is not advisable and I would advise against such a hasty move. Many who return here cannot wait to go back to physical form after the healing process has been completed. Unfortunately, they do so in haste and they find their next incarnation more stressful than the previous one. It is advisable to enjoy a period of rest and relaxation here on the Astral Plane before embarking on another life-experience on that lower level of existence where negativity pervades all areas of physical life."

"You mean take a vacation?"

"In a manner of speaking, yes," he stated. "It cannot hurt to rest for awhile. There is much enjoyment to be had here while in the company of life-long friends. I advise always to adhere to the four R's."

"Which are?"

"Return . . . Review . . . Rest . . . Relax!"

"I can't accept this nonsense about reincarnation. I'm sure this is simply a dream that I'm experiencing here with you and I will wake up soon in my own bed."

"That is a normal and natural response for everyone who returns. There may be exceptions now and then, but these are ones who are more advanced spiritually and who accept death as nothing more than another transitional phase of their ongoing life," Gabriel explained.

"I enrolled in a course on Buddhism once. The tutors were saying something similar, except that they saw life as one, long, never-ending river. As someone steps from one physical body, he or she steps into another one immediately. There was no return, review, rest and relaxation for them!" Mary stated somewhat forcefully.

"As to your thoughts, so shall it be."

"Okay, what about ones who believe that everything turns to black at the moment of death and there is no afterlife whatsoever?"

"Once again, it is the same answer . . . as to your thoughts, so shall it be. However, there will come a time when these ones will become tired of wandering around in their self-imposed darkness and they will begin to seek another alternative. Once that moment arrives, they will see the Light!"

"If what you're saying has one sliver of truth to it, explain to me how you view this never-ending saga of birth, life, death and re-birth?"

"I would say simply that the whole experience resembles a string of pearls," Gabriel stated, with eyebrows raised slightly.

"A string of pearls!" she exclaimed. "You'd better explain that to my somewhat-befuddled mind, which is on overload at present."

"Imagine a long string of pearls that is stretched out to its full length and resting on a piece of purple cloth. This is no ordinary string of pearls though. Every pearl is different from the one before and after it. Some are big, white and shining brightly. Others are grey and dull. Still others are small and white while there are a few little grey ones in-between. However, between every pearl on that long, long string is a clear, pure and sparkling diamond."

"I don't understand that description at all!"

"Look at it this way . . . individually; the small white pearls would represent a very short lifespan when the person concerned had passed over as a young child. Consequently, he or she . . . depending on the gender chosen freely before incarnation . . . would not have had time to become contaminated with the negativity of Earth. A large white one is consistent with a life lived in harmony and love, with little negativity being allowed to enter into one's thought-patterns. The small grey ones would signify a short life endured in negativity. And, so on it goes with our illusionary metaphor, with the different shades of grey depicting other lifetimes that were not lived in a manner that was to the liking of the returning soul-spirit," Gabriel explained. "With our diamond and pearl necklace, the diamonds in-between represent the rest periods spent recuperating between incarnations. Remember though, the long, long string that binds all of these pearls . . . or lifetimes . . . together is your ongoing and forever-long spirit-life. It is vitally important to remember this fact. This is the part, which is not accepted on Earth. It is why the old, worn-out and misguided *one-life-only* theory has gained such traction there and has become entrenched in the consciousness of many, unfortunately."

"Except, of course, for the Buddhists, as an example?" Mary interjected.

"Yes, I would agree. However, without our four R's of return, review, rest and relax, these ongoing and taxing lifetimes take their toll, eventually. Of course, there are exceptions to every rule. The exceptions here would be those who are operating at a very high energy frequency, due to the fact that they operate only by the Divine Love Principle in all that they say and do. This is a free-will choice on their part. By high frequency, I refer to the fact that their consciousness is attuned to Divine Love always and this shows in all that they say and do."

"You mean it's an energy thing?" she queried, before asking her next obvious question. "What happens with me now?"

"My suggestion would be that you walk in the garden for a short while. Allow all of the thoughts to drift through your mind. We can talk again a little later, after you have digested some of what we have discussed now. There is a door to your right. If you exit through there and follow the path, it will take you to a large lake. Boats and canoes litter the shoreline, so feel free to take one of those vessels and explore at your leisure. Return here when you are refreshed and we can talk some more. Try to accept that you have completed stage one and stage two. That is the Return and Review. When you have completed the Rest and Relaxation stages, you will be required to make a decision."

"What decision is that?"

"It is the decision as to whether you return to Earth in another physical form. If that is the preferred choice, much planning will be required, in consultation with your Guides-of-Light. This is necessary so that a placement can be arranged and one that is in accord with the higher ideals of your ongoing spirit-life, rather than the short-term wants and needs of a temporary physical existence."

"And, what is my other option?" Mary asked.

"This is to return to your permanent home on the Astral Level where your own very special spirit family awaits you with eager anticipation. If this is your choice, your etheric body will disintegrate slowly, just as your physical one is in the process of doing now. After that happens, you will be in your astral form. Once on the Astral Plane of existence, you will reside there until you feel the need to descend to the lower environs of Earth again. Hopefully, you will remain for much longer this time. That is their dearest wish, as well as my own."

"What of my family that I've left behind on Earth? They need me desperately."

"At this moment, your two families have joined together in a state of mourning as they make plans for your forthcoming funeral. They are coming to terms slowly with this final parting from you. Take your walk in the garden now, sweet one. Consider all that I have explained to you. I will join you there; or, you can return here. I am certain you will have many more questions. When you are ready, I will take you to your families who have remained behind in that lower realm. They will not see you, as was explained previously. However, this will set your mind at rest a little. They have no choice now. They must accept the inevitable, no matter how painful the parting has been. You must do so, also, in order to move on with your life – your ongoing, permanent life!"

Chapter Five

Slowly, Mary rose from the armchair and she walked towards the door that led to the garden. Gabriel stood and he watched her as she walked in a trance-like state. She descended the concrete ramp and he was lost to her view. She followed the path that led towards the massive lake. To her surprise, there were people in the water. They appeared to be in family groups, with adult males and females laughing together. Some children were present, also. She sat down beneath the branches of a large tree and she reclined against its massive trunk while, absentmindedly, studying the swimmers who were frolicking in the crystal-clear water.

Mary took stock of her surroundings for a few moments before her mind was besieged by many thoughts. These related to the discussion that she had undertaken with Gabriel not many minutes previously. Had that exchange really happened? Or, was this merely a dream-sequence that she was enduring? Perhaps, she would wake up shortly in her own bed in her safe physical world and life would go on as normal for her? To these questions, she did not have answers. Where to from here?

Finally, she made the decision to place all thoughts of this nature on-hold momentarily while she explored this magnificent garden. She would absorb the tantalising fragrance of the beautiful flowers and she would watch as the birds and the butterflies flitted from branch to branch. After that, she would return to the lake. There, she would attempt to come to terms with the explanation that her Guide, Gabriel, had given to her.

She knew, without doubt, that she must accept his offer to return with him to the physical world. There, she would view all of her family members and try to comfort them. If the situation was as Gabriel had explained to her, she would have no other option but to accept that she had died a natural death. At this present moment, she felt vibrant and alive, so she did not understand how it was possible to be dead.

This persistent thought was so abhorrent to her and so totally unbelievable that acceptance would be a long time coming, she knew. How could she have died? It was not possible. Death was something that happened to other people. It could not have happened to her. However, if this was a fact-of-life now, how would her family cope without her? And, what was to happen to her from this moment onwards, if this really was a present reality for her?

Finally, her mind accepted that this was nothing more than another dream-sequence. She would wake up soon. Everything would be normal in her real world.

Wandering around the garden alone, Mary tried to absorb what was happening to her. All that had been revealed to her was beyond her comprehension at this moment. She retraced her steps to the lake where family groups and other people were doing normal activities.

Here, she dropped down onto the lush grass on the bank of the lake. Mary dipped her feet into the cool, clear water while realising that her feet were bare. She noticed that she was wearing the lace nightgown, which had been on her physical body in the hospital bed. She wondered if the ones in the water could see her. If so, they would think that this was strange attire to be wearing in this pleasant and present environment. The day was bright and clear, with blue skies overhead and not a cloud to be seen anywhere.

She allowed a deep sigh to escape from her body. How was it possible to have a body, if she had died? To this question, she did not know the answer. What had Gabriel stated? He had mentioned an etheric body and an astral body. This, also, was beyond her comprehension now. There was much that she needed to know before understanding and acceptance would come, she decided. Then, she would be required to make a momentous decision, if Gabriel was to be believed.

She needed to see her family and, most especially, her children. Firstly, she would ask Gabriel to take her to them. If this was not a dream or, more succinctly, a nightmare, she would have to accept that her physical body could sustain life no longer and that it had died a natural death. Coming to terms with the fact that she was alive, despite her body having died, might take a little longer to absorb and to accept.

Secondly, Mary needed to discover what was to happen to her from this moment onwards. Where did one go from here, she pondered. Was there a place that was her permanent home, as Gabriel had stated? Were other family members who had passed beyond the veil-of-death already in that place and waiting for her? Would she locate her parents and other dear friends who had left Earth ahead of her?

Evidently, she was required to make a decision.

Chapter Six

Slowly, Mary made her way through the garden as she walked in the direction of the building where she had conversed with Gabriel. A bench seat came into view and he was seated there. Obviously, he was waiting for her.

"Come with me and I will take you to your family," he stated, as he rose from the seat.

She was elated. She walked beside him as they retraced their steps back to the enormous building, which she had left earlier. When they entered, Gabriel escorted Mary to an elevator that was situated in the foyer. Once inside and with her Guide at the controls, Mary felt the elevator descending. Suddenly, it came to an abrupt halt and they were in the foyer of yet another building. There were people wandering in through the massive glass doors that opened to a quaint bridge that spanned a moat.

Crossing the bridge in silence, they followed a cobbled-stone path for some distance before coming to the entrance to a tunnel. Once through the short tunnel, they arrived at an overgrown section of grass and bushes on top of an embankment. This unruly area seemed out-of-place in this pristine environment. Mary did not query him as they walked on in silence.

Finally, they scrambled down a rough pathway that led to a wire fence, through which they climbed before continuing along another rough track. Gabriel stopped beneath a massive oak tree and he took a hold of both of her hands.

"Just close your eyes momentarily. I will tell you when you can open them again. Will you trust me?"

Mary nodded her head in reply as she closed her eyes. When she was guided to open them, she was startled and a deep groan escaped from her. They were standing together at a graveside where a burial was taking place. The mourners were gathered around the priest who was conducting the sad and solemn ceremony.

All of Mary's family members were present, as well as her dear friends. Her children were being comforted by loved ones. Darren had his arm around Karen's shoulders while Lucy and Gran were seated on the chairs that had been provided by the open grave. They were gripping each other tightly, with hands interlinked. It was an extremely emotional scene.

Watching the scene before her, Mary had no option but to accept now the finality of the situation that was facing her in this present moment.

"Whenever you wish to be with anyone who is in physical form at any time, just close your eyes and *will it* to be so. Picture that person in your mind and request to be in his or her presence. In a blink, you will find yourself there."

Mary heard Gabriel's words as though these were coming from some distant place. Imperceptibly, she nodded her head, but the burial that she was witnessing in the graveyard was unbearable. She wanted to comfort them. She wanted to place her arms around them all individually and to assure them that she was alive still.

Slowly, she moved closer to her daughters. She walked by Darren and she stood on the other side of Karen. She placed an arm around her waist and her eldest daughter's sobbing increased markedly. Karen buried her head on Darren's shoulder.

From there, Mary moved to Lucy and repeated the embrace with her. Lucy clutched her grandmother more tightly in this moment. She crushed her older children to her – each one in turn. She loved them all so deeply. Finally, she moved to her second husband, Peter, as she endeavoured to support him. He was attempting to hide his grief and to be strong for his family. In this act, he was failing miserably.

Alana and Ben were standing on either side of him. Although barely able to stand himself, Peter was holding their two children extremely firmly.

Mary noticed that her first husband, Tony, was present. If those assembled around her open grave had known the full extent of his cruelty towards her and of his arrogant disregard for her feelings, they would have acted as-one and asked him to leave. Why had she kept that information from them? Why did she protect him to the extent that she had?

Perhaps, this was because she did not want her children to know how weak she had been and how cruel their father was. She did so to protect her children from her first marriage, she reiterated to herself. Her special friends knew the whole sorry saga. Those who were present were positioned quite a distance from Tony. Their demeanour was such that he would have been extremely unwise to approach any one of them. Obviously, he was not about to do so. He was present today from a sense of duty only, as well as to support their daughters, Karen and Lucy. That was patently clear to all assembled. He would leave as soon as it was practical to do so.

Chapter Seven

Mary watched as the coffin was lowered into the ground. The overwhelming feeling was one of disbelief. Until this moment, she had been able to delude herself into believing that this was nothing more than a dreadful dream, which she was enduring. In this moment, reality was upon her. She had died.

This fact of life was something, with which she would need to come to terms eventually. Currently, this was not possible. Watching the unbearable grief of her children and her husband, Peter, was more than she could stand. Glancing at Gabriel who was watching her intently, she pleaded with him to take her somewhere else. He nodded in understanding. Holding her two hands tightly, he guided her away from the grave. She glanced back over her shoulder one last time. Then, they moved to a small rotunda that was nearby and out of sight of the graveyard ceremony. Here, they sat side-by-side on the bench seat.

"The experience of watching your own burial is brutal, I know. It is necessary though. Otherwise, you will find it difficult to move beyond the earthly experience and onto greener pastures. Your life as Mary is over. You have a different identity here and a home that is waiting for you. It is your permanent place of residence and, it is waiting for you always at the end of every lifetime," Gabriel explained almost in a whisper. "Your name is *Melissa* when you are with us and between your incarnations elsewhere. We await your return eagerly always. Just as your earthly family treasures the years that you spent with them, your spirit family here waits patiently for your return after every visit down there, regardless of how long you remain on Earth. When you return, it takes a little while to come to terms with the transition. That is all."

"I don't think I'll ever move beyond this," she replied.

"You say that always . . . after every transition, you make that statement, as does everyone who returns to us . . . you are not alone in this belief; or, in the belief that you have only one life to live on Earth. That is the tragedy in all of this, you see. This is why the transition is so traumatic for most people. If ones of Earth could accept that this act has been carried out many times previously by all who are incarnate there at any point in time, I feel death would not be feared quite as much as it is. Also, their lives whilst in physical form would be lived in a more peaceful and, possibly a more loving manner. If you had conscious recall back to all of your other past lives while you were living in your most recent physical body, your whole attitude to life would have been very different."

"No matter how hard I try, I cannot see how I could have had more than one life."

"It is so," Gabriel replied. "It's an absolute fact-of-life. Perhaps you could view the whole process as a learning experience, with every lifetime being just one more semester in the college-of-life."

"What do you mean by my permanent place of residence?" Mary asked.

"I refer to your home here. It is waiting for you, as are all of your friends. You know them all so, so well. They are waiting anxiously to be reunited with you, even now as we speak. You will recognise them when you meet again, just as you will be pleasantly surprised by the sight of your home. After that, understanding will come, followed closely by acceptance. It is merely the false teachings of Earth that have dulled your memory temporarily and clouded your senses considerably. As with many others, your most likely reaction will be: 'Oh! No! Not again! How could I have been so blind and why did I believe all of the nonsense that was fed to me from birth?' It is as predictable as the sun rising in the east every morning."

Slowly, they rose and walked from the cemetery. Mary had seen all that she wanted to see this day. At a more convenient time, she would spend time with every one of her children individually. These plans were uppermost in her mind as they walked away. She did not look back.

"Where are we going now?" Mary asked, as they walked up the hill towards the embankment.

"We can return to the building where we conversed previously and, once there, I will explain a little more of this process for you. After that, you can take your time to consider your options. Spending a relaxing period at your home in this reality would be an excellent idea. You can enjoy a respite period with your friends and with members of your own extensive soul-family. Most of your earthly family in any given incarnation are from your own soul-family. It is when others of a lower energy and with other very different soul-family connections merge with your family on Earth that friction arises. You do realise that?"

"I don't understand that concept," Mary replied.

"Don't worry. It will all come back to you soon. Then, you will shake your head and laugh at your own folly in accepting the beliefs of Earth as gospel truth. I promise you it will be so."

While walking beside her Guide in silence for quite some distance, Mary allowed the thoughts to flow. The one thought that persisted was accepting the fact that she was dead . . . that *Mary existed no longer.* How was it possible to come to terms with a colossal idea such as that one was? All else paled into insignificance beside this mighty disclosure. What had Gabriel said? Her name here in this realm was *Melissa.* How was that possible? Mary did not know.

Finally, they entered the building. Gabriel led her to an escalator, upon which they stepped and ascended to the next level. This exercise brought another set of escalators to mind, so she broached that subject with him as he held a door open for her to enter the room.

"There was a man who was on that first travelator with me. He was travelling alone and he was dressed as a businessman. He was denied entry to the upper level and he was directed to the doors that were painted red and orange. He entered alone and he was sent to a set of steps that led to another travelator. Why did that happen? Why did the guards prevent him from coming where I came?"

"I cannot speak of specific personalities; you understand? Someone who is travelling alone is usually a person who has crossed over suddenly, as in the case of a sudden heart attack, possibly while at work," Gabriel stated. "The person may be someone who has shunned love in his or her many lifetimes and who needs to come to an understanding of the loneliness that he or she has inflicted on others previously. It is a very hard lesson and that would be why no one was there to greet a returning soul who is travelling alone. We are speaking of someone who has used the love of others to his or her advantage in many lifetimes, yet has forgotten that strong and powerful feeling in daily life. This person mistakes *desire* for *love* . . . by love, I refer to Divine Love. That is the most powerful feeling of all."

"But, why would the guards prevent that particular man from ascending to the level that I came up to?"

"Firstly, they are not guards, as you understand the term. These are great Beings-of-Light who are referred to as Guardians-of-Light. These are ones of a very high level spiritually, with a great capacity to feel love, this being Divine Love. As such, they can see the aura of a person very clearly and, more specifically, they are aware of the intent of everyone who arrives here. By the intent of the person, I refer to his or her consciousness and whether or not the person places the needs of others above their own wants and desires. This is shown very clearly in their surrounding energy field, which the Guardians-of-Light can view in a crystal-clear manner," Gabriel said. "In your former world of Earth, it is known as an aura; or, more specifically as one's auric field. Nothing can be hidden from the Guardians-of-Light and, most especially, someone's intent cannot be hidden. Do you understand, Melissa?"

Mary was taken aback by Gabriel's changing of her name. Whether or not this was deliberate on his part, she did not know. She was processing this thought when he spoke to her again.

"Just imagine for a moment that you are looking at a clown. You have people on Earth who dress as clowns to entertain children. Do you not?"

Slowly, Mary nodded her head, although she was uncertain as to where this conversation was heading.

"Looking at a clown dressed in his or her outfit, we can see all of the pompoms on the suit, including the one on the cap on the top of the head and the one at the area of the forehead. Just imagine that all of those pompoms were glowing with a different coloured light. On the top of the head, there would be a brilliant golden-white Light . . . this being Divine Light. Following on, there is one that has a purple glow and situated in the centre of the forehead. After that, there would be the blue one at the throat and the green one at the heart. Then, the next would be the yellow of the solar plexus, with the orange of the sacral area and with the red one at the base following on from there. In your world, these are referred to as energy centres or chakras. If someone presents to the Guardians and all of the upper chakras are closed or spinning in reverse, that person is directed to the lower astral plane for processing. Therefore, those who have all but the base and sacral chakras closed firmly would be of a very low energy level. The base or root chakra is the lowest one of all and anyone who is in this sorry state would be a person who was incapable of experiencing any aspect of Divine Love. When in physical form, this would be someone who performed unspeakable acts, such as murderers and paedophiles. These ones are base in nature, hence the use of the term base chakra," Gabriel stated firmly. "A person such as this would be directed to the red door and a travelator would transport the person concerned to a place where others of his or her ilk have gathered. It is the worse place to be sent."

"People like that are referred to as low-life sometimes," Mary commented. "The gentleman I saw was sent up some orange steps to another travelator."

"Anyone who is directed up there would be one who had preyed on others for all of his or her life and, one who would have exercised great power over them. He or she would be vibrating at the level of the sacral chakra. That is why the sacral chakra is often referred to as the power centre. Ones who have closed down all of their higher chakras over many, many lifetimes know no other way but to control others . . . and, to their own advantage always. There is much material written on your Earth that explains the chakra system. Many people understand the concept. A great spiritual master who has ascended to dizzy heights in a spiritual sense would have every energy centre pulsing with Divine Love and, this person would be considered to be an ascended master of great Divine Light and great Divine Love. There are many levels in-between," Gabriel said. "The Guardians-of-Light have their measure, you might say. They can see in an instant what the level and intent of a person is by a brief glance at the chakras. They direct accordingly."

"This is contrary to everything I have been taught. It seems incredible, especially as I belonged to the one True Religion on Earth. This was never taught."

"Every person who embraces a religion . . . and, I speak of all people down through all of the ages-of-time . . . has believed that the particular brand of religion, to which he or she belonged was the one True Religion. If it were otherwise, would they be there, do you think?"

To this question, Mary did not have an answer.

"Please, Gabriel, tell me what the colours of those energy centres represent. I need to know," Mary requested, as she remembered suddenly the colours of the elevator doors that were situated at the top of the escalators.

"These are well-known on Earth and are similar to the pompoms that I described on the clown's outfit. The brilliant golden-white Light at the crown is spectacular to witness. All Ascended Masters are at this level. Next comes the purple one at the third-eye in the centre of the forehead. Then, the blue of the throat is next, followed by the green of heart chakra. The solar plexus one is pulsing with a bright yellow glow while the two lower ones are the sacral, which is orange, and the base that is red."

"And, these all have a different meaning?" Mary asked.

"There are ones on Earth who are base in nature and, when someone such as this merges with your aura, you will definitely feel a distinct shudder, no matter how charismatic a character he or she is. This is indicative of someone who has closed down all of the higher chakras by free will. The sacral is power used without the energy of Divine Love to counter its misuse. The solar plexus is complete balance. Anyone who has closed this one is out-of-balance and a physical illness could follow in due course. The heart is the centre of Love, of course. This needs no explanation. If the heart chakra has been shut down, the person is in a sad and sorry state."

"I am not familiar with any of this information."

"You know it well, because you are a being of wisdom. Due to the negativity of Earth, it has slipped your memory. That is all," Gabriel smiled at her as he spoke. "Continuing on, we have the energy centre of the throat and this is blue while the third-eye is purple. So, it is all very simple. Depending on your spiritual understanding and the current level, at which you are attuned, this is where you are directed on your return to us. Coming from the crown, we have Divine Light, followed by the third-eye, which is Divine Wisdom. The throat is Divine Will. The heart, of course, is Divine Love while the solar plexus is Divine Order. The sacral chakra is Divine Power, as I explained previously. Many on the earth-plane misuse this one regularly and, this incurs a heavy penalty when they return to us. A karmic debt is added to their slate, one might say. The root or base chakra is Divine Life. That one does not require any explanation."

Mary was feeling overwhelmed by the information that Gabriel was imparting to her. Realising this fact, he suggested a short break. She wandered from the room, and without any difficulty whatsoever, she found her way back to the garden.

Chapter Eight

Leisurely, she strolled around the lake. Lost in deep contemplation, she walked slowly while trying to accept the information that she had received. She was haunted by the sight of the coffin being lowered into the grave. Was her physical body really inside that casket, she pondered. How was it possible when she was alive still?

She recalled how she had tried to fight off the signs of ageing while joining a gymnasium in recent years in order to keep her body active. However, once the illness was diagnosed, she had no other option but to rest and to fight its vicious onslaught. Was her physical body, in which she had walked around for fifty-five years of Earth-time really under six feet of dirt and dust while decaying rapidly? What an horrendous thought that one was, she told herself. She remembered how young and vibrant she had been as a teenager. How fast those years had flown.

Being thus occupied, she failed to observe a young couple running behind her. The lady, who was dressed in a swimsuit, ran ahead of her male companion. As she rushed by Mary, she called to her.

"Hi, Melissa, welcome home!" she called as she headed in the direction of the water. "Was it very traumatic for you this time around?"

Immediately, she dived into the water as Mary nodded her head in reply. Suddenly, the girl's male companion ran by Mary and, he moved in the direction of the water. He was intent on catching his companion and he did not appear to notice Mary by the water's edge. She watched momentarily while the couple frolicked together in the water. They were splashing each other and laughing as though they did not have a care in the world. The young girl's words began to swirl around and around in Mary's mind.

Was there truth in all that Gabriel had revealed to her? Had she really died? If so, why was that not the end of everything? Why was she wandering by this lake while her family members were in deep grief, because they had lost her? She needed to be with them again. She recalled Gabriel's words. He had said to picture the person in her mind and to state that she wished to be with them. She needed to will it to be so. How was it possible to do that, she wondered. How did one just will something to happen?

She sat down beside a tree and she reclined against the trunk. She closed her eyes. In her mind, she stated that she wished to be with her daughter, Karen. Concentrating on the vision that she had witnessed of Karen in deep distress as she stood by her mother's open grave, Mary relaxed as she willed herself to be beside Karen now. She was expecting her family to be at the cemetery still. Instead, she found herself on the back verandah of the home that her daughter shared with her husband, Darren.

Through the glass doors, Mary saw Darren inside the home while watching a football match on television. Karen was seated on a deck chair on the verandah. She was holding a large glass that contained a dark liquid. She knew that her daughter was drinking alcohol and, presumably, this was whisky, which was her usual habit at this hour of the night. Also, Mary realised this was not the first drink that Karen had consumed this night, as she appeared to be drowning her sorrows steadily. Mary moved to her and she placed her arms around her while hugging her daughter tightly. Karen began to sob. Then, the sobbing turned to an uncontrollable flow of tears and a deep sound of anguish escaped from her.

Why was her husband so uncaring that he would continue to watch the football match while his wife was in deep distress? Mary felt anger at this moment until she realised that Karen wanted to be alone so as to give vent to her pent-up emotions in private. The anger dissipated as quickly as it had arisen. Karen lifted her mobile telephone and pressed on the keys. She began to call Lucy's number. With relief flooding through her, Mary listened as these two sisters drew strength from each other on this dreadful night for them. Their conversation related to Mary and how much they loved her while admitting that they would miss her terribly. She had been the great rock in their lives since the moment of their birth. She had been there for them always.

This was a very long call, so Mary left the home. From there, her thoughts turned to Alana and Ben. She willed herself to be with her two younger children.

Mary located them. They were curled up together in Mary's king-size bed. Peter was seated in an armchair that he had moved into the bedroom, obviously. He was watching the same football match that Darren was watching. Alana was in a deep sleep while Ben was trying desperately to stay awake and he was attempting to follow the match on the television. However, his eyes kept closing. As she watched, he succumbed to sleep. Mary moved to the bed and she curled up between them. Shortly, she would visit Lucy, she decided.

She studied Peter and, as soon as he realised that the children were asleep, he allowed his tears to flow. He had stemmed the tide for as long as it was necessary, but now the floodgates had opened fully. He reached for the beer on the table beside him as he, also, proceeded to drown his sorrows this night. Mary's love for them all enveloped her and she wished desperately that she could be with them forever. Why had death come so swiftly? Why could she not have had another decade to enjoy their love and companionship? She had wanted to see the children through to adulthood, with her loving husband by her side. This wish was denied to her.

Mary remained with her second family until the match was over and Peter switched off the television and the light. He walked to the spare bedroom and prepared for bed while his wife watched from the doorway until she could bear it no more. Then, she willed herself to be with Lucy.

She discovered her second daughter on the couch in the living room. She was staring at the television screen that was blank. She moved to her and hugged her tightly as Lucy fought back her tears. In another bedroom, Mary found her mother. She was propped up in the bed with many pillows surrounding her as she watched a re-run of an old movie. Tears were streaming unashamedly down her face. These tears had nothing to do with the movie, which was a comedy. If it was meant to take her mind away from her daughter's sudden departure from this world, it was failing miserably.

A sudden movement to her right attracted Mary's attention. Gabriel was standing there by the bedroom doorway and he was studying Mary closely. The expression on his face was a combination of compassion and love intermingled there. He smiled at her.

"Come, sweet one. Nothing can be achieved here now," he stated. "You have witnessed your family and noticed their unresolved grief. You can come again and watch them as individually they go on with their daily lives and cope with their loss in their own way and at their own pace."

He held out his hand to her. Mary walked to him and she placed her hand in his comforting one. Together, they returned to the garden and, from there, they walked slowly back to the building where they had conversed earlier.

Chapter Nine

Seated on the blue couch once again, Gabriel studied Mary momentarily. She was sitting in an armchair and gazing with unseeing eyes through the window as she stared out at the garden. How long was she walking there before Gabriel came to collect her, she pondered. She decided to ask him. He was expecting her query, obviously. He answered before she had asked the question.

"You were wandering by the lake for only a short while. It may have seemed longer but, as time does not exist here, I cannot give you the exact number of seconds and minutes. Time is something that humankind invented. It keeps everyone running around in ever-decreasing circles as they attempt to accomplish more work and many other activities in an allotted timeframe. That keeps everyone on their toes. Does it not?"

"I suppose so. I had never considered that aspect," Mary replied. "Is my life really all over now?"

"Your life is never over. It is continuing even now, as we speak. You are here, in this now-moment, and we are conversing together. The reason that you were guided to return to your family to witness the burial of your physical form was to bring you to this understanding more quickly than may have occurred otherwise. Without this understanding, you would continue to cling to the notion that you were in a deep sleep in your own bed and this was nothing more than a dream, from which you would awaken shortly," he stated somewhat forcefully. "Your physical body requires much attention when you are occupying it. It needs to be fed, nurtured, clothed and housed. In order to accomplish these feats, the person occupying the body must work to earn a living to pay for the needs of that body. Some people have greater needs than others, depending on the belief-system of the one concerned. Here, there are no such requirements. In my world, you are free to enjoy the tranquil garden and to rest when necessary so that you can move on to your next chapter in peace and love."

"Can't I do that here?"

"Only temporarily, because this is merely a portal for the returning soul-spirit, so that he or she can accept the finality of what has occurred. When there is acceptance that the situation is final, a decision is required. You are almost at that point," Gabriel explained.

"I think many days have gone by in my old world, because the burial of my body would have taken place quite sometime after my death."

"That is correct," he replied.

Mary remained silent for a while as she attempted to understand the concept that Gabriel was presenting to her. She realised that had she been with her family and her friends after the burial, she would have been able to see them and to hear all that they were saying about her. Perhaps, this was why the often-spoken saying of *do not speak ill of the dead* was created. Possibly, it was for this very reason. The person who has died can see, hear and feel while not being able to communicate in any way with those who are holding the discussion about the deceased person. That was a very sobering thought, Mary decided.

"Tell me about all of the different levels that a person can reach, please, Gabriel."

He obliged and he began his explanation with the metaphor of the illusionary clown. He stated that when an Ascended Master decided to take physical form on Earth, he or she would do so for a specific reason. Usually, this was two-fold. One was to bring their great love and compassion down onto a darkened planet that was drenched in negativity. Possibly, the other reason would be to assist in expanding the spiritual understanding of ones with whom he or she was mingling at any point in Earth's history. It would never have been the intention of these Beings-of-Light that religions should be formed, so that their words and deeds could be used to enslave others. This had occurred often down through all of the ages-of-time on Earth. Gabriel explained that these great Ascended Beings operate at the highest level – or, vibration, if that is a clearer description. These Beings were the ones who came and went through the portal with the door that was glowing with a brilliant and shimmering golden-white light, he stated to Mary.

With the next glowing pompom on the clown suit, this being the one at the area of the third-eye, this would depict a person who possessed great spiritual wisdom and he or she would be operating at the level of Divine Wisdom. Then, this pompom – or, energy centre – would be open and shimmering brightly in a purple or amethyst colour. These Beings would return while utilising the purple elevator.

The throat chakra would be spinning freely and pulsing with a brilliant blue glow, because this is the area of Divine Will. The being concerned would be following Divine Will in every way. Therefore, this person would be following inner guidance and taking the main pathway that was predetermined prior to the incarnation commencing. Upon return, the blue elevator would be used.

With the heart chakra, this is the area of Divine Love. All great Ascended Masters would have this centre shimmering brightly and pulsing in accord with Divine Love. The green elevator would be the mode of transport for ones who have their three higher chakras closed while the heart is open and spinning freely.

The solar plexus chakra is the one that denotes balance, this being the balance between one's own male and female energy. It is the point of Divine Order. The yellow elevator would be used here in this instance, if all higher chakras were blocked with negativity.

With the two lower chakras, the sacral one is the point of Divine Power while the base or root chakra is the one that is responsible for Divine Life. Persons who are at this level would use the double doors with the lightning strike in the centre. The sacral chakra would be glowing with an orange hue, with all higher centres blocked. The base chakra person would be required to enter through the red door.

With an Ascended Master, as an example, he or she would be capable of creating miracles, for want of a better term, when in physical form. The Ascended Master could will a person to be healed of an illness, in accord with the Will of the Creator-of-All. No one else can do so. It is fruitless to attempt a healing such as this unless, of course, one is utilising the weapons of the negative world. This is a highly-unlikely scenario. By their words and deeds shall you know them; this is an oft-quoted phrase and it has a powerful ring-of-truth to it. Only those who are of the highest vibration or level can perform great achievements or miracles such as these. In times long past, great Beings-of-Light have walked the earth-plane often, with every chakra open and shimmering brightly.

At times such as these, their very presence would have caused great fear in those of the lower vibration who operated at this lower level due to their own freewill choices, which were made over many, many lifetimes. These lower ones have been afraid always of these Ascended Masters. Always, they do all in their power to discredit their words, downgrade their achievements and denigrate them endlessly, both before and after the death of the physical body occurred. Usually, the physical death of an Ascended Master is orchestrated by ones who operate at a very low level themselves and who are terrified that these Ones-of-Light will replace them in the earthly situation, especially if these low entities feel that there is a threat to their power-base at that moment-in-time. It is a tragic situation that occurs on Earth and a problem that appears to be insurmountable currently.

When all those with Divine Love shimmering in their hearts realise the truth of the situation, perhaps a change may be possible. That is a miracle yet to be achieved.

Chapter Ten

Once again, Mary walked by the lake. She was attempting to absorb all of the wisdom that Gabriel had imparted to her. At the same moment, she was trying to come to terms with the fact that she had died from the illness that beset her body and consumed it rapidly. This was not something that she could accept readily. Viewing her husband and her children, as well as the graveside ceremony, had given her a great jolt. Perhaps, even now, there was another explanation. Glancing ahead, she saw Gabriel. He was standing beneath the shade of a large oak tree. Obviously, he was waiting for her and she walked slowly over to where he was standing.

"Do you wish to speak with me again?" Mary queried.

"The moment has arrived when you need to make a decision, sweet one," he answered. "This is merely a portal, as I explained to you previously. There are many, many portals. Some are designed specifically for ones who are desirous of descending into physical form while others are here for the benefit of those who are returning to us following their sojourn in the physical realm, be that of a short or a long duration. The length of any lifetime spent in physical form on Earth is pre-determined by the one who plans the journey in the first place. The spans of life are arranged in segments of seven years. At the outset, you decided to visit for a set period of eight spans of life. Therefore, you were required to return to us prior to your fifty-sixth birthday occurring."

"Why on Earth would I do that?" she asked, while being staggered by this revelation.

"It was due to the fact that you felt this was ample time to accomplish all that you wished to do there."

"Did I do so?" Mary queried him again.

"That is for you to determine once you return to your permanent home and you can sit quietly while contemplating the situation," he replied. "I must take you to your home now. There, you will be greeted by your special friends . . . many of whom you will recognise immediately . . . as well as other members of your very extensive soul-family."

"Can I return here?"

"No, this is a portal for returning souls only, as I explained earlier. Once you are home again, you will come slowly to the understanding that you are seeking. You will do so in your own way and at your own pace," Gabriel stated firmly. "However, I should warn you that there will be much excitement and merriment when you arrive there. You are in for a great treat, believe me!"

Placing his arm through her arm, Gabriel guided Mary back up the pathway that led to the massive white building where they had conversed earlier. If Mary wished to describe this building, she would have to state that it resembled the one known as the *Taj Mahal* on Earth. Together, they entered at the ground floor level. Stopping in the foyer, he directed his next question to her.

"What is your decision? I must know it now."

"Are you asking me to choose between returning to Earth while entering the body of a baby? Is that what is on offer . . . a new identity with a new family while starting out again in physical form?"

Slowly, he nodded his head.

"Or, I can remain in this realm in the body that I am occupying now, whatever that is. Is that the choice?"

"Yes, those are the two options. Everyone faces these questions upon the return. You have passed through the Return and the Review stages. The Rest and the Relaxation stages await you. My advice is to remain here in this realm until you are ready to face another earthly experience. The body that you are using currently will dissipate slowly, if you decide to remain here. Usually, this exercise takes approximately three to five days of earth-time. The etheric body will disappear and you will be in your astral body completely. This is why ones who remain on Earth can see the departed person sometimes. It is because, in the early stages after a physical death, the etheric body is heavy and those who can see spirit-form will be capable of seeing the person who has died, supposedly. It is all very simple," Gabriel stated in a matter-of-fact tone. "What is your choice, sweet one?"

"I can't face another round of life in physical form just yet. I wish to remain here for the foreseeable future," Mary said firmly and with conviction.

"Then, let it be so."

Gabriel escorted her to the elevator that was waiting there. She stepped inside. He reached over to the panel and pressed on the indicator that was labelled as the rooftop. Then, to her surprise and alarm, he bade her farewell as he stepped back from the elevator doors.

"Why are you leaving me?" she called to him, almost in panic.

His beautiful smile was the last image that she had of him. The doors closed. The elevator began its rapid accent. Finally, the doors slid open and Mary stepped out into an area that, at first glance, resembled the interior of an old air raid shelter where people hid from the bombs that were being dropped from aircraft during the bombing raids of the Second World War. Puzzled and perplexed, she studied her surroundings. She did not know where to go from here.

Without warning, double doors that she had thought was a solid wall slid apart. She was peering out from her darkened prison cell into bright sunshine, which caused her to blink again and again. When she could focus clearly, she realised that there were many people waiting there. As one, they all began to clap and to cheer. Slowly, Mary stepped from the dark room and onto lush green grass.

"Welcome home, Melissa!" one man called to her.

As with a chant, everyone repeated his words of welcome as the applause continued unabated. Then, she was surrounded by this great group of people. Everyone was cheering loudly. Her homecoming was as joyous as it was unexpected. Buried deep within the folds of her friends, she was guided forward. Silhouetted against the blue sky was a shimmering white building and it was towards this structure that she was being led. Overwhelmed by the welcome, she studied her surroundings as the group, with Mary in the centre, stepped onto the large front verandah on the ground level of this two-storey building. With a deep sigh, she realised and accepted that she was home at last.

What a tremendous – though somewhat traumatic – journey it had been. Had she achieved all that she had set out to do at the outset? This was a question that would be answered in due course. For now, she would enjoy this wondrous homecoming party that was prepared for her enjoyment.

"Welcome home, my beautiful Melissa," the soft voice behind her stated. "I thought you'd never come!"

Turning slowly, she found herself wrapped in the arms of the love of her life, except that he was a taller version of her current husband. Peter was surrounded by a brilliant golden-white light, she noted, as she absorbed the deep love that they shared.

"How is this possible?" she whispered as she clung to him.

"I am the higher version of Peter, you might say. It will all come back to you soon. It always does," he murmured. "Just enjoy your spectacular homecoming. Truly, it is well-deserved."

He turned her to face the large group of people. There were so many faces. A glass was placed into her hand and she recognised it as a beverage that was similar to the one that she had consumed when she met with Elizabeth and others in the aircraft hangar upon her initial arrival in this realm. As she watched in stunned silence, everyone raised a glass high in the air. Peter stood behind her with his arms wrapped tightly around her waist. Suddenly, an extremely loud cheer rang out and the earlier greeting was repeated as they all called out in unison.

"Welcome home, Melissa!"

The Wall of Glass

There is a wall. This wall is made of clear glass. At various intervals along the length of the wall, openings exist. Every opening springs apart momentarily to allow entry and exit. On either side of this sparkling-clear wall is a magnificent garden that would be the envy of every king and queen on Earth.

This is a pristine environment where the sun shines permanently and, night does not exist on the upper level of the garden. The ones who reside on the upper level of the garden have no need of sleep, as they do not possess physical bodies. The ones on the lower side of the glass wall do not possess physical bodies either, but most are desirous of descending to Earth again to participate in the games that all are playing at that much lower level. Earth was a pristine environment once upon a time. However, as the consciousness of the ones residing there temporarily became immersed in day-to-day living, they forgot about the other world, to which they must return.

It was at this time that these ones of Earth began to be afraid of returning to the pristine garden that is their true home. They had become so preoccupied with the world, which they had created for themselves that they tried to hold onto it permanently. This was a fruitless endeavour, of course, because they had taken a journey to Earth and return they must to their true home. Their home on the Astral level was waiting for them at journey's end.

When they return, they must go first to the level of the garden that is on the earthly side of the glass wall. Here, they interact with their special friends and family members who have returned ahead of them. After they have completed the mandatory self-assessment of the life that they have endured and enjoyed on Earth, they are faced with a decision.

This, of course, is to choose where they reside for the next step on their road to perfection and full understanding. They can return to Earth while taking a new body and a new identity for the duration of that lifetime. Alternatively, they can choose to walk through one of the many entrances to the magnificent garden that exists beyond the illusionary veil of Earth's existence. Before they do so, however, they must make a commitment to the Divine Cause to redress any misdemeanours or errors committed during the previous excursion.

Let us assume that they make the freewill choice to return to the other side of the glass wall and to leave in abeyance the repayment of any karmic debt for a time. The garden beyond the glass wall consists of many sections and the area, to which ones ascend after an Earth excursion depends on many factors. The most important of these is the spiritual understanding of the returning ones. By this statement, I refer to a spiritual consciousness and understanding, rather than to simply a religious viewpoint.

Reaching the glass wall requires a little stamina, also, as these various entrances are positioned at intervals along its never-ending expanse. Before reaching the wall from the lower garden area, one must cross a suspension bridge that spans a deep ravine. In my next Discourse, I will describe the suspension bridge and the deep ravine in greater detail. The goal of all who take physical form on Earth is to return to the pristine garden beyond the magnificent glass wall. Some make it with ease. Some do not. The only requirement is a pure heart pulsing with the Divine Light and the Divine Love of Almighty God.

The Terrace

The terrace is situated within our garden. Our garden, therefore, consists of many sections or levels. Let us consider a place that we can call *the portal*. The portal is the place to where we ascend upon the moment of our physical death. Once we cross over the threshold (known as physical death), we are greeted by our friends and our family members who have passed beyond the veil previously. Here, we are joined by our main Guide and we are brought slowly to the realisation of the finality of the situation that is facing us in the present moment – just as occurred with our friend, Mary, in the story, **Transition.**

From the portal, we are taken to another garden. Let us proceed now from the portal area and walk slowly up a slope towards a suspension bridge that is a little distance away from where we are now. As we approach the bridge, we realise that it crosses a deep and very dark ravine. At the bottom of the ravine, we are surprised by the fact that there are people moving about down in that dark, dank area. Upon closer inspection, we spy some tents and other equipment that is associated usually with camping expeditions. Then, we move to the suspension bridge and step onto this structure.

Once across the other side, we are standing in a garden that is massive in size. There are people wandering around and most of these are in groups. They are chatting and laughing together as though they do not have a care in the world. There is a distinctly yellow hue to this area, almost as though the sun shines permanently here. We have reached the area that is attuned to the vibration of the **solar plexus** chakra. This is the place to where all those who vibrate at this frequency return after every sojourn down on Mother Earth.

We walk on and eventually, after what seems to be an eternity, we are stopped in our tracks by a massively high and impenetrable cliff face. The garden itself resembles an extremely large golf course with its pristine appearance and manicured lawns that are interspersed with tall trees. This is the area where many return after every lifetime endured and enjoyed on Earth.

The ones who reside between lifetimes in the ravine cannot rise to this level at all. However, their family and friends from this solar plexus level can travel down to the ravine via a platform that descends and/or ascends, depending upon which direction these ones wish to travel at any given time. The reverse cannot occur. Those who belong in the ravine, by their own freewill choices made when in physicality, must remain there indefinitely; or, until they choose to reincarnate on Earth. In that case, they must call upon the Guardians-of-Light who will arrange for one of their Guides-of-Light to visit with them to arrange for another incarnation on Earth. The ravine is the home of those whose energies are attuned to either **Divine Life (base or root chakra)**, or to **Divine Power (sacral chakra)**. When in physical embodiment, these ones crave power above all else.

Returning to the garden and to the terrace area where those who are attuned to **Divine Order**, at the level of the **solar plexus** chakra, live between incarnations, we observe a set of double doors. These doors are buried within the cliff face. As we approach, the doors slide open. We enter and the elevator ascends to the next level of the terrace.

We have reached an area that is bathed in a green hue. The doors slide open and we step out. We are in another immaculately and lovingly-tended garden. This is the area of the **Heart** chakra and those who have their heart chakras open and flowing freely with **Divine Love** can reside here during the time spent between incarnations on Earth. They can choose to visit the lower areas of Divine Order (solar plexus chakra), Divine Power (sacral chakra) and Divine Life (base chakra) whenever they wish while residing here, but they cannot access any area that is of a higher vibration or frequency than that of the heart chakra. It is not possible.

From here, it is permitted for ones who are attuned to higher frequencies and who are visitors to these lower levels, to access the escalators, which are positioned at various places along the cliff face that we come to as we walk in this particular area of the garden. The entire garden, we realise, is a series of terraces. These terraces are separated from one another by massively-high cliffs. Every terrace is vibrating at a different frequency and only those who are attuned to that frequency can reside there between incarnations on Earth. As water finds its own level, so too, do we upon our return to the Astral plane between lifetimes spent on Earth. This is why, when in physical form, we gravitate towards those who are our special friends between incarnations.

Sometimes, ones who are of a higher vibration enter our energy fields and we are buoyed by our association with them. Similarly, if ones of a lower frequency enter our auric fields, we experience discomfort, or sometimes a distinct shudder, especially if this new arrival belongs in the ravine during intervals between their lifetimes on Earth. That ravine is split into two sections, also. One section is where those who operate from the level of the sacral (or power) chakra reside. The other is where the ones who operate at the frequency of the base chakra live between incarnations. These lowest ones of all are the murderers and the paedophiles of society. Included here in the ravine are the ones who, down through the ages-of-time, have become known as the butchers-of-Earth. They have led great armies and they have committed grave atrocities, for which massive karmic debt has accrued. It would be impossible for them to repay those huge karmic debts while remaining sane when in physical form. They refuse to repay any debt while choosing to blame others always for the state, in which they find themselves now.

Stepping upon one of these escalators, we rise above the Heart level and we step onto another grass carpet. This terrace is similar to the other ones and, in the distance we spy another massively-high cliff. We have reached the level of **Throat** chakra and everything here has a distinctly blue glow about it. Those who reside here are ones who incarnate on Earth in order to teach others about spiritual truths and about the Law of Karma. This is the level of **Divine Will**.

We locate another escalator in the cliff face of this throat-chakra terrace and, stepping upon it, we ascend to the next level of the **Third Eye** chakra. Here, everything is glowing brightly in a purple light. Those who live at this level of **Divine Wisdom** possess great wisdom of a spiritual nature. This is where most wish to reside between incarnations on Earth. Many suffer great disappointment on their return to the Astral plane when they discover that access here is denied to them.

Above this area, there is no access, except for those who are vibrating at the frequency of the Masters-of-Light (in either male or female form). This is the level of the **Crown** chakra and it is pulsing with **Divine Light**. Great Masters-of-Light materialise there when necessary.

Between incarnations, we live, work, play and experience love at the section of the terrace that is available to us. We plan our next excursion to Earth, also, and we have every intention of rising to a higher level upon our return. Sometimes, and against the guidance of our Guides-of-Light, we set out to achieve almost-impossible goals. When we return, we are disappointed by our own efforts at the time of the mandatory self-assessment sessions afterwards. At other times, we are buoyed – elated even – at the great success that we have achieved as we discover that we have reached our pre-set goals.

This is how the whole system works. Whether we adhere – strictly or otherwise – to certain religious views, dogma or doctrines of a particular brand of religion when in physical embodiment makes no difference, if we do not live by God's One Great Law – and that is, of course, the Law of Unconditional Love. If Unconditional Love is our benchmark and our catchcry when on Earth while our Pure Intent is to spread this Divine Love and Divine Light, we will not be disappointed on our return to the Astral plane.

Peace on Earth, Goodwill to All and Love Unconditional to all who cross our path in any given moment – these are the Tenets of God's Law on Earth. For a peaceful Transition at the conclusion of this current earthly experience always abide by these Tenets of God and, all will be well. How could it be otherwise? However, this is a freewill planet. As always, it is a free will choice. Unconditional Love, combined with Pure Intent, will bring us Home in triumph and in great joy!

Discourses

Welcome – Onoraus

Come into my arms and rest awhile for my hugs are free. The Love of Spirit for our little ones in such distress is overwhelming and overflowing from our hearts to your hearts. The children of Light have so much to accomplish and such a very short time left, in which to accomplish all that they came to do. Walking in the Light and Love of God is the one step that will lead to all others. A step at a time is all that is necessary, but the first step is the most necessary of all if one is to begin the mammoth task that is ahead.

The task is to raise the consciousness of all who reside on Planet Earth. In so doing, the vibration of the planet is raised a little higher and, hopefully, the vibrations of some of her occupants, as well. It is a fervent hope of mine, dear children, that the lateness of the hour is not a deterrent to those seeking enlightenment for themselves and to enlighten others as a direct result of their own endeavours.

There is more to come by way of communication now that you have opened yourselves up to our Light and Love once more. We can assist you in so many ways now that you have opened yourselves up to our Light and Love. We can assist you in so many ways as you assist us so freely. It is time to return to your former state of Being where you would stand up and speak out. If you can work with us, your friends of Light, all will flow again for you in a spiritual sense.

Be strong, dear ones. Walk forward knowing that you have a great path to walk and your attempts to raise the consciousness of humankind will meet with success in many areas of your work. Go on with your plans with a carefree heart and Love for all, no matter how much they have hurt you.

Give your healing Light to those in need. Be at peace and know that you are Love and that you are loved.

Adieu,

I Am Onoraus

Onoraus
Gaia – The Mother

Gaia is the Mother. A mother nurtures, protects, heals, provides and loves, with an endless supply of Unconditional Love. The Love of the Mother is unsurpassed while, in most cultures, an image of the eternal mother nursing the infant in her arms is revered and respected by most. So, Gaia is the mother figure, regardless of the native-tongue or belief-system of any culture. The most well-known mother-figure is Earth herself.

Earth was revered as The Mother by the Essenes in times long-past. In that loving community, their Love for their Mother-Gaia was surpassed only by their unceasing and ever-increasing Love for what they termed, *Father-Sky*, the God-Source, their Source-of-all-life, Light, Love and Joy on Planet Earth. God was their own Source-of-All always and their prayers daily were centred around this central theme of Father Sky and Mother Earth providing their ALL in order that their physical forms could go on for another twenty-four hours of earthly existence. Beyond the next twenty-four hours, they did not bother to look, because this was irrelevant in their world. They had safe, secure homes to share with their families. They had a loving community, in which to reside and to work with others of like-mind and beliefs. Truly, their sanctuary was a heaven-on-Earth. They would strive daily to ensure it was so always.

Unfortunately, their *Light* became *too bright* for ones who were excluded to bear, so ultimately, they were slaughtered and destroyed. The attack came from without, but it was orchestrated by ones who had shared once their food, their hospitality and their Love. It was a boundless Love for All of God's Creations. It is possible for ones who walk in darkness to wish to remain in that state and to wish to bring all others down to their own chosen level of existence. It is an existence where the selfish-self rules rigidly.

If a person walks in God's Love and God's Light, that person is soft, gentle, kind and loving. All else comes from the personality-self that is steeped in negativity much of the time. This person cannot bear to be within the auric-field of someone who is *of Light* for too long, because The Light affects their own auric-field badly. They go into fear almost immediately and they respond and react to their fears in a negative manner. The higher the vibratory frequency of the Light-filled and Love-filled being, the more then is the size of the fear that is generated within the physical form of the one, who is in negativity by his or her own choice. For this reason, all loving communities on Earth are destroyed always on Planet Earth.

It is imperative that Earth or Gaia be protected. She needs immense help immediately now from those who reside on her. As one walks around on the ground beneath one's feet, does anyone stop to ponder that this is a beloved Creation-of-God, on which one treads for a time while in the current physical form that has been chosen for this particular sojourn on Gaia?

I ask this question only because as a Creation-of-God, she needs nurturing herself. She needs the protection, as well as the Love, of her children who walk upon her daily and who expect her to provide for their every need endlessly.

Gaia is in immediate and urgent need of help. She needs her children to stop for but one hour per day and to give her what she needs for her own survival. Gaia, at this stage, is at the point of giving up and asking God to intervene to save her from the ones who destroy her daily. Where will that leave the children who rely on her for their daily needs? In an unenviable position would be the answer. So, what is to be done?

The first solution would be for the children of Light to gather together on all of her energy centres on Earth's grid-system and to set up loving communities such as the one that the Essenes-of-old established at Qumran. These would be vulnerable at the outset, but when the tribulations come on Earth in earnest, many will see that this is the only solution and, in the final hour, they will attempt to join these loving establishments. However, this is where the problems will begin. They will try to change everything to their way of living, with their way of thinking that has destroyed Earth for centuries. They do not accept God. They do not acknowledge the Light of God. They reject the Love of God at their heart centres. Consequently, if they are permitted to force their will upon the majority of loving beings who established the community, it will be destroyed in a very short space of time.

If they cannot accept the Loving Principles and Guidance of the ones who established the community in Love at the outset, then for the good of the whole, they must be asked to move on and to go elsewhere to set up their own establishments while following their own rules and regulations. These have not worked in the past. If they had, then Mother Earth and those who reside on her would not be in the mess that exists currently.

No amount of Guidance – from above or gentle persuasion from within – has been sufficient to allow our beautiful little ones to extract themselves from their self-made dilemma. It is imperative for the survival of humanity, not to mention Earth herself, that these words of wisdom are heeded now. Stop the insane running at the behest of the personality-self, and listen within to the soft, gentle, kind and loving Voice-of-Spirit-Within. That is the first and most natural step of all. Go and sit quietly on a mountain-top somewhere and – all alone – ponder on my words of wisdom.

Humanity has created the mess, in which Gaia finds herself now. It is humanity that needs to solve the problem in a gentle and loving way.

In a time long past, there was one on Earth, at the beginning of the Piscean Age, and he came to show another way of living. His words have been distorted here and there while his great lessons-of-life have been misinterpreted by ones who wished to control others. These ones have gone now, but their legacy lives on in the words that they left behind for their faithful followers to follow slavishly. It would take a being of immense courage to challenge these words and directives, rules and regulations now. Rather than confront or challenge, just walk away; then, their *ship* will be nothing but a giant Titanic sinking into oblivion as she disappears beneath the waves. As she does so, the cables linking this gigantic ship to the continents of the world will snap one-by-one, and her directives will be heard no more. It is beyond a time where these misrepresentations can be returned to their pristine glory.

The original Precepts and Principles followed by the Essenes of Qumran were the same ones as set down in the original Ark of the Covenant that came from Atlantean times and that survived, by the Grace of God, those horrendous times of destruction on Earth. It is a repeat of those horrendous times that we are endeavouring to prevent – or, at best, delay – with our warnings, our predictions and our gentle, loving persuasion. Time is very short now. Do not be misled by ones who tell you otherwise. Gaia is dying. She is choking to death from the pollution of her waterways. Her ice-caps are melting at an alarming rate. Before what you term the *industrial revolution,* this was unheard of, and unseen on this planet. Turn back the clock two hundred years and live as ones did in the past. Shut down the oil wells; turn off the generators and begin to nurture, respect and love Gaia, for she provides your all. Every basic need that you have for survival in physical form on this planet is met by her. Can you not open your eyes a little and see that this is so?

What I am proposing is a radical change of lifestyle, but what is the alternative? The alternative is Divine Intervention, as occurred at the end times of Atlantis; and then, life began again on a pristine planet. Humanity was forced to rely on Father-Sky and Mother Earth, as the Essenes did voluntarily and lovingly all those centuries ago.

For many decades, this guidance and these warnings have been given to ones-of-Earth who will listen. Not many have, admittedly – but those who did and who have stepped out in faith now were destroyed in many ways, that being emotionally, physically, financially and by whatever means were available to those who walk in darkness and who know no other way, despite the words emanating from their lips and the great works that they, themselves, purport to do for God on Earth. So, deception abounds.

It is only by following one's own intuition coming from the Wisdom of Spirit-Within every individual that a way can be shown. Every way will be different as every being is different. Follow that gentle and loving Spirit-Within and walk in God's Light and God's Love only, from this moment forth.

If someone wishes to see a bigger picture, let us say that there are other ways to have one's current lifestyle. It would require a parcel of land that is what would be termed *freehold land*. By pooling resources with others of like-mind, pure intent and similar vibratory frequency, it is possible to have a place of safety for those who desire to escape what you term the *rat race* and who are anxious to have a safe place for one's family and friends, so that they can survive the turmoil and tribulations that are on your doorstep now, as I write these words of wisdom and caution.

Be discreet, even secretive, as you set up these establishments, because once you are seen as being *different*, you will become a target for those who live in fear and negativity. Love Unconditional will see you through these troubled times.

I cannot be more specific with regard to timing, but I can paint a picture for you, and this may give a small clue to some likely events. However, these are not set-in-concrete, as you say, but they are the most likely scenario that will occur, based on past events that occurred on Earth.

With regard to power that seems to be an essential part of daily life now, then turn to solar or wind power and store these in batteries. Have your basic water supplies and toiletry facilities that do not interfere with Earth and your own environment. Do not pollute the air or the water. Treasure the land, for it will provide your daily needs with regard to food supplies. The rain can fall easily on unpolluted landscapes, if God so wishes, but the first move must come from ones-of-Earth who show sincerity and love for all, including all animals, mammals and bird-life, which have within them the same Spirit-of-God that you yourself, possess. Without that spark-of-God, no one and nothing can survive in physical form ever.

So, there are a few clues with regard to living one's life in a pure and simple form. As far as timing goes, I refer you to the Planet of Jupiter that was hit by an asteroid, as you term it, and this sent great shock waves through that planet. Had this event occurred on Earth, the result would have been catastrophic, for it would have caused major loss of life and damage where it landed. It would have caused, also, a corresponding implosion on the opposite side of the planet as, unseen by the cameras of Earth, this occurred on Jupiter. What would have become of your skyscrapers and cities then, not to mention your hideous nuclear reactors? The thought does not bear contemplation, does it? Yet, to the amazement of all in my Realm, the event was not seen for what it was. What was it then? That great happening was a warning shot across-the-bow for all to witness.

If the great Being-of-Light who was known in your world as Jeshua-bar-Joseph (or, Jesus, son of Joseph) was born in the year 6BC, as seems to be the general consensus on Earth now, and if he were born at the commencement of that great Age-of-Man, known as the Piscean Age, perhaps Jupiter's spectacle happened at the moment of that anniversary and perhaps, from that moment onwards, his thirty-three year lifespan began. This would mean that there would be great changes in those last thirty-plus years. Those changes needed to commence at that time and they needed to begin with a massive change in the thinking of humanity.

Let us try a *what-if* scenario. What if the last century of Earth-time began with the horrific and deliberate assassination of Emperor Franz-Josef's nephew and heir that heralded the commencement of the hostilities, which became known as the war-to-end-all-wars – or, World War I? Has war ceased on Earth since then? Of course, it has not, because those who *live by the sword* do so in every incarnation that they have on Earth and their current ones are not exceptions to that rule. What if that terrible assassination heralded the countdown to the last century on Earth as a third dimensional planet and that, with the commencement of the Aquarian Age, great changes will come as Gaia begins her own ascent as she raises her own vibratory frequency to the level of the fourth dimension? Can the ones who are vibrating, by their own choice, because of their dense negativity, remain on her in physical form?

This event will be achieved with God's Great Assistance and God's Great Love. After that, the Golden Age babes will begin arriving en masse. Some have arrived already and they are recognised easily by the Light and Love of God shining brilliantly from their eyes.

The negative ones will leave the planet in droves, via the physical death experience, but they will not do so before they wreak as much havoc as is possible to achieve in the short time that is left to them. Know this as fact. Where does that leave the children of Light? In a great dilemma one would think unless, of course, they have heeded the warnings coming from deep within themselves, from their own heart centres, and they have acted on these warnings by silently, secretly and lovingly, in great sincerity and trust, set up their own *places-of-safety* as a refuge for their own family and friends who live only in God's Love and God's Light.

These are a few matters that needed to be brought to the attention of those who have eyes that can see beyond the five basic physical senses. Whether these children of Light, choose to act upon these warnings, remains to be seen. There is only one fact that is relevant here. Father-Sky has heard the pleas of Mother Earth, because her children would not listen as she begged for their assistance incessantly.

Gaia is on the move, dear child of the Light and Love of God. Are you going to move with her, in secret? Or, are you going to bury your head in the sand and pretend that life-on-Earth can go on as *normal?* Look on the planet as your astronauts see her, from afar, and you will have your answer as you witness her degradation and destruction. Set up your secret places. That is my advice to you. This advice is given in Love, with your best interests at heart and with the interests of Gaia as a main priority.

I AM a Lord of Light and I go, as a trouble-shooter does, at God's Direction, to bring peace and Love, along with positive and loving solutions, to places where trouble exists. There are many such Beings-of-Light watching over Gaia now as a great moment-of-truth and retribution dawns. I call it such, because the mistakes of the past, with regard to pollution and forest destruction – to name a few – have caught up with the inhabitants of the planet. It is not too late to redress the situation, but this current moment of Earth-time may be the last one that is available to those who are incarnate here now. That is a sobering thought; is it not?

So, change your way of thinking urgently. Change your way of living even more urgently. Life on Earth cannot go on the way it is for very much longer.

If the last one hundred years of the Piscean Age began with an assassination and the last thirty-three years of Grace began with an asteroid – and these time-frames may overlap each other – then time is short indeed. My words, as with many others written in a similar vein may be described as *mere rubbish* and *total fantasy*, even scaremongering. But, can the children-of-Light afford to ignore these and other warnings? Allow the children of darkness who have chosen to live in ignorance continue to do so until the bitter end. Do the children of Light who are wise, loving and resourceful in the extreme, need to remain with them to meet the same fate as they have orchestrated, by their own callous and thoughtless treatment of our once-beautiful Gaia? She was once the most beautiful jewel-in-the-crown in this, God's Twelfth Universe. Let her be so again.

I will leave you in my Peace and my Love, dear children of the Light and Love of God, as I leave you to ponder my words on a mountain-top, or in a deep meditative state somewhere, as you lose yourself in the Silence that is God Everlasting. These words have appeared on a page with the aid of a pen held in the hand of my own twin flame, Constella, who is incarnate on Earth currently. She is the one who will bear the brunt of the criticism that will be levelled when these words are made public.

Respond in Love, dear ones. Respond only in Love. Always remember that Spirit comes from God and Spirit is soft, gentle, kind and loving. How could it be otherwise? All else comes from the personality-self and conscious-mind combined, and these live in separation from God and God's Great Love for ALL Humanity. This is illusion taken to the extreme.

Walk away, sweet ones. Walk away from the illusion and from the negativity created by all those who live, happily or otherwise, in their own form of this illusion.

Please remember – Love is ALL there is. All else was born of and in illusion.

Peace be with you,

I AM Onoraus

SUMMARY

Symbolism

Needless to say, the Discourses regarding **The Wall of Glass** and **The Terrace** are symbolic. However, there are different levels that ones who pass over to the realm of Spirit at the time of their own transition are assigned. The level or terrace, to which one ascends, will depend on several factors, not the least of these being the degree of spiritual understanding that a person possesses. Karmic debt from this immediate past life and all of the other debts hanging over one's head from previous lifetimes is the determining factor, also. If one operates on a pay-as-you-go principle, the debt will be minimal. If one refuses to repay karmic debt for lifetime after lifetime while adding to the score with every subsequent life on Earth, the karma could be quite massive and a depressing situation for the one concerned.

The more debt that is repaid, the *lighter* is the Being concerned. With Light comes illumination always. If one opens oneself up to Divine Light, understanding of a spiritual nature comes quickly. If one follows the doctrines and dogma of certain religious institutions while in embodiment on Earth, the more one is stymied spiritually. This places great power in the hands of the self-appointed leaders of these institutions, also. Power corrupts. Great power corrupts greatly. Remember this fact always.

Read the Discourses in this book with discernment and draw your own conclusions. If reincarnation is an absolute fact-of life and we are all on our own individual spiritual journey, regardless of which realm we choose as our home at any given moment, we are fellow-travellers and we need support from others from time-to-time as our journey becomes tiresome and lonely.

Be wary of the ones who you choose as your fellow-companions, because some may have massive karmic debt that is beyond their ability to repay. Therefore, they may try to delay your journey; or worse still, they may attempt to hitch a ride with you, shall we say. Either way, your own spiritual journey could be derailed for a time – perhaps, even for the extent of one lifetime. You may become involved in seemingly worthwhile religious pursuits, as opposed to your own spiritual advancement. This event when it occurs in life causes great disappointment on your return to the Astral plane of Spirit as you realise that another lifetime has been wasted, so to speak, because you did not achieve the great goals that you had set for yourself before incarnation.

The greatest misconception on Earth is that the death of the physical body is the end of life. Life goes on endlessly. How could it be otherwise? You are Spirit first and foremost. You are a physical being who is taking a journey away from Home temporarily. When you step from your current physical form at the end of this lifetime, your physical body disintegrates, because you require it no longer. It is similar to removing a heavy overcoat when you enter your home after being caught out in a snowstorm. If ones-of-Earth could master this concept, life would not be quite so difficult when in physical embodiment.

If one could accept the fact that this is not the first excursion into physical life and that it will not be the last one for most, daily life would not be a grind and, hopefully, would be seen as a means to an end. The greatest prize of all is to reach a level on the Astral plane of Spirit where one is not required to return to Earth again. There is great joy and excitement when someone reaches that great goal. Truly, it is so.

The two main factors preventing ones-in-embodiment from reaching their final goal are clear. One relates to karmic debt and the fact that most keep repeating the patterns of past incarnations due to their inability to clear past trauma and the debt associated with it.

The second reason concerns spiritual awareness and understanding. This is where the current religious institutions come to the fore. If these establishments are promoting still the old, worn-out, one-life-only concept, they are doing a great disservice to their flock and to humanity as a whole. One must ask the question of who benefits from a deception such as this great one that was forced upon humanity fifteen centuries hence.

Keep your own counsel. Follow your own guidance that comes from your mighty Spirit-Self within. Walk your own pathway back to your Home that is waiting for you, and to your friends and soul-family who await you eagerly. Shine your great Light on all who cross your path in daily life. Send out your great Love to all who are in distress and need your assistance. This can be accomplished from afar, as most know.

By your Light and your Love, I refer to Divine Light and Divine Love that burn fiercely within all who walk a path back to the Light and Love of our great Divine Spirit. A way has been shown within the pages of these four small books. Take the words and meanings to your heart. If these do not feel right for you, discard them. If these resound within you, embrace them. It is oh-so-simple. Be at peace and know that you are loved more greatly than you can ever, ever imagine in your wildest dreams.

Adieu, Sweet Ones,
I Am Onoraus

Meditation One – Onoraus

Meet Your Loved One Halfway during Meditation

Walk with me awhile. There is a pathway that winds through tall trees with bush on either side. This is a secluded area where no one comes. We can be all alone here.

A little up ahead, the trees and bush thin out a little and we spy a large suspension bridge up ahead. Beneath the bridge, there is a dark, dank area that is decidedly out-of-place in this pristine environment.

Walk with me now as we cross the bridge together. Without glancing beneath, let us proceed to the other side. This is an area that resembles a well-tended golf course. However, there are no golfers present this day.

If we were to veer to our left, there is a slightly wooded area with a few tall trees. There is a two-seat swing with a brightly-coloured canopy waiting for us. Sit down on the swing and allow it to rock gently back and forth. This swing has an uninterrupted view across a deep ravine. On the other side of the ravine, there are people moving about while laughing and joking together, almost as though they do not have a care in the world.

The sky is a brilliant blue, without a trace of a cloud present. This whole area is bathed in brilliant sunshine and it seems to have a yellow glow to it.

This is our very special place. It is our meeting place. Anyone can come here, whether day or night, to meet with a loved one, who has passed over to the Astral Realm of Spirit.

As you allow the momentum of the swing to lull you into a detached and peaceful state, call your loved one to you as you make way for your special one to sit beside you. If you so desire, you can call upon your Guide-of-Light to be with you, also, as you ask for special protection to encompass you as a cloak would do while protecting all of your chakras and your spirit body from unwanted attention from anyone who was residing here at this level between incarnations on Earth.

You can raise your vibratory frequency during meditation to visit here. Your loved ones can come down to this level to meet with you here. If you wish to speak with your Guide-of-Light as you seek clarification for a problem that is troubling you, now is the time to do that, also. In this way, the veil-of-illusion that is known as *the death process* is wrenched aside and open communication with your special one is possible.

As you have crossed the bridge over the ravine, those lower entities cannot reach you. Also, you have asked God for a cloak-of-protection to encompass you completely, so you are safe from harm.

Do not allow interruptions from the physical world to disturb you either, for this is your special time alone with your loved one, or with your Guide. Open communication is not necessary either. Simply enjoy the great love that you share as you sit side-by-side on the swing, which is your special place that no one else knows about, because it is your secret.

Understand that, at this moment, neither one is in physical form. How could you be, because you have left your current physical form resting in your meditation place on Earth while you came to visit in the realm of Spirit?

Some may call this la-la-land, or other derogatory names. That is fine, as you know where you are and what you are doing in your special place during your deep meditative state. However, when you return to your physical form, you will need to close down all of your chakras one-by-one to tiny pinpoints of Light. Then, it is advisable to place a Shield-of-Light over your chakras in front, stretching from the Alpha Point above to the Omega Point beneath your feet. Bring another Shield-of-Light over the back while stretching from the Alpha to the Omega, thus sealing these together at both sides. For added protection, a mirror can be placed over each shield while reflecting all negativity back to the sender as you go on with your day.

Daily meditation sessions such as these can and will help greatly as you walk your paths back to full enlightenment while in physical form on Earth.

Do not forget the one great task that you set out to do before incarnating this time. Do you remember? Was it to ask your own Higher Self to perform this great task, on your behalf while you were here on this earthly journey?

That special task has been revealed within the pages of the complete book.

God speed you on your journey from here. Hopefully, this will be *The Final Journey* to Earth for you as you come Home to us in Divine Love and Divine Light.

In my great Love, I leave you.

I AM Onoraus

A more detailed version of this mediation, entitled *Final Meditation,* is revealed in Book Two.

God Speed, Gentle Starseeds

God speed, gentle starseeds,
so trusting, so true;
God speed, gentle starseeds,
in all that you do.

Your paths are so narrow,
so tiresome, so dark;
You long for security
as your road you embark.

Come, gentle starseeds,
take My Hand as you go
to tomorrow's new landscapes;
wherever life does flow.

Come, gentle starseeds,
leave all in the past.
Your thoughts turn to Home
as you open your hearts.

Allow God's Love to infuse,
to inspire and transform.
Come, gentle starseeds,
as God's Love you do draw.

You'll find a good reason
to follow your dreams.
Come, gentle starseeds,
follow where I do lead.

My Heart's overflowing
with Love for you all.
God speed, gentle starseeds,
hold My Hand lest you fall.

God speed, gentle starseeds,
over land and sea,
in city or country,
lands war-torn or free.

God speed, gentle starseeds,
come softly to Me.
In sweet, sweet surrender,
God speed thee to Me.

Stella McMillan – 26 December, 2001

The poem, **God Speed, Gentle Starseeds,** was published originally in 2013, as it was included in the seventh book of the **Stella McMillan Series:**
SUSPENSION – Between Two Realms –

Lamb of Love

The Dove of Peace descends this day.
The Lamb of Love comes to the fray.
The turmoil of Earth continues to play.
In a land far away, his head he did lay.

Far, far from turmoil of earthly care,
far, far from fear of earthly war,
in a place of beauty, free from fear,
the Great Southern Land protects him there.

His blanket is one of protection from harm.
His parents the Light of all who come
to see, to know, to follow, to form
the nucleus of a family formed in Love.

Divine Light, Divine Wisdom, Divine Will
are the hallmark signs of this child of Love.
Divine Love is his only signature still.
With Balance, Power and Life, he is above.

Above all, above Earth, above turmoil, strife –
guile unknown, he offers hope in life.
The Lamb of Love comes to still the flame,
to lighten the load, to heal – not enflame.

To enflame with a passion for God Everlasting
to a world torn apart, hatred rising,
He comes in Love, in Peace, in Blessed Joy.
Welcome him all, our precious golden boy!

Stella McMillan – 30 September, 2012

The poem, **Lamb of Love,** was published in 2013 in the book,
SUSPENSION – Between Two Realms –

Consciousness

To those of a *limited consciousness,* Earth is here to be exploited by them. Her riches are there for the taking.

To those of an *expanded consciousness,* Earth is here to be protected by them. Her riches are there to be held in trust for future generations.

To those of an *enlightened consciousness,* Earth is a precious treasure – there for all to behold. Her beauty is a source of joy and wonder.

Only those of an *enlightened consciousness* can view Gaia, the Mother:

From The Rim

From The Rim

From the Rim of Earth, I view her beneath me

The canopy of the night sky enfolds me.
The darkness of Earth troubles me.
Her oceans, her landmass, struggle to breathe.
She trembles; she quivers – longs to be free.

From the rim of Earth, I view feather-fingers.
These creep imperceptibly; their promise lingers.
Dawn spreads slowly over land and sea.
There is great promise. *Light* is all I see.

From the rim of Earth, I view an horizon of Light.
Love follows, on angels' wings, Divine Light.
Light cleanses. Love heals anew. So bright!
A new dawn is here – a wondrous sight.

From the rim of Earth, I view a new era of Love.
The vision so clear, viewed from above.
The darkness shatters and dissipates fast.
Humanity awakens joyfully at last.

From the rim of Earth, I know of a future bright.
I See; I Feel; I Know; I witness Light.
Love Everlasting, peace on Earth, goodwill all.
Divine Will, Divine Light, Divine Love re-born.

From the rim of Earth, I know hope rising;
Hatred, violence, retarded consciousness subsiding.
Love conquers all. Abandon old ways dividing.
As one, strangers embrace in Love unbridled.

From the rim of Earth, I view The Mother in fear.
She quakes; she quivers; the rock a-near.
With one, mighty shudder, she succumbs to fate.
Her children notice her plight too late.

From the rim of Earth, I view panic arise.
All running in panic, nowhere to hide
In God's Love, all could easily abide.
Fear is dominant emotion to rise.

When fire is quelled, damage reviewed.
Earth now populated by so very few.
The Mother now shattered and drained.
Her energy abated; her distress restrained.

"Where to from here?" all ask again.
"Help The Mother heal," comes the refrain.
"How?' is the question; "gently" comes reply
as the sun beats down from a clear sky.

Temperature rising; water so scarce;
food disappearing fast; animals scared.
Hope on horizon; rain appears from nowhere.
Crops peep from rejuvenated Earth.

As God takes away, God gives aplenty.
To ones who survive, appears great bounty.
Blessings are counted by those on surface.
Miracles recounted as life has purpose.

Purpose of life on Earth comes into question
by ones who possess a mind probing reason.
Reason is simple; world out-of-balance;
ones remaining rise to the challenge.

Earth on the mend; Mother smiling again;
her children toil in ways of times olden.
Happiness reigns. Hope springs eternally.
Father Sky, Mother Earth joined fourth-dimensionally.

All are One. Oneness resumed with above.
All toil together in Universal Love.
All play together in unbroken bond.
All pray together, bound by universal code.

Divine Intervention a necessary sequence
when children run rampant, denying consequence.
Unfortunate, but true, when Light, Love denied;
to Buddha/Christ Light, most were blind.

All clear; all cleansed; all healed presently.
The Mother shining so brightly in galaxy;
her rightful place resumed in heavenly sky.
Her vibratory frequency currently sky high.

From third to fourth dimension a quantum leap –
her population fought to keep her deep
in the quagmire of third dimensional life.
Her courage, in rising so fast, brought strife.

With turmoil behind her, Mother seeks to heal.
Her children shaken, saddened by experience real.
Many loved ones missing; didn't answer 'the call'.
Believed life could go on with no change at all.

Impossible feat to accomplish for most –
rising to fourth dimension a cause lost.
Those steeped in denial of Creator-of-All
were first to experience gigantic fall.

Wailing, weeping, as earthly return denied.
Understanding reason impossible for ones blind.
Blind to True Reality by own choice.
All others, in God's Love, rejoice!

Stella McMillan –10 October, 2012

The poem, ***Consciousness – From The Rim***, was published
previously in 2013 in Book Seven of the ***Stella McMillan
Series: SUSPENSION – Between Two Realms –***

Author's Note –Transition – Book One

Let us explore the levels that were described during Mary's Transition in Book One. These related to a travelator, an escalator and several elevators. Alternatively, we could play with the scenario that was described in **The Terrace**.

Both of these examples – fictitious examples, of course – were given so that an understanding of spiritual matters could be achieved more easily. It is possible to be religious, as well as being spiritual, when one is living a full physical life. Many people are exactly that while others are religious without any aspect of spiritual understanding at all. These ones accept everything that they are told as the absolute truth. Therefore, religious leaders, who teach these innocent ones – whether they be adult or child – have a grave responsibility on their shoulders. If we take the example of the place to where Mary ascended after her Transition, we can see that the various levels described all correspond with our chakra system; as with the story of **The Terrace** where there were different levels, to which one could rise, spiritually speaking, that is.

Returning to **The Terrace** example, it is easy to see these various stages of spiritual understanding. The ones who return after every incarnation experienced on Earth and who are obliged to live in one or other section of the deep ravine are to be pitied. On Earth, they are responsible for some horrendous deeds. In physical embodiment, they will deny that reincarnation is a fact of life. They may pretend to believe in God, but their deeds are never those of a God-like Being. In the Discourses, their pathways have been covered adequately.

With the next level, that being the one that is in tune with the Solar Plexus chakra, these are the good people of Earth. For the most part, they lead ordinary lives and they do not harm anyone, unless that person does harm to them or their loved ones. Then, they feel justified in retaliating in some way. In this act, they create usually an extra karmic debt. Their main purpose in incarnating again is to clear the slate – not to add to it. These ones follow the dictates of their ego-personality self for the most part and rarely – if ever – operate from their spirit-self.

Climbing to the next level, we have these wonderful beings who operate solely from the Heart Chakra. These are the loving, giving individuals who do not know how to receive. They are the givers of Earth, as opposed to the ones on the lower levels who are takers and who regard the givers as somewhat naive and foolish. The ones who operate predominately from their Heart Chakra are not here to learn to give, for they do so abundantly. They are here to gain greater spiritual awareness and, in so doing, they can rise higher upon their return to the Astral plane after the death of their current physical body. Still, they do not accept reincarnation as fact when in embodiment on Earth. This concept is beyond their ability to understand until they pass beyond *the veil*, as Mary did. Mary was at the level of the Heart Centre, as far as her spiritual understanding was concerned. Past-lives were not something that she considered consciously when in physical embodiment. It took some time for her to accept the possibility of reincarnation once she had made her transition from physicality on Earth.

With the next level of the Throat Chakra, this corresponds to Divine Will and is blue in colour. Did Mary do God's Will in all areas while in physical form? That is for her to determine only. We are not here to judge her or anyone else. However, had she been attuned completely to Divine Will, she would have been able to access the higher level that vibrates at a Throat Chakra frequency. The Third Eye is the next chakra on our scale, which is similar to a piano scale, one might say. This level is attuned to Divine Wisdom and its corresponding colour is purple or amethyst.

At the Crown Chakra, we have the golden-white Light – Divine Light – emanating. The Crown Chakra is indigo usually, although all great Ascended Masters of Love and Light operate at this level or frequency with Divine Light being visible for all to see. Everything that they say and do exudes Divine Love, Divine Will, Divine Wisdom and Divine Light. However, the ones who reside in the ravine – or, who are required to enter via the red and orange doors with the black lightning strike down through the centre – are fluctuating between Divine Life (Base/Root Chakra) and Divine Power (Sacral Chakra).They cannot rise above this area. This is because they refuse to accept any being that is greater than they are. They refuse to repay karmic debt; or, to acknowledge that they owe same. Their intent, always, is to cause as much strife, war, hardship and dissent as possible in the time allotted to them in any lifetime. On the next terrace above the ravine, the good people of Earth are attuned to Divine Order whose colour is yellow. Moving higher still, we have those on the Heart Chakra level. This is Divine Love in action. Its colour is green and its intent is to spread Divine Love everywhere.

So, from the top, we have:

Divine Light – golden-white Light – Crown Chakra

Divine Wisdom – purple/amethyst colour – Third Eye Chakra

Divine Will – blue in colour – Throat Chakra

Divine Love – green in colour – Heart Chakra

Divine Order – yellow in colour – Solar Plexus Chakra

Divine Power – orange in colour – Sacral Chakra

Divine Life – red in colour – Base or Root Chakra

As water finds its own level so too do we, upon our return to our True Home on the Astral plane between incarnations. Remember always that everything and every decision that is made comes back to two main factors. These are *Unconditional Love* and *Pure Intent*.

When we have learned these two simple factors – and, we accept them fully – all else will pale into insignificance. Our sojourns to the plane of Earth are at an end. We have graduated – hopefully with flying colours – from the College of Earth.

I hope that the books of the *Stella McMillan Series* have been helpful in aiding those who have read them to come to an acceptance of Cosmic (or Karmic) Law and to a greater understanding of the reasons why we seem to incarnate endlessly on Earth. If we do not accept reincarnation and we do not seek spiritual solutions to earthly dilemmas, we will remain trapped on this endless treadmill for as long as it takes.

Accept that *reincarnation* is an undeniable fact of life.
Accept that, in all things, our *pure intent* is the overriding factor in all that we say and do on Earth.
Accept that, at all times and in all areas of life, *Unconditional Love* is our ultimate and only goal.

There is a pathway through the mire that physical life-on-Earth has become now for the children of Light. It is a secret and sacred pathway that all must discover alone, in association with one's own Higher/Spirit-Self, because this is a purely personal journey that is undertaken in Love, hope and trust. As has been stated previously, everyone who is walking a spiritual path to the exclusion of all else must discover the secret and sacred information for herself or himself. It is secret and sacred for a very good reason. It is similar to the situation that Onoraus described (in Book Two) as happening at Qumran. The way can be found in a deep meditative state. Only then can the truth that is unique to that particular individual be revealed from within.

This is how the whole situation operates. Once discovered, the information cannot be passed to another, no matter how loving and trustworthy that person appears to be. Safeguards have been put in place to prevent a repeat of the horrendous times that occurred at the end of our beautiful Atlantis, due to this secret and sacred information being placed into the hands of ones who were not ready to receive it – at a spiritual level – and who did not come by these methods by their own efforts.

If one is living a full physical life and this person has no interest whatsoever in the spiritual aspect of life, then the books of this Series will be of no interest whatsoever to the reader.

When someone is conscious of another realm of existence and he or she becomes involved in religious pursuits – whether as adult or child – this person will reject out-of-hand the concepts and proposals outlined in this Series of books.

There are those who are seeking actively and enthusiastically the spiritual truths that are presented in the *Stella McMillan Series*, which culminates in the complete book, **Transition – *The Final Journey* –**

If what has been presented thus far in **Transition – Book One –** is beyond what is considered acceptable at this stage in one's current life, the complete book will be of no interest to the reader.

Transition – *The Final Journey* – has been written for the benefit of those who fall into category three of the above explanation. These are the *spiritual warriors* who are here to finish off the last leg of their own personal journey and who are desirous of showing others the path that few can find or are prepared to walk in earnest.

To all *spiritual warriors* whose hearts and minds are wide open, please read the final books of this publication with discernment. From then onwards, it is wise to *keep one's own counsel.*

Transition – Book One –

This book is unrelated to the seven-book Series that preceded it. **Book One** of **Transition** describes the Transition of Mary as she leaves her safe world of the physical and she embarks on a new adventure as her ongoing spirit-life continues in another of its never-ending cycles. Mary is left to ponder on whether the birth/life/death/re-birth cycles are real. Her new life appears real to her in this now-moment after she passed beyond the veil of physical life.

Transition – Book One – is presented as food-for-thought. Possibly, this story may give credence to the seven-book Series that preceded it.

Transition – *The Final Journey –* that is published here contains Book One, Book Two, Book Three and Book Four, as well as the *Guidelines to Self-Healing.* This book has been written for the benefit of those who are desirious of making this lifetime their own final journey to this planet that is steeped in negativity. Be cautious. Be discreet. Be secretive as you strive to make this trip down here to the planet – that is known currently as Earth – **your** *final journey.*

Stella McMillan
24 March, 2019

For more details:
stellamcmillan.com
stellamcmillan.com.au

Transition

The Final Journey

Book Two

Onoraus
Qumran

Qumran was a place of great healing, great Love and great understanding. With its destruction by the Romans, much knowledge was lost – irretrievably so. In this current climate on Earth, this great knowledge is missed sorely and needed desperately.

Let us say that there is a pool. A pool can represent cleansing and healing, but it can represent, also, a pool of shared knowledge and understanding – that being a *pool of wisdom*, so to speak. So, what is this great knowledge that was lost all of those years ago? In those days, the ones who had become Masters, in a spiritual sense, took all of their instruction from the one known as *The Master*.

This great Master-Teacher was not in physical form, yet the ones who adhered strictly to his inspired teachings could see him clearly with their own physical eyes and could hear him just as clearly with their own physical ears. They observed his great Light, listened intently to his great wisdom, understood and appreciated his great compassion, yet it was his great and all-encompassing Love that they felt when in his Presence. He was, and still is, the greatest Teacher of Spiritual Wisdom that this world has known ever, in all of its various and varied existences. He has come to Earth many times in physical form to give his message of peace and love, with compassion being his overriding theme.

In every incarnation, he has been vilified and discredited by those who feared him. In many cases, his physical body was destroyed - cruelly so – in order to placate those in authority on Earth at that time in her history. After these events, his followers – those who remembered his Love and compassion – adhered strictly to his codes of conduct that he established when in that particular physical form. Unfortunately, as another generation took over from the previous ones, the cracks began to show as negativity and dissention began to take a hold. The negative ones eventually took charge while winning the day, so to speak. His words of wisdom were altered. At first, it was a little here and a little there, but after a while, the movement that he founded was torn asunder, thus causing breakaway movements to form.

This great Master-Teacher has come at the beginning of every Age-of-Humankind on Earth. So, every two thousand years, he appears. He is glorified by some and vilified by others, but ignored he cannot be, because his great wisdom, great Light, great compassion and great Love for all of humanity is on display for all to see. Beyond the sight of those in physical form, he teaches and guides still. His words of wisdom were laced often with words of warning and many of these have been exaggerated in some cases while being downgraded in other scenarios. Consequently, many of his ardent followers, to this day, are in confusion as to what he was preaching in any of these incarnations; but, as always, his original message was simple. It was compelling. It was shunned by most who found it too difficult a concept to incorporate into everyday, daily life at whatever time in Earth's history he appeared.

Whether we speak of great Master-Teachers of Earth, such as Melchizedek, Enoch, Moses, Pythagoras, Zoroaster or any other identity that he may have used, we speak then, in awe, of this one great Master-Teacher.

Last time that he appeared in physical form, he promised to return. In actual fact, he has never left. He walks among all of his loyal followers to this day, but his special followers who were devoted totally to him at Qumran have a special place in his heart, for they know no other destiny than to follow him, regardless of the walk-of-life that they have chosen in any subsequent incarnation and regardless of the gender of the form, in which they walk around to this day.

Whatever he asks of them, they do without question, without fear and without one thought given to the consequences of such actions, which are only ever based on the principles of Love, compassion and peace.

At the Temple at Qumran, many poignant truths were taught. He guided his loyal followers to guard these Precepts with their lives, and he warned them when imminent danger was upon them to seal these Precepts that he had given to them in large vats and to place these in caves for safe-keeping. In their wildest dreams, his followers could never have imagined that these Precepts would remain hidden for some thousands of Earth years; but so it was, my beloved children of Light.

Many of the children of Light who are incarnate on Earth now are the ones who were ensconced in the complex at Qumran and who voluntarily offered their services to others, by being teachers, writers, painters, musicians and healers. These followers were known as *The Essenes of Qumran*. They were a breakaway group of religious monks whose wives and children lived nearby to the temple and monastery, for want of a better description for this great complex of Light, known simply as *Qumran*.

Returning to *the pool*, this was where ones who were anxious to join, would be taken first and foremost to wash away symbolically all trappings and connections to the *outside* world and to commit to a life of service to the Temple, around which the community flourished. They were self-sufficient and all of the needs of their families were met amply. There were no restrictions placed upon these men with regard to close contact with their wives, children, parents and other family members, for their service was a voluntary one always and loyalty to their Temple was as important as was loyalty to their loved ones. Both were of equal importance, but they had no other lives outside of the Qumran community.

However, this was their free-will choice, also. Always, it was a voluntary code-of-conduct, as prescribed by the one known as *The Master.* Many could *see* him, whereas others could *feel* his great Presence and his great Love whenever he walked amongst them. There were never any restrictions placed upon the members of this community. Guidelines for communal living were given and these were given in Love and in compassion, but never were there any repercussions if ones chose to operate for a time outside of these Guidelines. It was only when ones whose energy-fields gave off a negative pulse and whose deeds and words gave offence and pain to others that intervention occurred. Those-in-charge simply asked this errant one to leave permanently in the interests of the community as a whole.

When these negative ones grew in number, they approached the priests in Jerusalem with outrageous stories of happenings taking place in Qumran. As this loving community had been a thorn-in-the-side, so to speak, of the priests for a very long time, the fate of this loving community was sealed. Qumran ceased to exist, except in the soul-memory of its followers. To this day, many children of Light remember Qumran and long for its return on Earth. However, whenever a community such as this, following the Principles and Precepts is ,established, then the negative ones move in and its destruction and/or abandonment is assured. Such is the way-of-life on Earth at present.

In the Golden Age on Earth, many such communities will be established and this communal-type of living will thrive. Those who cannot live by these Principles and Precepts will be society's outcasts then, instead of it being the other way around, as it is now.

This, then, is a brief outline of the way it was in Qumran. To a degree, the ones known as the *Armish people* have sought to establish communities based on these lines, but restrictions on individual freedoms were never a part of the code-of-conduct at Qumran. Everything operated on a voluntary basis with personal responsibility being the uppermost consideration and with peace, Love, compassion, understanding and respect for the feelings and needs of others overriding all else. Love of a Divine Being existed everywhere, yet living within the heart and soul of every living creature, human or otherwise, was an understanding that was never in question. The Master's overriding Love for God underlined everything that he said, did and advocated. God was – and still is – his ALL.

The Great Master-Teacher walks among us still, to this day. Many know him by different names, and/or identities, depending on which incarnation it was when they were one of his ardent followers. His message is simple always. His message is the same always.

In the Golden Age of Love and En-Light-enment on Earth, his overriding message will be the same once again. However, the difference will be that the negative ones who have controlled the planet totally for thousands upon thousands of years – even back before Noah and The Flood occurred – will have been removed completely. Their own ardent followers will have no one to lead them and they will be in disarray for a time. After that, they will form themselves into groups; then, they will begin warring amongst themselves. As a house that is divided-against-itself cannot stand, they will fall.

In the meantime, these peaceful, loving communities will begin to flourish all over the world. They will establish themselves on the grid-system of Earth and draw on her great throbbing energy to survive and to flourish in God's Love and God's Light. In a time such as this, the Principles and Precepts of Qumran will come to light and, once again, *The Master* will lead, guide and instruct those who are open to receive his great wisdom, great understanding, great compassion, great Light and great Love. To be within his great Presence is to know Love Unconditional intuitively. Peace will reign on Earth once again. As it was in the beginning, so too will it be again.

In my next Discourse, we will consider *the pool* at Qumran in more detail, so that a greater understanding may be gained by those who are open to receive.

Peace be with you,
I AM Onoraus.
23rd December 2007

Onoraus
The Pool

In understanding the importance of *The Pool* to ones who had chosen to be a part of the community, it is necessary to acknowledge its use at Qumran.

The ones, who came with Love in their hearts and with willingness and a desire to be a part of the community, were required to live apart from the members at the outset. Whether this was just one person or a family or group, this was a requirement. During that period of adjustment, the new arrivals were given instruction into the workings of the community and of the requirements for participation. There was a set course of instruction that all must agree to adhere to and to implement in their daily lives. This instruction was important in that it stressed the need to conform to the Principles and Precepts of those residing at or near Qumran.

The members who were fully-fledged adepts lived permanently within the Temple complex, as monks in monasteries do now. Their families lived nearby in a village-type setting that was surrounded by fields where their daily food and other resources were grown for their own use only. They did not sell their excess provisions, instead electing to store these in large storage vats or buildings erected for this purpose. So, new arrivals lived outside of the village and attended the Temple where the priests/elders instructed them in those all-important Principles and Precepts that were spiritual in essence.

During this time then it was possible for the ones-in-charge to assess the suitability or otherwise of the new candidate for initiation. These elders had achieved a very high state spiritually and, consequently, were able at the very least to see and to read the aura of the new initiate. From that cursory glance and by close contact during the sessions of instruction, the personality and the intent of the candidate could be studied. At the end of the set course, the candidate was offered then a place within the complex; or, he or she was advised to attend a different establishment if the person was considered to be unsuitable for whatever reason. In the case of the latter, it was important to consider the good of the whole, rather than the needs of the one desiring access. It was this group of disgruntled ones who were in negativity and who felt slighted by the elders that devised a plan to destroy the community as a whole.

The elders knew that, because of their negativity and their ego-based pride and spiritual vanity, they would cause dissension and, eventually, the cancer of negativity would work its way surreptitiously into their loving community. The wise elders were on guard for this constantly, but unfortunately, they could not exercise control over anything that these negative ones did or said once permission was refused for them to join. In the outside world, they could show their true colours and their true selves for all to see.

For those who were admitted, temporary shelter was found for them within the village, if they were a family group; or, within the Temple complex itself, if the person was single and alone. Set chores were given and these were undertaken with enthusiasm always by the new arrivals. Then, the new arrivals, singularly, were invited to undergo an initiation ceremony and to become novices within the Temple, thus moving on to a deeper understanding of spiritual truths, if that was the desire. Within a family unit, if one was not ready for such a commitment, that one was allowed to come to this commitment at a time of his or her own choosing.

Once one became a novice, there were three more sets of instruction to complete before being able to become an elder or priest/priestess, as the case may be. No one was precluded from these high levels of attainment, due to race, gender or age. All were welcome to move forward at their own pace, as long as their hearts were filled with Love Unconditional and their Intent was pure. These were the only requirements.

When one agreed to accept the Principles and Precepts of this loving community without question, the Initiation was offered. When accepted, the candidate was directed then to the Temple where, at a set hour, an Initiation Ceremony began, with the whole community in attendance.

The new Initiate wore a long white gown or robe during the ceremony, with a garland of white flowers adorning the head. The attendants chosen to escort the Initiate to the cleansing pool (or baptismal font in modern churches) were of the same gender – with some older and some younger. The Initiate was led to The Pool, which was surrounded by fire and crystals, thus the four elements of water, fire, earth and air were represented.

The white robe was removed by the attendants who, themselves, had undergone Initiation already and who were well-versed in the Ceremonies and Principles of the community. The Initiate then entered the water wearing only the garland of flowers. At either end of the wide pool, which today would resemble what would be termed an extra-wide lap pool, there were deep steps that stretched the width of the pool. The purpose of the deep steps was for the benefit of young children who were being baptised or initiated at the request of their parents. For children, this first Initiation was a precursor to their own full Initiation that was offered to them at probably between twelve and fourteen years of age (usually at what was considered to be *puberty* for the individual concerned).

Returning to The Pool and the adult Initiation Ceremony, the attendants would walk then with the white-robed Initiates to the other end of The Pool. Chanting the Prayer-of-Initiation continually while underwater, the Initiate would walk then the length of The Pool as the garland of white flowers floated free from his or her head. Walking completely naked from The Pool at the other end and having been cleansed symbolically of all sin, the new Novice was dressed in the white robe again while dripping wet still. Then, a sash would be placed around the waist and a headband placed on the head. The colour of the sash and the headband denoted the degree that one had achieved within this spiritual community and was dependent on the level of attainment within the non-compulsory area of the Temple structure that was hierarchal in nature.

There were seven degrees and the white sash of purity was the first one given. The Initiate was the Novice now. The gown/robe, which was white for those undergoing the seven steps of instruction, was worn always within the Temple complex and on ceremonial occasions. Ordinary clothing was worn within the village and while working in the fields surrounding it. Within the village itself, meals were served in a communal building three times a day and always, at the outset, a priest/priestess was in attendance to say Grace before the meal was taken. Always, those who were of a higher standing in the community were given preference and they were the first to be served their meals. All others followed, in their turn, to the area to be given their share of the food. Nursing mothers with young children were given the greatest respect of all, for they were the ones who, through great pain and sacrifice, brought forth new life into the world. These women, regardless of spiritual achievements within the Temple were accorded the greatest deference and respect of all. They were served their meal first, while seated at the table, by the priest or priestess in attendance for that particular meal, this being the one who presided over the ritual of eating and who recited Grace in thanks to God.

Such was the way it was at Qumran. Such is the way it can be again and, most especially, will be when the Golden Age manifests itself on Earth within the time-frame of the Aquarian Age.

Within the Temple complex, the main focus in the Temple itself was prayer and meditation. Central to these was the drawing down of the Divine Light of God from above while the one in prayer and meditation raised his or her own vibratory frequency to the highest level possible, thus becoming a Beacon of Light while in embodiment. From there, the Divine Light of God that was manifest in this beautiful being was directed down into the heart centre of Mother Earth. In this manner, these beautiful ones at Qumran were assisting voluntarily, consciously and lovingly, The Mother – this being Earth herself – to raise her own vibratory frequency to a higher level, in order to counteract the negativity of those of a very low vibratory frequency who were incarnate on her at that time.

Unfortunately, Mother Earth is in a worse state now than she was then. So, what needs to be done – and, done quickly – is for like-minded, loving beings of pure intent to gather together and to form communities that operate on a similar basis to the one at Qumran. In so doing, everyone would be assisting Mother Earth to heal herself and to rid herself of the negativity that is choking and suffocating her daily and nightly now.

Qumran was run less on ceremony and selfish, personal pursuits and more on being the spiritual conduit between what they termed *Father Sky* and *Mother Earth*. It is when the ego-based, selfish pursuits and the pride-based, spiritual vanity take centre-stage that the real purpose is lost and disintegration of the group as a whole occurs. When the pomp and ceremony becomes more important than the raising of the vibratory frequency, then the community as a whole is on shaky ground, so to speak. The ones who came to infiltrate at Qumran were sent on their way by the elders who met as a group and who deliberated long and hard over every choice that was made. So, when the community could not be destroyed from within, it was done so from without, because its very existence threatened the authority of the *puppet-priests* in Jerusalem. And, there lies the story of the demise of Qumran.

If the loving children of Light were to form Qumran-type communities on all of the energy centres on Mother Earth's grid-system, then Earth would respond quickly and beautifully, as God intended. It is the negative ones who are incarnate on her in great numbers now and keeping her down at a low vibratory level that is the root cause of the problem. Many of them vibrate at a low level themselves, and this is at the level of the base/root chakra. Defeating them will not be easy. It can be done only with God's Divine Light, God's Divine Love and in peace at all times, regardless of the provocation, which will be extreme in many cases.

Returning to The Pool at Qumran, the reason why one was immersed fully in the water, as opposed to how the Baptismal Rite is carried out now in most churches, was to cleanse the aura completely. To cleanse the *aura completely* is to cleanse away all negativity from the etheric and astral bodies. This debris has been collected from birth as one goes about attempting to function in an out-of-control negative world – as Earth has become now. That was the purpose of the Initiation Prayer or Chant stated continually while walking underwater from one end of the pool to the other end.

After one reached the highest level on the seven-step set of instruction into the seven Principles and Precepts of the Temple, then a different robe was issued to mark such a great achievement. The colour of this garment was the same as the second step on the ladder of seven steps. The colours corresponded with the seven colours of the rainbow and the tone of the musical note played during every Initiation at The Pool was the note that corresponded with that colour on the musical scale. This note was played continuously on a gong while the Initiate was underwater cleansing his or her auric field. By this calculation, there were a total of twenty-one steps on the ladder of completion. It would be an exceptional student of a high vibratory frequency and spiritual understanding who would be permitted to undertake his or her first voluntary Initiation before the age of twelve years.

The Essenes at Qumran held strictly to this code. The one exception was a young lad of five years of age who was so far advanced for his age that a dispensation was permitted. His name was Jeshua-bar-Joseph – or, Jesus, son of Joseph. Qumran was destroyed, because it had spawned, educated, encouraged and nurtured Rabbi Jesus in his formative years. Even though he had left there by the time of his fourteenth year, his parents had been a part of the Essene community and his father was one of the esteemed elders within its higher echelons. Therein lies the real reason for the destruction of the Temple complex and the villages that surrounded and supported it. Qumran went the way of all others that drew down daily and nightly the Divine Light of God to Mother Earth for her protection and assistance.

The negative ones who control this out-of-control world can never allow such an occurrence, because they are in fear of God's Divine Light as they shun God's Divine Love, regardless of the words that they are uttering and the excuses that they are giving as they do so. When, fourteen hundred years after the death of Jesus, the Light of God began to rise once again on Planet Earth, they brought forward another round-of-atrocities to destroy that Golden/White Light of God emanating from God's children of Light who were incarnate then in physical embodiment. People, to this day, are fearful

114

still of witches and wizards, such was the extent of and the success of the propaganda machine of the ones in charge of Earth at that moment in Earth's sorry history. It is such a sad and sorry state of affairs, is it not?

The questions that need to be asked:

Can the children of Light rise up just once more to assist Mother Earth to raise her own vibratory frequency?

Can they do so just one more time?

If so, can they do this sooner, rather than later, for *later* may be just a little bit too late this time around, dear ones?

With regard to the elders/priests and priestesses, they reached every level through a pre-set series of instruction, with an Initiation Ceremony taking place in the Temple, followed by another baptismal underwater walk through the Initiation Pool. At the end of the seventh Initiation Ceremony, a different coloured robe was given; then, another seven steps were taken, under instruction, with a different coloured sash and headpiece issued for that robe. In this way, twenty-one steps were taken to reach Completion, the ultimate goal of all.

It was considered to be the highest level attainable while ensconced in a physical body on the third-dimensional planet of Earth. This was the basis of the teaching at Qumran. The community was formed by a group of Jewish priests who was disenchanted by the way that their Temple was being run, with the moneylenders in the Temple being but a small part of their disgust at what was occurring behind the scenes within the Temple walls in Jerusalem at that time. The Essenes were a breakaway group. They were sincere, loving and dedicated to God at all times and in every way.

They had a practice of devotion that has been adopted in many monasteries and, in cloistered societies of nuns in the world currently. This practice revolves around a flame that is kept burning at all times, night and day, within the main

Temple or chapel and at least one person is there, kneeling before the altar to keep the flame of Love burning brightly on Earth. This practice is known by many as *The Flame of Perpetual Devotion* or *of Adoration*. No matter what occurs, the Flame is never left unaccompanied and the practice is worked usually on an hourly roster system, twenty-four hours per day. Within the Christian faith, it stems from the torment of Jesus in the garden of Gethsemane when he asked the question of his followers: "Can you not stay by me but one hour?"

By giving this outline of the Essenes and their loving community at Qumran, I am seeking to show the importance that they placed upon their Temple, the Flame within it and the Initiation Pool of cleansing and renewal. Their gowns, sashes and headbands, along with the colours and the level of attainment that these denoted, were a vital part of their community that was devoted to God and to the drawing down of Divine Light and Divine Love to Mother Earth.

By using this example, I am seeking to light a flame of desire within the hearts and minds of the children of Light who are desirous of walking away from empty, chaotic, out-of-control lives, in which they are trapped now. One does not need to leave behind family members and friends, if these loving ones are ready to walk away, also; but, remember always that everyone has freewill, which is a God-given gift and their own precious birthright, so do not, in your love and zeal, fall into the trap of trying to force your will upon another, no matter how sincere your intent may be at the time. When they are ready, they will follow at their own pace and in their own time. You cannot bring someone forward to your current *reality*, but by the same token, you may not be able to go back to their present *reality*, for want of a more apt description in words-of-Earth. Therefore, a decision is necessary. That decision is for you alone to make, in God's Love.

The Flame-of-Love that was Qumran burned very brightly for a time on Earth; then, it flickered briefly, after which it was extinguished. It is alive and burning fiercely in the hearts and souls of all who passed through its Portals-of-Light at that time. That is why the discovery of the Dead Sea Scrolls caused such excitement, because at a soul level, a memory stirred in the hearts of all those who were former members – priests/priestesses and Initiates alike – as word of the discovery spread around the world and reached the ears and conscious minds of those former members incarnate on Earth now in different physical forms, regardless of which race, gender or skin tone has been chosen for this round of earthly experiences and lessons.

So, as promised, I have given an explanation of *THE POOL* and its reason for existing at the loving Essene community at Qumran all those centuries ago.

Will it all come full-circle to operate once again and, this time, operate successfully on every energy centre on Mother Earth's grid-system? That remains to be seen.

I will leave you now to contemplate my words of explanation and my hopes for the future of Earth and her loving children. Just remember the symbolism of the glass that can hold but one substance. If that substance is water and the glass is half-full, the remainder is occupied then by air. If water represents *ego* in our analogy and air represents *spirit*, then one is battling the other. If it is full to the brim with water (ego), the spirit withdraws, thus leaving the ego to run rampant. Without Spirit, no life exists anywhere at all. When the ego is in full control, life expectancy is not long, believe me.

So, what was your own spirit-self's proposed contribution to the overall Divine Plan for Planet Earth? Has it begun to contribute yet? Or, is the ego in full control while working on self-orientated pursuits? If the latter is so, then disappointment may be great upon its return to the Astral Plane of Spirit at the end of this current sojourn into physicality on Earth. That is another point to consider and to contemplate.

With all of this food-for-thought, I shall leave you now.

Peace be with you,

I AM Onoraus of the Light and Love of Almighty God.

4th January 2008.

Onoraus
Final Meditation

Walk with me awhile. Let us walk up this slight incline towards a suspension bridge that spans a deep and wide ravine. The road is unsealed and very wide. We step onto the bridge and cross-over. On the other side, the area is green and lush, with a carpet of grass that stretches all the way to a massively high cliff-face that is some distance away from where we stand at the end of the bridge.

Bright sunlight illuminates the whole area, which seems to have a distinctly yellow glow permeating everything and everywhere. Instead of walking towards the distant cliff, let us veer to our left and enter a slightly wooded area. We follow a dirt track for some distance as the trees sway slightly on either side of the track. There is a soft breeze brushing against our faces and through our hair.

At the end of the track, which comes to an abrupt end where the deep ravine begins, there is a multi-coloured two-person swing with a large canopy covering it. This inviting chair looks across the almost endless and almost bottomless ravine. The view is spectacular and the day is fine and clear. As we approach the multi-coloured swing, we realise that someone is seated there. The excitement mounts when we realise that it is our own special Twin Flame who is waiting there for us.

There is a great difference between twin-souls and our Twin Flame. Twin-souls are ones whom we know so very well, because we have incarnated together in many, many lifetimes, as well as interacting together regularly on the Astral level between incarnations on Earth. However, our Twin Flame is different. This person is the other half of ourselves. We were breathed into life as the one entity. While the male aspect separated to explore in the various universes in order to develop fully the female aspect of itself, the female aspect did likewise. When these two aspects come together again as-one, their whole universe stands still.

Returning to our multi-coloured swing, we reach out and join hands with the other half of ourselves. We look across the ravine and, in the distance, we spy another mountainous area that has two extremely-high peaks, which are protruding into the brilliant blue sky. Nestled between those two peaks, there is a white building. It has a flat roof that is covered in a carpet of grass while the building itself is circular. There are white marble steps leading up to its grand entrance.

As we sit on the multi-coloured swing, we make a decision to visit this gleaming white structure. The one thought enters our minds simultaneously and, holding hands still, we rise and walk to the edge of the massively-high cliff that faces the ravine.

We have left our physical bodies in a deep meditative state in our earthly environment. Now, we leave our etheric bodies sitting on the swing. Together and with hands clasped, we fly in our Astral form over the deep ravine. We land on the marble steps and in front of the massive golden door. As we approach, the door opens automatically and we sail on through its portals. Once inside, we are standing in an exceedingly wide circular corridor that encircles the entire inner structure of the building. We traverse the corridor together and acknowledge that we have walked around the magnificent Holy-of-Holies at its Core Centre. Then, we return to the front entrance again.

The circular inner dwelling, known by all as the Holy-of-Holies, possesses twelve doors, with every door depicting a symbol of the religion, to which one belongs. We enter through the door of our choice. Once inside, we realise that twelve beautiful Angels-of-Light guard all of the twelve entrances. Only those of a high spiritual frequency or vibration can enter here. Slowly, we walk towards the centre of the room and stand beneath the Golden-White Light that shines down from above. The Golden-Light of God enters through the opening above our heads.

As a moth to a flame, we rise above and, with arms interlinked, we glide through the circular dome while leaving our Astral body awaiting our return before the magnificent Holy-of-Holies.

As we fly away in Spirit-form, the *pulsing* begins. From our Core-Centre, this *pulsing* vibrates throughout our entire Being. In this Now-Moment, ONENESS commences for us. We are AT-ONE with our special God of Divine Light and Divine Love. Our whole world stands still as we become ONE with each other once again. As it was in the Beginning so, too, it is now. Twin Flames unite in absolute union with each other and with our God-the-One. At this moment, the *pulsing* becomes all-consuming.

What a truly blissful State-of-Being!

When the time comes for us to return to our world of the physical on Earth, we need to retrace our steps while returning firstly to reconnect with our Astral form in the Holy-of-Holies. After that, we return to the multi-coloured swing and reconnect with our etheric body. From there, we return to the entrance to the suspension bridge. Sadly, this is where we are required to bid farewell to our Twin Flame. After a loving embrace, we walk slowly over the suspension bridge. We give a wave to our precious other-half as we walk from the bridge and down the wide dirt track to our home in the world of the physical where we re-enter our physical body, so that we can continue our current physical life on Earth.

What a tremendous experience we have enjoyed. Now, it is time to close our chakras/energy centres to tiny pinpoints of Light before entering the world of the physical to continue our work for Divine Love and Divine Light here.

Before leaving our comfortable chair, we bring a Shield-of-Light down over our energy centres at the front – stretching from our Alpha Point to our Omega Point. Similarly, we bring an identical Shield-of-Light over our chakras at the back – stretching from our Alpha Point to our Omega Point. As an added insurance, we can cover the outer sides of our shields with mirrors-of-Light that reflect all negativity back to the sender as we go about our daily work in the physical world.

We are buoyed by memories of our contact and interaction that we have experienced with our beautiful Twin Flame as memories of the *pulsing* re-surface. As we go on with our day, our feet hardly touch the ground. *We are floating on air!*

I AM Onoraus

DISCOURSES

Constella
Light of the World

Compassion and Love are the Light of the World. In all worlds, Divine Light and Divine Love when combined with an overwhelming compassion for one's fellow travellers on life's long road provide a powerful tool for change.

To bring about positive change in a world that has lost its way, a combination of Love, Light and compassion will work miracles always. A healing of the soul is possible.

An illness occurs when the soul is in need of healing at the deepest level. An illness or ailment is a call for help and a call for acknowledgement of the soul's deep-seated pain.

Listen first to the soul's plaintive cries for help. Physical healing can take place only after the healing of the soul.

In Search of Love

In search of the way of life, a change is needed. Change cannot occur until an acknowledgement comes that change is necessary in the first place. After that, the change will follow automatically, because the combination of Divine Light, Divine Love and compassion will fill the soul. All that can happen from there is a fulfilment of the soul's purpose. The external way of accomplishing this feat will happen in the fullness of time and at the appropriate moment.

First comes the acknowledgement. Second comes the change.

It may be dramatic and unexpected. It may be a slow dawning of enlightenment and the way that was shrouded in mystery will reveal itself without any effort on the part of the one or ones involved in the process. Either way, change will occur.

The soul needs to soar. Otherwise, it will become bogged down with external happenings and daily work, worry and chores. Then, the soul will begin its slow decline at a deep level as it seeks solace. Depression may follow-on from here.

Allow the soul its flight. Miracles can occur from there.

The Challenge

Given that there is conflict on a global scale, as well as within families and in the community, to which one belongs, one must question why this is so and what can be done to redress the situation.

The earth is a hotch-potch, with diverse groups and religious beliefs abounding in all areas on her surface at any one moment. If one were to view our earthly mother from the realms of what is termed *space*, one would see the picture as it really is.

It is not a pretty picture. There are wars occurring in many places. Children are starving and suffering. Women are treated as little more than slaves in some places.

Man's inhumanity to man comes to the fore here. These words were written centuries ago by a wise and creative poet. The weak are trampled by the strong. Those who live by the principles of Love and compassion – the Divine Principles of Life in all realms – are seen as being ripe-for-the-picking, shall we say. Until one comes to the full understanding of the cause and the reason for this state-of-affairs on Earth, nothing can change in a positive manner.

There can be no positive change until a need for change is acknowledged.

There can be no positive change until there is a willingness to tackle the massive problem.

It is a daunting and a seemingly impossible task. The problem is caused by an out-of-control ego. The ego is fuelled by the male-dominated energy. In extreme cases, this is without the balance of the feminine essence of Love being present in the being or beings concerned. This is not a physical love essence that is missing. It is the Divine Love Essence of God that is being denied, regardless of the religious or cultural beliefs that a person may hold currently. Those beliefs can change, but the lack of Divine Love within that individual cannot be overcome until he or she acknowledges that there is a problem. Pride and ego will prevent that acknowledgement in most cases.

It is only when the person's entire world that he or she has set up in the physical world falls apart completely that an acknowledgement of the need for change within oneself can be faced. Usually, pride and ego will come to the fore in that moment and one's current predicament will be blamed on others. It will be declared forcefully that someone else is to blame for the situation, in which this hapless person finds himself or herself.

Why do these situations arise in life, as experienced on Earth?

It is because the Love Essence of God that is within us all has been suppressed to a great degree in some. In others, it is less so. The more that the Divine Love of God is suppressed, the deeper one sinks into an abyss. Then, the ego seeks to take charge in an effort to reverse the situation.

The solution to the problem is not to give free rein to the ego-personality self. It is to bring the Divine Love Essence of God into Perfect Alignment with the Divine Light Energy of God.

Perfect Balance can occur only – within an individual – when the feminine essence of Love and the masculine energy of Light have merged completely in a fifty-fifty partnership.

From then onwards, the individual has no need to incarnate on Earth ever again. The true purpose of these continuous Earth incarnations has been revealed and acknowledged.

That purpose is – and always has been – to learn the lesson of Love, Light and Compassion – THE DIVINE TRINITY.

ALPHA

There is an Alpha. There is an Omega. If the One who is known as God, The Great Divine Spirit, Abba, Ra and many other titles down through the Ages-of-Man on Earth, is the Supreme Being Who guides us all, it follows then that He/She is the Alpha Point.

The Alpha Point is the brilliant point-of-Light that is our Guiding Star, our Compass on the dark sea of physical life and our Reference Point. The Alpha Point is calling us Home. Why do we disregard the call?

Is it because our earthly endeavours and our physical life are more important?

Is it because we have strayed so far from our Sun – our Original Source – that we can hear the call no longer?

Is it because, in order to return to our Original Source, we must abandon earthly pleasures and pursuits, as well as repaying all past karmic debts owed to our fellow-travellers on the long road to Home?

Could it be that we have neglected to learn the one and only lesson that there is to learn?

This, of course, is the lesson of Unconditional Love. If we have reached now the Omega Point, is it not time to turn our faces towards Home? Is it time to seek our Alpha above all else?

To do so, we must acknowledge firstly that there is a Supreme Being Who created us.

We must acknowledge secondly that at the very heart of our being, we possess a tiny spark of Alpha.

To return to Alpha is our birthright. It does not matter how far we have journeyed from Home. Alpha is calling to us always. Alpha is similar to a lighthouse on a dark ocean. Alpha is our comfort during storms at sea. Alpha prevents us from destroying ourselves on the shallow shoals and hidden rocks beneath the waves.

The religions of the world since time immemorial have attempted to package and to market Alpha – sometimes for altruistic reasons and often for selfish motives. All pass away eventually and all that is left are decaying monuments that bear testament to their folly.

Alpha cannot be packaged any more than the brilliant sun can be packaged and marketed for personal gain.

From where did we all come?

To where will we all return eventually?

It is Alpha. Alpha is our ALL. Alpha is our Beginning and our Ending.

Imagine a Sun – a Brilliant Shining Ball – up in a cloudless blue sky. Imagine this Sun pulsing with Divine Light and Divine Love. As our Sun pulses, It expands and contracts. This is constant movement that is unstoppable. It is as natural as breathing is to a person who is in physical form.

There is a contraction that is followed by a burst of expansion. In that moment of expansion, another life bursts forth. It finds its way out into the world. It is free to pursue its own pathway from here. It can play in the realm of Spirit. It can descend to the world of matter. It is a free will choice, for free will is its birthright. Unfortunately, many have descended into matter. This was meant to be a temporary state, but for many, it became a permanent and stagnant existence.

All the while, Alpha is calling it Home. Many have been stuck firmly at the Omega Point and either cannot or will not respond to the Eternal Call. The Eternal Call continues unabated. Those who respond and make a conscious decision to turn towards Home need to be applauded, for they have taken the first step, which is acknowledgement, followed by physical action and decision-making.

The Omega Point could be described as equivalent to the Base or Root chakra. Those who have closed down all of their higher points are vibrating at the lowest frequency possible. Those whose vibrations are at the level of the Sacral chakra – the point of Power – have a definite need to control others, because by controlling others, they are fulfilling a need within themselves and this makes them feel real. It gives them a purpose in life. Those whose vibrations match the level of the Solar Plexus chakra are the fence-sitters. They can allow themselves to be controlled by those of a lower frequency; or, they can allow themselves to be influenced by ones who are vibrating at frequencies that are higher still on this vibratory scale.

The ones who respond at the Heart level are attuned to the Love Essence of Alpha – the Point of Divine Love.

Those who are vibrating at a higher frequency than Love are at the point of the Throat chakra, the communication centre and the point of Divine Will. Their will – by their own free will choice – is attuned to Divine Will to the exclusion of all else.

There are those who possess great wisdom. This wisdom did not come from books or learning dispensed in schools or universities. This Wisdom came from a multitude of experiences enjoyed and endured on Earth and elsewhere between physical incarnations. The Point of Divine Wisdom is the Third Eye chakra.

At the highest point on our imaginary piano scale, we have Divine Light. This is the Crown Point and these ones are inspired by Divine Light that they draw down deliberately and purposely through their Crown chakra. These ones vibrate at a frequency that is rarely seen in physical life. The great prophets and secrs of Earth have been prime and pure examples of the Divine Light and Divine Love Principle in action. Their appearances on Earth in times of great turmoil have led ultimately to the demise of their physical forms prematurely in many cases. This has occurred in the cruellest and most base way possible, because it was carried out by ones who were vibrating at the level of the Base chakra only while being directed by ones who were vibrating at the level of the Sacral chakra – the point of power. At the same time, these acts were witnessed by ones who were the fence-sitters and who did not dare to intervene, because they vibrate at the level of Divine Order.

The ones who are at a frequency that is equivalent to Divine Love would have watched in horror while wondering if they would be the next on the list of casualties. This level is the Heart level. The Heart level is the highest frequency that ones on Earth reach. It is not that they are incapable of reaching greater heights. It is that the greater heights have been obscured deliberately by those who have a vested interest in so doing. Misleading the beautiful and loving children of Love has been a constant theme for many a millennia on Earth. The most effective method of achieving this goal is through organised religion.

Those who vibrate at the highest frequencies of Divine Will, Divine Wisdom and Divine Light have found their own way through the mire. They have found what all others are seeking – some more earnestly than others.

These ones of Divine Will, Divine Wisdom and Divine Light have located their own Source and Point-of-Reference within their own being. They have found the Source at their own Core Centre. Their own individual Core Centre is their original Spark-of-Light that was born within them at their moment-of-creation. It is their personal Point-of-Contact with the Source-of-All – **The Alpha Point**.

The Alpha Point

Imagine a point of Pure Light. Look through your Third Eye chakra and observe this Pure Light.

At first, it is a tiny pinpoint. The more that we concentrate our attention on The Point, then the larger the circle of Light grows and the more brilliant its glow becomes.

Step into this great Circle of Light now as we watch it expand and contract continuously. We study our surroundings. This is a garden that is bathed in the Light and Love of God. This fills our senses and a calmness envelopes us.

Up ahead and a little to our left is a quaint timber bridge that crosses a stream, which is gurgling with crystal clear water that is flowing over smooth river rocks. We cross over the narrow bridge that resembles one, which could be located in a Japanese garden.

On the other side of the bridge, we notice a gleaming white building. It is a massive structure that is sparkling in the morning sun. Obviously, it is a place of worship and it possesses twelve doors. Every door represents the entry point of the place of worship of one of the great religions of the world.

We can enter through the door of our own personal choice. From there, we cross the large room without looking from side-to-side. Then, we approach the door that is directly opposite our point-of-entry and, which is glowing with a brilliant, continuously-pulsing White Light. The door opens automatically as we approach and we sail on through its opening. Inside, there are twelve angels who are standing as silent sentinels beside all twelve openings.

We have entered the Holy-of-Holies that is available at every moment, whether day or night, and regardless of creed, skin-tone or gender. Young and old alike may avail themselves of this great place of worship.

Upon entry, the calmness that we felt earlier is replaced by an overwhelming feeling of Love, this being Divine Love.

Glancing above, we observe a Point of Pure Light. Mesmerised, we stare up at the Point of Light above our heads. The more we focus our attention upon this Divine Light, the larger and more brilliant the Light becomes.

As we stand in rapture beneath the Light, we feel arms surrounding us and we know, without turning, that we have been joined by the other half of ourselves – our own Twin Flame who was breathed into life at the very same precise moment as we were. We are two halves of the same coin.

As our Divine Essence and Divine Energy merge as-one in this now-moment, we experience the most intoxicating and overpowering feeling of Love and our entire world stands still. There is complete stillness. There is complete silence.

In the Silence, we are ONE. We have become ONE with each other at the same moment as we have become ONE with **The Alpha Point**.

True union with GOD, THE ONE, is achieved.

Praise Be to Almighty God.

ALPHA – A Meditation

Focus on a Point-of-Light. Close your eyes and, through your Third Eye, concentrate your full attention on this tiny speck in front of you.

This is the Divine Light of God.

Watch as the Point becomes a Golden Ball while you focus your undivided attention upon it.

It is glowing while growing ever larger.

It is pulsing continuously.

It is shimmering continuously.

The more you focus on this great shimmering Ball of Light, the more you are drawn under Its Spell. As a moth to a flame, you draw ever closer until the moment of complete abandonment arrives and you become ONE with the Flame of Light as your Core Centre and Divine Light merge completely.

How is this moment of complete absorption reached?

The simplest and quickest way to bring about this ONENESS is to chant one word over and over again while concentrating, with your physical eyes closed, upon the pinpoint of Light.

That word is: *ALPHA*

When we are ONE with Divine Light and Divine Love, the external ceases to be a reality for us. All thoughts are directed towards GOD, THE ONE.

I Draw Up the Alpha Light from my Core Centre Within.

I Draw Down Divine Light from my Alpha Point above.

I Activate my Core Centre deep within.

I Direct the Christ Light from my Core Centre to the Heart Centre of Mother Earth. At this point, I connect the Alpha and the Omega. In the Silence, the Pulsing begins.

I Am AT-ONE with THE SOURCE-OF-ALL while listening to THE HEARTBEAT OF GOD!

Stella McMillan – (July/August 2015).

Divine Jade

Who Is She?

There is a secret and sacred Truth.

All must seek her alone.

Sealed lips only must speak her name.

Who is this precious gem?

She is:

Divine Jade!

Divine Jade

In a moment of Truth, Violet Flame awakens.

Sight is revealed in a flicker.

Ruby Red awakens.

Cord lengthens as Touch is revealed.

Yellow-Gold flickers awake.

Fragrance is the prize as blossoms breathe
out their sweet aroma come fresh from the Breath of God.

Blue Soul arises.

The call of the dove is heard.

Memory stirs, as Vital and Radiant,
The Spirit emerges.

The Divinity of Royal Jade
– more radiant than one thousand suns
of Earth – is revered.

No power can hold her. She is –

Divine Jade

The Rose and The Rock

As the Rose of Divine Love opens, the Heart is revealed.
As the Heart revolves slowly, the Light appears.
As Divine Light awakens, the Crown is revealed.
As the Fire of Divine Power activates, the Core Centre
awakens.
As Divine Jade arises, Blue Soul appears.
As ALL become ONE, the Holy Trinity is exposed for ALL
to witness.
The Glory-of-God is revered.

Only great Masters-of-Light – with the Divine Balance of yin
and yang – can manifest this State of Divine Grace on Earth
when in embodiment.
All others aspire to do so.
Pure Intent in all matters and Unconditional Love at all times
are prerequisites.
Miracles can occur when:
ALL is in Balance
ALL is Love
ALL is Light
ALL is Power Sublime

The black rock of negativity shatters and dissipates beneath
the Sun of our Golden Dawn. Divine Jade is revealed.
No force on Earth or elsewhere can defeat DIVINE JADE.
As Divine Jade becomes ONE with our ALPHA POINT, Blue
Soul consummates its Divine Union with ALPHA – our
GOD-the-ONE

Eternal Call

A diamond of great rarity fell to Earth
It was pure; it was clear; it was superb.
Dust covered its purity as its journey began.
Whispering winds rolled it along in the sand.
Sands of time cracked its pristine surface a little.
As mud filled its cracks, sun made it brittle.
A Hand lifted it high; its Creator's Breath soothed.
Rest and refuge was its harbour beneath the moon.
Again, this diamond fell on Earth's surface,
though no longer so pure, nor so clear, but still superb
beneath the collection of dust, sand, mud of Earth.

In all its lifetimes since before time began,
the Heart of the diamond pulsed beneath sand,
mud, dust, grit and grime – alive at its Heart.
In time with the Creator's Beat, it was never apart.
Light, Love, Wisdom, Will, Order, Power, Life Divine
were the Hallmark Traits of this diamond sublime.
Difficult to recognise by a glance at its surface;
there was little to recommend it to ones of taste.
Others saw only its outer shell – not its Core.
Illusion reigned supreme. Unrecognisable, though pure –
still pure – a diamond of great beauty roamed on Earth!

Its covering was its protection against pain.
No matter the trials of rock, wind, sun and rain,
at its Heart, it pulsed still to its Creator's Sound.
To *Ohmn-of-Life*, its soul continued to pound.
Many, many times, it returned – at its Creator's Call –
to Nirvana to recharge, regenerate after its fall.
In all diamond's excursions, its covering grew more dense.
In all diamond's travels, the journey made less sense.

Until diamond discovered the truth of the trek
was to come to the understanding of its hidden depth.
At its Core Centre, it was a diamond of great rarity!

As a rolling stone gathers no moss, diamond's need
was to rid itself of sand, mud, grime and to heal.
To all Earth's physicians did diamond appeal.
But, none could help, for they, too, must heal.
'Physician, heal thyself' became the catch-cry.
All sought a way to redeem and to try
to return to their original seed – the diamond sublime.
Some had shut off Divine Light; others Love Divine;
Divine Wisdom, Divine Will, many denied.
With Divine Order out-of-balance, Life
was left to partner Power – Creator's Tune lost!

As every diamond on Earth's surface grew more dense,
The Mother suffered pain, loss, degradation immense.
Her heart heavy, she sank to despair. Her desperation
caused a response that shook every vibration
within her Being and every diamond upon her surface.
Fear reigned. Panic followed. Despair on every face.
Nation fought nation. At every Age, the Diamond Master –
Amilus, Enoch, Melchizedek, Pythagoris, Gautama,
Zoroaster of Persia – appeared to lead the Race.
In many forms, to many nations, He came –
this Diamond of Light Divine; Love Unmeasured!

He was glorified, deified, crucified, vilified.
He forgave; then, came again and again to Earth's tribe.
As Jew, as Greek, as Indian, as Persian and more
to lead by example, to heal, to teach the *LAW*.
The *LAW-of-ONE* was his theme; his simple way
misunderstood; his simple life too difficult a way.

The tribe rebelled – broke away; Planet's diamonds lost.
Aquarius brought point-of-no-return. Ignored by most;
water-carrier, with pitcher held high and aloft.
Piscean Christ's lessons forgotten or scoffed.
Hope for diamond's return all but lost!

"Where to from here? Many asked in vain.
Return to the Creator to be healed of pain.
Illusion's way not the answer diamond sought.
Diamond's Heart pulsed, but time was so short.
Unseen, unheard, Creator called and called.
The Master's Voice was that of Maitreya, the Lord.
He came in many guises. All awaited His next birth.
Shoemaker-Levy was *shot-across-bow* of Earth.
Next comes *the rock* so large, so close, so fiery.
Will it shave by within a whisker, is query.
Or, hit with a shudder, scattering diamonds a-plenty?

Earth *on-the-move, ready or not,* Creator does cry.
Diamonds run hither-and-thither; nowhere to hide.
Creator's Love Song continues; unheard by most.
Ohmn is the sound wave; *LOVE* all but lost.
Planet shudders and shakes; fire out-of-control.
Rock demolishes satellites; oceans roar; waves roll.
Never has the like been witnessed before.
Even Noah, in Age of Leo – after Atlantis did fall,
could envisage a disaster to equal Earth's upheaval.
Second Woe is all over in one, swift reversal –
All over in *no-time*; survivors ponder the cause!

Cause-and-effect is answer, of course; Cosmic Law
overrides law of king, prince, pope, priest and *ALL*.
Diamonds called *HOME* – *"Come, one and all."*
Time for tea-party; time for reflection/overhaul.

Life is ongoing for our diamonds on journey
as they trek from one life to another endlessly.
Lack of understanding at spiritual level, the cause;
time for tea and rejuvenation; *ALL* must now pause.
Pathway is winding; Life never-ending in reality.
True Reality beckons; Akashic Books open to scrutiny.
Karmic debt accounted as ledger displayed!

Planet now cleansed – not healed at core.
Return requested – most diamonds implore.
Request denied for many with unpaid score.
Lesson of Unconditional Love most did ignore.
Sorrow great; wailing, wishing greater still
as many ponder the reason, ignoring Divine Will.
Divine Light brought Illumination, but centre locked.
Divine Wisdom, Divine Will, Divine Love blocked.
Divine Order out-of-balance for most still;
Divine Power, Divine Life flout Divine Will.
"Piper to be paid" brought life to a stand-still!

"How can this be?" became catch-cry of *ALL*.
Creator's Song unheard – on deaf ears *Ohmn* did fall.
Uncomprehending, diamonds request immediate return.
Love's Lesson unlearned. The Mother badly burned.
Cause-and-effect misunderstood by most souls.
Rejuvenated planet needs to heal and console.
Children's destruction too horrific to describe;
pollution, degradation, money ruled tribe.
Only Pure Diamonds trusted with Earth's care.
All others a thousand years watch from afar.
Wail, weep, while Creator unmoved; Song unheard!

Clear all dust, sand, mud, grit and grime.
Start at outer level, one layer at a time.
Only answer is this – to heal oneself now.
Only then can *Eternal Ohmn* be re-found.
Only then can God's children hear *The Sound*
Of Creator's song once again; once more rebound.
Diamonds of great rarity fall to Earth again,
when *ALL* is pure! *ALL* clear! *ALL* superb then!
Mother Earth hears the *Ohmn Sound* clearly.
Why, then, cannot all be attuned really?
Diamonds listen! Diamonds hear! *Divine Light* awaits!

Stella McMillan
(during the blue-moon time-frame on 1ˢᵗ January 2010)

First published in ***AWAKENING TO AWARENESS,*** the
fourth book of the ***Stella McMillan Series***

The Veil
To *know* the meaning of Life
is to lift the veil of Death.
To lift the etheric film beyond Life
is to peer into the mist beyond Time.
Through the mist is revealed Reality.
In this Realm, *ALL* ways are seen!

To peer into another Reality
is to look both ways – *ALL* ways.
To peer forward beyond the *NOW*
is to look into the Future.
To search backwards before the *NOW*
is to look into the mist before Time!

To *Know* True Reality
is to look every which way.
For that which has gone before
and that which is to go beyond
is all the same – the *ONE,*
a part of the *ALL – Super-Consciousness!*
Stella McMillan
15th May 2007

First published in **ERROR of UNDERSTANDING**, the first
book of the **Stella McMillan Series**

Transition

The Final Journey

Book Three

Tenets of the LAW OF ONE

Tenets of the LAW OF ONE
Introduction – Onoraus

Gentle Starseeds of Light, the following Discourses are given to you so that you may find a peaceful and loving pathway through the maze of experiences that makes up your life on Earth. Along with other books from the pen of my Twin-Flame, Constella, these writings, the *Tenets of the LAW OF ONE*, comprise a complete set of steps that can be taken on the road back to ONENESS with our Creator. Ultimately, that is the goal of all, even though at a conscious level most may not acknowledge this to themselves (or others) while in physical embodiment. I commend all of these Discourses to you. Many Masters of Light have contributed to these four simple books that have been a labour of love for all concerned since they were commenced in October, 1999.

Take them to your hearts, I beg of you. Please do not allow false pride, petty ego, inherited belief-systems or the outmoded concepts of the conscious mind to rob you of your inheritance. Your life (Real Life) is too important to you for you to allow this to occur. World events may intervene in your lives and many of your future plans may come to nought. When this occurs, most people tend to go into shock, for want of a better description; then, they become depressed, for they cannot see the future as clearly as they did once – or perhaps, they cannot see a future at all.

That is why these Discourses have been written and are being presented to you at this time. Your world is changing. It is changing very rapidly and there are more changes to occur. These cannot be stopped. The juggernaut has begun its roll, as you say. As all of the old concepts and dogma slip away, what will there be to hold on to in this world of matter? Truth is the answer to that question. There is no other Truth but God. All else is illusion.

It is easy to live in an illusionary world when everything remains the same, day in and day out. But when rapid change occurs – then continues to occur – even the most lethargic and lazy souls begin to question. When the leaders of a society do not have the answers, the illusion begins to be seen for what it is truly. Then, the seeker may begin his or her search for Truth. Who, in this world of matter, has that Truth, Which is God?

Deny that reincarnation is a fact of life and you give power to the ones who have controlled this planet for aeons of time. Open your minds to the concept that this transitory existence that you call *life* is but an illusion and that True Reality lies beyond the veil that you call *death*; then, you have taken your first step back on your road to recovery. That road to recovery will come to an end for you personally when ONENESS is achieved. Let this be your only goal from this moment onward. From a willingness to open up one's self to *new* thoughts, ideas and concepts and on to your moment of completeness is a long journey for many. For those who began this process a long time ago, the journey is nearing an end, so perhaps it is time to lend a willing hand to those coming behind you on the path to enlightenment, completeness and, of course, self-healing. Be guided by the words in these books until you find your own way onto your own unique pathway HOME. Whatever information you need for your journey will be absorbed by your subconscious mind. Whatever is superfluous to your current needs will be discarded by your soul/spirit within. All that is being asked is that you read this series of books with an open mind and Love in your heart. That is not too much to ask; is it? I think not when one considers the overall picture and ponders upon just what is at stake here. I will leave you to decide, my beautiful and ever-loving Starseeds of Light.

Be at peace. Know you are loved more dearly and greatly than you could ever imagine; or, that you ever thought was possible. I will leave you in Love and surrounded by my love for all of you. I know all of you personally and by your cosmic name, as well as by your ever-loving vibration/frequency. Until we meet again beyond the stars, stay true to yourselves, no matter what or who comes into your life to delay or disrupt. Place your trust and faith in God and in our Creator's Love for every one of you who walks this path back to ONENESS. May your Light shine more brightly than the brightest star in your universe and may your Love know no bounds.

This is my last contributions to these Discourses. I trust you will find them helpful and enlightening.

Adieu, sweet ones.

In God's Love,

Onoraus

Prologue – Constella

In the coming days, months and years, many will come to a clear understanding of spiritual matters and spiritual truths. In order to speed this process a little, I have written a Discourse, which covers comprehensively the *LAW OF ONE Tenets*. I present this for the perusal of the Starseeds of Light.

Many are asking what can be done now to prevent a third and most horrific world war. In the EPILOGUE of this simple booklet, I have outlined suggestions. Take these to your hearts and if they feel comfortable to you, then put your thoughts into physical action to aid the planet, as well as all of humanity residing upon her presently.

I ask only that you read the following words in Love, in silence and in peace while meditating alone. Then, I would ask simply that to your own self be true. It is a simple request. Your response, or lack of response, could make a great difference to the survival of Planet Earth and the life you know today; or, to the destruction of all you hold dear. Consider well and act accordingly.

Do not allow yourselves to be misled by others. Hold on to truth, no matter what, and that means your own truth – not someone else's idea of what your truth should be.

Prayer is the only answer to peace. Prayer alone, or in a group setting, is vital to the survival of the planet. Who or what else could save her at this late stage, do you think? Continue to live the illusionary lifestyle that most earth-dwellers believe is *real;* then, know that your future on this planet is tenuous indeed.

These are strong words, but they are given in Love. Please read the words that follow with open-ness and Love in your hearts. They are given in Love to give you hope.

In God's Great Love, I commend these –the *Tenets of the LAW OF ONE* – to you, gentle Starseeds of Light.

I AM Constella

MAJOR TENETS

Tenet One

In God, we trust.

In God, all our needs are met.
In all else, we are on our own.
On our own, we struggle and strive in our quest for uncertain goals.
On our own, we seek fame, fortune – the baubles of earthly life.

In God, we love.
In God, all our love is returned one-thousand fold.
In all else, we are on our own.
On our own, we can love unwisely.

On our own, we become one with another, not necessarily knowing the love we seek – that being Love Unconditional.
So, love God above all others.
Love God Unconditionally.

This is the **Tenet of Divine Love.**

This is the First Tenet of God – The First Cause –The Mother-Father-God Principle from Whom All comes.

The Origin of ALL species is GOD – THE ONE.

Tenet Two

Divine Love fills all beings.
Divine Love comes from GOD – THE ONE.
Divine Life fills all beings.
Divine Life comes from GOD – THE ONE.
Divine Light fills all beings.
Divine Light comes from GOD – THE ONE.

If Divine Love, Divine Life and Divine Light
fill all beings, whether in physical form or in astral/etheric
form, then who has the right to hurt or harm another
who is filled with God's Divine Source?
The Divine Source – GOD – THE ONE – fills all.
The yin, the yang, plus the qi, is Divine Source.
Without the three, there is no life – not in any realm of
existence.

To hurt or harm, in any way at all,
a being who contains the Source and Essence of all life
is a crime against humanity and a crime against the Source of
ALL – GOD – THE ONE.
First comes the thought to hurt or harm.
Next comes the passion that gives fire to the thought.
Then comes the physical action to manifest that thought.
All three play a part, but the crime is enacted with the thought
unmanifest.

The Power of Thought is grossly underestimated
in the illusionary world of matter on Earth.
So, the three are One – GOD – THE ONE.
That Source flows through all beings, to a greater or lesser
extent, depending on knowledge, understanding, compassion
and love.

Nevertheless, the Source, The Essence of God,
flows through all, regardless of gender, size,
skin colour or tone, number of legs, shape of physical form
or the belief-system or racial origins of a particular species.

Every creature, large or small, gives off a frequency.
This frequency is colour and sound combined.
This frequency/vibration indicates how much or how little
of the Source/Life Force of GOD – THE ONE – is flowing
through that creation of God at any particular moment in
Earth-time.
As with the seasons, the frequency can change.

In any moment, a fear – real or imagined –can alter the
frequency by altering an emotional state or response.
Divine Love, Divine Life, Divine Light, flows through all
beings everywhere.
Hurt or harm another creature of our GOD – THE ONE,
our God of all creation, and we hurt our God.
We harm ourselves, also, by lowering our own frequency at
the same moment.
Love all, for God's sake, as well as our own.

This is the Second Tenet of God.

The Tenets of Life (An Explanation)

The first two *Tenets of the LAW OF ONE* are those that will ensure eternal life for those who abide by them. During physical life upon Earth, this path is almost insurmountable in the eyes of most, because of perceived obstacles. These obstacles are placed upon *the path* by one's own self – the Spirit Self/Higher Self – so as to defeat one's ego-self/lower self.

To defeat one's own self and to complete the obstacle course that one has set for oneself, at a higher level, when vibrating at a higher frequency during resting times between physical incarnations, it is necessary to understand and to have knowledge of the four minor *Tenets of the LAW OF ONE.*

If one were to look at a strand of pearls, as an example, then possibly one could perceive *the path* a little more clearly. Let us suppose that all of the pearls in the strand of pearls are of equal size, yet every pearl is a slightly different colour. Let us suppose, also, that between every pearl, there is a small diamond. Now, assuming that every pearl represents a physical incarnation and every diamond represents the cleansing and clearing process that one undergoes between incarnations when we return to being our own Higher Self, then that will help to understand perhaps a little the picture that I am painting here.

In this *diamond state*, we return to our permanent home and we review our university or kindergarten experiences upon Earth – in our last incarnation – the *pearl* state. In this other world where we live in our astral/etheric bodies, we have a permanent home, which has been our abode between most incarnations. I say most, because there have been times when we have become caught-up in the conflicts and causes of this illusionary, pretend life on the planet known currently as *Earth* and, we have forgotten all about who we are really (in True Reality), who we are here to represent by our Love, Life and Light (our God-Self), what we came to achieve (our path – our Earth mission this time around) and, tragically, who are the members of our own soul-family, with whom we share our Love, joy, fun and laughter in our true home (our *diamond* state) between incarnations and what we all came down here to do as a group – as a soul-family.

When we have forgotten our true purpose during an Earth experience, we return to the diamond state in a pitiful state and often, we have been devastated, during our compulsory review of our immediate past-life sojourn on Earth, by our actions, reactions and lack of action where our own brothers and sisters are concerned. Most especially, this relates to our lack of compassion and Love shown to those from our own soul-family who may have chosen to be a part of an *opposition* family on Earth during that incarnation. In such times, we have lowered our frequency considerably and our vibration is too low at these times to return to our true home, so we are obliged to go and join other members of our soul-family who have fallen by the wayside, so to speak, in other incarnations and we reside now in a world where the frequency is lower and the Love, Life and Light of the Source does not shine as brightly as in higher worlds, because the inhabitants have closed off their receptors (energy centres) more than is advisable or acceptable.

Quote: 'Behold, for there are many mansions in my Fatherland. If there were not, I would have told you so."

The lowest world of all is Earth. Its frequency is so low that one needs a physical vehicle (body) in order to be seen and felt by others walking around down here. When the astral/etheric/spirit body decides to leave, being for the most part a pre-arranged schedule of the Higher Self, the physical vehicle disintegrates and that particular identity is no more on

Earth. Regardless of the status, the wealth, the power that any particular identity/being has achieved, or the influence he or she has been able to wield during a physical incarnation, the diamond state is the fire that trims away the illusion and brings the being concerned face-to-face with True Reality once again. This is a truly awesome experience for many.

There are ones who are incarnate upon Earth now and these ones pay homage to beings who existed in times past and who built temples and shrines that have lasted for centuries-in-time. But, they pay homage to an illusion while the one to whom they pay homage has returned to Earth in a heavier vehicle, because he or she lowered the vibration of their own being during previous excursions on Earth. Does that make sense to anyone?

So, let us return to the strand of pearls. The strand itself is the ongoing Life Force or Source. The pearl is the Earth experience and the diamond in-between is the prism of fire that cleanses and heals – the golden-white Light of God.

There are some who began incarnating at the first pearl after the golden clasp and they lowered their vibration immediately. They have not learned one lesson since that first pearl experience and now, as they approach their own golden clasp once more in their final lifetime on Earth, they are in fear and trepidation, because the fire of the last diamond will be the most severe of all for them. They have lowered their vibration so much with every pearl experience that they resemble the blackest pearl imaginable. Others have cleansed and healed themselves so much during and in-between every Earth experience that they will pass through their final diamond experience as though swimming across a crystal-clear pond to meet their dear friends on the other side. Most have pearls that are grey, followed by white, followed by pink and the final diamond process will be a mere adjustment of their energy centres. The ones who are the blackest of all have closed off all of their energy centres, except for the lower two, and they exist in the reality of Earth by draining the Love Essence of God that they need for survival from those who love them and who continue to support them while in embodiment on Earth.

These black ones are energy *vampires* and need to be avoided at all cost. They control every power source on Earth to this day, be it a religious power-base, a military power-base, an educational power-base, a media-based power-base or one of the greatest aphrodisiac of all and that controls all others – the financial/monetary power-base.

The vibratory frequency of these ones, who are in total control on Earth is so low that they cannot and will not survive the final diamond state, through which all must be ready, willing and able to pass when the time comes for them to do so. Every being that is in embodiment on Earth at present, is experiencing their last or their second-last pearl experience. The final diamond state is fast approaching for all.

Life can go on no longer on Planet Earth, because Earth can sustain life no longer, due to the violence, pollution, and rape that she, as an entity-of-God, has undergone at the hands of her inhabitants, but most especially, it is due to the loveless state, in which most people on Earth live now. By loveless, I refer to the closing down of the energy centres one-by-one in order to survive physically in this loveless world. When one shuts down the energy centre relating to love and compassion, then one has made a huge difference in one's own vibratory frequency, descending by one's own freewill choice to the lower negative state, of which I speak. This is why the planet can sustain life no longer.

There is a soft, inaudible, silent Voice that whispers on the breeze. All life hears this Voice, because It is the Voice of God. Its whispers cannot be drowned out, no matter what the state of the vibratory frequency of the individual or life-form. The trees hear It. The birds, the wild-life and the great creatures of the ocean hear It. Every human being is hearing It now. It comes through the strand that holds the pearl and diamond necklace together. It is the three-fold Life Force of Divine Love, Divine Life and Divine Light. Or, for those who prefer a different terminology – that of the TAO – the yin, the yang and the qi. It cannot be shut out, because the soul/spirit hears It and breathes It into every cell and atom, into every fibre of one's being. The timbre or tone is echoing and reverberating throughout space. Those *gods* from beyond Earth's atmosphere, who took up residence some six centuries hence, have heard It. Their ill-conceived plans for Earth's dominance, through its hardened population of a few dark souls, have come to nought and have been shelved. They head for greener pastures now. They leave their puppets in physical form quaking in fear and trepidation of that which is to come; that must come.

The blood of all of the prophets of God martyred on Earth since time immemorial is on their hands and no matter how many times they cry out the words: "Out, damn spot!" the indelible bloodstains remain, forever marking them as traitors of God's Love.

The Word that is whispered on the breeze now gives hope to this world of darkness and death – this hell – known as life-on-Earth. All life hears and most are gladdened by the Word that is being spread the length and breadth of the globe and throughout the fabric that is known currently as *space*. That Word is:

"It is finished. Let God's Will be done!"

Minor Tenets

There is One God for all of humanity. In that One God, we love and trust. This is the basis of all religions of this world. To a degree that a religion has moved from the basic tenet, then that is the degree, to which it has moved to become a power-base for the self-aggrandisement of man.

There is a Master-Soul – a Master among men, women and children – whose lives upon Earth have been a pattern for humanity to follow. This Master of Love, Life and Light has trodden many, many pathways in physical form. He has brought his Love and Compassion to every race on Earth, whether we speak of times long-past in Atlantean times; or, we speak of him as the Prince of Peace of more recent times, in an Age just past.

There is not one religion on this plane of Earth today that did not have this Master of Love, Peace and Compassion as its founder. That is why he watches, with a heavy heart this day, those who claim to be following his teachings and who claim to be acting in his name and in God's Love preparing for another war-to-end-all-wars on Earth now.

He has come to Earth in physical form at the beginning of every Age of Man. He has come in Love – God's Love – with peace and compassion as his only agenda.

In every lifetime, this great Light – the Golden Frequency, upon which he operates – has so affected the negative ones that they have plotted and planned together to bring about his physical destruction. In the lifetimes where he has allowed this to occur, he has been led as a lamb to the slaughter to his violent physical death. In other lifetimes, he has practised and preached peace, compassion and Love.

There was never a time when this was not the main focus of his teaching. Regardless of what men did, at a later time, to alter his teachings as they sought to control the population of the day, using his image, but their own interpretation of his laws and rules for their own benefit, his message of peace, compassion and Love remains the basis of every religion that was founded as a result of his life in that particular incarnation. There was never a race of people on Earth to whom he did not come to share his Love, to give his message of peace, to enlighten his followers and, in so doing, to raise the vibratory frequency of Planet Earth herself.

His message was never about violence, hatred or war; nor was his message about subjugation of the *weaker* ones of the human species, for it needs to be understood that every being who is in embodiment at this time, at one time in Earth's history, has had an embodiment as a male and as a female, so the notion that all men are made in the image of God and that all women are *soul-less* is a concoction from the minds of men who were required subsequently to live by these rules in the form of a woman. That is the Law of Karma in action.

The teachings of the Illumined One – this Master of Souls – is clear and unequivocal. It is the teaching of Universal Love, embracing the themes of peace at all cost and compassion for all, regardless of creed, race, colour, shape, size or gender.

If these are not the tenets of the religious organisation, to which one gives allegiance currently, the wise will lift up their eyes to see this Master Soul – The Illumined One – smiling down at them; then, they will walk away totally from a man-made belief-system that has adopted violence, hatred and revenge in place of the Master's original message of peace, compassion and Love for all.

Honour The Illumined One and live by his message, for to live in peace, compassion and Universal Love is to honour him who came oh! so many, many times – in God's Love – to give the *Tenets of the LAW OF ONE – THE ONENESS OF ALL LIFE.*

The Tenet of Karmic Consequence (Cause, Effect and Redemption/Renewal)

The Law of Karma in action is the Tenet of Cause and Effect. Redemption and/or Renewal is the sum total of all of our lifetimes lived in peace, compassion and Love, balanced against all of our lifetimes lived in an unloving state while promoting and living by the rule of violence, hatred and vengeance.

It all comes back to the symbolism of the pearl and diamond necklace. The removal of the Law of Cause and Effect and the Law of Reincarnation from the Holy Books of Earth has resulted in a shift in consciousness for the planet as a whole. It has altered the whole fabric of society. It has altered the way that society, as a whole, views the animals, birds, sea creatures and plant-life. It has altered the way that one human being relates to another.

If one can delude oneself into accepting that there is no God and that this lifetime is the only one that occurs, then this alters the pattern of one's thinking during that lifetime and the way, in which one leads that life. When a person such as this faces a death situation, he or she is secure in the knowledge – false though that is – that he or she will simply slip into a deep sleep, never to wake again. What a shock it is for one such as this to come to the sudden realisation that the physical body has gone to sleep permanently, but that the person is in a body still, with a consciousness that is real and just as alive as it was always. Then, the being realises that the belief-system, to which he or she adhered – strictly, in most cases – was as false as the premise, upon which it was based.

"Where to from here?" is the usual response for one such as this in a situation such as I have described. It is a long road back for that particular soul/spirit from that point.

There are many, many people who incarnate upon Earth and who believe that they need to adhere – strictly or otherwise – to the teachings of their chosen religious leaders. Because of this belief-system (often passed down from generation to generation), they listen intently to the words of these religious leaders and, in many cases, obey to the letter the rites, rituals and sacrifices that they are promoting. In order to keep their *flock* in line, it is an unspoken rule that the one who does not adhere and give allegiance to that particular doctrine or belief-system be ostracised from the family unit. Is such a regulation coming from Love?

Let us return to the pearl and diamond necklace. If the strand holding these stones (lifetimes) together is pulsing vibrantly with the Life Force of God, then why would such a one be listening to and adhering to rules and regulations coming from the mouths of ones who, in many cases, have blocked off that Life Force from God and, therefore, are vibrating at a lower frequency than the one who is the *parishioner,* for want of a better word in this language? Power is a strong and addictive aphrodisiac, regardless of which organisation a person chooses to join to further one's selfish ambitions in this regard. There are many who join power-based organisations, regardless of what their main focus is, with high ideals and love in their hearts. But, power corrupts. Wearing a uniform – whatever the design or focus – and administering rules and regulations of others makes the *self* feel very important. The further up the ladder one climbs, the greater the importance that is attached to the role one is playing within the organisation of one's choice.

There are many, many thousands of men and women within religious organisations on Earth today and these ones have a great love for God, for his prophets of old and for humanity itself. In every subsequent lifetime, their pearls grow brighter with the Light and Love of God. But, the tragedy is that whilst in embodiment, they allow themselves to be at the beck-and-call of others who are dominant in the self-same organisation, yet whose light grows darker with every life experience upon Earth. Was it not the priests in their fine robes and with their eloquent speech who condemned Jesus to death? What robes do you think that they are wearing this day, in their current lifetime on Earth? Do you really think that they are wearing the robes of the loving and humble parishioner? Could anyone be so naive now? They could, because it was men who wore fine robes and who spoke with eloquent speech that convinced an unsuspecting public many centuries ago that reincarnation was not a fact of life. Was it the self-same men, do you think? Could that be a possibility?

If one looks only at one's current lifetime, rather than at the whole picture – the strand of pearls and diamonds – then, one has a rather restricted and, dare I say *blinkered* view of life as a whole. That is a fair assumption, I feel. So, rather than accepting only what the five physical senses detect, adding to the inherited belief-system that has been altered by time and by ones with hidden agendas, perhaps it is time to take a fresh and unbiased view of all of life. View life as an ongoing pearl and diamond necklace with the golden clasp (entry into the Golden Age) as the greatest prize of all. Rather than seeing certain events in life as negative happenings, see them as the Law of Cause and Effect in perfect action, leading to a culmination that is known as *Redemption/Renewal*.

This is the Tenet of Karmic Consequence – of Cause, Effect and Redemption/Renewal.

The Tenet of Relinquishing ALL DESIRE

To desire or want something is to rely upon self to achieve that desire.

To desire pleasures above God's Love is to deny God.

To desire possessions above God's Love is to deny God.

To desire other people above God's Love is to deny God.

To need (as opposed to *want*) a pleasant experience within the realm of the physical world in order to release tension and stress is a worthwhile exercise. This needs to be encouraged, for the path of life on Earth can be overwhelming at times for God's children as they endeavour to overcome all of the tests and trials that they have set for themselves in any particular incarnation. This is considered a need and not a want or desire.

A desire is when one pursues something with a passionate resolve to have same, regardless of cost to self or others. In all things, let there be moderation. The *something* that one pursues with passion and dedication could be *pleasures*, *possessions* (including wealth) or *people*, or a particular person to whom one is attracted and feels one cannot possibly live a life without these people, or this person, as a pivotal part of that life.

These three *P's* are the traps one has set for oneself in life and will be, in all probability, a pattern that needs to be broken, having been responsible for one's downfall in previous incarnations on Earth and perhaps elsewhere.

To relinquish **ALL DESIRE** is the Tenet that needs to be observed to succeed in this area of one's life.

The Tenet of Denying ALL PRIDE, POWER, EGOTISM, HYPOCRISY and DECEIT

This Tenet is the taking of the previous Tenet of Relinquishing ALL DESIRE to its absolute limit.

Humility is the greatest of all attributes and goes hand-in-hand with peace, compassion and Love. Anyone who possesses all four of these attributes is a giant among humanity and shines as a beacon for all to follow. Unfortunately, a great being such as this emanates a sound and a frequency, as well as a brilliant glow, in his/her auric field. I say it is unfortunate, because the lack of understanding on Earth is so great where vibratory frequency is concerned that ones who are in negativity (due to their own low vibration) feel threatened by a Great Being of Light.

When one allows fear, ignorance and negativity to rule, then that person can have one reaction only. That is the reaction of attack. Many who wear the *mantle of greatness* on Earth today are ones such as these negative ones who wear this mantle of false humility while possessing great pride, great power and great ego. Hypocrisy and deceit are their constant companions. All too often their own followers follow their lead and mirror themselves on their self-appointed leaders. It is the blind leading the blind into ever-greater darkness and, for ones who possess still a little of God's Light and Love, it can lead to the deepest depth of despair that is imaginable. For ones such as these, it is a matter of time only before they begin to shut-down their own chakras; then, illness and the slow destruction of their own physical encasements follow. Physical death is but a matter of time; then, another pearl experience has been wasted, because the lesson of denying pride, power, egotism, hypocrisy and deceit was not learned in that lifetime.

The Tenet of denying ALL PRIDE, POWER, EGOTISM, HYPOCRISY and DECEIT is the one that leads to humility in all areas of one's life – a truly blessed state of Be-ing.

The Tenet of SILENCE

To become the tool of the ego-self when in embodiment is to deny the spirit-self the time, the space and the peace to be alone with our GOD – I AM.

To allow the ego-self full rein (when one is occupying a physical encasement in any lifetime on Earth) is to relinquish total control to the ego-personality. When in such a state, the person concerned will reject totally ALL of The Tenets of the LAW OF ONE.

To find a place, however small, where one can be alone with God and to allow time to stand still and for the peace of God to enfold is the first step to recovery for the spirit-self.

The ego-self, if given full rein, will keep the mind and personality so busy and so engrossed in physical pursuits that the spirit-self is forced to withdraw. The further the spirit-self is forced to withdraw (because of busy-ness), the less of the Life Force of God can be maintained in the physical encasement. The more one denies the ego-self by following closely the Tenets, the closer one will draw to God, the Source of ALL.

The Tenet of denying busy-ness and accepting SILENCE, so as to be in the Presence of God during prayer and meditation, is the greatest of all Tenets and leads to enlightenment and Love beyond measure.

This is the **Tenet of SILENCE**.

The Tenet of Accepting NO TRUTH but GOD

Accepting no truth but God is accepting that God alone is TRUTH EVERLASTING. Accepting man's version of what they (and their own egos) believe God's Truth to be is to be the blind fool being led along a path to oblivion and darkness.

God speaks to the soul-spirit of ALL.

God speaks to the soul-spirit of ALL in the land of silence.

God cannot speak to those in human form through their heart centres if those heart centres have been closed off, so that they can follow blindly the dictates of ones who have hidden agendas (masked by hypocrisy and deceit) and, who wear the *mantle of greatness* with great pride while wielding great power, displaying great ego and duping the population as a whole with their own version of truth, which is no truth at all.

The Tenet of accepting NO TRUTH but GOD is binding on all of humanity.

This was the message that was at the basis of all religions on Earth, along with the message of peace, compassion, Love and goodwill to ALL, regardless of race, creed, colour, gender, shape or size. This includes all creatures great and small, whether the form is human or otherwise. Humanity was given tenure of this planet, known now as Earth, on the clear understanding that this planet and ALL of its inhabitants, including trees and plant-life, came under the protection of humanity's love, care and stewardship. At the beginning of the Aquarian Age of Humanity, it is time for humanity to be called to account, not only for its stewardship of the planet as a whole, but also for its adherence (or otherwise) to the *Tenets of the LAW OF ONE*.

The Book of Remembrance is being opened at this moment. This Book – or, Akashic Records, as it is known –

records the sum total of all lifetimes lived upon Earth. The strand of pearls is being examined now for faults and flaws before the final diamond state is undertaken. The ego-personality can deny the existence of all other lifetimes while it is in charge fully when in physical embodiment, but no one – NOT ANY ONE PERSON ON EARTH – can defeat death at this point in time.

At a future moment when the planet's vibration has been raised considerably, this will be possible. At this moment, the vibration of the planet is being kept low – deliberately so – by many of her inhabitants who are in total fear of the final outcome, which they know at a deep level within themselves is approaching fast. With the moment of death comes *clarity-of-thought* and the ego-self is in charge no longer. The spirit-self takes charge and the spirit-self judges itself more harshly than any judge, jury or earthly king could do ever.

Were the spirit-self to be allowed the time, the space and the peace to be alone – TOTALLY ALONE DAILY – so as to drift in God's Love, God's Light and God's Life Energy or Essence, then one would know GOD'S TRUTH. No truth other than God's Truth would be acceptable; nor would it be countenanced.

The Tenet of SILENCE and the Tenet of GOD'S TRUTH are inseparable. Every Master of God, including the Master of Masters, the Illumined One of the Most High, has made the *Tenets of the LAW OF ONE* the basis of their preaching and teachings when in embodiment on Earth. Anyone who has altered, for their own reasons and their own self (ego) aggrandisement, these Tenets, has made a rod for humanity's back. If humanity, as a collective consciousness, is prepared to follow blindly ones such as these and to accept their words as truth, then the future for Earth and her inhabitants is bleak indeed.

If humanity, as a collective consciousness, could accept the strand of pearl analogy and the concept that as soon as one steps from any physical encasement at the point of physical death, one is confronted with God's Truth, which brings clarity-of-thought immediately, then life on Earth would undergo a massive change overnight. The result of this would be an immediate lifting of the planet's vibration and the regeneration and rejuvenation of *all life* on Earth.

Living by the **Tenets of the LAW OF ONE** would ensure a continuation of this planetary shift-in-consciousness and vibration. Perhaps, all of the prison doors could be thrown open then and the ones governing this planet would be excess to requirements, because all would be governed and guided by the spirit-self, as the ego-self would be no more.

The greatest threat to all is the ego-self. Master the ego-self; be guided by the spirit-self; cleanse, clear and self-heal the astral/etheric/physical self while in embodiment and live, love, work and play in God's Light, peace, compassion and Love for the remainder of one's time on Earth and in Earth's environs – known as the astral plane – between incarnations.

That has been the promise of salvation offered to humankind by all of the Masters of Light and Love who have trodden Earth's stage in peace, harmony, joy, humility, goodwill and, most of all, Love. Honour them all, including the Master of Masters, the Illumined One, who began the charge back to the Light and Love of God many millennia ago, long before time began on Earth.

Observe the *Tenets of the LAW OF ONE,* so that when clarity-of-thought returns all will be well and the diamond state will be a process of pure bliss. Be at peace and know that God's Love surrounds all, regardless of belief-systems and vibratory frequency. God's Love infuses those whose energy centres are open to receive. That degree of open-ness depends upon one factor – if one walks in PEACE, HUMILTY and LOVE upon Earth and promotes GOODWILL TO ALL. Following the *Tenets of the LAW OF ONE* will ensure that the future is as bright as the brightest star in your constellation.

I AM Constella, Master of Light and Love, from a constellation not far removed from your own and where the Light and Love of God shines so brightly that all I can wish for, hope for and pray for is that Earth's vibration will mirror that of my own constellation in the NOW moment.

May the stars in your eyes (that are your eyes, for they mirror your soul) be so full of God's Light and God's Love that reaching for the stars is your ultimate goal.

I leave you in peace. I leave you in Love. I commend these, the *Tenets of the LAW OF ONE*, to you. May the joy you share and the joy you experience, know no bounds. Give allegiance to GOD – THE ONE – and give your power to no one, for you are the Master of your own destiny – here and elsewhere.

In God's peace, joy, harmony and Love, I bid you farewell. Until we meet again beyond the stars, adieu, beloved children of the Light and Love of God.

I AM Constella.

Author's Note (Transition – *The Final Journey*)

Without doubt, this book, entitled **Transition – *The Final Journey*** – is a hotchpotch in that it covers many different issues for those who are walking a spiritual path. Commencing with the Transition of Mary into another reality, before moving onto other Discourses and explanations that are spiritual in essence, these writings are a culmination of a lifetime of searching. From there, it moves to an explanation of self-healing.

We can search for Truth endlessly, but what we regard as Truth Everlasting today may be different completely from what we accept as our own version of *Truth* tomorrow. Is reincarnation a fact of life? There are millions of people who believe this to be so. There are religions that are based upon this theory while other religions cling firmly to the one-life-only concept. If there is one-life-only and during this lifetime, we are meant to become perfect, what happens to those who cannot achieve this great feat of perfection?

Every week on Earth, during any given millennia, thousands pass through the veil that is physical death. For those who are *spiritually-aware*, shall we say, this may be a simple act of lifting a light veil or curtain and walking into another reality, as Mary did in our fictitious story. For others, the veil is almost impenetrable, because they fight their own transition vigorously. It is fear that causes them to fight the inevitable ending of that particular physical life. It is a fear of the unknown.

For some, it is an acceptance that they will close their eyes, drift into a deep sleep and never wake again. When they come to the realisation that they are alive still and fully conscious while possessing a body that resembles the physical one that they have discarded, shock sets in and this is followed by confusion. How can they be alive still? They have no answer, because they have swallowed the one-life-only story while walking around in physical form.

Slowly, they come to the understanding that they have passed through this *veil-of-illusion*, which is known also as *physical death*, many, many times previously. As Mary did, they arrive at this truth with great assistance from their Spirit Guides who are Beings of great Light and Love – that being Divine Light and Divine Love. So, why the illusion and the purpose of promoting the one-life-only theory while in physical embodiment on Earth? Could it be that some of the religions on Earth have chosen to delude their followers for their own selfish reasons? Is this possible? After all, if one can reach *heaven* only through that particular religion, this gives great power to its leaders.

Let us explore the story of Mary's transition a little more. If the Guardians-of-Light allowed Mary to step aboard the escalators with her entourage and to ascend to the higher level while they refused permission for the businessman to do the same, what could the Guardians see in the man that Mary could not see? Perhaps, it was that his aura was dark and murky? Or, was it that he was displaying, also, other symptoms, for want of a better word?

When the businessman made his final journey, he would have been offered healing, as Mary was. He would have been asked if he wished to have all of his weapons that he had accumulated over his recent life removed. Also, he would have been asked if the crystal/rock could be removed from his Sacral chakra/energy centre. However, a condition would have been placed on this last offer. The condition would have been that, in his next lifetime on Earth, he would agree to begin repaying some of the great debt, which he owed to Karmic or Cosmic Law. That rock (crystal) would not have been in his etheric body only, because the etheric body disintegrates and disappears within a short period after the death of the physical form. This man's rock would have been lodged firmly in his Astral body. It would have been removed willingly by the Guides-of-Light once he agreed to this simple condition. However, his next lifetime would have been a nightmare for him, because those of his ilk, with whom he associates both on Earth and on the Lower Astral level between incarnations, would have regarded him as a traitor to their negative cause.

They would have forced him to pay dearly for his capitulation and for his act of treason, as they would view it. So, with the rock of a crystalline substance lodged in his Sacral chakra at the level of his Astral body on a permanent basis and by his own freewill choice, he was destined to remain on the Lower Astral level until he could arrange another physical lifetime on Earth. As the Lower Astral plane is a dog-eat-dog existence, he would have elected to remain there for a very short period of time and he would have asked very quickly for a return to Earth in a new physical body. He would have chosen the parents to whom he wished to come as a new-born babe. He would have mapped out his next incarnation carefully and precisely. Certainly, he would not have elected to be born a pauper. He operates from his two lower chakras only. Therefore, he would choose a family where wealth and power were the accepted and expected requirements of physical life. Possibly, he would choose a male body as opposed to a female one, because he would be able to exert more power and control over others when operating in a male-dominated society, as he would see it.

Returning to Mary, all of her weapons that she had acquired during her lifetime were lodged in her etheric body. These would have been removed during her mandatory healing session, as she reviewed her immediate past life. She would have agreed willingly to repay any karmic debt, which she owed to Karmic Law. That is the great difference between those who operate at a higher frequency at all times and those who choose, of their own freewill, to operate in a negative capacity on Earth, as well as between incarnations on the Lower Astral plane. These ones will never accept, at a conscious level when in embodiment on Earth, that there is anything but a one-life-only, in which to become perfect in God's Eyes, shall we say. Also, their energy level or vibratory frequency is too low for them to access the higher levels, or to cross the suspension bridge, if that is a clearer explanation. They are at this level by their own freewill choices. They are the only ones who can change the situation in a loving, positive way.

For the children of Light, their weapons are at the etheric level only in most cases. These are cleared quickly and easily upon their return to their true home, as happened with Mary in our fictitious story. The exception to this rule would be the children of Light who had been the well-respected spiritual leaders of pure intent operating in various situations in former lifetimes, and the Atlantean ones come to mind here. Those leaders were targeted mercilessly in more than one lifetime. Consequently, those deeper weapons will be lodged in their Astral bodies, as well, and these will need to be cleared in these instances. Also, they may have cords-of-attachment hooked into some of their chakras and these will be there, because in this current life, someone who has been in control of their lives previously has returned this time around and may be in a position of power over that person again. Once again, it is the Higher-Self who knows all.

Those who are required to return to the Lower Astral level after every incarnation have weapons and cords embedded in various places/chakras at the level of their Astral bodies. These weapons cannot and will not be removed from their Astral bodies until they make a firm commitment to commence repaying some of their karmic debt, which for some is massive. There is one thought that may bring some clarity.

The question is this:

If there is only one lifetime available for every person who has been born on Earth at any given time in Earth's history, where are all of the billions of people who have gone before us? Would some have been so perfect that they ascended straight to *heaven*? Are others so corrupt and so evil that they went straight to a place known as *hell* from the moment that they closed their physical eyes for the last time? Perhaps, there is a place in-between, which is known as *limbo*, as some religions preach. But, what about all of the ones who leave Earth via the death process in any given week? Where are they? Are they in one forever-long queue that is snaking around and around the planet of Earth while waiting to be processed? Is this really how the one-life-only concept operates? If so, it is a tragedy for many, because their belief and trust in God is brought into question when True Reality is upon them after they make their latest transition. The realisation that they have passed through the veil-of-death many times previously shakes them to the core and they are angry at the ones who have perpetrated this deliberate fallacy during their latest life experience.

Perhaps, the story of Mary's transition, once she moved onto greener pastures, may not be so far-fetched, after all? This is a question, with which one will need to grapple, for those whose minds are open to new (and age-old) theories and who are seeking more spiritual enlightenment than the religions of Earth can offer. With the children of Light, for whom this Series of books has been written, there is one question to be asked. If these gentle ones do not have weapons lodged within their Astral bodies and the ones that they acquired at the etheric level in any incarnation on Earth are removed before the etheric body disappears, why then do they continue to incarnate on this planet?

The reason is two-fold. Firstly, it is to bring their great Love and their great Light down to a very dark planet that is steeped in negativity, due to the actions, reactions and inaction of some of its inhabitants. Also, they have a great Love for their fellow-travellers on this long, long road to Home, so they come to offer assistance where they can. They come, also, to assist Mother Earth to rise-above all of the negativity that permeates every atom of her being.

However, the second reason is a little more complex. This relates to a severe wound that they suffered during their very first lifetime when they offered their service on Earth. Let us call this tragic event an *Original Trauma*.

For most, this will relate to trust and betrayal by ones whom they loved deeply and trusted completely. These gentle ones were not prepared for the traumatic effect of the dense negativity that hit them when they arrived for the first time. They suffered a deep wound at their Core Centre. To counter this attack at a future time, they lodged deeply within themselves – at their Core Centre and Soul Seat – an insurance policy, one might say, and this was in the form of a pea-sized crystal. If we call a crystal by a name that is in common usage in this day-and-age, it would be described as a *microchip*. Therefore, this crystal at their Core Centre contained all of the data from every lifetime spent on Earth. This was done, so that they would see danger coming and take evasive action before they could be destroyed again. As stated earlier, this was counter-productive, in many cases, because their in-built intuition, upon which they had relied always, was compromised and, in many cases, sidelined.

For those wishing to repair the damage, there is a two-step releasing, clearing, cleansing and healing process that is outlined in the final section of this book. It is entitled: *Guidelines to Self-Healing*.

As this crystal/microchip was implanted during an earthly incarnation, it needs to be removed during a physical incarnation on Earth. However, here lies the rub. When incarnate on this planet, they forget to do what they came down specifically to accomplish. This is because they become caught up once again in the games-of-Earth that everyone else is playing. Consequently, they experience great disappointment upon their return to the Astral level after every incarnation.

If the one-life-only theory is a smoke-screen to keep everyone locked into the birth/life/death/re-birth cycle endlessly, why cannot the children of Light who are soft, gentle, kind, wise and loving break the cycle?

Why do the children of Light continue to incarnate endlessly on Earth?

Could it be that, as the crystal/rock/microchip was acquired on Earth, it needs to be cleared, then removed completely, during an incarnation here on this lower level?

If so, why is this not possible? Is it because when we arrive here, we genuinely cannot remember why we came?

Could it be due, also, to the fact that our intuition has been compromised, so we do not realise that the answers to every problem are buried deep within us?

If this is the case, read the section, *Guidelines to Self-Healing*, at the conclusion of this book. If the information appears ill-informed and inaccurate to the reader, toss the book aside. If the information contained therein feels accurate and one feels guided from within to pursue this course of action, please do so.

Release, clear, cleanse and heal at the deepest level and remove all instruments, implements, cords-of-attachment and belief-systems that are keeping all of us trapped on this treadmill of birth/life/death/re-birth endlessly.

This is a personal choice. A way has been shown in these Guidelines. No one can do this great work for another. If someone is claiming to be able to do so – and worse still, is charging money to accomplish this task on your behalf –do not be misled when the end is so close.

In **Book Four** (of this publication), which is entitled **Earlier Discourses**, there are many profound and beautiful writings that came from the Masters-of-Light many years ago. Several of these Discourses have not been released before now while most were published previously in 2000 in my book entitled: *UNDERCOVER STARSEEDS*. Please take the time to read these words of wisdom from these wise Masters-of-Light; then, *to your own self be true*. That is the best advice of all.

There were three other small books that I self-published between 1992 and 1999. These were entitled: **THE GOLDEN AGE, FAMILY OF MAN** and **THE REAL BOOK, REAL BEGINNING.**

The first two of these were published with financial assistance from a beautiful lady whose name is Kathryn. I thank Kathryn most sincerely for her generosity of spirit and her belief in those wonderful words of wisdom that came from a great Master-of-Light. Perhaps, at a future time, I will re-release these three books as the one publication.

This concludes the writings of the *Stella McMillan Series*. Chapter One of Book One, *ERROR of UNDERSTANDING,* was written in 1971. The original manuscript containing the first Trilogy was submitted to publishers in 1991. Of course, it was rejected out-of-hand back then. Now, by necessity, the entire Series has been self-published. The road has been long and difficult. It is at an end now.

May the peace, Divine Light and Divine Love of God overshadow everyone on every step of the journey from here and onto to our ultimate goal as we make this lifetime: *The Final Journey.*

Stella McMillan
20 July 2018.

Transition

The Final Journey

Book Four

Earlier Discourses

Ephram

There is joy for all who walk the path to true enlightenment. In a sense, all are walking this path, but many have lost their way. They stopped to play for awhile in a reality that was not their true state. The tragedy is that they forgot to re-start their journey and they are trapped within a dream state that, for most, has become a nightmare. It is such a pity, for they had so much to offer to the whole.

It is the *whole* that I wish to speak of now. The whole is the collective consciousness of the human race, as it is known. If one were to look at the planet as a whole Being and the ones living, loving, laughing, playing or crying out in pain, as being her children, then that places a different perspective on the reality, of which I spoke earlier. It is in this reality of Earth that the children of Earth and of God have become lost.

Over the centuries, many Masters of Light have come to teach another way of living and another way of thinking. Unfortunately, their legacy has been distorted over time and religious establishments have been founded based upon their different teachings. These establishments have drawn imaginary lines in the sand then and, have paved the way for this *them-and-us* mentality amongst the followers of that establishment, regardless of the fact that this was counter to the wishes of the Master to whom they give adoration daily. It is the divide-and-rule principle taken to its ultimate conclusion. Religious wars have been fought over the centuries and these have been a source of great consternation to the Masters concerned, for they never wished for such extremism to come out of their teachings. In all cases, their overriding message was one of Love – and only Love.

It is the collective consciousness of humanity that needs to change and to change rapidly. As time-frames go, in earthly terms, we are long past the point of no-return in terms of the spiritual versus the scientific imbalance. This is what brought about the total destruction of Atlantis, Le Muria and Mu. Humanity was required then to start afresh, on a pristine planet, and to begin again the building of cities and the learning to live in God's Way and God's Love on Earth. Even beginning again as Neanderthal man and woman, the lessons of Atlantis have not been learned and the consciousness has not been raised sufficiently to enable a smooth transition into the Golden Age upon Mother Earth. It was known always that there would be a *time of sorting* prior to the introduction to the Golden Age. The Golden Age will be the predicted one thousand years of peace, after which a small amount of negativity will be released upon Earth in the form of new arrivals who have known little else in their lives on other planets and star-systems. They will be as disorientated by the Love Essence present in the Golden Age as those new arrivals are now when they have known only Love in the environment, from which they left to incarnate upon Earth.

The overall picture is not as positive as we had hoped at this point in time on Mother Earth. With regard to the sorting time, it was known that as ones of a negative persuasion left the planet, via the death experience, they would be refused permission to reincarnate back upon Earth. These ones who have not raised their level of consciousness at all, and in some cases have gone backwards, so to speak, will be directed to other planets where life is barren and lifeless. They will be required to begin life again as Neanderthal man and woman. They are banned from *The Garden* again.

The ones who are gentle, kind and loving and, who have proven their commitment to God and to their own quest for Enlightenment are beginning to incarnate upon Earth. But, who is left to *enlighten* them upon their arrival? Would it be the ones who are in charge of the established religions? I think not. No, my children, it is you – the children of Light – the beautiful Starseeds – who are locked into situations that are not to your liking, but that you feel powerless to change. It is the Starseeds who must lead by example now, for there is no one else. Sitting around waiting for a new Master to come, or for an old Master to return, is useless. The baton has been passed to the Starseeds now; and, in this final hour of Earth's history as a third dimensional planet, the Starseeds must rally now as never before. Forget the petty egos of others and suppress one's own ego for the good of the whole.

The consciousness of humanity must rise so that the vibrations of the children can match those of the Ascending Mother – Earth herself. It would be a tragedy and a scenario that does not bear thinking about if the majority of Earth's current population was required to begin reincarnating upon that other third dimensional planet where nothing exists at this present moment-in-time. The sorting has begun, my children. The sorting has begun. Could not the Starseeds begin to put aside their own personal lives and endeavours for a time in order to assist humanity now, in its hour of greatest need? Is not this what you came to Earth to achieve all those millennia ago? It is, dear ones. Truly, it is.

I will leave you now to ponder the wisdom of my words. My peace I leave with you and my love surrounds each and every one of you individually. I know you all personally and I love you all dearly – collectively and, as the individual and beautiful beings that you are. Stay centred. Remain true to your path, which is the path of Enlightenment. Renew your commitment to the Cause, Which is the First Cause, Who is God Everlasting.

Peace be with you,
Ephram, Archangel, Messenger of God.
21 January 2000

Yoganandah

In a world that is devoid of Love, that being the Love Essence of God, it is very difficult to motivate ones of Earth to strive toward a new way of thinking and a new way of living. Having forgotten what it was like to live in a world where all was peace, joy and Love, they can accept only that which they have known for all of their physical lives. When one finds peace in the garden and love in the hearts of all those around, then this is a true state of bliss. Judging ones around you means that you are in fear of an attack of some description from them. This fear is where most people on Earth live. It is judging and analysing others to be ready to ward off an attack if one were mounted against you.

Children of Light have no need to fear. Children of Light will turn always any attack into a positive situation, because at the heart of the matter, it means that the one who mounts the attack is in emotional pain and the attack is merely a cry for help. This is but a case of one of God's children crying out to another of God's children for assistance. Of course, when encased in a physical body, it is difficult to recognise the warning signs and to take preventative action. When the attack comes, the *victim* is hurt and is in dismay. Retaliation seems to be the only recourse and the cycle continues endlessly.

There have been many books written on the subject. There has been much correct information regarding the victim/perpetrator scenario and just as much misinformation. Unfortunately, it is the misinformation that is circulated freely while the truth of the matter remains hidden usually. And so, the cycle continues.

There will come a time when the cycle will be broken, but this is an individual *moment-of-truth* for every being. This moment will mark a turning point in that individual's evolution and a large step upon the path to

Enlightenment. Turning the other cheek is never easy when one is under attack. If there is no one to attack and to counter-attack after the first retaliatory encounter, then how can there be a war of any description, large or small? Whether the act of aggression takes place in the playground, the workplace, the home or on the battlefield, without an enemy or a victim, how can there be a war?

If one were under attack on a battlefield and heavily outnumbered physically, would not a withdrawal be in order? Could not this be the way to handle situations in the workplace or the home and to teach in the playground? It does not have to be permanent. It can be a temporary arrangement until the heat of the battle is over. Then, it may be time to negotiate and to find the cause of the problem.

It is not God's Way to fight and argue, to gossip and cause dissent. God's Way is Love. It always has been. It always will be. Regardless of which religious views you express and, in which you place your faith, if this is not the teaching, which is the teaching of Unconditional Love and acceptance of ALL, no matter what their station in life (the so-called *station* of the physical life that is), then, it may be time to reassess your place within that establishment. If its rules and regulations are counter to Unconditional Love and they are pursuing a divide-and-rule principle – a *them* and *us* policy – then, it may be time to question the motives of the leaders. This is not a judgement. This is discernment. This is questioning to yourself whether or not you belong in an institution, which does not practice, at every level, the Unconditional Love that is God.

It is an individual choice, of course, but sooner or later, that choice will need to be made by every individual. That choice will be that person's moment-of-truth and the first step taken on the road to recovery. The road to recovery leads to the road to discovery, the road to self-discovery. That is an exciting path to walk. Discovering that the little self is not really all-ego, but all-Love, is truly an exciting moment. Discovering that there is a beautiful, joyous, loving Being inside just waiting to blossom forth and share its Love with all, is truly an eye-opening moment of truth.

If everyone on Earth allowed that Being of Love to express itself fully on one particular day every year – hopefully on the same day – then, there would be so much Love on and around the planet that everyone would be intoxicated. With any intoxication, it can become habit-forming. Perhaps then, it could spread to the other three hundred and sixty-four days of the calendar of Earth and, we would have a consciousness-raising like no other. We would have a third-dimensional planet changing to a fourth-dimensional planet overnight. What a sensational happening that would be. Of course, it would be vital to block out all negativity from an outside influence, so it would be necessary to turn off all radios and televisions and to refrain from opening a newspaper. It would be simply a case of face-to-face communication with one's fellow man and woman. What a wondrous state-of-Being, especially if that communication were to be done in Love, and Love only, to the exclusion of all other sentiments and emotions.

The other factor in the equation could be intoxicants and depressants. These could have a bearing upon the outcome of a Love day. So, refraining from drinking coffee, tea, alcoholic beverages or beverages containing caffeine would be a good way to commence this Love exercise. Of course, smoking and other forms of drug-taking would hardly be conducive to overall peace, joy, harmony and Love, would they?

It is, as always, an individual choice, because Earth has been a free will planet always. Perhaps, for one day a year, the free will factor could become subservient to the

Love factor. From there, it could spread to a quarterly event. Let us start with a 21st day. Let us start with a 21st September day and progress then to a 21st March day. In no time at all, everyone will be looking forward to a 21st December inclusion and then, of course, a 21st June inclusion. Who knows where it will go from there? But, we must start somewhere and we must start soon.

Time is running out on Earth for ones who wish to remain at the third dimensional level, which is almost a loveless state. Trying to break old patterns and habits is very difficult indeed but, on a free will planet, it is almost impossible, because old patterns and habits are comfortable. Therefore, it is easy to put off until tomorrow the breaking of these insidious masters that control us.

Give up one today! There is a suggestion. Do not just try to give it up. Give it up! Whatever the cost to self, you will feel better for it. Once the withdrawal symptoms have passed, the self-esteem and self-love will rise to replace the old habit. The loving Inner Being will glow with pride and another step forward has been taken – a step forward for LOVE.

I Am Yoganandah. My legacy is one of lasting Love, which is surrounding you now as you read my words, which are given in Love. I hope that they will be received in Love. The more Love Essence that we can spread daily then, the more Love Essence will flow for it is a self-perpetuating, never-ending stream that can become a torrent, if only you will allow this Love to flow from the Core of your Being, from your Core Star. Everyone has a Core Star. Has your Core Star been opened today, so that the Love Essence can flow to those around you? It may cause confusion to some as your silent Love reaches them. Watch for their reactions. Record it in your diary, if you wish. It may make interesting reading later, especially if you have another with whom you can share your Love adventures.

Open your Core Star today and send Love out to the world. After all, it is the *intent* that counts. The more that you send out, the more you will receive. As long as you do not allow the trials and tribulations of physicality to bring you down, your new-found fountain of Love Essence will create such an aura of Light and Love around you that you will be positively glowing. The wattage can only increase from here, my lovely ones.

God Bless You,
Yoganandah.
22nd January 2000

Onoraus

When one is immersed in a full physical life, it is difficult to see a way to fulfil the path and the dream that was planned prior to incarnating into the current physical body. The personality changes little from lifetime to lifetime, but the changes that are apparent to ones who look through the eyes of Spirit are remarkable, in most cases.

Everyone who takes physical form does so while believing that the path that has been set, in consultation with the Spirit Guides, will be able to be walked with relative ease by the one taking on embodiment again. However, two factors stand in the way of this successful completion. The first is the one concerning the obvious and that is a karmic debt of some description from a previous lifetime. This weighs heavily upon the incoming soul/spirit being. There may be a debt that has been awaiting a cosmic solution for many a decade or century. With every subsequent life experience, this has been delayed by the debtor.

In this final lifetime (for most) in third dimensional embodiment, the time has come to repay these outstanding debts. Unfortunately, this is adding to the burden that Mother Earth is carrying as she begins her ascent to the fourth dimensional Being that she truly is. You see, the repayment of a karmic debt will bring pain always to the debtor. If one causes pain to another, then that degree of pain and suffering must be felt and experienced by ones who chose, of their own free will, to inflict pain and suffering upon another in some past incarnation. This is Karmic Law or Cosmic Law and cannot be changed. Whatever one causes another to experience, then that experience returns eventually to haunt the perpetrator. If ones of Earth understood this principle fully, they would hesitate before inflicting pain and suffering upon any of God's children; or, indeed, other innocent creatures, such as birds and animals. Perhaps, even fishing for sport may be looked upon in a different light.

These are some thoughts for you to ponder as you give serious consideration to your spiritual life, as opposed to your physical or even your religious life. Let us examine for a moment a tragedy upon your earth-plane. As an example, let us picture a happy family scene upon a picturesque beach. The beach is deserted, except for one happy little family. The palm trees are swaying in the breeze. The children are playing on the sand with their father and making sand castles. The mother is under the shade of a brightly-coloured beach umbrella. Every now and then, she raises her eyes from the book that she is reading to check on her little brood. She smiles happily to herself as she watches them at play with their father. Her love for them all is overwhelming.

Her eyes look down at the picnic basket and she decides to take a quick swim before serving lunch to her family. The day is very warm and she feels the need to cool off a little before lunch. She walks to her little family and gives lavish praise to her children's endeavours and their sand creations. She bends down and kisses her husband on the top of the head as a farewell to him. He tells her jokingly to watch out for sharks.

With a laugh and a wave of her hand, she enters the surf while never dreaming of the danger, or of the painful death that awaits her. Within minutes, these jaws of death grab her around the midriff and razor-sharp teeth bite into her abdomen. There is no time to call out for help. The first her family know of her dilemma is to see the thrashing movements in the water – a hand raised here, a tail and a fin raised there, followed by blood mingling with surf. The family rush to the water's edge and stare in horror and disbelief. Of their wife and mother, there is no sign now.

The father's dilemma is great. Does he rush headlong into the foaming surf? This is his first reaction, because of his deep love for his beautiful wife? Does he stay with his terrified and horrified children who need a parent to protect them? Does he reach for his children, gather them in his arms and run for help from the deserted beach? The sight of a severed limb rolling in with waves further up the beach makes his decision for him. Numb with shock, he grabs his children in his arms, turns his back on the surf and walks in a determined, brisk manner up the beach towards his car to go for help. Beside him and unseen by all of them runs his wife, for her soul/spirit has left the physical body and is in total shock, also. The attack happened so fast that she believes she has escaped from the jaws of the shark. Her husband runs so fast that she cannot catch up to him at first. She cannot understand why he does not hear her calling to him. He is so preoccupied with comforting the children that he does not look around to wait for her. She cannot believe that he has abandoned her so easily. She reaches him and reaches out to grab his arm as he places the children into the car. Still, he is in such shock that he is oblivious to her presence.

She shouts at him, but still he hears not. She jumps into the car beside him, but he looks straight ahead as he drives crazily along the dirt road leading to the highway. Once again, she places her hand on his arm, but it seems to slip through the flesh of his arm. At the highway, he jumps from the car while telling the children to remain in their seatbelts. He flags down the first vehicle that comes along and the driver of the massive rig brings his vehicle to a screeching halt as he tries to avoid the man standing in the centre of the highway. He is waving his arms frantically and in obvious distress.

The lady concerned watches with dismay; then, she joins the two on the roadway. Now, this new arrival will see her and jolt her husband out of the shock that he is suffering. The driver will point out to him that his wife is standing beside him. When this does not occur and the driver begins to radio for urgent assistance, she knows that something is horribly wrong. She becomes aware suddenly of another reality that is superimposed upon her original one. In front of her stand three people with their arms outstretched to her. Two of them are her grandparents looking as she remembered them from childhood. They have been deceased (as earthlings know *deceased*) for many years and beside them is her dear, departed father who left them suddenly via a heart attack after celebrating Christmas dinner several years ago.

In total confusion, she looks back at her little children who are crying now as their father stands by the driver. Both men walk back towards the car as other traffic streams by, the drivers unaware of the tragedy that has occurred. She rushes to her children; then, she realises that they cannot see or hear her. She realises she cannot hear them, but that she is more or less reading their thoughts. They are crying for mummy. They want only their mummy. She places her arms around each one of them individually, but they do not feel her.

Her grandmother places her arms around her and draws her close to her in a hug that is filled with Unconditional Love. She leads her to her father and grandfather. They step aside and a blinding and beautiful White Light –A Golden/White Light – appears and she is drawn towards it as a moth towards a flame. She turns to look back towards her family, but they fade into the distance now. The music that resounds around her is so beautiful that she feels she is floating on air. The Love that is surrounding her now is so soothing and so overpowering that she feels intoxicated by this Love. And, the peace that enfolds her defies description in words of Earth.

Of course, the newspapers and the electronic media have a field day with the story while spreading horror and fear amongst the population of the day. The sceptics question how such a tragedy could occur, if a God of Love exists. Looking only through physical eyes, is this an unfair question? Perhaps, it is not so.

Let us look more closely at the other lives of this brave lady. I say *brave*, for indeed she is so. Before incarnating, she had agreed finally to repay a karmic debt from many, many centuries earlier, in Earth's timeframe. This karmic debt had been weighing heavily on her mind for many a lifetime, but always at the last moment, she delayed repaying that terrible debt. You see, there had been a time when she had incarnated as a male into a wealthy and influential family. It had been the intention of the incarnating soul/spirit in that particular incarnation to make a difference to the thinking patterns of humanity at that time. The man had become a lawyer and had married when quite young. It was a marriage that was to take him off his pre-set spiritual path and onto the social-climbing ladder of his wife's choosing. In later life as a judge, he had been placed in a position of casting judgement upon a man who he knew to be innocent of any crime other than being a follower of the one known as Jesus, The Christ.

On that occasion while bowing to peer and family pressure, he had sentenced the man to be torn apart by a wild beast in an arena, with others cheering on the beast in a display of frenzied emotion that would have sickened even the most hardened of men, not to say women. Not only did he cower to this pressure, but also, he had given into the pressure placed upon him by his wife whose influential brother was demanding that the man be made an example of for all other Christians to see. The callous brother was demanding that the man's wife and children be made to watch the victim's suffering from a ringside seat. The newly-appointed judge knew that his own career and his marriage were on the line. After many a sleepless night, he caved into the pressure and gave the order.

After watching the spectacle first-hand at the direction of his wife and his brother-in-law, he was horrified and appalled by his own cowardice and by the horrendous pain and suffering that it had caused to so many people, not the least of whom were the little children watching their father torn to pieces while supposedly-human beings cheered and shouted as wildly as is seen now at a weekly football match. That night, the lawyer drank poison and ended his own life in that incarnation. The reports of his death were sketchy, but alluded to a heart seizure.

In the latest incarnation, it was necessary for a female embodiment in order to fulfil other requirements for the spiritual evolvement of that soul/spirit in that particular incarnation. The incoming soul/spirit came into the last incarnation in trepidation while knowing that the final moment would be sudden, unexpected and very, very painful, but not knowing what form it would take.

With her family all alone on a deserted beach, she was torn apart and torn from them as they watched helplessly from the water's edge. They were all alone as the earlier family had been in a sea of frenzied, horrible humans – heartless and cruel – while calling for blood.

That karmic debt had been played out, because one very brave being chose of her own free will and, on another level, to do so on that beautiful, carefree day. Unfortunately, there are many who continue to incarnate upon Earth to this day and these ones have massive karmic debts that have accrued against them. They steadfastly refuse to repay, of their own free will, this indebtedness to Cosmic Law. That is why this time of sorting is upon those who inhabit physical bodies on Earth now. We have come-full-circle from the end-times of Atlantis to the end-times of this civilisation as it is known at this point in Earth's history.

Walk your paths, your spiritual paths, with your heads held high and do not allow pressure from anyone, no matter what their standing on Earth's stage-of-life, for you are the one who has to account for your actions, reactions or inaction, as the case may be. To *account* means a self-assessment, in the company of your Guides, with whom the current incarnation was planned and, under the watchful eye of your own Higher Self. There is not an Authoritarian Judge who judges harshly all misdemeanours or so-called sins, as many religious establishments would have you believe.

Could this explain why reincarnation was so thoroughly and so successfully wiped from the collective consciousness of humankind some fifteen centuries hence? If one believes that this is the only lifetime, in which to *get it right*, so to speak, then that places a great deal of power in the hands of the established religions to whose rigid rules and regulations many people adhere, as sheep do to a shepherd. Is this not tantamount to a middle-man in the market place? Who has the right to set himself or herself up as a go-between, acting as an agent between God and another of God's children? Who gives that right to ones of Earth? Is that right self-proclaimed? Or, is it a decree from the only God there is, the Source-of-All, our God of Love, our Loving Creator of All?

Who, indeed, gives this Right of Passage, I ask you!

In the next discourse, I will give the second reason for incarnating into physical form on Earth at this time and the ways, in which these ones tend to stray from their pre-set spiritual paths. In my great Love, I will leave you for now. I will bid you adieu and ask you to ponder on my words well before reading the next discourse.

I Am your devoted servant and Guide to all of you, my sweet children of Light, my Starseeds Extraordinaire.

I Am Onoraus, Lord of Light.

23rd January 2000

Zu Deus

In a moment-in-time, a decision is made. This decision is based upon reason and free will. It is not necessarily a decision of the soul/spirit. It is, in all probability, a decision of the ego-personality. The ego-personality, in some past incarnation that is lost in the ethers of time (Earth time, that is, because time exists nowhere else at all), lost its connection to its Divine Source, the Source-of-All-Life and Creation, known upon Earth as *God.*

Let us stay with this premise for a short while. Let us imagine for a moment that a cataclysmic event occurred, at a personal level, for all Starseeds. Let us imagine that all Starseeds came to Planet Earth for a specific purpose and that was to assist those already in embodiment upon the planet to raise their consciousness, and thus their vibrations, to the level of a fourth dimensional frequency.

You see, prior to the Atlantean experience, or the disaster-to-end-all-disasters (however you may wish to describe that fateful and horrific event in Earth's history), everyone and everything, was vibrating at a fourth dimensional frequency. It was a virtual Garden of Eden, one might say. The weather was perfect, as God had intended. The garden and its inhabitants were blissful and serene. Everyone cohabitated in perfect harmony and Unconditional Love was all that anyone knew. It was much as it is now in the higher echelons of the Astral plane where one rests and relaxes between incarnations upon Earth.

The bodies were vibrant and healthy. They were fourth dimensional bodies, so it was not necessary to feed them. There were plentiful supplies of fruit and nuts for those who felt the need to partake, but this happened rarely. If it did, it was because someone had lowered the vibration of the body a little and it required revitalizing. Let us say that the bodies were vibrating somewhere between the upper and lower levels of the Astral plane. On the lower levels of the Astral plane, there are ones who, though in spirit-form at present, have a firm belief that they must eat three square meals a day. As with any belief system, the same rule applies . . . *as to your thoughts, so shall it be.*

Returning to our Garden on Earth, if one did partake of a piece of fruit, for example, one asked permission of the tree or the vine first, because this was in accord with God's Law of Love. It was recognition, also, of the fact that the tree or vine was another living creation of our Loving Mother-Father God Who provided for our every need or whim before we knew ourselves that we had a need in a particular area. With faith, trust and most particularly Love, Earth could return easily to the Garden again.

It would take a giant wake-up call to open the eyes of the leaders, those being the Starseeds or Light Workers, to enable them to see the bigger picture again. It would take a resolve on the part of the Starseeds to repair the damage that has been done to them during their original and subsequent sojourns onto Mother Earth.

What occurred to change our *Garden of Eden* into a third dimensionally-vibrating huge rubbish tip, for want of a better description? Man and woman of Earth changed their thinking-patterns and, in so doing, lowered their own vibrations to match those of the animal kingdom. The animal kingdom was a loving environment, also, once upon a time. It became a predator/prey arena when man of Earth became aggressive towards this kingdom and chose to eat the flesh of God's beautiful and innocent creatures. The balance of nature was changed irreversibly and forever with that first act of depravity. Nothing as base and as cruel as this had been experienced upon Earth ever. The more that the flesh of the animal was eaten, the more the vibration of the planet's inhabitants was lowered. The more the vibration was lowered, the less spirit could remain within the physical encasement.

Instead of spirit-filled beings enjoying a temporary sojourn on Planet Earth, we had the spectacle of bodies becoming heavier and heavier with every passing day. Between incarnations, these little ones would realise the error of their ways and their thinking, but once upon Earth again, they lowered a veil of illusion over their eyes and lived as their fellow-humans had begun to live. And so, it continues to this day. Worse was to come, however, for on one terrible day, a being whose vibration had become so terribly low that he flew into a passionate rage against another of God's children and, he slew the physical body of his brother, another of God's children of Light. What a tragic event for Earth!

This catastrophic event caused the heavens to stand still and to shudder in dismay and horror. Never had such an occurrence occurred before and it was an event so shocking that the whole vibration of the universe – the twelfth universe, in which Earth is but one inhabiting planet – was lowered dramatically in an instant. For it needs to be understood clearly that whatever affects any one being anywhere has a dramatic effect upon *the whole* of Creation, because ALL of life is interconnected and inexplicably joined to the Source, from which it came. It cannot be any other way, dear children of mine. It cannot be any other way.

It is time now to undo the deeds of the past and to move on to greener pastures, or to return to the *garden*, in other words. With this great deed (or sin, as some would term it) perpetrated against another of God's children occurring, the *garden*, as everyone knew it, ceased to be. From there, it has been a steady, downward slide to the point where the Piscean Age ended and the Aquarian Age began. That is when God decreed that *enough is enough*, for the freewill factor had overridden completely the Love factor upon Earth. The point-of-no-return had been reached. The imbalance was total and could not be redressed without Divine Intervention.

A Master came at the beginning of the Piscean Age, as a last resort, one might say. His message was for the people of his time and, also, for all people of his Age upon Earth. For the most part, his message has fallen on deaf ears as have the messages of all of the other Masters who preceded him. It is such a terrible shame and such a terrible waste of time and energy. There is a chance, slim though that may be, that the Starseeds could yet be rallied and come to the fore again.

Harking back in history a little now, I will reveal that when the dreadful and terrible deed occurred when one of God's children destroyed the physical body of another of God's children, then a call went out through all of the universes for volunteers to come to the aid of the ones-in-embodiment upon Earth who had lost their way and were in such terrible distress, because of their negative thought patterns, which had changed the consciousness of humanity forever. In the heavenly realms (for want of another description), it was decreed that help was needed to rescue our little ones from their own dilemma, which was of their own making, because it was a case, as always, of the silent majority following the wayward leaders in a subservient manner. No one spoke out when the first animal was killed. No one spoke out when the first child of God was attacked in such a brutal manner as to render lifeless the physical encasement of that particular child of God.

In such a short period of Earth-time, what had seemed so shocking and so abhorrent in the beginning became the norm until the children of God broke up into tribes and began attacking one another. This then followed on to the present day when nation attacks nation over resources – God's resources – such as oil and food supplies; or, over territorial gains and losses when the planet was created by God for the use of the children of God when they felt the need to go to that particular playground to play.

If one does not look through the eyes of Spirit, which is what we all are at our Core, then one can see only a distorted and partial picture of the whole scene of Creation. It has become convenient on Earth to place a veil over the eyes so that one sees only that which one feels comfortable seeing – through physical eyes only. It has led to so much unnecessary misery, pain and suffering on Earth that it must come to an end now, at the dawning of the Aquarian Age.

There are new energies being released upon Earth. These began at the beginning of the twentieth century as a trickle, which became a stream by the middle of that century, just after the war between nations known as World War Two concluded. From then onwards, the stream of new energies became a river. Now, at the start of the new millennium, this river has become a torrent that will drown every person on a world-wide scale. Soon, it will become an avalanche – an avalanche of Love – that even ones with the most hardened of hearts cannot ignore.

The world has operated on the energy of the male – the masculine energy – for the entire Piscean Age. The Aquarian Age is the Age of the feminine energy, the Age of Love, caring, nurturing and renewal. It cannot be stopped. It is a Divine Decree and the free will factor of Earth has been overridden now. The fight that has been ongoing between the sexes on Earth ever since Emmeline Pankhurst and her sisters picked up their first banner to fight on behalf of all oppressed women must end now. This explosion of female action coincided with the release of the first trickle of feminine energy to the planet, in order to redress the imbalance of male energy that had been forced upon the population from the time of Joan of Arc and the Inquisition. This male energy imbalance occurred, because of the great fear the male of the human species has of the power of the female to give life, to renew life and to regenerate itself. It is a deep-seated fear that has its roots in superstition and ignorance. Hence, the witch-hunts designed to destroy all vestige of feminine energy. The emergence of a male God-head to whom all must pay homage stems directly from this fear.

You see, my children of Light, my precious Starseeds, you are all made in the likeness of God, regardless of which gender you have chosen in this particular lifetime. You are children of God, children of the Great Divine Spirit. Spirit is Light. Spirit is Love. Spirit is soft, gentle and kind. Spirit is God. Without Spirit, you cannot exist on any level of Creation. Spirit is androgynous, as is the Great Divine Spirit, the All-Loving, All-Caring, Omnipresent, Omnipotent, Father-Mother God Principle.

You are Spirit. You are Love. You are Life Everlasting. You are soft, gentle and kind. Anything else is illusion and comes from the ego-personality, combined with the conscious mind that has separated from the soul/spirit, because of a lack of faith and trust in the Source-of-All to provide for your every need. The soul/spirit has needs. The ego-personality has wants. As Spirit, your needs will be met always. It cannot be any other way. As physical beings, being led around by the ego-personality combined with the conscious mind, you have wants. The two are not necessarily the same. Whatever the ego-personality *wants*, it must attain for itself by physical means. Whatever the soul/spirit *needs* to fulfil its pre-set path in this particular life-experience on Planet Earth at this particular moment-in-time will be met always – be that a roof over your head, a daily meal (or bread) or a shoulder, on which to lean or to cry. It may even be a need such as a shelter, or a stable, in which to bring forth a son or a daughter in times of upheaval and strife on Earth.

Aeons of time ago, before the calendar and clock were invented upon Earth, a call went out for volunteers, as I mentioned earlier. This call was echoed and reverberated throughout all the universes in the kingdom of God. Many, many Light Workers, or Starseeds as we shall call them here, answered that call. Their vision and their unselfish offers were accepted gratefully by the Lords of Light and the Brotherhood of Masters who were concerned for the well-being of the planet and her inhabitants. When I use a male terminology, it is because this is the terminology that has become familiar to ones of Earth over time immemorial. It has nothing to do with who inhabits a male body or who inhabits a female body. We are all Spirit in my realm of existence – Pure Spirit – and as such, Spirit is a perfect blending of the masculine/feminine, the yang/yin principle. This terminology is not used to cause offence or to stir already troubled waters on Earth. The gender problem is an earthly problem, which thankfully has not spread to other areas of Love and Light. The battle between the sexes on Earth is causing sufficient consternation and confusion now without adding more fuel to the simmering fire.

Returning to my story of the Starseeds and their selfless Love and sacrifice, it was decided to allow these volunteers – very enlightened Beings in their own right – to begin inhabiting human-like bodies on Earth and to turn the tide back in favour of Love and Light, while hoping of course to raise the consciousness and vibration of the inhabitants, and thus the planet, in a very short space of time; or, in no time at all really. That had been the agenda anyway and, one that was thought to be achievable easily, given the highly-evolved spiritual nature of the Starseeds who were chosen for this rather short-term exercise – or, so it was thought.

Almost immediately, the First Wave of Starseeds was contaminated. They were not prepared for the effect of the massive wave of negativity that hit them at birth. Why does a baby cry at the time of its first breath? It has entered an alien territory and it is required to breathe to survive. When one has been floating in a sea of Love between incarnations on Earth, this adjustment takes time. After the adjustment comes the indoctrination of all of the false and faulty beliefs of Earth. These do not exist anywhere else at all. They are a concoction of the minds of men (and some women), because men have controlled this out-of-control environment for aeons of time.

The next event that occurs in the life of the newly-arrived infant is mandatory, depending upon one factor and one factor only – the sex of the baby. There are relatively few exceptions to this rule. The rule is that, in the male of the species, all feminine instincts are squashed and the child is given to understand that these are counter-productive in a *man's world*. In the female, the opposite occurs. When one considers that the masculine energy is the action-taking attributes – the doer, if you like – while the female is the loving, caring nurturing one – it is this great imbalance that is causing the war between the sexes on Earth as the feminine energy is rising. So, too, is the anger rising in the hearts and minds of all women in all countries of the world, because this power can be suppressed only for a short while. With the increase in the feminine energies flowing to the planet, men will suppress it at their own peril from now onwards. My sincere wish is that it does not manifest itself in the war-like attributes of the action-taking male. My fervent hope is that it will manifest itself in a life-giving, natural, loving way, because both parts of *the whole* have been hurt equally by this suppression.

Both the male and the female resent the fact that they are co-dependent upon the other. Why is this so? If they were operating as Spirit first (which they truly are) and physical second, then they would have an equal balance of male/female energies operating within them from birth. They would be truly androgynous while operating in either a male physical encasement, or a female physical encasement, depending upon the life-path that they have chosen for this particular incarnation.

It is such a simple explanation, but one that is very difficult to grasp when in physical embodiment; or, as some describe it, when wearing a coat-of-skin. An apt description, I feel personally.

So, what happens now? Do we blame the parents for the dilemma, or their parents before them? No, my children of Light, blame, retribution and retaliation are tools of a negative world and have no place in a world of Love, or in our *garden*, to which we are desirous of returning. In fact, previous generations were hoodwinked, also, into believing that that is the way it was meant to be.

Returning now to our First Wave Starseeds who set out to accomplish the impossible, only to be stymied at birth, they resemble a cartoon character known on your planet as *Superman*. This particular character has a problem when he comes into contact with a substance known as kryptonite, as the comic-strip story proceeds. This is precisely the effects that the negativity on Planet Earth had upon our newly-arrived Starseeds. They became disorientated immediately and fell into the trap of believing, like their human counterparts, that the physical body was paramount; whereas, in truth, it was but a coat-of-skin of a chosen gender to be worn for a short period of time on Earth.

They came to change the thinking of the earth-dwellers but, instead, their own thinking became contaminated; or, if you like, their own in-built computing systems became contaminated by the virus that was affecting the entire population. They came to eliminate the virus, but were themselves contaminated by it before this chore could be completed.

Several Masters of Light and Love did come over the Ages to stir the Starseeds into action. Those Masters were able to avoid the contamination themselves, but their messages were so outlandish as far as Earth's population could see and understand that they were either martyred for their pains; or, their great messages were unheeded. After their deaths, religious institutions were founded on their words (or, their *reported* words/messages) and a divide-and-rule principle was invoked to keep every Master's establishment in competition with the other. This aggressive, competitive streak was born out of a totally-male energy taken to the extreme, without the qualities of the female energy to balance it.

So, as far as the story goes, we have a sad and sorry state of affairs existing on Planet Earth, especially when the Piscean Age was coming to the fore, at the end of the Age of Aries. Knowing that an Age lasts for two thousand one hundred years, in Earth's timeframe, helps to understand a little of the recent history of the planet.

In my next discourse, I will continue the story of the arrival of the Second Wave of Starseeds. This occurred way back in time, when Atlantis was in its infancy and the negativity was nowhere near the frighteningly destructive state that it is today. This is a sorry tale of woe, I know. But, it is one that can have a happy ending, if only the Starseeds can be persuaded to stand up and be counted once more. You were slaughtered in great numbers during the witch-hunts of the Inquisition and you have come under sustained attack in every lifetime, so that you cannot rise up one more time. But, it is that *one more time* that is being asked of all Starseeds now, regardless of the colour of your skin, the gender of the current physical body or the belief-system, to which you give allegiance currently. It is an urgent task and a pressing need, dear ones. Truly, this is so.

I will leave you in my peace and my Love, for I love you all individually and AS ONE.

I Am your devoted servant and brother in Light and Love,

I Am Zu Deus, Lord of Light.

24th January 2000

Mary

Greetings and salutations, dear ones of Light! You are all so special to me. How you have survived relatively intact the traumas of your lifetimes on Earth is a source of amazement and delight to me. I love you all so dearly and I surround you with my Love whenever your own individual endeavours do not work out in the way you plan and disappointment sets in for you. My arms surround you in comfort during your sad times and again, when you are joyous and happy.

I know all of you individually as the happy, delightful, refreshingly-honest and irrepressible Spirit Beings that you are when not in those heavy, physical encasements that you don for your sojourn into earthly life. It is such a shame, is it not? You are such free spirits in your natural state of Being, which of course is Love. But, the Love Essence of God does flow freely through each and every one of you during your daily lives. This occurs because you are Spirit first and physical flesh second. Did not Jesus say words to this effect – "I Am in this world, but I Am not of it." That was the essence of his message.

The Beam of Light that is you – the real *you* – goes through the centre – the Core – of your Being. So, you are all made in the Likeness of God. That Spirit, or Beam, is androgynous. If you are in fear, in pain, in suffering or in negativity of any kind, then you are out-of-balance. Your energy centres on your Beam of Light, which keeps the ebb and flow of life going, have become blocked. If the higher ones are blocked, stopped, reversed or functioning at a slightly slower pace, then you have cut off your connection to the Source-of-All-Life-and-All-Love. In the terminology of Earth, that is the Loving Mother-Father-God-Principle on Earth, the God-Source.

It is all so simple really. When that occurs with the higher centres, you are functioning only from the lower centres, which are the ones that deal solely with the physical level of life.

You are, in totality, such large Beings of Light and Love that only a small portion of yourself can inhabit these bodies vibrating at such a low frequency on Earth. Therefore, you have what is termed a *Higher Self*. In truth, you are the one Being of Light, but a small portion has descended into physicality for a time and you have done so for a specific purpose. My dear friend, Zu Deus, has explained a little of that purpose and I know he wishes to elaborate upon it even further, so I will not encroach upon his territory. But, try to see yourself from our perspective. Let me reiterate here the story of the diving party, about which Constella has written in a previous Discourse.

A party of intrepid Starseeds sets off from land in a large launch. They sail far out to sea; then, drop anchor. They have, before leaving, planned a course of action in consultation with their own Higher Self. They wish to dive to the ocean floor to assist others who have dived some time earlier, but who have got themselves into difficulty now and have become disorientated. They need help and the new recruits, who have dived many times before, are eager and willing to help their sisters and brothers of Light beneath the waves.

Before entering their dive suits, they go to the main control room and they check their main computers. The pre-set plan is perfect. They know exactly what they have to do upon arrival in their underwater world. They check again with their own Higher Self and, then they re-check their meeting places along the way with their fellow divers who are all from the same soul-family, we might say. They plan to meet up with one another at various points along the way and they plan, also, to meet as a group of close friends quite regularly, because they know that they will need to share Love and to support one another, because this dive is not going to be just a *one-day-wonder*; or, if you like, a picnic-in-the-park.

There is great concern in that Higher Realm for the ones who belong under the sea and for the ones who went to rescue them, for all have succumbed to the negativity that has crept, much as a cancer does, into that underwater world. What has occurred is that the ones on the ocean floor have lost connection for the most part, with their own on-board computers on their launches and, more distressingly, with their own Higher Self. Can you see the picture I am painting here, dear ones? In many quarters on your earth-plane, it is referred to as *the separation*, which refers directly to the separation between the conscious mind-ego/personality and the soul/spirit-Higher Self. In truth, it is a separation from God that was never intended to occur. This separation has been preached about, talked about and written about from time immemorial, believe me. But until now, no one has been able to come up with a way to redress the problem – and, it is a major problem – except by rhetoric or by urging others to *repent of their sins*. Let us leave our divers for a moment as they re-check their maps and their gear, and remain with the premise that sin does not exist.

What is a sin? Perhaps, it could come under the heading of an act of aggression towards another of God's children. But, is that any concern of ones on Earth? Has not my dear friend, Onoraus, explained already a little about karmic debt and Cosmic Law in these Discourses? This is a debt, usually freely acknowledged at the self-assessment session after every incarnation on Earth, for once one leaves the physical body (or, dive suit, if you prefer), the first happening for most is that clarity returns immediately. Clarity-of-thought brings with it the realisation that, perhaps, we have repeated old karmic patterns and gone down a similar pathway in other lifetimes. Perhaps, with this clarity comes the realisation that the one who has been your sworn enemy in this incarnation just concluded is, in reality (true reality, that is) your dearest and most trusted friend. What if, as clarity returns, you have both led great armies against each other on one of Earth's battlefields (and, there have been many)? Many, many people may have returned to the realm of Spirit from their physical bodies, because of this great feud, which was permitted to get out-of-hand on Earth. Innocent children and their parents, whether or not they were wearing military uniforms of some design or other, marching under some so-called spiritually-designed insignia, have returned to the Astral plane. The first reaction is one of horror when the person who could have turned the other cheek, or negotiated a lasting peace treaty, realises the extent of the irreparable damage that has been done.

In absolute despair and with deep sorrow, he/she awaits the return of the dear friend who was the sworn enemy on the battlefield. After a self-assessment where the loving soul-spirit is none-too-gentle on the little self, the dear friend returns to the Astral plane. A similar scenario occurs as with the return of the first one. They embrace while sobbing in each other's arms.

After the self-assessment, followed by the mandatory clearing and healing of the traumas of that lifetime, an appointment is made, individually, to see the Lords of Karma. These are Beings of great Light and Love, as well as understanding – androgynous by nature – and filled with Divine Love and compassion. This is not a *kangaroo court*, as ones of Earth would possibly see it. The damage has been done and the matter needs to be redressed, in accord with Cosmic Law. There is not any blame or stigma attached to these sessions. The two Beings concerned went to the earth-plane with the clear intent of incarnating into the two warring factions. Their intent was to bring about joy, peace and most of all harmony to the whole area.

What happened to change their pre-set pathways? These were Beings of great Love and Light themselves and they could have made a great difference to the planetary vibration and to the lives of many thousands of people had they followed inner guidance coming directly from their own Higher Self. But, unfortunately, they had not counted on how devastating and how disorientating is the cancer of negativity that pervades Earth and that almost chokes the new arrival at birth, especially ones who come from the upper echelons of the Astral plane where they float along in a constant stream of the Love Essence of God.

There is a problem with the separation of the soul-spirit from the conscious mind/ego-personality. It is a very serious problem and one that I wish to speak of more deeply now; but, before I do, I will complete my thoughts about *sin* so-called, as people on Earth perceive sin.

The churches in your realm define this as an act, a word or a thought, which transgresses God's Law; or, perhaps their own laws, depending upon their own interpretation of what God's Law should be. That, I feel, is a fair summation of the so-called *sin*, which will suffice for now. It is, also, something that is committed with full knowledge, full will and full consent.

Now, in the above scenario, where two loving Beings of Light mistakenly took a path of action, believing in their hearts that each one acted for the good of the whole, then who is there to cast the first stone? They needed to have the *INTENT* to commit a crime against God's Law, or Cosmic Law, if you like. What these two Beings did upon Earth, in our hypothetical story, is that they embarked upon a course of action that had terrible and tragic consequences for many thousands of God's children; but, as the great leaders that they were, it had been their clear *INTENT* to protect and to care for their own people and to save them from the enemy who was determined to destroy them. As a consequence, many would have suffered terrible deaths, grief, loss, pain, suffering, heartbreak and terrible wounds – physical, emotional and mental – that would never heal in that lifetime. So, where is the *sin*? It is called by another name, my dear children of Light. It is called *FEAR*.

FEAR is the opposite of *LOVE*. God is *Love*. *Fear* is born of illusion, which is the state, in which most upon Earth have decided of their own free will to dwell now, at the beginning of the Age of Aquarius. How many more Ages must come and go upon Earth before the Starseeds open their eyes and wake up to true reality? You came to Earth for a purpose. You came to end the *separation*, which is caused by *fear*. Where did the separation and the fear begin? The separation occurred, because a fear arose in you that God would not support you at all times. Therefore, you decided to go it alone, so to speak, and your conscious mind, combined with your ego/personality, split from the soul-spirit, in all probability (for most, that is) when you incarnated upon Earth for the first time, eager, willing, enthusiastic and ready to help those dear friends who had gone before you and who had become disorientated. They had lost their way upon arrival, because of the dense negativity caused by *Fear*. That is what sin is, dear ones. It is the fear that God will not support the dear children of the Source, the God-Source.

Is such an event possible? Of course, it is not. But, the belief has become so entrenched upon Earth that it has become *knowingness* for most and, that is the great tragedy – the great *sin* – of Earth.

Let us return to our divers now. They are on their launch still and the meetings and briefings are at an end. They have checked and re-checked their on-board, individual computers, through which they will have contact with their own Higher Self should the unthinkable happen and they, themselves, as with their brothers and sisters before them, become disorientated and distracted from their intent, thus abandoning their pre-set path. Their final act before they dive is to re-check their own in-built computer in their individual dive suits – their mini-computer (which is equivalent to the soul), because it contains all data, past and present, of the particular Being concerned. All past life adventures on all different planets and star-systems are recorded here, regardless of the outcome of all of these missions on the path to Full Enlightenment.

What happens upon their arrival will be dealt with in my next Discourse, dear ones, for it is a subject close to my heart and one that requires much explanation and much study on your part if you are to understand fully all that is being revealed to you in these Discourses.

My Love, as always, surrounds each and every one of you, my very precious Starseeds. Until we meet again, avoid the traps that fear and negativity set for you. Their three deadly weapons are despair, depression and drug-induced states. These are deep holes, from which it is difficult to extract oneself when in embodiment, if one allows oneself to trip headlong into that deep abyss. Try to stay positive in the days ahead and to draw to you the Love Essence of God, in a meditative state, be that in a place of worship, such as a temple, a mosque, a church, a shrine or in your own home. Remember that everyone who prays, prays to the same Divine Being of Love and Light, regardless of the name that is given, in the language of the day, to this Supreme Being, the He/She Deity, without Whom no life at all can exist in any reality anywhere.

Practice tolerance and spread peace and joy wherever you go. A smile does not cost the earth, does it, my little treasures? How many smiles, filled with God's Love, can you dispatch this week? Perhaps, you could start a diary, or a bank book of smiles instead of money. That would be a great way to begin to heal the pain of separation from your Source, would it not?

Dear children of mine, in case you had not realised it, I Am the one you have come to know as Mary. I Am not regarded as the Mother of the world for nought, dear ones. I represent the Mother-Figure, the nurturing, loving, caring aspects of the feminine energy, with which Earth is being literally bombarded at present in order to repair the imbalance that has occurred with the above-normal increase in masculine energy that has built up during the past few Ages of humanity on Earth. This is not a *good* or a *bad* scenario. It is a fact of life on Earth. The pendulum of yin and yang is dreadfully out-of-balance and needs to be returned to the central point as a matter of urgency. We, in the Higher Realms, have answered the call of the Enlightened Ones of Earth and these energies are being directed to all now, as a matter of urgency.

You have come full circle from the terrible, end-times in Atlantis, but the hope for the future this time is that the children of Light called out for help to us in the nick-of-time. We cannot intervene on a free will planet without being asked to do so. A request has been received. It was received in Atlantis, also, but on the eve before the button of self-destruction was due to be pushed was just a little late for our intervention to be of any great assistance to our dear children in embodiment. This time, the result will be different. This time, there will be a positive, loving conclusion. This time, the children of Light, our precious Starseeds, will be successful. They will rise as one (vibrationally), thus giving our precious and sorely-tested Mother-Earth the boost that she needs to take her beyond the pollution and negativity of third dimensionality. This time, the science of the mind will not outstrip the Love of the Spirit on a free will planet. The Love factor will prevail and be in perfect harmony with free will.

Those who cannot accept such a happening and who cannot raise their vibrations to keep pace with that of Mother Earth as she soars upwards reaching for Father Sky, these ones will not be happy with their new situation upon another third dimensional freewill planet as they try again to master self, in all its forms and facets, and to begin finally their own individual path to True Enlightenment.

Dear children, remain true to yourselves in all things and true to your own path, not someone else's path, because no two paths are the same. If you waste time and energy carrying another if that one is capable of walking or crawling by himself or herself towards True Enlightenment, then you do not do either one a favour so, please, remember these words.

My Love surrounds you always. My Light is upon this world always.

I Am Mary.

25thJanuary 2000

Jesus-Sananda of the Light

Dear children, your lives will change so much and for the better if you could but let go of your fears and trust in the One Who loves you so very much.

Reading these Discourses will give you a greater understanding and a broader outlook than most established religions and philosophies could do ever. Your understanding is hampered by outdated belief-systems that have been passed down from parent to child, just as the outdated practice of handing down family estates to the eldest son has passed away to be replaced by a more enlightened framework, shall we say.

These were belief-systems and practices that belonged in an era where the understanding of the earth-dwellers had not reached the great heights that it has now and a framework was needed for a society devoid of moral values. When one views historic events, for instance, one needs to look at these happenings in the context of the understandings and belief-systems of that particular time or era.

Great Masters have come at the beginning of every great Age on Earth. These Masters have shown a path on the long road to True Enlightenment. But, their words and their messages need to studied and evaluated based upon the understanding of the people to whom these were delivered in that particular era.

Time on Earth has moved on in every Age and, with it thankfully, there has been an increase in understanding, both in the mental and the physical aspects of life. The rules governing health matters in the fifteenth century, for example, are no longer relevant to today's more sophisticated society, but those rules were adhered to rigidly, because that was the understanding of the health professionals of the day; so, too, does the same story apply to religious and spiritual matters. Science has moved on. Astrology has moved on, but somehow, leaders of religious institutions have prevented their followers from moving on and some are entrenched deeply in the dark ages, shall we say. Therefore, once again upon Earth, science and technology have outstripped the spiritual side of life. Without a perfect balance of the two, a catastrophic outcome is likely.

If people in general shun mainstream religions, because they can accept no longer outmoded teachings and belief-systems that belonged to a bygone era, the gap between the scientific world and the spiritual one will widen to become a gulf too wide to be bridged. The difference between science and spiritual matters is that one can be proven beyond reasonable doubt, so that the sceptics can have no doubts on a certain issue. Spiritual truths cannot be proven beyond any reasonable doubt so, therefore, they come under the heading of esoteric matters. Those who work only from the left brain and operate on purely masculine energy, regardless of the gender of their own physical bodies cannot accept, understandably, a belief-system that cannot be proven beyond reasonable doubt, whereas ones operating in a balanced state, or ones operating from predominately feminine energy being governed by the creative force from the right side of the brain possess a *knowingness*. The wonderful gift of knowingness is a creative force that comes directly from the Source-of-All.

If there is a great imbalance on this planet between those operating solely on masculine energy and those who are either in a balanced state, or a state where feminine energy is dominant, then that planet and its people are going down a road to self-destruction and self-annihilation. It is only a matter of time before these imbalances cause the population, and consequently the planet itself, to reach a point of no-return. It has happened before upon Earth, in the final days of the Atlantean era. Divine Intervention, at the final hour, was necessary and life began again in its infancy once more on

Planet Earth. Does history have to repeat itself, my children of Light? Or, is it time that the veil of illusion was removed?

The information contained in these Discourses is not new. It has been floating around in various books and publications for decades, ever since this information was released to *Channels of Earth*– mediums who were open to receive messages from the Higher Realms – mainly because the Creative Force within them was higher than those who operated purely and solely from a masculine energy, which causes the individual concerned to analyse logically and to dissect every new piece of information that he or she receives.

Let us take the Original Bible, for instance. How were these messages from God received? If it were not for open and willing Channels who devote their lives to the service of humankind, there would not be a Bible as such. If it were not for the wonderful musicians who opened themselves up to the heavenly realms as Channels, would there be such beautiful musical scores and compositions for earth-dwellers to enjoy?

No, my children, there would not be. From time-to-time, there have been trance-mediums who have given great service to the world by predicting forthcoming events. This was not done for their own self-aggrandisement and glory, as many so-called prophets do now; but, it was done for two reasons. One, of course, was to give warnings, so that humanity could change its ways and its thinking, collectively. The other was to bring to the people of Earth the knowledge, or the knowingness, of a Greater Force or Source than their own and to make people everywhere aware of another reality operating above, beyond, below and around their current field of illusionary experiences.

These dedicated ones have paid very dearly for their great service to humankind. For the most part, it was a thankless service, for which they were rewarded with cruel martyrdom. Is it any wonder that willing channels are so very rare in this supposedly-enlightened Age that is fast-approaching? Will the Age of Aquarius be any different, I wonder.

Let us hope so, because if man and woman's spiritual life and ideals do not begin to outstrip the scientific and sceptical worlds based upon greed, power, competitiveness, lust and exploitation of women and children, as well as the total disregard for the plant and animal kingdoms whose stewardship was placed in human hands aeons ago, then an Atlantean-style scenario will be the result. Neanderthal man and woman will be the first step back on the long, long road to enlightenment again for most of humanity.

It is not a pretty picture, my beloved children of Light. You came to Earth for a purpose and that purpose has not been fulfilled. Time is fast running out. Within the pages of these Discourses – these original Discourses – will be given a method of silently and secretly changing your own thinking, your own lifestyle and your own energy field, so that you can raise your own vibrations to those that are very close to a fourth dimensional frequency.

There are a few guidelines that will help, also, such as not eating the flesh of animals. This can serve only to keep you vibrating at a much lower frequency than those who have elected, of their own free will, to change their diet. Alcohol, cigarettes and drug-taking of any description have the same effect on the physical vibration so, if you must partake of these, due to pressure or for whatever reason, then do so infrequently or in moderation until such time as your consciousness has risen to a level where such happenings are not a part of your everyday reality.

My comments earlier regarding *original discourses* stem from the likelihood of these discourses being dissected and altered by others to fit in with their current mode of thinking and – dare I say it – because they see a *quick dollar* in the exercise for themselves and, as a by-product, an ego-elevation at the same time. This is how misinformation is spread on Earth and often by genuine and well-intentioned people. Did not the Bible of Earth become altered here and there, because well-intentioned people felt the need to do so? Once again, it was felt at that time that the very survival of Christianity was at stake, because an outside-force was knocking-at-the gate, so to speak. Therefore, as I have mentioned earlier, it is not wise to judge historical happenings without viewing these within the framework of the understanding and mores of the era in question. However, history does have an awful habit of repeating itself on Planet Earth; does it not?

Living and working in your current communities and in the environment of your own choosing is not at risk here. What is being asked of you is very, very simple. It may be a little time-consuming and probably, a little unpleasant for a time, but it is so very vital for your spiritual advancement now that I would urge you strongly to begin as soon as possible. The guidelines that will be given will be straight-forward and precise. They must be passed from one to another free of charge, for this will ensure that no middle-man (or woman) can profit by their release and distribution. It is an individual path and one that can be achieved by the Higher Self and the lower self (that being the one in embodiment) working closely together to achieve a certain result. If another person tries to teach you this method, or tries to charge you to teach you this method; or, worse still, tries to pretend that he or she can do it for you, then run from that person as fast as you can. Use discernment and all will be well.

The method given can be copied freely and given to ones who ask specifically for it. Pass it on in Love and the Golden/White Light that surrounds the original copy will be passed on to the subsequent ones. If a fee is charged, the Light will cease. This is a fine, etheric web of Light that the beautiful Starseeds will weave and, which will spread around the globe, mirroring the grid system of the Earth herself. Do you see the fine web we are weaving, my little ones?

This will be done in secret and with a minimum of fuss. Join with your friends of like-mind to gain support, to give comfort and to share experiences. Make these pleasant, social evenings, but follow the directions to the letter, as well as inner guidance coming from your own Higher Self. This time spent alone with your Higher Self will be so very valuable to you as you draw closer together. The separation can only grow smaller. Eventually, clarity will come followed closely by a greater understanding and your *knowingness* will increase daily.

Do not, I beg of you, push your views or new-found wonderment onto others, for there is nothing more *off-putting* than a new convert to a certain cause and one who sets off to change the world before changing himself or herself first. Remember, your first priority is to self – Higher and lower. As you find yourself smiling more and having a new-found sense of self-confidence, others will begin to notice. They may notice something else, also. They may notice a certain *glow* around you that is associated usually with the first bloom of a new love affair. But, my lovely ones, your love affair will be with yourself, your own Higher Self.

Your Core Star will begin to open a little more widely every day and, in your mind's eye, this may resemble a lotus flower or a beautiful pink rose, the symbol of Love. See it as either, but know that, without a doubt, your old friends will move out of your life. This may upset or hurt you at first, but the truth of the matter is that they are in negativity and your new-found *glow* will be upsetting them vibrationally and, they will not be able to be present within your auric field for very long.

Others, then, will come into your life, attracted by that glow of Love surrounding you. They may pluck up the courage to ask your secret, in a round-about way, of course. Use discernment, my little ones. Do not rush headlong into a full disclosure at the outset. Be guided by your own Higher Self, through your inner guidance. When in doubt, err on the side of caution, for one must remember always that sealed lips are worth a thousand words. The Starseeds have been thwarted many times in their endeavours in the past, when victory seemed within their grasp, because they did not remember the old adage of *sealed lips are worth a thousand words.*

So, for your own sakes, keep these exercises to yourselves until you are certain that it is your own Higher Self guiding you to reveal your secret, for it may be the ever-ready ego-personality, combining with the conscious mind, hurtling ahead of the soul-spirit and the Higher Self. Be wise. Be cautious. Be silent. Be diligent in the practice of these exercises but, most of all, be consistent. And, I have just one other word of caution. These may continue for quite a considerable amount of time. These will happen silently and imperceptibly, for the most part, but they may take many, many months. They may, at times, cause a slight feeling of irritability and/or a slight feeling of edginess. Try to rise above these periods, because they are a necessary part of the process. Take a long walk or a cold shower at times such as these. Or, perhaps, spend some time alone in silent meditation. Do not, I beg of you, attempt to drive your car, because you may be a disaster-waiting-to-happen at times such as these.

As the method is explained more fully, you will understand the nature of my concern. I would be disappointed to see my beautiful Starseeds give up too soon, just as they were reaching the final conclusion to every earthly incarnation that they had ever experienced, just because of a little discomfort or irritability of a minor nature.

I am certain that most awakened Starseeds would understand what I am meaning with the above words of caution. Keep your own counsel but, most of all, remain centred and try to stay calm at all times. Remember the words of one author on Earth who reported that *God does not rush.* So, if you find yourself rushing, ask yourself why you are doing so. God does not rush, because God is Spirit and not controlled by a man-made clock or calendar. You are Spirit first, my children, and physical second, so why do you allow yourself to be controlled by a clock or a calendar? In physical form, you may need to refer to them from time to time as you travel on public transport, etc. Otherwise, you may be doing much more walking than you would wish. However, in everything, there is balance and the word *controlled* is to what I was referring.

Prune your self-imposed daily schedules down to a minimum, so that the work ethic does not override everything else in your lives. If you do not need to live in a big house, for example, try a caravan by the beach. It would cut down on household chores by at least sixty per cent, would it not?

Every individual is different, with different needs, different aspirations and a different spiritual path to walk. So, it is for every individual Starseed to decide, in consultation with the Higher Self after much meditation where the conscious mind has been brought to a complete state of stillness (and the ego/personality has been persuaded to sit still for thirty minutes or so), to formulate a plan for future spiritual advancement. This can be done simultaneously with your chosen physical path while that remains relevant to your current needs.

When you are in a state of complete calmness and you feel as though you are floating on air, your vibrations are rising rapidly. Before you complete the method that will be taught to you, as a result of these Discourses and your willingness to take that one extra step necessary to complete the task, then you will experience this state only during deep meditation sessions, either alone or with others where the energy surrounding the group is raised considerably. Can you imagine experiencing that state of calmness and the feeling of floating on air at all times when you are in physical form?

It is not an impossible state of *Be-ing*. Many great Masters of Light have achieved it before you. Now, with the raised consciousness of the Starseeds, it is possible for many thousands of Be-ings to experience this state of pure bliss.

We are not asking the impossible of the children of Light. All we are asking really is that you, firstly, remove the blindfold from your eyes and read these Discourses. Secondly, we – your friends of the Higher Realms of Reality – are asking simply that you remove the veil of illusion and consider these new pieces of information, or view them in a totally different light, as the case may be. Thirdly, there is a need to remove the blinkers that have been in place firmly for many centuries, through many incarnations; then, throw out the old, worn-out concepts and beliefs from a bygone era and replace them with a new and vibrant philosophy. Then, and only then, as the scales fall away from your eyes, your path to True and Full Enlightenment will become clear to you. The choice, then, is yours as to whether or not you walk it in Love and Light. The method accompanying these Discourses will be the fastest and most comprehensive way of so doing that you will find anywhere in your world, because it does not rely upon anyone else in your world – only a willingness to tune into your own Higher Self – and, it will not break your bank balance either. If it does, a middle-man or woman has slipped in there between you and the Higher Part of you.

Please remember that every person, regardless of the coat-of-skin he or she is wearing and regardless of the role he or she is playing upon Earth's stage currently, is equal in God's Sight. You are not any better than anyone else. You are not a lesser person than anyone else. Everyone can access this information from within themselves.

It is being revealed here in these Discourses, because no one is bothering to access it. Unfortunately, some have brought through some of the information and then, despite the fact that it was given freely to them, have begun charging exorbitant prices to teach or to release the information. When one considers how highly-evolved these ones think that they are, one must pause to wonder why they do not think that there will be a karmic debt accruing as a result. That is an observation, dear ones, and not a criticism. If one does not observe, how can one then discern? It is one matter to observe and discern. It is most certainly another issue to criticise and judge.

In a moment-in-time, when you face your own, individual *moment-of-truth* (and, this will be different for everybody), then you will *know* the validity of these Discourses. Your Knowingness and your clarity of thought will be clear and in accord with each other. Then, you will know that the separation between the little self and the Higher Self is very small indeed. When you have reached a state where you are twenty-five per cent the lower self and seventy-five per cent the Higher Self, then that is approximately where you will need to be before you can hope to start the final stage of your Earth mission as *Starseeds Extraordinaire*.

If you raise your vibrations any higher, you may have difficulty remaining in physical form, as you may begin drifting off while leaving the physical body trying to walk around without you. Now, that would be counter-productive, would it not? It may get you into all sorts of trouble. So, this is all that is being asked of our beautiful Starseeds at this point in time.

Remain centred and mull over my words and the words of other Master/Spirits in these Discourses, which have been a labour of Love for the writer. When you are sufficiently comfortable with the words and their meanings, I would like you to take your greatest martyr of the Piscean Age down off his old wooden cross, because he was more about living than about dying. Would you not agree?

There are many drawings, sketches and paintings that have been accomplished by spiritual artists over the past few decades. If you need a symbol to replace that of the Piscean Age, in this dawning of Aquarius as the water-pitcher walks across your skies, then look no further than these, for they present and represent the living Christ, as seen through the different eyes of the different artists and painters of Earth.

No two will see the same image, any more that any two writers will write the same words on a page, but the effect upon the inner self, the soul-spirit within, will be the same for everyone. With these words, I will leave you, my children of Light. We have been together many times before. We will be together so many times again and these will be happy, joyous ones that are to come. Believe that and be joyous and free.

In my great Love, I will leave you. My Love encompasses Earth and all of her children, as does the great Love of Mary, the Mother-Goddess Figure of Earth. Allow that Love to infuse each and every one of you as you begin the next stage of your spiritual journey on the road to HOME. It is not quite so far as you think, little ones. Come to my waiting arms and I will carry you, as a caring shepherd would carry a sheep that was too tired to keep pace with the rest of the flock. Love all who come into your path this day and every day that is to follow from here. Time is short on Earth, but not so short that it will prevent you from walking your path to True and Full Enlightenment in the period that is left to you. Practice humility, for the ego/personality does tend to be somewhat troublesome and wayward at times, does it not? Humility, patience, tolerance and LOVE will bring you HOME far sooner than you think.

Raising your own vibrations is the only way to reach that goal. Take the method that is being shown to you now and embrace it fully. Do not form religious/spiritual establishments, enclaves and institutions. Go it alone, with your friends in Spirit by your side and with your friends in the physical by your side when you feel the need to ground yourself. The Starseeds who will not make it HOME, unfortunately will be the ones whose pride is high and whose humility is all for show. It is because this person believes, truly and deeply believes, that he or she is so advanced along the spiritual path that he or she has attained True and Full Enlightenment already.

Believe me, if that were the truth, then that person would not be in physical embodiment any longer. Perhaps, he or she is still walking the earth-plane in a physical body, because the lessons of humility and tolerance have not been learned. It is worth your careful considerations, dear ones. Remember that, in most cases, the tortoise comes home first, because his/her ego does not get in the way and *burn-out* does not result. Can you imagine a tortoise that suffers from *burn-out?* It is a little too ridiculous for words, is it not? So, err on the side of caution and take a few lessons from the tortoise. Withdraw into your own shell and keep your own counsel. These are wise words from one who loves you more than anyone else.

Be at peace and allow my Love and my Light to surround you.

I Am Jesus-Sananda of the Light.

26th January 2000

Zu Deus

In the whisper of the trees and the breeze flowing through them, a Voice is heard. In the ocean deep, through the coral reefs and the underwater boulders, the web of life continues. The reeds in the river know this Sound. It pulsates through everyone and everything. It is the soft, gentle Voice of Spirit whispering Its sweet melody of Love.

Only in third dimensional life is It ignored, drowned out by another voice and that is the noisy, demanding, selfish and self-centred voice of the ego-personality self who drowns out the Original Voice, the Voice of the Holy Spirit within us all.

Why does the ego find it necessary to do so? It is because, my children of Light, the ego feels threatened by the Voice, because It is the soft, whispering Voice of Love, the Love Essence of God. Knowing this, the ego keeps the conscious mind and the personality so busy and so hassled that it cannot hear this beautiful, melodious Voice coming from within all of us. It does this because the Voice, if listened to consistently and at a conscious level, threatens its very existence, because that still, silent Voice of Spirit is showing another way to live one's physical life – indeed all of life!

The ego, which is a word meaning *self*, was born in fear and out of fear. It was born, then nourished and nurtured by the fear that God would not support us in all that we did. If all that we did was in accord with God's Love (and, why would it not be, for we are all children of the Light and Love of God?); then, how could Love do anything other than support us?

It is a very simple concept, but one that one finds difficulty in accepting with ease when in physical embodiment and also, often between incarnations, if one's level of understanding and Love are so low (vibrationally) that one returns to the lower levels of the Astral Plane for rest and recuperation between incarnations. These lower levels do not vibrate at a level that is much higher than that of Earth, because as with earth-dwellers (most earth-dwellers, that is), their collective consciousness mirrors that of their counterparts who are in physical form still.

If one could see the two levels – the Astral Plane and the Earth plane – as two huge bubbles of Light and within these bubbles, life is busy, hassled and frantic, in some quarters, while in other parts, it is free and slow-moving, as a river meandering its way to the sea, while taking time to enjoy the scenery and the wildlife on its banks as it goes by, casually following direction and guidance from the silent, melodious Voice that directs all of life. That is the difference between the two worlds. How clearly one hears the Voice Within, will depend upon the thoughts, the belief-system and the vibratory frequency, upon which one is operating at this present moment.

Being self-centred and self-absorbed, the ego-personality self needs to keep the vibration low in order to survive. It takes great strength of character to firstly, listen for that still, silent Voice from within and, secondly, to shut out the voice of ego for a period of time every day to discover the direction that you have pre-set for yourself in this lifetime. If one ignores the Voice for a sufficient length of time, in any lifetime, then the soul-spirit within will begin to feel a hopelessness, which does not stem from fear and doubt, but from a Knowingness that the pre-set path will not be walked in this lifetime, regardless of how many assurances it was given before taking physical form this time around.

It is then that the soul-spirit begins to shut down and to slowly reduce the life-force within the physical body. In time, when time has run out to even begin the path, the soul-spirit informs the Higher Self that all is lost and physical death follows soon after that. Of course, this does not occur in all cases. Sometimes, when a person leaves physicality suddenly, due to what is termed in your realm as an *accident*, this is merely someone who has completed the pre-set path, sometimes ahead of schedule, because the still, silent Voice was listened to and its directions were followed. As with the river meandering to the sea, this person reached his or her *sea* and returned to the level of the Astral Plane, to which that person was entitled to go, after having completed a life successfully.

In the first instance, the ego returns triumphant while knowing that no progress of a spiritual nature has been made and the soul-spirit – the True Self – has lost out again in the school of life on Earth. In the second instance, the soul-spirit has returned triumphant to claim his/her certificate of merit, or perhaps a diploma, which entitles the bearer who has graduated from another level in the college of life on Earth, to progress. This, in turn, means that a higher level is the prize in the Astral realm and, that the vibrations of the returning soul-spirit have risen considerably.

If one looks only with physical eyes, one sees only that which the ego-personality, combined with the conscious mind, wishes for the one in embodiment to see. If one opens one's conscious mind (and removes the veil of illusion) to accept, for instance, the messages and explanations of another life – a spiritual life – that is superimposed upon this one, namely the Astral realm, then one is challenging one's current thinking and belief-system and this, in turn will send the ego into a frenzy. If one were to accept all that is revealed within these Discourses, because one's own inbuilt Voice of Love was confirming their validity for you (and for no other reason), then the vibration, it can be assumed, is very high in the case of this person.

Let us assume for a moment that this occurs with a young girl who we shall call *Sarah*. Sarah comes across these Discourses and, upon reading them, she is charged with excitement. She cannot wait to share their content with her close friend, Paula. Now, these two are close friends, because they have been together in many incarnations, as brother/sister, as twin sisters, as father/daughter, mother/daughter and, of course, as lovers. These are the roles that they have played over time on Earth. They are from the same soul family and, for the most part, they are at a similar vibratory frequency. Therefore, their auras are of a similar hue and the sound emanating from their vibratory frequency is at about the same octave range. So, it is not surprising then that they are close friends and gravitate towards each other most of the time, both socially and emotionally. Let us assume, also, that they have been indoctrinated from birth within the framework of the same religious institution. However, there is one noticeable difference between them and this difference, instead of weakening their close friendship, which is purely platonic, strengthens it.

That difference can be explained in the way the world-at-large sees them. Sarah is feminine in outlook and demeanour. She is the nurturer, the carer and the dreamer. She loves romantic movies with happy endings and she loves to spend quiet nights at home with a good book, but she loves romantic, candle-lit dinners, also. As a child, she loved to dance, to dress up in beautiful, flowing gowns and to play with her dolls. She is the homemaker and she is proud of this role. Paula, on the other hand, is the tomboy who could hold her own on any pretend battlefield as a child as she fought for supremacy in the rough-and-tumble world of her boisterous, older brothers. The sensitive nature is there, of course, but she tries to mask it with a brusque exterior and a forthright, often even confrontational, manner. She is the doer, the action-taker and she can hold her own beside any man in his world.

What sets these two friends apart from each other is that Sarah is operating on probably a 60%-40% mix of feminine to masculine energy while Paula is operating on a 60%-40% mix of masculine to feminine energy. This is not good or bad, right or wrong. It is just how it is with these two friends. Perhaps, in this lifetime, one of the tasks that each has pre-set for herself is to adjust that imbalance, and so they would have planned to be together for this first stage of their lives, that being the stage between birth and twenty-eight years of age (four times seven years), in order to work towards the accomplishment of this factor.

You see, as they are now as a couple (as friends), they form a perfect circle of energies, that being 100% feminine and 100% masculine. So, as long as nothing occurs to alter that arrangement, they can face together anything in life and achieve a successful outcome. This is how most, if not all, successful marriages, partnerships and business and social arrangements work on Earth and in the lower level of the Astral plane. It is only when another player comes onto the stage, such as a man with whom Sarah falls head-over-heels in love, that the balance is altered and each one of the original players, that being Sarah and Paula, needs to readjust her energies in order to survive and for the new relationship to survive.

If the man who sweeps Sarah off her feet, for instance, was operating on a mix of 80% masculine energy and only 20% feminine energy, he would not only be totally out-of-balance himself (as many men in Earth's patriarchal society are), but also, he would cause then, as a matter of course and a flow-on effect, Sarah to adjust her energies accordingly – that being 80% feminine and 20% masculine. This is a totally unacceptable arrangement and can, if allowed to continue indefinitely, lead to a situation where respect for each other flies away and domestic violence can ensue. In this case, Sarah has not learned the lesson that she came down to learn and that was, in tandem with Paula, to adjust their own individual energies a mere 10% in the opposite direction.

Sarah has a massive imbalance of 30% now and she cannot survive in an out-of-balance, male-orientated world indefinitely in this state. It is only a matter of time before a victim consciousness sets in, within her thought-patterns, and she will bring that to reality in her daily life. Because she has devoured, from an early age, all the literature and movies that have fed her imbalance, such as hero/heroine storylines and prince/princess fairytales, she has strengthened her main weakness, if you like, so when a man who resembles her dreamtime prince-charming came into her life, she reached for him as would a drowning person grab for a passing life-raft. There will be a major upheaval in her life not long after her twenty-eighth birthday unless she redresses this great imbalance as a matter of urgency.

Paula, on other hand, has been thrown off balance by Sarah's demolishing, almost overnight, of their pre-set spiritual plan or path. She feels hurt and betrayed. She reasons with herself (as those operating mainly on masculine energy always do, for *reasoning* is the way that the male of the species deals with all dilemmas and problems), that she should be happy for her best friend, because she has found *true happiness and love* with this new man in her life. Paula, mistakenly, believes that these feelings are ones of jealousy and selfishness while, in actual fact, they are feelings of misgivings, because she knows her friend is on a path of self-destruction – spiritually, emotionally, mentally and physically with this man. Nevertheless, she chides herself, because she reasons that her feelings stem from jealousy and selfishness on her part.

Paula is left to go on with her part in the spiritual attainment of perfect balance on her own. Now, she can take up with a partner who is similar to the way that Sarah was, be that male or female, and enter into an arrangement that is acceptable mutually to each one, be that sexual or platonic.

Let us follow Paula's story for a time. Let us suppose that she decides to follow inner guidance, thus listening to the soft, still, silent Voice within. In so doing, she becomes involved in the healing arts, but as a doer and not as a passive carer. She decides to become a surgeon, because this satisfies the masculine energy of the action-taker within her. Along this pathway, she falls in love with another who is similar to the way that Sarah was in her pre-prince-charming days as far as the energy balance of 60% feminine and 40% masculine is concerned. In the relationship that follows, both are working towards adjusting that imbalance in a positive way, albeit at a subconscious level.

Paula has taken a positive step on her spiritual path, because she has listened to the small Voice Within. Sarah has taken a step, or perhaps two, backwards on her spiritual path, because she has, by age twenty-eight years, fallen into the trap that the ego, fed by the media hype regarding male/female perfect love matches supposedly *made in heaven* and, she has ignored the still, silent, ever-encouraging Voice Within.

For Sarah, it is a long road back to the centre-point of the pendulum where the perfect balance of male/female, yang/yin energies is concerned. Paula, on the other hand, is well on her way to achieving that perfect combination by twenty-eight years of age. She can start then the second cycle of her life between ages twenty-eight years and fifty-six years (another four times seven years) with optimism and hope for the future, because she is free to work towards the goal of overcoming lesson two, which she had pre-set for herself to achieve within that time-frame.

This, my children, is the difference between looking through physical eyes, seeing only the ego's perspective, and looking through spiritual eyes, the eyes of Love. Unless Sarah comes to her senses and turns her life around completely, in a very short space of time, she will know great disappointment on her return to the Astral realm of Spirit. Paula, on the other hand, may be on the road to achieving her next diploma from the college of life on Earth and may be able to rise to the next vibratory frequency upon her return to the world of Spirit.

This is an overall view of two friends and their current endeavours in embodiment upon Earth and their dreams, plans and aspirations on the Astral plane between earthly incarnations. However, let us go back a little in our story. Let us return to a time when Sarah and Paula were happy together, as close friends, before the arrival of the third party whose energies caused Sarah's extra imbalance.

Let us suppose that Sarah and Paula, both aged twenty-five years, attend the same church and meet socially with the same set of friends. Let us suppose that (as an example) Sarah comes across these Discourses, reads them and is excited by them. Why would she be? Because she does not use reason, as Paula does, and because, at this stage in her life, her feminine energies are to the fore and she is listening to the soft Voice of Spirit within her. She is determined to follow the guidelines accompanying the Discourses. When she has read and re-read them many times, she has decided that this will be her main goal in life from then onwards.

She is quite astounded by Paula's reaction to them, because Paula, upon the first reading, has closed her mind. She has used reason to judge them and, judge them harshly she does. Why is this so? It is because she has been conditioned, due to the 60%/40% mix of masculine/feminine energy, to reason, dissect and draw a logical conclusion with everything in her life. The only area where this is not the case with her is with her religious belief-system, because with this, her thought-patterns were programmed from birth and she was conditioned from a very early age to accept the family and parental values and beliefs of the Christian faith, into which she was born. That is the difference. Also, her ego/personality and her conscious mind set up barriers where the Discourses were concerned, because with any belief-system, if someone or something is not *for it*, they are assumed automatically to be *against it*. Therefore, it is perceived at a subconscious level as the enemy. Enemies must be attacked; otherwise, they may weaken the current belief-system. If they (whoever *they* may be) were to be in agreement with the current thought-pattern and belief-system of the person concerned, then in so doing, they are strengthening that system and belief. It is the old story of polarities, as opposed to balance.

In a balanced world, this could not occur. In an out-of balance world, where the male energies have dominated for Age upon Age of humankind, it is a dangerous situation indeed. It has caused more wars between nations upon Earth, in God's Name, of course, than Methuselah has had breakfasts.

So, my children, sadly in their own way, Paula and Sarah have discarded the revelations of these Discourses by the time they have reached twenty-eight years of age. Perhaps, as they move towards the middle of their next twenty-eight year cycle, they may have been guided from within to give them another chance. Let us hope so, because a closed mind does not belong in a perfectly-balanced being, human or otherwise.

Sarah discarded her copy, because of a need within her to reach for her idealised lover of her stories and fantasies. This person does not exist in your reality, dear ones, so please save yourselves a great deal of anguish and self-sacrifice by searching in vain for the movies' version of prince-charming or princess-charming, as the case may be.

Paula discarded her copy of the Discourses, because her logic and reason were operating in unison with her ego/personality and these miscreants judged the Discourses harshly. This was because these threatened her inherited belief-system, a belief-system that is flawed. I say it is flawed in the sense that it is outmoded and outdated, as it belongs to a bygone era that invented the images of witches and devils, in order to keep its parishioners and followers on the path towards God and sanctity. That there may have been a few other selfish motives thrown in for good measure is not without precedent in Earth's history, but we shall leave that subject for another time and perhaps another set of Discourses – time permitting on Earth, of course.

It is slowly – ever so slowly – from here, my beautiful children of Light. Remember always the story of the tortoise and the hare. Remember, also, Paula's reaction to the Discourses, which surprised Sarah who thought that she knew Paula so very, very well. Be as sly as a fox, as wise as an owl, as cautious as a dingo stalking its prey to feed its young and as brave as all of the Masters of Light who have walked before you this secret and well-hidden path to True and Full Enlightenment.

Remember that, as your vibrations rise, then clarity-of-thought will come so very clearly, as will Knowingness, spurred on by and guided by the small, ever-present, all-knowing Voice from within, the Holy of Holy, Pure Spirit.

In your earthly Bible, it is predicted that 144,000 will rise up. It is speaking vibratory frequency, of course. In my estimation, being the eternal optimist that I am, I feel that this will be just the beginning of the groundswell of spiritual awakening and vibratory Ascensions into Light and Love.

The best advice that I can give, as you begin your journeys from here, is to forget about the physical body, in which you are residing presently. Sit for one hour per day, every day, following the guidelines accompanying these Discourses. As you do, try to think only of your Astral/Spiritual self and to imagine yourself coming into balance totally, as male/female energies mixed perfectly together. Then, your androgynous soul/spirit can slip back silently into your physical body, regardless of its gender or skin colour. Is this not a more simple way of coming into balance? I would advise that it is.

Several decades ago, some cassette tapes were released via a beautiful and clear channel/medium into your world. These set the spiritual/New Age world afire. Some openly criticised the new information released free-of-charge to Earth and would not have anything to do with it. Other beautiful Starseeds were excited by these and began spreading them the length and breadth of the planet, painstakingly translating the words into other languages and carefully keeping the text as close as possible to the originals channelled by an American gentleman by the name of Eric Klein. His labour of Love set the Starseeds into a whirl, those who accepted them, that is. It was a little like our fictional story of Sarah and Paula. One grabbed it and devoured the information. One discarded it and ran from it, judging it harshly.

So, it will be with these Discourses, my lovely ones. So, it will be!

However, for those who criticised the original information contained within those tapes, before you judge these Discourses in the same manner, I would ask you to consider this question. The story of the divers leaving their launch and going to their underwater world as outlined here in these Discourses by Mary and as told in more detail in a previous set of Discourses by Constella, is so obviously a metaphorical account that no one would consider it otherwise.

The point I am making here is that the most criticism, which was levelled at the original cassette tapes – so beautifully channelled by the softy-spoken Eric Klein – was due to the fact that the Starseeds were lulled into a false sense of security, because the tapes gave them to understand that they had no need to work towards their own True and Full Enlightenment, as the one known as *Ashtar* and his band of space brothers and sisters were coming to rescue the Starseeds without them lifting a finger to help themselves.

To my way of thinking, this is similar to Paula's reaction to the words and information revealed in these Discourses. Therefore, I would ask these ones within the New Age movement to carefully re-consider all the information that they have discarded. They may have thrown out a few jewels and several precious pearls amongst their rubbish pile. The original cassette tapes were no different in their storyline from the metaphorical story of divers going to an underwater world. It is the perception that caused one to see, hear and believe the same information from a different perspective. To judge and to criticise material, simply because it is from an unfamiliar source, is to reveal a closed mind full of fear.

The churches, in days of old, called their followers *God-fearing* people. But, God is a God of Love, so how did fear come to be associated in any way, shape or form with our Loving Creator, the Source-of-All? It came from the minds of men who had hidden agendas and who wished to keep their followers well under their control. Control is something that is alien to someone in a God/Love-filled world. Therefore, we have two opposing forces – one of fear and one of Love. In a Love-filled world, there will not be found one closed mind or one belief-system. Why is this? It is because all float along in Love and follow their own Knowingness to the letter, never seeking to hurt, destroy, detain or control another of God's Creations from the tiniest insect to the tallest being in human form.

Everyone knows that the life-force within *all* is a Sphere of Light and Love connected directly to the Source and that whatever happens, either positively or negatively to the smallest creature affects the whole as well. It is not possible for it to be any other way. As a pin-prick on your smallest toe is felt by the whole body, so too will any movement of energy affect the whole of Creation. If only for a moment, the impact is felt. And, always, for every action, there is a reaction – large or small, negative or positive. That is Universal Law. That is the way it is, my children. That is the way it is.

So, have a thought for others – all others – as you go about your daily life. Leave no stone unturned to assist another and to give service where you feel it is needed.

See the two large bubbles of Light that I spoke of earlier as two gigantic worlds pulsating with and because of God's Love. Between them, there is an imaginary escalator. As one person goes up after every incarnation, he or she passes another brave soul-spirit coming down to take charge of a new body to experience for a time, third dimensional physicality and third dimensional reality. That is the way it is, sweet ones, and it has been that way for aeons of time. However, the time has come now, at the beginning of the Age of Aquarius, for the new energies that are bombarding the Earth and her inhabitants to make a difference. It can be only a source of much confusion and consternation if the reason for the feelings and emotions that people are experiencing now are not understood. Ignored they cannot be. Controlled they cannot be. Harnessed and used positively as a catalyst for change for the better, they most certainly can be. The choice, as always, lies in the hearts and hands of the individuals

251

concerned upon a freewill planet. Give your Higher Self a chance to show you the way from here. That is my advice. It is very sound advice. I cannot conceive of an easier or better way to raise one's vibratory frequency and it will be inexpensive, too, in monetary terms. All it requires is will, intent and to a degree, a little patience as you devote some of your precious time every day to your own spiritual advancement.

As the Life-Force, which stirs the trees, moves the oceans and motivates the river is allowed to flow freely and to guide your lives, there will be renewal and regeneration, also. It may not reverse the ageing process and it cannot be bottled, packaged and marketed as the *fountain of youth* by enterprising marketeers (or, racketeers, as the case may be), but it can make a great contribution to your overall feeling of good health and well-being. This is a by-product of the process, upon which you are embarking now, should you wish to avail yourselves of the information, which is given freely to all who feel guided from within by their own Knowingness to request the material.

I will leave you in peace, Love and optimism, because I know that you will not let yourselves down on this issue. Stay the distance, dear ones, for it will be truly worth the while and worth all of your efforts. The path to True and Full Enlightenment has never been easy and this is most especially true on a third dimensional planet. However, with the incoming boosts of energy, everyone is a little off-balance at present, to say the least. When the dust settles a little, the planet herself will be vibrating at a higher frequency so that, for those with the will, intent and commitment, the path to True and Full Enlightenment will be the easiest that it has been upon Earth since the early days of Atlantis when she was very much a fourth dimensional, living creation of God.

Stay the distance, little ones. The children of Light will make it easily from here. All that you need to do is to reach out and grab with both hands what is being offered to you. Enlightenment, in all of its glory, will be but one step or two from there.

The Love of God surrounds you all. The Light of God infuses you all.

Peace be with you,
I AM Zu Deus.
28th January 2000

Selene

All about this great universe of ours, there is a Force to be reckoned with and which challenges us to our very souls and to the depths of our Being. It is born of Spirit and Its Voice cannot be heard by physical ears, but Its direction for all individuals is clear and precise. We know, at a heart and soul level, what is being asked of us in any realm or reality.

In the world of the physical, It is sometimes referred to as one's conscience. But, really, It is more than just a meter or a gauge to tell us right from wrong. It is our directional compass that guides us as we struggle blindly through adversity. That struggle may be with another, or with one's own self. The Voice/Compass that guides us along on our sea-of-life does not cease when our time-span in physicality comes to an end after every incarnation.

It guides us then on to and through the next phase of our life, for that life is ongoing and never-ending, because we are the children of a God of Love Who keeps expanding our horizons and drawing from us the best that we can give or offer. This is not a hurried, rushed existence. It has its quiet moments and its times of great activity. It is Spirit's Voice of hope, of Love and most especially, laughter, for laughter is a great boost to the soul and to the energy levels of the Spirit within every one of us. Because our lives go on for all of eternity, we do not have a need for rush and bustle. If there is a frantic rushing hither and thither in our lives, the Voice/Compass that guides us so lovingly and so compassionately has been drowned out (hopefully, temporarily) by the ceaseless demands of the ego-personality, spurred on by the conscious mind who, along with the ego, makes plans to keep those heavy schedules so demanding that there is not any time for stillness, for silence and for our meditations. And, our homes are so full to overflowing with unnecessary clutter that there is not any space left for our quiet space, into which we can withdraw from the world-at-large and from the dictates of our ever-loving family members.

This is how it is for most people on Earth at this time. It takes super-human effort to make changes to lifestyles such as these. As you read my words, I feel that most of you will be saying or thinking or feeling that it is not possible for you to change anything in your life at present. Perhaps this is true, but when looking from my perspective, it is quite simple. When looking through your eyes, it seems a vicious circle that is self-perpetuating. When you return to the calmness of my reality between incarnations, you wonder why you could not see the simplicity of it all when in physical embodiment and you set yourself another goal for the next time that you incarnate. Well, my special and dear friends, that time and moment has arrived. Your Voice/Compass will guide you and show you how it can be done within the framework of your present lifestyle.

I cannot tell you, because I can listen only to my own Voice/Compass from my Source-of-All-Love, Light and Laughter. My Directional Guidance is all that I can listen to and It meets all of my needs. Your Voice/Compass will meet all of your needs, also. It cannot occur any other way in this universe or in any other one. I can give you a clue though. It will be simple. Your answer to every question will be simple, straight-forward and what you in your world term *getting back to basics.*

Do not fight Its direction, dear ones. It is your survival mechanism and first-aid kit while in physicality. If your life is busy, out-of-control, hectic, frantic or filled with confusion, despair, depression and complications that seem beyond your ability to control, then this is the reason. This is the answer to your every need. You need to *tune-in*, as a matter of urgency, to your Voice/Compass whose frequency and call signal to you never ceases.

If, at a conscious level, we do not know that it is there, how can we seek the time, the space and the silence to listen? We cannot, dear ones. We cannot hear It. At times, we sense It. But, for the most part, we ignore these vital, directional signals, because if they do manage to penetrate through the noise, the nonsense and the senseless and ceaseless demands of the selfish ego, their message is in direct contrast to the direction that the ego is taking us. It, the ego, is leading us by the nose around and around and around in ever-decreasing circles until the soul-spirit gives in, realising the futility of the exercise and of this out-of-control lifetime on Planet Earth. The soul-spirit within advises the Higher Self at a subconscious level that this lifetime is beyond repair or redemption, if you like. It has passed beyond the point where it is possible to complete all that one had pre-set to accomplish, in the time-frame that one had allotted to one's own self, for the identity that the current physical body had assumed on Earth's stage and at this point in Earth's history.

The physical body – male or female, black or white, child or adult – is merely an overcoat, or a coat-of-skin, worn to cover the soul-spirit while it attempts to defeat the ego-personality again while walking around on Earth and being seen, by the physical eyes of others who are themselves walking around in other coats-of-skin of varying shapes and sizes trying to defeat their own ego-personalities. Learning to listen closely to one's own still, silent Voice/Compass and only to It is the one and only way through the maze that is life on Earth.

If one can achieve this great feat amongst the pollutants of Earth – the noise, the negativity, the pornography, the sounds that are given in the name of *music*, but which are so discordant as to throw one's soul-spirit *off-*

balance completely and the sicknesses that plague our little ones during life – then, that Being is a miraculous and awe-inspiring giant who receives much admiration on their joyous return to the world of the Astral plane after their pre-set and pre-determined allotted time-span on Earth as that particular identity in physical form has concluded.

There is one other question in this equation. That is the factor of the conscious mind versus the unconscious minds. Now, let us for a moment suspend logical thought (if the ego will allow such a happening) and consider another scenario. Let us suppose that the sub-conscious or unconscious mind is the storehouse of everything that has happened to us. Let us suppose that the spirit-within is the beautiful Beam of Light pulsating within all of us and totally *in tune* with the Great Divine Spirit, from Whom all life everywhere emanates, expands and contracts; then expands some more in an endless sea of Divine Love. It is from this Great Divine Spirit, this God-Force or God-Source, comes the Voice/Compass as I call it that is our directional beacon through all of our lifetimes, past and present, whether upon Earth or elsewhere.

Now, the soul is our archives, if you like. This is the repository where is stored all of our memories of past experiences in all their myriad of forms. The unconscious mind is the terminal for the collection of all of these experiences. Let us imagine for a moment a large studio where someone is working away quietly, recording on video tape every experience, large or small, from this current lifetime of your present incarnation, that being on Earth at this time.

When the lifetime is at an end, the video tape continues through the self-assessment afterwards and records, also, the aftermath or result, shall we say. The *footnote* or *postscript*, if I may call it by either name, records the karmic consequence in detail, whether of a positive or a negative nature. Therefore, these transgressions or meritorious awards are balanced, at a later stage, and an overall picture evolves of the state of spiritual attainment and evolvement of the person concerned.

There may come a time in your physical life when you are struck by either an illness or an instrument. Let us say the instrument, in this case a ladder, falls against your shoulder. Depending upon which shoulder is injured, it may be a message regarding the imbalance of your male/female energies. Now, the injury may heal and only on rare occasions does it hurt you. But, in later life, a condition known as arthritis occurs in the area where the original (in this lifetime) injury occurred to the shoulder. That is the scenario if one looks through physical eyes. With many of Earth's population who do not believe in reincarnation, that is all they can see or will see. However, let us take this scenario one step further and look through the eyes of your Higher Self.

You have chosen, before incarnating this time, to clear a little debris from a past incarnation, as it has been sitting in the *footnote* of one of your videos for many a lifetime and it really is time for it to be cleared, because if it is not, it will keep raising its ugly head in lifetime after lifetime until the matter is resolved. This is because that is the nature of habits and patterns, which follow on from our thought-patterns or inappropriate way of thinking, at a conscious level. So, the ladder has fallen and the injury has occurred. This is the Higher Self, through the unconscious mind, giving a reminder to you that this is where you had pre-determined you would be when you chose, of your own free will, to clear this injury. If it is done and the memory is removed from the unconscious mind, which has a long, long memory, then the healing will be complete. It will not come back to haunt you in future lives and it will not cause the painful condition of arthritis to occur later in this one.

What was the original injury or trauma in the old video? Ask the Higher Self for guidance. Let us say it was caused by a blow from a sword on the battlefield many centuries earlier. Who was the one wielding the sword? It was a sworn enemy of that time. Has this person, wearing a different coat-of-skin, just entered your life while using a new and different identity? The answer, in all probability, will be in the affirmative. It may be just a fleeting appearance in your life. It may be the new shopkeeper at the bakery down the road, or the one who came to your home to repair the washing machine.

When this person enters your auric field, no matter how temporarily, an old memory stirs. The unconscious mind sets up warning signals, which could make you, if you were *tuned-in* to your Voice/Compass, feel discomfort or to be ill-at-ease in this person's presence. You may never see this person again in this lifetime, or you may see them daily for a time; but, he or she was the catalyst, the trigger, to send the unconscious mind into a frenzy of activity as it reaches into the archives to find the video, which recorded the lifetime where this person had a marked, or profound, effect upon your life and perhaps even caused your physical death.

Do you see how it works and how closely everything is interconnected? Now, if you are on your spiritual path, listening to your Voice/Compass and following inner guidance, you will ask your Higher Self for help to rectify the problem. Healers who can help may come your way. Or, there may be another way that your Higher Self will show you, so that the old traumatic event can be erased from that original video and from all subsequent videos where it had raised its ugly head again.

Coming back to the present lifetime, if it can be cleared and healed from the unconscious mind, then that is one less burden to carry around with you as you move from reality to reality and, so it goes on. This, then, will clear the footnote or postscript from the end of your video from that long-ago lifetime. In so doing, your energy field will undergo a change. Your energy levels will improve to a large degree, in most cases; then, as a result, you will feel much lighter, because of this discarded excess, negative *baggage* from the past being removed. Little ones, I am painting a picture here for you. Please try to see your lives through spiritual eyes and try to sit for a time daily, in a quiet meditative state, to review the old patterns and habits that you are, in all probability, repeating in every cycle of your current lifetime.

When I say that with the removal of just one, etheric weapon, embedded for many centuries within your etheric/astral body, you will feel a lightness, I mean by this statement that you will raise your own vibratory frequency markedly and your auric field would become clearer, as well. So, in the long term, it is truly worth the small effort involved. In drawing this little picture for you and bringing this to your attention, in a metaphysical manner, I am giving a slight hint as to what Constella and the other great Beings of Light who have written the Discourses in the book, ***UNDERCOVER STARSEEDS,*** are alluding to and perhaps in so doing, I have stolen their thunder, as you say on Earth. But, they are full of Love and walk the same path as I do, so I am certain that they will forgive me if, in my enthusiasm, I have let the cat out of the bag, so to speak. I am using a number of clichés; am I not?

I think that perhaps I will pass on another little clue. If the removal of just one traumatic event from the memory recorded in the archives of the soul could bring so much relief and such a clearing, as well as the removal of one etheric weapon from the unseen bodies (etheric/astral), then what would be the result (at a vibratory level) if every one of your past hurts, weapons and traumas were removed all at once? Would you not experience great relief, great clarity, great release and, most of all, a great shift in positive energy that would raise your vibrations to such a point that you would be close to an Astral being? Does it all sound too good to be true? Does it sound as though it would be better than winning the lottery?

Now, here is another scenario, which I am certain that Constella and my other friends in Spirit, will not mind my bringing to the attention of your conscious minds, so that you can mull it over or discard it at will. What if, as these traumatic events happened on the physical plane of existence, they can be cleared only while in a physical body? What if when in a physical body, the Starseeds became so caught up in the games and schemes of Earth that they forgot why they came? What if when they return to the Astral plane for rest and recuperation, as well as recreation, they chide themselves and exclaim: *"Oh! No! Not again!"* This is, because, dear children, it means another round of physical merry-go-round experiences.

What is it that the Starseeds came to do? There are three areas that they intend, in every lifetime, to address. The first is to open one's eyes to spiritual truths, instead of accepting the indoctrination from the belief-systems of their pre-chosen parents or guardians. Secondly, having done this, they intend then, in conjunction with their own Higher Self (and, with no other being, in physical form or otherwise – and this, I stress most strongly), to clear and to heal all past traumas and their aftermath from their unconscious minds, as well as their etheric, emotional and mental bodies. This must be achieved with the understanding between the Higher and lower self that it is done with full knowledge (of the reason for and not necessarily the events in question), full will on the part of the lower self and the full consent of the lower self. Only then can the Higher Self begin the clearing and the transformation. But, if this is not understood at a conscious level, how can it be achieved at all?

The third proviso is an obvious one. That is the wiping clean of the slate, so to speak. This means that any indebtedness to karmic or cosmic law must be addressed. In other words, all *footnotes* and *postscripts* at the end of every video that there has been ever, upon Earth (and possibly, in some cases, elsewhere), must be erased. Now, the Higher Self is in a position to know what needs to be cleared while in physical form, such as large, negative debts and what can be renegotiated and left to be served at another time, in another field of service, perhaps in a teaching or healing role upon the Astral plane between incarnations.

You see, little ones, it is very, very simple, but everyone forgets why they came when they get down on Earth and they begin repeating old patterns, because they are locked into an energy pattern that is repeated for lifetime after lifetime after lifetime. They choose parents with the same habitual energy patterns in the hope that they will see first-hand the problems and, then rectify these problems in their own behaviour and their own thought-patterns; but, old habits become like old friends and it is very difficult to break an old, negative *friendship* that has been a part of one's reality for aeons of time. It fits like an old overcoat that has passed its time, but one that it is difficult to discard. So, the merry-go-round of physical life continues on – endlessly.

Fourthly, having cleared and healed one's lower self, with great and loving assistance from one's own Higher Self, then one is in a position to understand more clearly the next step, which is to lead others to this understanding and to quietly, without fanfare and certainly without charge, to teach others what you, yourself, have been taught. In this way, there will be a secret and silent changing of the collective consciousness on Planet Earth and a rise in the vibratory frequency of her children. This, in turn, will give a great boost, in a vibratory sense, to the planet herself. It is all so simple, is it not, dear children of Light and Love?

These Discourses contain much information that is contrary to popular thought and can and will cause much dissension and debate when they are released to the general public in the mainstream of public life. Also, they challenge many entrenched belief-systems of the religious establishments in the world today. Despite this, many of our Starseeds will take them to their hearts and read them constantly. This could lead, in some instances, to what you would term *overload* or *burn-out,* because in their enthusiasm, they are trying to consume too much too soon. As with everything in life, moderation is the key.

When it is nearing completion, the clearing and healing that is the gulf separating the Higher and lower self (known in some quarters as *the separation*) will be decreased markedly and, an increase will be seen and felt in what are called now *psychic abilities,* such as clairvoyance, clairordiance, clairsensory and mediumship abilities. These, of course, bring with them great responsibilities and heavy karmic penalties for misuse. We do not wish that old merry-go-round to re-start when the Starseeds are so near to completion and are Homeward-bound toward their new state of True and Full Enlightenment; do we?

So, caution and moderation are the paths to follow, dear ones. Now, here is my last little piece of advice for these Discourses. After the first reading of *UNDERCOVER STARSEEDS*, put the book aside for a few days, perhaps meditating and mulling over in your minds all that has been revealed. Then, place the book on your bedside table and, before going to sleep, ask your Higher Self to guide you on what you need to know in this moment-in-time. Then, turn over and, go to sleep.

Next morning, before you even open your eyes perhaps, ask your Higher Self to draw close to you and to place his/her protective cloak around you. Then, ask to be shown the answer to your question of the previous night. Open your eyes and sit up as you reach for your copy of the book. Flick through the outer rim, the edges of all of the pages a few times with your thumb and forefinger. After that, close your eyes again and allow the book to fall open at any page at all. Wherever your gaze falls onto a sentence, begin reading from there. You will know where to start and you will know when to stop, especially if your bus to work is coming around the corner of your street.

This is a suggestion only, of course. It is not a hard and fast rule. There are not any such restrictions in our realm, because these are not necessary. They are excess and superfluous to requirements in our world of Love. Why is this? It is because, at a vibratory level, we are *in tune* with one another and with everything that there is. Why is this? It is because we listen to the sound of that sweet, silent, melodious Voice from within our hearts, souls and minds and we follow absolute and total direction from the Compass that accompanies the Voice of the Great Divine Spirit, the Source-of-All-Life, our Loving Mother-Father God of Creation in Whose Likeness every single being, creature, plant and tree is made.

In God's Everlasting Love will I leave you now, beloved children of Light, my beautiful Starseeds, au revoir!

I AM Selene, Master of Light.

29th January 2000.

Zacharia

Having a sense of the inevitability of the death of the physical body, it is possible then to begin the next step on the road to Enlightenment while realising that one cannot change the inevitable, but accepting that one can but do the best that one can in the time available, or allotted, according to the belief-system of the one seeking answers at this moment of time on Planet Earth.

After making such a strong statement to begin my first Discourse for this little book, I feel it would be polite of me to introduce myself now. I AM what is termed in your world as an *Ancient Being*. If I were to show myself to physical eyes, probably it would be in garb resembling that of Old Father Time. This is because, in your world, ones who appear *ancient* are then given respect that is accorded to ones that are supposed to be wise. In your Eastern cultures, this is so. In your Western cultures, it is not so, sadly, because more often than not, they are treated as second-class citizens who, like sheep, need to be put-out-to-pasture where, because of their age and frailty, they become the victims of cruel wolves. Is this not so, my lovely ones?

So, I AM Zacharia. I AM a teacher, a healer and a sage. I AM proud of these titles, because I have worked tirelessly, unceasingly and enthusiastically towards these goals for a time-span that far exceeds the life of the Planet Earth herself. I may seem to be blowing-my-own-trumpet, as earthlings term it, but I do so for a very good reason. I do so to remind you that you are not any different from me. The Being that you are, in totality, is Pure Love and Pure Light, because you were created by and as a part of the Supreme Being Who we shall call *God* for the purpose of this transcript.

Having digressed a little from my opening statement regarding the inevitability of death in your arena of Earth, let us move on a little from there. Imagine, for a moment, that you were laying in a bed in a busy hospital ward. The screens are drawn around you. There is a lighted candle on the bedside table and all of your friends and relatives are sitting around in silence, not knowing what to say to you or to one another. They are all, without exception, praying for a miracle that will *save* you, even in this final hour as you lay on your death-bed.

Without doubt, in our imaginary story, it is you in the bed. Do not doubt this as we proceed. Who can you turn to for help now? Can your family do anything to help you? Can your friends come to your assistance? The doctors, surgeons, nurses have all performed their tasks to the very best of their abilities, but it was all in vain. Assuming that you have accumulated wealth and possessions in this current incarnation, can these be utilised to change your destiny from here?

No, my little ones, nothing is possible to stop the inevitability of your current death. The tragedy is that you have passed through this experience on Earth hundreds and possibly thousands of times before, but your current thought-patterns will not allow you to accept this fact-of-life – eternal life – so you lay there in great fear as your relatives and friends sit there in great distress, frustrated by a feeling of helplessness and unable to accept that one they have loved so deeply is leaving them, supposedly forever.

If what is being proposed in this set of Discourses is truth, can you see now why I call this a *tragedy?* The tragedy is in the ignorance of ones who believe in a *one lifetime only to get it right* system. The tragedy is, also, in the fact that one is being led around by the ego-personality who wishes, for its own interests, to keep you in a deluded state, which is the absolute antithesis of the Enlightened State.

So, what is your state-of-Beingness at this present moment in time? Do you believe that there is but one lifetime and, after this, all the billions of people who have ever walked the Earth in all of its billions of years of existence are standing around in an endless queue awaiting the final Judgement Day by an Authoritarian Judge known as *God?*

Is that your perception, my little ones? Is this not what the churches of the Western world are asking you to believe and to accept in blind faith, because they say that it is so? Well, I am giving you another perspective to consider. Who is correct and who is incorrect is for you to determine. If the ego has its way, I know what your choice will be. This will sentence you to many, many more lifetimes on the merry-go-round of karmic experiences on Planet Earth, or elsewhere, where the vibration is so very low that no one can think or see anything other than the physical world, in which he or she is residing at a given moment. This will mean that the five physical senses of sight, sound, taste, touch and smell are all that one uses to function in that world. Are these not the same five senses that the animal kingdom uses?

There is one exception. Animals use, also, their instinct. In humans, this is called *intuition,* but this is squashed almost at birth in probably three-quarters of Earth's population. This is because, when intuition is given full-rein, the ego is required to take a back seat. For most people, it is a long time since the ego was forced into the back seat. Probably, by a rough calculation, it would be ten to twenty millennia. That is a long, long time in Earth's history; is it not?

So, let us ignore the dictates of the little ego-personality, combined with the conscious mind, who is trying to distract you now, in the hope that you will go on with your physical activities and discard these Discourses permanently. Will it succeed yet again, my lovely ones? Will it succeed?

What is it that one takes when one crosses over into the reality of Spirit? If one has followed inner guidance (intuition) to the letter, then one will have a loving heart. That Being will be filled with Love, with Light and with Compassion. What is it that one will have if one has followed the dictates of the ego to the exclusion of all else? Nothing, my lovely ones – there will be nothing but a shadow of karmic debt trailing behind him or her. Another round on the karmic wheel-of-life is inevitable, I am sorry to say. What a tragedy!

I AM Zacharia of the Light.

03 February, 2000

Adele

Songs of praise drift from our realm to your realm.
Songs of praise give rise to hope in our realm.
Songs of praise raise the vibration of ALL everywhere.
This cannot be denied by ones of Earth.

Songs of praise to God on High give thanks.
Songs of praise give rise to elation of the soul.
Songs of praise provide a source of sustenance to ALL.
This cannot be denied by ones of Earth.

I wish to speak this day of music. Music is the balm of sweet, pure Love that sweeps over the soul and washes it clean of negative emotions. It cannot be stressed enough the importance of music, dance and song in uplifting one from the doldrums and the humdrum of physical life on Earth.

In light of this, why is it that there are some religious belief-systems and establishments that ban music of any kind? If there is not an ulterior motive, for example, absolute control with total submission to the will of the leaders of these establishments, then what is the purpose of banning something that is so beneficial to ALL? By All, I am referring to the collective consciousness.

The feeling nature of music supplements our emotional needs and provides a calming element when life seems out-of-control. It is possible for ones who have sunk into negativity upon Earth to provide a noise factor, which they may label as *music*, and perhaps this discordant sound is what the church leaders of some religious establishments are endeavouring to ban. The sound that these discordant notes provide, when strung together, does much damage to the vibration of ALL who hear them, regardless of whether or not they are listening to them at a conscious level and/or by choice. Never, under any circumstances, could this discordant sound produced in negativity to bring ALL down to that negative state be described as *music*.

Music is love in action, producing a sound that is melodious and uplifting to the soul/spirit of the listener. That is the difference, dear ones. When music is played to a large audience, it has a profound effect upon every individual who makes up that audience. Christmas carols sung by ones with crystal clear voices, for example, provide a source of joy for all who hear them. Such an event can raise the vibration of everyone upon the planet, because of the cumulative effect that Love, combined with music, can and does provide.

Discordant sound that is sometimes registered as a half-beat has the opposite effect and, in some cases, this sound can affect a crowd in an extremely negative way, working through the subconscious levels of those listening and affecting adversely their emotional bodies. It has caused riots and loutish behaviour of an extreme nature, especially when compounded by the unwise use of alcohol, stimulants and drugs of a dangerous nature. It is this extreme element that has led to a blanket ban on music by some churches. This is extreme, also, and is similar to banning sunlight from the lives of its followers. In all things, the pendulum needs to be in the centre.

In our realm, we have a large choir made up of ones with beautiful and melodious voices who meet in an amphitheatre, which would be considered large by Earth's standards. It is a very high structure without a roof. On every level of this circular structure is a balcony. All those with similar voices meet on their own balcony and sing in harmony. The same songs are sung and the same ones gather together. There is never a moment when the amphitheatre is empty or devoid of music. If there was a roof, it would have lifted off ages ago, because the music that these beautiful ones provide is done in Love as a service to ALL.

In sending out their beautiful Songs of Praise continuously, they are raising the vibrations everywhere, because everything – negative or positive – affects the whole. Nothing that is of a negative nature or persuasion emanates from this amphitheatre, which is and was designed for the upliftment of ALL and to give thanks to our Creator-God, regardless of the name ones of Earth give to the Mother-Father-God-Principle, the Source-of-All.

It is wise and prudent to remember this difference between true music and discordant sound when making arrangements to attend concerts and gatherings upon Earth. Discordant sound can upset the equilibrium of the physical body long after the sound has ceased, because it reverberates in the atmosphere for a long, long time, just as other pollutants do on your Earth plane. Some you can see and others you cannot see with physical eyes. They are nonetheless dangerous, because they are unseen.

Giving some thought to these revelations may help to distinguish between music and discordant sound and may explain mood changes in many people on Earth. Mood changes can lead to other unpredictable behaviours, such as sending a dozen red roses to someone you love on the spur-of-the-moment. Conversely, it can cause a negative response, also. Suicide can be triggered by this discordant sound, in extreme cases.

Songs of Praise on Earth, when these join with Songs of Praise from our amphitheatre on high, will raise the vibrations of ALL on the planet in a very short space of time. Our heartfelt thanks go out to all of our singers, musicians and creators of song who work unceasingly and in great Love in both realities to provide this source of joy and Love and the beautiful balm for the soul/spirit, which true music is and always will be.

I thank you for reading these few words on my favourite subject, which I asked to be included in this wonderful book, another example of co-operation between my realm and your realm. These joint efforts will continue indefinitely until the dividing line between our realities is no more. What a wondrous time that will be!

In my Love, I leave you. This Love, which is the Love of our Creator-God, is the life-balm of ALL. Without this Love, no one could exist or survive at all, on any level of existence. It is your birthright and your life-support, dear ones, so treasure It, please. True music will increase Its Flow tremendously. Be at peace, be still and listen. The musical tones of the birds in the tree-tops is a source of joy and Love, also, as they raise their voices in Songs of Praise to greet the morning sun.

I AM Adele,

Musical Director of Music-of-Love-and-Light for ALL from the Amphitheatre on High

12th February, 2000

Onoraus

My children of Light, I AM Onoraus. As promised earlier, I will elaborate on the second reason for incarnating into physicality on Earth. The first one was, of course, karmic debt. The second one relates to the learning of lessons in the school of life on a third dimensional planet.

As has been explained earlier, also, there is but one lesson, that being the lesson of Unconditional Love. However, the road to that state of Being is strewn with the corpses of those who tried and then gave up, due to excessive stress. So, let us analyse stress. What is stress? Stress stems from a fear in the subconscious mind. The side-effects of this fear cause massive problems for those in embodiment. Because of this underlying fear, there is stress that is alleviated temporarily by over-indulgence. As a result, obesity occurs in some while anorexia can occur in others. Of course, the obvious result that we see in society today is an abuse of drugs (prescribed or otherwise), alcohol, cigarettes and beverages that lower the vibration of all the bodies, such as coffee, tea, or chocolate-related substances, to name but a few.

If one can defeat the underlying cause of stress, that being the fear that is allowing the stress to occur, then one can defeat any of the associated problems relating to this stress-factor. Does this not make sense? Of course, genetics play a part in this little drama, but then one must ask the question of why one chose those particular parents who had this genetic imbalance in the first place. The answer is that those parents were chosen for the same reasons that they chose their parents. That reason was to learn lessons and to repay karmic debt. It means, also, that the parents chosen were fighting a similar fear, which was manifesting itself as obesity, for example. They tend to eat too much to over-compensate for their lack of self-worth. This lack of self-worth stems from the fear, which is the root cause of the problem. Therefore, they try to *hide* from the world-at-large by covering themselves in layer upon layer of fatty tissue, of which they are ashamed and then, of course, the problem is exacerbated. Their reason for choosing those particular parents was that they wished to see the problem for themselves first-hand and to overcome this same tendency in themselves.

This seems such a difficult concept to grasp when in physical embodiment on Earth. It applies to all *evils*, for want of a better word. It is the explanation for alcoholism, domestic violence that occurs in generation after generation and a violence that is built-in and must be fed by killing other human beings or animals. These urges are fuelled by movies and videos that are freely available and watched by many children of tender years, as well as adults. If this problem exists in a family and is suppressed in most members of that family, then that does not clear it. That merely means that it is ongoing and eventually, someone who cannot control himself or herself, will incarnate into that family and massive violence will be the result. The victims may not be only from the immediate family, as has been witnessed in cases where this has spilled over into the street, the school, the local shopping centre, amusement park or restaurant.

It is a complex problem, which could be solved easily if one were to learn the lesson of Unconditional Love. It is very difficult to act in Love toward someone else when one is in negativity oneself, due to excessive stress. There are television programmes, which devote much of their time and energy having one set of characters slur and slander deliberately another set of characters, thus presenting the view that this is normal behaviour in the home, school or workplace. For every action, there is a reaction. If the action is soft, gentle, kind and loving, then the reaction will be the same, even if it is not shown immediately by the one who received the kindness. If it is a negative action, in most cases, there will be a negative response and in all probability, this will occur immediately. Regardless of the original action, there will be a flow-on effect, be that positive or negative. It seems to be the role of the media these days to promote the negative, for the positive is no longer *newsworthy* and does not *sell*, yet they *wash their hands* of any blame when a massacre occurs.

So, if the parents chosen have a problem, which appears to *rub off* onto the children, then this is the answer. The child has chosen the parents, or parent, to learn the lesson, with which the adults are struggling still. Once the lesson is learned, then that set of circumstances need not be a part of any future incarnation. However, if the original fear is held still within the subconscious mind, then it is a matter of time only before it manifests itself again. Then, the lesson will need to be re-learned at a future time. This is why it is so very important and, dare I say *vital*, that these fears, which cause the stress that causes the problem to surface when in physicality on Earth, are released and cleared, and the damage that they have caused is healed once and for all time.

The fallacy that is being promoted within some sections of the New Age movement is that ones who elect to incarnate into these situations do so to experience what they *feel* during these times. If this supposition is taken to its ultimate conclusion, it would mean that a child-of-God incarnates upon Earth to *experience* what it feels like to kill the physical body of another child-of-God who is incarnate on Earth for another reason. Could such a preposterous situation occur when the Creator-of-all is a God of Unconditional Love and wishes only Love for the children of His/Her Creation? I know that this is not so and so do you, my beautiful children of Light, so do not allow yourselves to be misled by such nonsense, I beg of you.

If you are prone to alcoholism, for example, then your emotional body is overflowing with unreleased trauma, which needs to be released, cleared on all levels of oneself and healed totally. Otherwise, the problem will surface in every lifetime. Someone who is able to *keep a lid* on these emotions under normal circumstances may become what is termed a *binge-drinker* occasionally. In this way, the release valve is opened for a short period of time, then that person can go on with their normal life until the next time that the stress-factor rises to an untenable level; then, the valve will need to be opened again. However, the danger with this practice is that it can become addictive in itself and, also, there can be great damage to the body of self and others during these times of uncontrolled release of the pressure of extreme stress. Make no mistake. That is the cause of binge-drinking or drug-taking, for that matter. The next step for ones who are under extreme pressure (or, who think in their minds that they are under this pressure) is suicide, of course. That is the greatest tragedy of all.

If stress is the problem, then fear is the cause. That fear is held at a very deep level and needs to be released. There are ones on Earth who understand this problem and do try to treat the problem and the root cause. However, they are labelled as *quacks*, for the most part, because their thinking is not that of the majority of Earth's population who is fed this information from the media and from a source that has a vested interest in keeping everything just as it is. After all, their own livelihoods could depend upon this factor. So, do not be misled or led around blindly *by the nose*, because someone has a university degree and letters after their name. Their degree may be from the universities of Earth only while the one who is releasing, clearing and healing in a spiritual sense may have their degrees and diplomas from a far greater school of learning than any seen upon Earth.

I will temper, however, the above statement. There are many practitioners who are trained in both arenas and who operate on a highly spiritual level, even though they may not promote the spiritual side of their being to others. There are many practitioners who work in the healing arts in the New Age movement who hang a shingle over their door, but who are doing more damage than good, because they are operating from ego more so than from their own spiritual nature. It all comes back to discernment and what is most appropriate for the individual.

Within the last section of this book, *Guidelines to Self-Healing* has been presented so that a way can be shown where one can go-it-alone and release, clear and heal for oneself, in association with one's Higher Self. Let us look at a healer who works solely from the spiritual aspect. Let us call the person, Noel, for the purposes of this explanation. Now, Noel is a spiritual healer and he has been so in many previous lifetimes. Noel begins to explore his gift with his friends and then, as others hear of his methods and his success, his talents have begun to be recognised. Noel can work from one of two ways now.

He can exploit his gift and charge quite a substantial amount for his services. Or, he can give his services for free, asking merely for a donation to guarantee an exchange of energy between himself and his client. After all, he is using his valuable time that could be better spent perhaps earning a living for himself in the broader community. He is using his expertise, which was gained not only in this lifetime, but also in many past incarnations where he was treated none-too-kindly by the authority figures of the day. So, he has earned his *stripes*, shall we say.

This is a matter for him to consider and no one else. He will do, if he is following inner guidance, whatever his in-built guidance system is recommending. It is for the one seeking his services to decide whether he or she is prepared to take advantage of these services that Noel is providing. However, there is another matter here and it does require a mention. If Noel, as he goes about his releasing, clearing and healing, asks for the permission of the Higher Self of the client and for the co-operation of that Higher Self, as well, then the fear and subsequent trauma will be released slowly and in a controlled manner that is conducive to the wellbeing of the one seeking the service from Noel. If on the other hand, Noel releases without asking for the involvement of the Higher Self of the client, even though the client has given permission for this to take place, then the free will factor applies and the Higher Self cannot intervene. Noel is going-it-alone, shall we say, while working solely with his Higher Self as the Higher Self of the client takes a back seat, for want of a better explanation.

Now, this situation is fine, also, and a criticism is not intended. My observation would be that if Noel were a *pure and clear channel* for the life-giving energy of Spirit, that being the Love Essence of God, then he would be capable of healing as Jesus and other Masters-of-Light have done on Earth. If he is not a pure and clear channel, it is because he has not released, cleared and healed himself at a very deep level. Therefore, he is channelling energy from Spirit through his own bodies – or levels – and these are not clear themselves.

This is not to say that Noel is not doing good work and not providing a wonderful service, especially if it is being done on a donation-only basis; but firstly, the client could do this releasing, clearing and healing for himself or herself, instead of relying on another of God's children who has taken the time and the effort to learn about spiritual healing (regardless of the name/s given it on Earth) in this and other lifetimes. Without the involvement of the Higher Self of the client, then the danger is that too much will be released at the one time and, as a consequence, much damage could be done to the physical and other bodies.

This damage could send the client's body out-of-balance for a time and, during that time when its reserves are low it could attract another illness to itself. Therefore, the healing itself could be blamed for the subsequent illness and this would be the cause for more criticism to be levelled at spiritual healing. It happens, because the healer is not a completely clear channel himself and he does not know when to stop the releasing in a session, because he is not picking up clearly the signal from his own Higher Self, due to his complete absorption in the process that is taking place at his hands. Does this explanation make it clear that the only One who knows, without a doubt, what needs to be released in any one session is the Higher Self of the client? I hope it does.

There is not a criticism being levelled at the healer who believes he is providing a wonderful service and so he is, but Noel needs to realise that he is not the one who is releasing, clearing and healing. He is but the instrument. My children of Light, you can bypass the instrument and become the healer yourselves, as long as you have the clear intent to do so and as long as you involve your own Higher Self in every session. It is not as complex as it may seem. You may not understand what is occurring at a conscious level, but at a subconscious level and at the level of the Super-Consciousness which is you, you do understand . . . and, more importantly, you *know!* It is the Higher Part of you that is releasing, clearing and healing the lower part of the One Being, so that ultimately you can become the One Being again. You are similar to two parts of a magnet. There is a blockage there that is keeping you separate and apart. The lower part descended into illusion for a time, but this was meant to be a temporary situation only. You have become stuck in that illusion. It is the Higher Part that can and will extract you, if only you will ask.

The second part of this equation is that of re-programming the subconscious mind after the old files have been cleared from the memory bank of your computer. Let us start with Unconditional Love. If we have cleared, or are in the process of clearing the trauma and its aftermath that is buried deeply, then we will not be *reacting* quite as quickly as may have been the case in the past where situations arose that upset us. So, this is a start. If we do not react, then the moment will pass, hopefully, and a situation that could have provoked conflict has been avoided. That is Unconditional Love in action, my lovely ones. It is contrary to what most of your soap-operas depict, but it is God's Way, the way of love.

If the situation does not resolve itself by you feeding it Love only, then hand the matter over to the One who Loves you the most of all – hand it over to God and do only that which you are guided to do from within. In other words, turn the other cheek, for it is the meek that will inherit the Earth – that being the fourth-dimensional Earth during the Golden Age. Slowly and without you realising it, your thinking will change as Love towards others is your main goal in life. Then, the re-programming will be taking place without you realising that this is happening. That is how it will take place and it will be slow, subtle and silent. How else would God work with His/Her children of Light?

Do not expect miracles and instant cures. It took hundreds, perhaps even thousands, of lifetimes on Earth and elsewhere to build up this shield-of-resistance to Love. It cannot be removed overnight. However, I will be so bold as to say that if the methods outlined to you in the *Guidelines* are followed to the letter, in complete faith, then by this time next year, in Earth's timeframe, you will not be the same person that you are today. You will be Lighter, freer and more in control of yourself – your Whole Self – than you are now and your Guidance and Knowingness will be unrecognisable when compared with what it is today.

You will *know* where you are going and what you are meant to be doing. You will not need Noel, or anyone else, to help you along your own pre-determined path to True and Full en-*light*-enment. Let us hope that Noel and others like him do not criticise and denounce these *Guidelines*, because of a fear that they will be superseded and their own livelihood as healers will disappear overnight. Beware of this fact, dear children of mine, and look behind the scenes when listening to ones who may have a vested interest in keeping everything as it is. If that is the stand they are taking, then their fear is great . . . perhaps even greater than your own deeply-buried fear. That is a little food for thought, is it not?

If they can release, clear and heal as Jesus did, then perhaps they are clear Channels-of-Light. If they cannot produce these so-called miracles, without even laying-on of hands, then they are in a similar situation to what you are yourself. They are locked into the birth/life/death/re-birth cycle of Earth and are living in illusion. Can they, then, guide and heal you better than your own Higher Self can do? I do not think I need to answer that question. Your Higher Part will do so for you, if you need an answer. That is the difference.

I am here merely to bring these matter to your notice, and hopefully to *grab* your attention for a short period of time. That is my service to you. I have no other motive at all. It is for you to decide what is *Truth* for you and what is not applicable to your needs. You have the freedom of choice, because that choice is a free will gift from our loving Creator-of-All. Guard it well and use it wisely. That would be my advice to you as you commence this new and exciting journey towards the Subtle Light that so Loves you that another massive effort is being orchestrated to *save* you from yourself.

In the light of what has been revealed in these Discourses, does that last statement of mine make sense to you? Hopefully, it does, my children of the Light and Love of the God-Source. You are truly magnificent Beings of Light and Love. It is merely the trauma that you have suffered that is keeping the separation so painful and so real to you. Change your thinking and your patterns and all else will fall into place for you, as you take the first step on the last journey Home.

We await every one of you with open and loving arms. The Homecoming Party is about to begin. Will you be there, my little one? Will you be there?

I will leave you now as you ponder another Discourse in this book. Let us hope it has more impact than its predecessors and that this book can shake the Starseeds into an awakened state, so that they can rescue themselves from their own predicament. There is not time for any more wake-up calls, dear ones. Please act upon this one now as a matter of urgency. Nothing in your daily lives is more important than your own releasing, clearing and healing at a deep, deep level.

You cannot help another until you help yourself first. Ask yourself this question:

"Am I so indispensable to those around me that if I were to return to the Astral Plane of Spirit this moment, would they cope and continue with their lives and, if so, what would be my greatest disappointment when True-Clarity-of-Thought returned to me at the self-assessment session following my return to Spirit?"

That says it all; does it not?

In my great Love, I will leave you now. Adieu, my beautiful ones!

I AM Onoraus, Lord of Light and Love.

18th February 2000

Jesus-Sananda of the Light

Holding on to past hurts and hates is not conducive to a happy life. In an instant, life could change for you, often irrevocably. This trauma is added then to all of the other traumas that are stored within the subconscious area of your soul/spirit. This imprint is added to all of the other ones from previous times, both in this lifetime as well as past lifetimes. An illness of any description can be traced back by ones who look through spiritual eyes and the source of the physical problem can be located and alleviated.

Unless the source is found and the problem addressed at the deepest level, a cure for the illness is not possible. The illness may be healed temporarily, but a cure is not possible. How, then, can the problem be eradicated at such a deep, deep level? It is simple, sweet ones. It is so very, very simple.

Place yourself in God's Hands. Be guided by inner guidance coming from your own Higher Self or Holy Spirit within. The Higher Self is in a position to know immediately the cause of the original problem and to be able to trace it back to an original trauma that occurred in a distant past life. In every lifetime after that one, the problem would have occurred at about the same age that the original one took place. The exception to this would be if one had chosen to return to Spirit, via the death process, before reaching that particular age in an embodiment.

The body is but a *diving suit*, as Constella has described. That diving suit is the focus of attention for most upon Earth. Keeping it healthy, fed, clothed, fit and beautiful is the goal of most. Keeping it in luxury is the sole pursuit of many. Seeing the body as nothing more than a diving suit that one has donned for this particular Earth experience is a new concept for most. Let us toy with this idea for a time.

You slipped into this diving suit while it was in your mother's womb. After your birth into this reality, it was necessary for the first seven years – from infancy to childhood – to learn to cope with the diving suit's capabilities and to learn all over again how to operate its various functions.

From seven to fourteen years of age – that being from childhood to adolescence – one was learning to cope with the mind games that everyone else was playing.

From fourteen to twenty-one years – that being from adolescence to adulthood – one's body was formed and the mind was formed. The ego-personality was in control fully, in most cases.

From twenty-one to twenty-eight years of age, the die was cast and the life had begun. By the twenty-eighth birthday, the first one-third of one's life-span was completed.

Now was the time to remember what you, the person inhabiting the current diving suit, had come to Earth to do. Now was the moment to consult with the Higher Self and to acknowledge one's readiness to begin the task or tasks that the soul/spirit had pre-set to do. If one had left the physical body permanently during the first one-third of the life, then that would have been in accordance with the pre-set plan and would have been the directive given to the Higher Self prior to stepping into the diving suit.

There are not – and never have been – any such occurrences as coincidences or accidents. Everything happens for a particular reason and is a part of a Higher Plan conceived by you prior to stepping into your diving suit. Supposing you experienced a so-called *accident* at a moment in your life when everything, that the ego-personality, combined with the conscious mind, had planned for years was about to come to fruition. Let us say that at twenty-eight years of age, after many, many years with your nose to the grindstone, you had graduated from university and your role as a skilful surgeon was assured. Let us say that a *freak accident* occurred and you lost the use of one or both hands.

The result would be that the ego-personality, combined with the conscious mind, would go into shock. This would be followed by the 'why me?' scenario. An adjustment to the new situation would take some time. However, the soul/spirit, combined with the Higher Self, would have planned the incident meticulously and in every detail, including the timing, of course.

This is because you had pre-set a path before incarnating and this required the knowledge that a surgeon would possess, but that knowledge may be required elsewhere. You may have planned to go to a third-world country and to work as a teacher while imparting your wonderful and great knowledge to less fortunate students. You may have promised them you would come, before incarnating. Because of this promise and this service that you intended to carry out for humankind, they may have placed their faith in you and in your commitment to them. They had incarnated, as a group, into families within that third-world country. Do you see the bigger picture emerging here?

As a soul-family, you have given a commitment to the Spiritual Hierarchy that you would all become surgeons, for example, and you would work solely for the good of the people of that country. For this great service, unselfishly given, great merit and reward would be given to every member of that soul-family upon their return to Spirit.

Just as the diving party lowered themselves beneath the waves into their underwater world, intending to meet up at a certain point for a particular purpose, so too did our group of surgeons. Therefore, the one who elected to learn the skills necessary to teach the others of his/her soul family would have been guided to offer service to a particular university in the country that had been chosen. After several attempts to guide the would-be surgeon to accept the *lesser* post had failed, a more drastic approach would have been necessary.

The Higher Self – in conjunction with soul/spirit of the surgeon – would have suggested and then implemented, another way to bring this person to the university in the third-world country as a teacher.

The remainder of that soul-family would have been guided to attend and the whole family would have met up, as pre-planned. Much is orchestrated during the dream-state, between the Higher Self and the soul/spirit of the one in embodiment. This is without the knowledge of the conscious mind and the ego-personality, which goes into shock frequently when drastic measures are implemented, at a higher level, to bring the person concerned back onto his or her pre-set spiritual path.

Seeing the body as a diving suit, rather than the totality of everything, is a way, in which one can be more *in-tune* with what is occurring in the current lifetime.

Coming back to our surgeon/teacher and his band of students, there may come a time when all of the students have graduated and he returns to his former life in the country of his birth. After that, he may regain the use of his hands to go on to another part of his life, perhaps in the latter half of his mid-life years, between twenty-eight and fifty-six years of age, when the third part of his life begins. It is all in 4 x 7 year sections, known as Part One, Part Two and Part Three.

On the other hand, the students in the third-world country might use free will and decide to follow their own ego-personality self, led by their own conscious minds, and shunning inner guidance from their own Higher Self, they might take up positions at hospitals in different countries. This may be counter to their pre-set paths, which may have been to improve the lives of the population of the country of their birth. Some may stay and some may leave. The ones who fulfil their life-path know such great joy upon their return to Spirit. The ones who side-step every endeavour of their

Higher Self and work against their pre-set path know such deep, deep disappointment upon their return.

This is how one sees the world when looking through the eyes of Spirit. When looking through the eyes of the physical, or the peep-holes of the diving suit, everything seems distorted. Trauma and tragedy are seen as negative happenings. Obviously, there is a positive side that is apparent only to those who peer through spiritual eyes.

Many books have been written on this subject in recent years. Often-times, they – the writers – are coming from different perspectives but, for the most part, their messages are similar. It is a subject worth contemplating at length and studying so that an understanding can be reached. Seeing the physical body as a disposable diving suit that has been allocated a set period of time upon Earth to achieve certain goals and objectives, as well as to learn certain lessons as set by the soul/spirit, in conjunction with the Higher Self, makes more sense than the current thought-patterns of humankind. Seeing a Part One, Part Two and a Part Three stage in one's life can help, also, in coming to this understanding. From the understanding comes the Knowingness.

When the Knowingness has arrived, the person has arrived at a spiritual moment-of-truth. It is his or her choice then to accept or reject this understanding and this Knowingness. Many do reject it, because it is easier to pull down the veil of illusion once again than to confront TRUTH head-on. Confronting Truth head-on may require then another decision and the changing of one's current lifestyle and thinking. That becomes too difficult for most when their own families and their contemporaries in their work and social setting are all living in illusion and most plan on doing so for the remainder of the life of the current diving suit.

It takes a being of great resolve to choose, of his or her free will, to break away and to swim against the tide. To swim against the tide, it takes great stamina, also.

This is the state-of-play on Earth at present. This is what is being asked of the Starseeds now. Remove the veil of illusion from your eyes. Acknowledge that a change is needed both in your thought-patterns and your behavioural patterns. Open the peep-holes of the diving suit until you are looking through the eyes of Spirit.

In so doing, you are making great changes in the consciousness of the *whole* and assisting to raise the vibrations of every living soul on the planet. This is what is needed now, urgently, as Mother Earth raises her vibrations. If this change does not occur soon, Mother Earth will be vibrating at a frequency that is so much higher than the vibration of most of her children, so that major disasters will and must occur, because of this major imbalance. It is occurring already and has been for most of the Piscean Age.

The horrendous wars, the man-made disasters, will continue and perhaps even escalate. The disasters that are termed *natural* will increase, also. When a pendulum has swung far too far in one direction, can there be any other result, my children of Light?

My beautiful Starseeds, the time for procrastination is at an end. No one is coming to *save* you, or to *rescue* you. Individually, it is up to everyone to carry their own baton and to run their own race. Step out of your diving suit, during meditation, and listen to your own hearts. Therein your answers lie. Therein is the path you seek. What are you waiting for?

Many have stepped out in faith already and most have been crushed. Why?

It is because the Starseeds who had promised to walk beside them and to help carry the load are so engrossed in *ego-self* pursuits that they do not want to know anything about spiritual paths and spiritual truths.

We need thousands upon thousands of Starseeds in every nation to take up their own baton this day and to walk the promised path to Enlightenment, as well as to raise their own vibratory rate through meditation and *right* thinking. That is the need. That was the urgent need several decades ago.

Now, it is almost at the point of no-return. Encouragement has been given. Information has been given in many different forms and in every language of Earth. Enlightenment has been given on a massive scale. For the most part, it has been ignored. There is not another *Saviour* coming. The Starseeds are the saviours of humanity. The time is long-past when the saviours could work at a leisurely pace. The final hour has arrived.

A commitment is needed this day. And, willingness is needed. And, a degree of sacrifice is being requested now. It is the sacrificing of the *Ego-Self* for the good of *The Whole.*

I cannot be more specific as every individual is different and unique. Every path is different and unique. But, now is the time to say to yourself:

"I must be about my Father/Mother's business now".

What is that business? It is not about making changes, for change's sake. It is not about making decisions at a conscious level, because that will lead only to changing one set of circumstances for another. It is not about heading for the hills and spending the remainder of one's life meditating in a cave.

It is about freeing yourself from bondage first. Then, and only then, can you assist others to do the same for themselves. No one can do this for another, no matter how much money changes hands. Please be clear about this. The Higher Self is the only one who can and will do this for its own lower self in the diving suit. That is the answer, my beloved beings of Light. That is the answer.

When the Higher Self has concluded its work, then each and every Starseed will know, without a doubt, where the path lies for them. I cannot be more specific about the process, but these Discourses will reveal *All*.

The clue is in the clearing of all traumas from every lifetime in physical embodiment. Fear has caused a separation from the Higher Self. It is a fear that God will not support you. That fear needs to be eradicated at a very deep level indeed. The Higher Self cannot, and will not, override the free will factor. It is for the one in embodiment to allow. It is allowing fear and trauma to be eradicated while in physical embodiment. This can be done silently, secretly and with a minimum of fuss. It cannot occur overnight. It did not accrue overnight, so consequently, it cannot be eradicated overnight. This stands to reason.

So, my beautiful children, a commitment is required. It is necessary to give the Higher Self permission to begin the clearing and the healing of *All* traumas, no matter how deep. Once permission has been given, the Higher Self can begin this massive task. An hour per day is the minimum required now for this exercise of releasing the soul/spirit from bondage. That is one hour per day to the exclusion of *all* else. After that, a request can be made on a daily basis that the clearing and healing continues during sleep.

You will experience uncomfortable dreams and even nightmares. When this occurs, ask for a reprieve from clearing and healing on the next night to give yourself time to adjust to the new energies coming into your bodies – all of your bodies on every level.

You may feel irritable. You may experience anger that can trigger an eruption over a very minor cause. Take yourself away from situations such as these quickly. Know the cause and go for a brisk walk, if possible. But, please, whatever you do, do not allow your one-hour per day every day to be interrupted or delayed. Nothing is more important in your life now than this clearing and healing.

Come to us in Love and Light. Tell us of your decision and you will have our undying Love, which you have already, and our unceasing caring and support. Nothing in your physical life, physical endeavours or physical pursuits is more important than this is now, my children.

There is one other matter that I wish to touch upon here and it may trigger fear in many. I ask you to bear with me.

In the final days of Atlantis – and this lifetime for most is a mirror-image of that life – there were many Starseeds who permitted crystalline implants to be inserted into their own etheric bodies. These implants were neither positive nor negative in themselves. However, the reason for their impregnation was to allow the Starseeds to raise their own vibrations very quickly and easily. This was the positive side of these implants. The negative side meant that if their life situation was traumatic and not to their liking, they could descend easily into doubt, depression and negativity. At times such as these, they were used by ones who were not of Light and who knew how to use a beam of light to activate these implants externally.

It was the misuse of the crystals and the great power of crystals that caused the catastrophic destruction of Atlantis. There are many (on Earth now) who have an uncanny fear of crystals. There is a very good reason for this fear. That fear needs to be cleared, also. The Starseeds who had these implants in Atlantis will find that these are appearing in their etheric bodies now, as it is the time that they have pre-set for their clearing. This is another request that needs to be made of the Higher Self. If you do not have these implants, then it does not matter, but ask anyway, as you have no way of knowing at a conscious level. If you do have them – and, most do not – then, it is time for their removal permanently. The lessons of Atlantis cannot be learned until such time as these are eradicated from your etheric bodies.

This was a subject that I was loath to broach, because there is such a deep-seated fear involved for all Starseeds. However, this fear must be faced, cleared and healed now. So, ask, my children, and you shall receive all that you request where the clearing and healing is concerned. Do not be misled into thinking that the possession of these implants is a positive and powerful attribute that makes you superior to your fellow-brothers and sisters of Light. If anything, the opposite is true. Allow one hour per day, every day, for the remainder of your physical life. When you and your Higher Self are *One*, then the clearing and healing can cease. When that day arrives, you will know, without one shadow of a doubt. You will know, because the diving suit can be set aside and you can operate simultaneously on both levels of reality, that being the Earth plane and the Astral plane. Then, death will be non-existent for you. You will have overcome ALL that you came down to overcome aeons of time ago.

It has taken longer than any of us imagined that it would. It has been far more traumatic and tragic than we ever thought possible in the beginning. It is that beginning that we are returning to at this point-in-time upon Earth.

One hour per day every day for the remainder of your physical life this time around is what is being asked of you. Is that too high a price to pay for the joy you will know when you come *HOME* in *LOVE*, surrounded by the Higher Self who is you?

Look through the eyes of the physical and you may answer in the affirmative. Look through the eyes of your own soul/spirit and there will be no doubt in your answer. Please read and re-read these Discourses, so as not to allow the momentum to cease and to allow negativity to overcome you.

I cannot state that the clearing and healings will not be traumatic for you, but I can say that they will make you a clearer and happier being the longer that you persist with them. Please do not allow them to become similar to a New Year resolution that does not survive past the month of January.

This Discourse is important. It is so important that I feel it alone needs to be read weekly to keep the goal before your eyes – physical and spiritual.

I will leave you in my great Love, which surpasses all of your expectations of Love upon Earth. I will leave you surrounded in my Light, which will surround you instantly when you read and re-read this Discourse. This Love and this Light will infuse you daily, my beloved ones, as you sit for your hourly session in a meditative state. Please do not remain any longer than one hour, because the Higher Self will continue for as long as you are prepared to submit. This could be counter-productive, as too much is not any better than too little. It could be very traumatic for you, so make one hour your goal, on a daily basis – no more and no less.

God bless you, my beautiful Starseeds of Light,
I AM Jesus-Sananda of the Light
19th February 2000

Zacharia

Sometimes, it is easier to walk a safe and secure path than it is to walk a spiritual path.

To walk a spiritual path requires much faith. With faith, it is a matter of following the *Knowingness* from within. Without faith, the ego-personality has a field day and leads the person concerned around by the nose. This is how it is for most in physical embodiment at this time.

How will it be in the Golden Age then? It will be peaceful and joyful. It will be a place of serenity where everyone is following their own Knowingness that comes from within.

Between incarnations, everyone rests on the Astral plane of Spirit. In the Higher States of the Astral plane, this is how life operates. Everyone is doing what he or she needs to be doing at any given moment. If, for a time, someone loses contact with the Guidance from within, then there are Spirit Guides on hand to assist and to guide. So, this is how it will be on Earth, also. Everything will operate on a communal system with no one owning anything, but with everyone having their own place and their own space. There will not be exorbitant rent to pay, because those who charge these amounts in monetary terms will not be a part of the Golden Age. This is because these ones are coming from the perspective of the ego-personality only. Ones such as these will not be able to be a part of the Golden Age upon Earth, simply because they are so entrenched in their physical existence that they are unable to see another way. Their own vibrations will be too low for them to be a part of the Golden Age.

It is sad. It is not how it was envisaged, but if one is unable to place one's spiritual life ahead of one's physical life, it is obvious that more lessons need to be learned. No one can wave a magic wand to transform someone who is unable to see that a transformation is necessary. When freewill overrides the Love factor on Earth, or anywhere else for that matter, the person concerned is functioning, by his or her own choice, at a lower vibration than was ever intended. Therefore, when Earth does raise her vibrations completely while becoming once again the brilliant fourth-dimensional beauty that she is, then ones whose frequency is below that of the planet, upon which they are residing, will have no choice but to leave.

Many will leave via the death experience. From there, it will be decided what the next step is for them. There will be many factors involved. Their level of spiritual understanding and their acceptance or rejection of another way of thinking and another way of living will all be factors that are considered before a decision is made regarding their future. Another factor, of course, will be what degree of karmic debt is attached to them.

In a way, it is a day of reckoning for everyone. Until now, the self-assessment, which is mandatory after every death experience is a loving experience where ones of a lower vibration do tend to make many excuses for their behaviour during incarnations upon Earth and they do tend to blame others for the sorry state of their previous life experience in physicality. They allow their karmic debts to accrue while hoping that they will never be required to repay them. However, with the commencement of the Golden Age, their own moment-of-truth will arrive.

It is virtually a case now that those returning to the Astral plane of Spirit are facing these long-overdue debts squarely in the face and they are being asked to account for their non-payment. It is a much more serious situation than an overdue credit card, bank overdraft or a missing library book. So, the day-of-reckoning has arrived already for many and, as well, they are being refused permission to reincarnate upon Planet Earth.

The horror of coming to a realisation that their next incarnation on a third dimensional planet will not be upon Earth is sending all into shock. Realising that they are beginning life again on a barren, undeveloped planet as Neanderthal beings is so traumatic that most cannot function at all where they are resting now between incarnations. *But,* my children, how many warnings must be given before man and woman of Earth take heed? How many Masters must come to show the way of Love and Light, only to be martyred for their efforts? Time has run out now, little ones. The lives you are living now, in your self-selected, illusionary world have concluded. So, perhaps, it is time to take stock of your spiritual achievements in your current lifetime and to do a voluntary self-assessment for yourselves, based upon the knowledge you have of this incarnation with its pitfalls and its heights. The checks and balances are there. Are you proud of your spiritual achievements thus far?

Please remember that your own physical achievements do not count for much when you return to the Astral plane, because those were merely a means to an end. They were there to keep you occupied and focussed as you set about learning lessons of a spiritual nature while on Earth. They were there to be a gauge, if you like, of your ability to turn the other cheek when under attack, or to give a helping hand to a fellow-brother or sister of Light when the need arose. Putting one's own needs ahead of another who is in difficulty is not conducive to a higher vibratory frequency being achieved. Conversely, placing the needs of others above one's own needs all the time is counter-productive, also, as it shows a lack of self-love and self-esteem. Always, there is a fine line between giving too much and in taking too much.

So, my children, how would you fare if today was the day when you were called upon to do the final self-assessment after leaving the third dimensional Earth for the last time?

I will leave you to ponder this question now. Please take time to be alone and enjoy the silence, so that your own Guides and Helpers of Light can draw close as you consider carefully all that has been revealed in this Discourse and in all of the other Discourses in this book.

May the peace, the Love, the Light and the Joy of the God Source be your Guiding Light this day and during all of the remaining days that you will spend upon our beautiful Mother Earth. The question of one's own vibratory frequency is one that needs to be addressed as a matter of urgency. To raise the vibratory frequency, one needs to clear and to heal all past hurts, pain and trauma from this and every other lifetime. Also, it is necessary to open one's eyes to True Reality and to raise the level of one's own understanding while breaking age-old thinking-patterns and behavioural patterns. Meditation is another exercise that would be helpful during this process of reconciliation with your own true self, your Higher Self.

Begin today, dear children, and all will be well. It is the *intent* that counts in everything, as well as the *willingness* to move forward in peace and Love towards the pre-set spiritual path that has been in place for aeons-of-time. Your spiritual path is a vital *cog-in-the-wheel*, being your unique contribution to the overall Divine Plan for Earth.

Begin today, dear children. Please begin today and keep the momentum going every day. It is a simple task and a simple request. Ponder your response to this request What shall it be, dear ones? What shall it be?

I AM Zacharia of the Light
20 February 2000

Mary

It is with great Love and affection that I come to you this day. I AM Mary and I wish to write the final Discourse as far as my contribution is concerned to the book, *UNDERCOVER STARSEEDS.*

With the dawning of the Aquarian Age, as with every Age on Earth before this one, a Christ has come and One will continue to come until such time that it is deemed to be no longer necessary for ones from our world to come to your world to instruct the population – or, those who will listen – on how it is that one needs to live one's life whilst in embodiment upon Earth. That is why a Christ has come always. The Aquarian Age will be no different, so an Enlightened One is due to be born into physical embodiment upon your Earth in the not-too-distant future. As I was the one through whom the last Christ came, I have been chosen to foretell of the future coming of the next Enlightened One, Who will lead Earth and her inhabitants into the Golden Age. What a glorious time that will be, my beloved children of Light!

So, where will He or She be born? And, to whom will such a One be born? What exciting questions to be asking one's own self, or one's Higher Self to be precise. Why is it assumed within the New Age movement that the One Who is to come will be taking a male form? The Master Kut Humi is the One who has been named by many to be The Christ of the New Age of Enlightenment. The Aquarian Age and the Golden Age, as these run simultaneously, will be the Age of the Feminine Energy of Love, nurturing, caring and giving, so why then would The Christ of the Golden Age be taking a male form? That is an assumption that is not based upon any form of truth and, as such, one would need to be wary of pursuing that thought.

My little ones, the Master of Light and Love that is to come will be the One Who is androgynous by nature and, therefore, a True and Enlightened Master in every sense of the word, but it does not follow that He/She will take a male form during an Age when the Feminine Energy is surging forth on Earth. That is my point. It may well be that the Master Kut Humi who has had many embodiments upon Earth, will be The Chosen One of the Golden Age. Whether or not the One know as Jesus-Sananda of the Light chooses to take on embodiment one more time is a matter for him alone to decide when the time is right in our Loving Father-Mother God's Eyes, shall we say, for he above anyone else is attuned totally to the Divine Will of God.

Kut Humi, it is conceded, was John the Beloved of your biblical times. It would seem fitting that this Master should wear the shoes of the next Christ upon Earth. If it is so, then the One for Whom many wait in anxious anticipation may be born as a girl-child to a poor, uneducated family in India, for example. It is assumed by many that the new Christ will be white, male and be born into a wealthy family, perhaps within the United States of America. If one studies former Christs that have chosen to take embodiment upon Earth, it will be seen that they have chosen families that are not wealthy, not influential and not necessarily the dominant race in world affairs. That is another thought worth pursuing as one questions and studies these matters. There have been books written over time and some have mentioned former Christs of Earth by name or by inference. One such a book was channelled by a beautiful Channel in 1907 on Earth. His name was Levi and his book was entitled: The AQUARIAN GOSPEL of JESUS THE CHRIST. It is well worth a read, even in this so-called enlightened day and Age.

I come to you in Love and much Love surrounds you now, as you read my words, but my heart is troubled by many misconceptions that abound at this time, and ones that some are believing, and accepting as Truth Everlasting. Truth Everlasting is God. God is Love. There is nothing else in my world or in your world – in True Reality. In your reality, which has become distorted over time, truth as you know and accept it is far from Truth Everlasting, believe me. If you accept what is written in these Discourses, then you will *Know* this at your Core. That is the point I am making. So, if there is someone who, in the not-too-far-distant future, is proclaimed as The Christ of the Aquarian and Golden Age, then do not accept this as fact, please. Question and query all information that is being given to you, no matter what the source, and this includes these Discourses. These, as with all other channelled material, have come through the conscious mind and the subconscious mind of the person writing or speaking the words.

There is not any channelled material that is one hundred per cent accurate, no matter how clear or how confident that the Channel himself or herself is on that subject. Anyone who claims to be a Channel from a Higher Realm and who claims to be one hundred per cent accurate at all times is deluding himself or herself and, therefore, the ego has become engaged. It is another of those chicken-and-egg situations, I am sorry to say. So, please my little ones, be on your guard and do not accept anything at face-value now, because too much misinformation abounds on your earth-plane.

I wish to return now to the new Christ, Who is to come and to the parents of this child of Light and Love. They will suffer much hardship and dissent will be common among other family members, as well as with ones who they thought to be their dear friends. I speak here from experience. It is not easy to accept that you are different from everyone else and that you have been singled out to perform a task that appears to be mammoth when seen through the eyes of one so young. In some religions on your earth-plane now, my memory is revered, but in my time, I was ridiculed and treated almost as a leper for being *with child* when my husband-to-be and I had never been together in a physical sense and were certainly not of a *married* status in the eyes of the religious leaders of the day. My great *sin* was punishable by death by stoning. Could ones who would inflict such a death upon a young mother carrying an unborn child ever be considered to be *of God?*

It was only through the intervention of ones such as Elizabeth and Zacharias that I did not suffer a fate such as that. It would have prevented The Christ from being born to me at that time, and no doubt that was the intention. Did they not, a few years later, put to death every male child under two years of age? This was another vain attempt to prevent The Christ of the Piscean Age from being born and from continuing with his great work. Do you really think it will be any different for The Christ of the Aquarian Age and for the parents of that child? I feel you know the answer to that, my little ones, so if one is born into a privileged family, and is presented to the world-at-large as The Christ of the Golden Age, then please keep your own counsel and beware!

That is my advice to you and it comes from one who knows the pitfalls of taking on a role such as that. The joys associated with that role were of such a height that no one could know but me. The pain and heartbreak associated with the role of Mary were many and were soul-destroying at times. The faith and the Love were there, but that faith and that Love were tested to the limit on many, many occasions, not to mention during the final days and hours of the life of the beautiful and beloved Jesus.

I bring this to your attention now in an attempt to forewarn you of one who is to come and who will be heralded as *The Christ*. This one has been warned of many times in your earthly prophesies. He will confuse and mislead many. Many wars will be fought on this issue unless ones of Light and Love wake up and heed the call of the Enlightened Ones Who seek only peace and Love for Earth and her inhabitants. Please believe that, my precious ones.

There are many ways that you can help yourselves to become, once again, the great Beings that you are. In so doing, you become a *Christ*, an Anointed One, an Enlightened Being again. You were selected, chosen and appointed as *Ambassadors-to-Earth*, because you were *Christed* Beings already in your own right, having earned the right to be so many, many moons ago on other planets or star-systems – some perhaps in other galaxies or universes in God's Kingdom.

You, the Starseeds, answered the call for assistance aeons ago and you are being asked once again to remember back to that time so many Ages ago that we have all forgotten the exact moment. Remember, dear children of the Light of our Creator, and respond again now to this latest call for assistance and prepare the way for others to follow you along the path to Oneness again. *Oneness* means an end to the separation that has kept you in physicality, and often in deep negativity. Remember who you are really and what you came here to do originally, before you came under sustained attack from ones who were your brothers and sisters-of-Light-and-Love once. That scenario and situation is lost in the mists of time but, when you are with them in the physical, there is an attraction and a deep-seated love from long ago between you, so you trust them again – only to be betrayed again. They can bask no longer in our Creator's Love and Light. They shun that great Love and they cringe when that wonderful Golden/White Light comes near them.

My children, my beautiful Starseeds, open up your eyes to True Reality. End the separation from your Self and come on Home to us, for we will salute you as the wonderful, loving, gentle Christed Beings that you are and always will be. In the not-too-far-distant future, there will be so many *Christs* on the earth-plane that the darkness will shrink before them and all will marvel in the glory that is – and always will be – our Creator-God. The Light and Love of God will shine forth from your eyes for all to see and your auric field will be positively glowing.

So, it will not matter then who *The Christ* of the Aquarian Age is, because He or She will be lost in a virtual sea of Christs on Earth. What a wonderful day that will be and truly then will the Golden Age be a reality on our beautiful Mother Earth who will be glowing in her new-found freedom from negativity as she basks in God's Love and Light while vibrating at a frequency that is far, far above what she was at the end-times when the continents of Atlantis, Le Muria and Mu passed beneath the waves, never to be seen again by physical eyes until the dawning of the Golden Age of Love and Light upon her. Father Sky and Mother Earth will be One once more, vibrating together in harmony, joy and peace. For one thousand years will this be so, my precious ones. It will be the Starseeds, the extraordinarily beautiful, loving Beings of Light that will achieve this great feat as they respond yet again to our calls from on High for assistance to aid the planet in her final push to rise beyond the depths of negativity that is choking her currently.

Trust in the Guidelines that are given, sweet ones. It is their simplicity that will attract the most criticism, but it is that very simplicity that will make the difference and will make your task of ending the separation a complete and resounding success. That success is assured, Beloved of God. All that is in question is the timing of your great Ascent into Light.

Dear children, the understanding of what you term the *immaculate conception* is lacking greatly. I know that you understand when life is at an end on Earth, the soul/spirit is withdrawn, with God's Blessing in most cases. The exception to this is when free will overrides the Love vibration and a life is taken by another. It takes God's Blessing, also, for a life to be conceived on your earth-plane. This is not understood. For every pregnancy, there is a soul/spirit waiting to come down into your realm. But, not every pregnancy goes to full term. This is because the Higher Self of the mother, in most cases, and/or the Higher Self of the father do not deem it appropriate for a child to be born to them at that particular time as it may take them off their pre-set spiritual path. So, if there is a pregnancy or a fertilisation, shall we say, and a baby is not the result nine months later, why would this be?

It is because another event needs to occur to produce a baby in your world, other than the obvious of a male and a female coming together in a physical way to achieve that result. New life needs to be injected, for want of a better term, into a fertilised egg to ensure that a baby is the result of the copulation and subsequent fertilisation. What form does this take? As with the withdrawal of the soul/spirit at the end of a physical life, there needs to be an infusion of the soul/spirit at the beginning of new life into physical form. How is that achieved? It is achieved by the coming together of Twin Flames in a Perfect Union of Divine Love, with the Thought uppermost that a new creation in third dimensional physicality is the desired end.

Thought and Love combined with God's Blessing can create anything that is needed at any time. That is how it is possible to have what is termed an *immaculate conception.* On fourth dimensional planets and star-systems, this concept is understood and accepted as natural and normal. On a planet where the inhabitants believe firmly that they are in control of everything, then this concept of God having a part to play in the arrival of new life on the planet is difficult to accept. It is with grudging respect that many accept that God is in control where the withdrawal of the life-force is concerned, because they have no other explanation. It is not often acknowledged that God has any part to play in the infusion of the life-force into the newly-created foetus.

If God can create new life, in a physical sense, by the coming together of Twin Flames when Thought and Love are combined and if God can end a physical life by the withdrawal of the life-force by a similar operation, then how simple would it be for God to fertilise an egg for the purpose of bringing forth a new Christ on Earth through the womb of a virgin-mother? It is simple, easy and it is done in the twinkling of an eye. What is not understood is that physical death is new life in our realm. Physical life – a new life – born into your world is a *death* in our realm. Both require the coming together of Twin Flames, with Thought and Love combined, to achieve the desired result. Without God's Blessing, Twin Flames do not, cannot and will not come together for this purpose. Therefore, ultimately, it is God Who determines who is born into your realm and it is God Who determines who returns to our realm. That is the bottom line, as you say.

God does not intervene on a free will planet unless and until a critical moment has arrived, and the planet and its inhabitants are so out-of-balance spiritually that the point of no return has been reached. Then, and only then, is Divine Intervention considered necessary. Such a decision is not taken lightly. It has been taken already where the affairs of Earth are concerned. My little ones, it is God – the Source of ALL Love and Light – Who has determined now that many cannot and will not be permitted to reincarnate onto your earth-plane, because their past misdemeanours (to put it mildly) have been repeated so many times that they cannot be allowed to rule Earth in such a negative way as to cause the destruction – the total destruction – of Earth and her people.

Immaculate conceptions have been numerous on Earth. Few are publicised in the way that the one in which I was involved was. Conception is a two-fold operation, little ones. This is not to criticise your IVF programmes that help many couples to bring forth a new little one into your world. The medical profession has been guided to these advances for the benefit of all.

If there is a physical problem that is preventing a part of this two-fold operation taking place, then the parents-to-be may be guided to a physician or to a clinic that can help to overcome their particular problem so that, together with God's Love, a new infant can come into your world. Looking through the eyes of Spirit, it is simple. Looking through physical eyes, the theory of an immaculate conception is as alien to the thought-patterns of humans as is the theory of reincarnation. Change the thinking-patterns, dear ones, and open your eyes to True Reality, so that you can survive and thrive when the changes that are to come, arrive fully in your world. That is sound advice, believe me.

What if, during your sleep-time, you left your physical body and came to my realm. In my world, you have a life that is ongoing and never-ending. In the last chapter (of **UNDERCOVER STARSEEDS**), you will be given a description of Constella's home upon a hill in my world. But, everyone has a home in my realm, whether it be beside a lake, on a hilltop or near a beach. Everyone has a home. During sleep, you leave your physical body and go Home. There, you carry on your life as you would normally and without interruption. When it is time for your physical body to awaken from its well-earned sleep, you slip back into it and begin your mission on Earth.

You see, your physical body is your vehicle. Now, that vehicle could be left-hand driven or right-hand driven, depending on the gender, and the car could be white, black, brown, bronze, yellow or red. It could be any shade that relates to these colours. But, first and foremost, it is a vehicle, into which you slip to accomplish the task that you came to do on this particular planet. When the task is completed to your satisfaction, you advise God of this fact and permission is given for you to discard that particular vehicle. Then, after a period of counselling, relaxation, re-orientation (depending on how badly one had been affected by the negativity of Earth) and rejuvenation, you return to the life that is ongoing as the Being of Light and Love Who you are truly and always will be.

The problem is with the veil of illusion that exists and with the negativity that surrounds the *sleeping* vehicle that is garaged in its bed every night. When you are in your True State and your True Home whilst out of the physical body, you know exactly what you are going to do and how you are going to do it when you awaken the body (vehicle) next morning after your re-entry into it. If you decide not to re-awaken it, then that is fine, also, and is your free will decision that would have been made in consultation with your Guides, because in that True State and in your True Home, you are the one that we refer to as your *Higher Self*. You know what your Earth mission is and you know, without a doubt, what your part is in the overall Divine Plan for the planet known as Earth.

It is when you become disorientated in the atmosphere of Earth that problems arise, and then the Earth Mission is compromised, at best; or it is distorted or discarded, at worst. This is when meditation becomes most necessary. However, the lives of the ones of Earth are so very, very busy that it is impossible to find the time to meditate daily. Without that meditation, you cannot hope to remember what it is that you are meant to be doing. Consider for a moment the most efficient and effective form of torture on your Earth. It is the depravation of sleep for the physical body. Without sleep and without a meditation time, you cannot be in-touch with yourself – your True and Higher Self. Therefore, you cannot know what it is that you are meant to be doing or where your future lies. That is why that form of torture is so very, very effective.

So, when you return to your physical body every morning, find and take time to sit peacefully with your eyes closed and try to remember what it was that you planned for this day while you were in your other Home and while you were out of your vehicle, whatever colour and gender that has been chosen for this incarnation. The busier the lifestyle that the ego has chosen, the more difficult will it be for the soul/spirit to reach its goal in this lifetime. That is the crux of the matter.

As promised in my earlier Discourse, I wish to return to the divers who dived beneath the ocean in their sophisticated dive-suits. You see, when they shut-down their own inbuilt computers in their dive suits, they leave them resting on the ocean floor in that underwater world and they return to the launch on the surface above. There, in consultation with their own advisors and Higher Consciousness, shall we say, they review their progress and try to counteract any problems and mistakes that have been made during the previous day's work under the waves. Does this not occur now with ones who work in such a way with vessels that have sunk and which contain treasures and memorabilia from a bygone era?

Your present careers are but a means to an end. They are to provide you with the means to give food and shelter to your physical bodies (dive suits) while you are in that world and that reality. They are not the reason for the dive in that particular dive suit. They become the main focus of your life from a very early age, because you are programmed by others from a very early age. It is an ongoing problem and the cycle must be broken now.

If you are not meant to be devoting all of your energies, solely and completely, to your career (whatever that may be), then what are you meant to be doing in that time that is allotted to you between your physical birth and your physical death? You are meant to be releasing old patterns and clearing all traumas from all of your bodies. Then, and only then, you will be guided and you will know, without a doubt, what your real Earth mission is. Until then, the ego-personality self will convince the conscious mind that the chosen career is all that there is.

When that particular career comes to an end, what then? If you arrive at work tomorrow and you are confronted suddenly and unexpectedly with your instant retirement or redundancy, what then? It is a sobering thought, is it not? Yet, it is happening to many on your earth-plane now as technology becomes more advanced and sophisticated, so that replacing the human workforce with mechanical labour is seen as the norm.

There is a date when someone is born, and there is a date when someone dies to physical life on Earth. In-between those dates, there is a dash on a tombstone. What was the purpose of that life? What occurred to that person during that *dash?* Did he or she achieve what was envisaged when that person took physical form in that lifetime? Was that the only lifetime for that person and is he or she waiting in a holding pattern in a place called *Limbo* until some great Day of Judgement? That is what many religions would have you believe.

Their theories are that you have but one lifetime to get it right, so to speak. What chance is there then for a child of five years of age? Is it fair that someone should have a *dash* that lasts for ninety-five earth-years while another has but five years in order to achieve a perfect result? Does not the theory of reincarnation make more sense, even to the most casual observer, than the theory that a God of Love gives everyone but one chance – and, one chance only – to become *perfect* during a set timeframe on a planet called *Earth?* And, following on from this theory, is it then assumed that Earth is the only planet in the vast Kingdom of God that is inhabited?

My children of Light, these are theories that were around when you lived in caves and scavenged for food on a planet that was inhabited by what you term, *Neanderthal* man and woman. Science has moved on, so why have not the thought-patterns of the inhabitants of Earth? Could it be that you are being kept in ignorance for a reason and that if you begin to question the powers-that-be, you will be committing a grave *sin*? Why? Is it because you are rocking the boat and threatening someone's comfort zone? These are questions for all of you, individually, to consider now.

We, of the Light, can present only the facts as we see them, from our perspective. From your perspective, where you have been kept in darkness and ignorance for thousands of years, these Discourses and the information that they contain will seem blasphemous, to say the least. Is it because they challenge the established religions of the day? Did not Jesus challenge the established religions of the day? What better way to distort his messages than to form another religion to compete with the other religions that were in existence already? Can you not see the picture that is being painted here?

Why is it assumed that because you study other planets and star-systems that seem lifeless to ones in your world, then no life exists there? Of course, life exists there, but your scientists cannot find any evidence of its existence. This is because the places that they are studying are vibrating at a higher frequency than those who are exploring there, or who are studying these places from afar. You can be seen and studied, also, and from the perspective of ones who are vibrating at a fourth dimensional frequency and operating solely on the Love Factor, then you do resemble beings who are far from enlightened and who are in need of great assistance at this present moment in time.

That great assistance is being offered. It has been offered many, many times before now and it has been shunned and rejected, because it is easier and simpler to pull the veil of illusion down further over your eyes than it is to make the effort to think for yourselves and to draw conclusions for yourselves that are different from those expressed by parents, peers and offspring.

That is how it is, dear ones. This is not a criticism. It is merely an explanation of how your plane of existence is viewed from the perspective of ones who do not reside on your planet. You may feel that it is easy for ones on the outside looking in to see how the changes are necessary for your planet and its inhabitants to survive, could be made. And, this is truly so. It is acknowledged. We, of Light, are bombarding Earth with so much Love and so much Light now, as never before, that it must make a difference. It will be impossible to ignore in a very short space of time in your sphere of existence.

The inhabitants of Earth will have two free will choices. They can bring the veil of illusion down even further and pretend that nothing is changing. This, they will do at their peril, because they will not survive physically on a fourth dimensional planet in their current third dimensional forms; or, they can go with the flow and begin to raise their own vibrations to keep pace with the Ascending Mother, that being Earth herself. She can wait no longer for her children. She is moving and she is moving very fast indeed. In a few Earth years from now, you will be amazed at the Lightness and Brightness of those who are moving with her. Catching up to them and to Mother Earth will be a momentous undertaking so, please, my little ones of Light, begin now. Then, the peace and joy of the Golden Age will be your birthright to have and to enjoy to the fullest extent possible.

See the dive suit for what it is. That is the first step in accepting what is being offered to you in these Discourses. It is a vehicle that has an in-built computer that is clogged to overflowing with misinformation, misconceptions and, above all, damaged files that have been corrupted beyond recognition by viruses that are ongoing and self-perpetuating. That is a very good description, I feel, to explain the state of the physical bodies that you inhabit currently and which you have vowed to yourself to clear and heal in this particular lifetime.

Do not disappoint yourself, I beg of you. Release, clear and heal for the remainder of your days in this current embodiment; then, you will come Home to us triumphant and rejoicing in your new-found freedom. More importantly, your days of incarnating on a third dimensional planet will be over for you and the nightmare of this ongoing cycle of birth/life/death/re-birth will be at an end forever. That is the promise contained within the pages of these Discourses. For those who have the courage to embrace this concept that is *new* only to those of Earth, then the freedom and the rewards are beyond your comprehension currently.

There are many in your world with a great love of The Bible. They read it and study it daily. This is, of course, to be commended, but they would, in many cases, give their lives for the words that are written, believing them to be Truth

Absolute. And, indeed, they were when The Bible was first written. However, over time and by deceit, by design or by just an oversight, there have been many alterations. If the words of these Discourses are correct, then how can the Bible be accurate if all traces of reincarnation have been removed? Did this happen by deceit, by design or by just an oversight? This is a question that students of The Bible will need to address soon, because one day the Real and Original Bible will come to light and all will be astounded at the Truth within its pages.

In light of what I have suggested within the pages of this particular Discourse, I will leave you to be the one who discerns the Truth of the matter, especially with regard to the fact that the feminine energy is the dominant Love Energy of the Aquarian and Golden Age as Earth redresses the great imbalance of the male energies that have ruled her for too long now.

The book, **THE AQUARIAN GOSPEL OF JESUS THE CHRIST**, by Levi, to which I referred earlier has been transcribed directly from the Akashic Records, with the permission of the Spiritual Hierarchy. In this book, the reader will find discrepancies with some passages in The Bible. It is for the reader to decide and discern where the discrepancies lie. I will give an example. In one passage that refers to the *end times*, there is a reference to an Age when women will rule. If one were to locate the corresponding passage in The Bible, it may be of interest to note that all references to woman ruling are missing. Students and lovers of The Bible will point to this discrepancy and comment on the fact that the book Levi has compiled is erroneous. To them, this will be the obvious explanation. But, is it? Or, is there perhaps another explanation?

If there is an extra sentence in one that does not appear in the other, then there are two explanations. One is that Levi inserted the extra sentence. The other explanation is that the extra sentence was omitted from the text of The Bible by a person or persons unknown by deceit, by design or by just an oversight. Is this what occurred with other Truths that were in The Bible originally, such as all references to reincarnation? You, my children of Light, will need to be the judges on this and other matters raised in these Discourses. Your inner guidance will give you the correct answer. Your personality-self, combined with your conscious mind, will give you the answer that it feels is the safest one for you to accept at this time. Follow inner guidance, dear ones, and your victory over the little self – the ego-self – is assured.

At this time, when the water-carrier is walking across your skies, at this time of Aquarius, then it is appropriate, I feel, to begin to reassess one's thinking on these and other issues. Signs have been given before now. A few may be still to come. Does one wait until the final sign appears before action is taken at a personal level? When that final condemnation that is predicted arrives, will anyone recognise it for what it is anyway? That is the question.

Blessed and lovely ones, come and see me during your nightly visits to your other Home and we will continue these discussions at that time. We will have a most enlightening and entertaining time, I can assure you. There is no need to make an appointment. Just call me and I will come to you as you drift off to sleep. Together, we will solve all the problems of Earth and any that may be troubling you, as well. Trust in that, my beautiful Starseeds of Light and Love, and trust in my great Love for you – every one of you. You are all so very dear to me. Together with all of the Masters of Light and Love, we will bring forth the glory of the Golden Age upon Earth. It is long overdue; is it not? Most of you are members of the great Brotherhoods of God and some are Lords of Light, also. A Lord of Light has a title such as this, because he/she is what would be termed on your earth-plane as a *trouble-shooter.* These Beings go to wherever they are directed to serve and where they can be of the greatest assistance in times of great trouble. At this time and during this transition period into the Golden Age, Earth is besieged by Lords of Light and all are androgynous by nature, because they are great Beings of God's Light and Love. Many have contributed to the book, ***UNDERCOVER STARSEEDS.***

May the Peace of God surround and infuse you now. May the Divine Love of our Creator-God pulsate through every fibre and atom of your Being as you begin this, the final stage of your Earth Mission and your last assignment on the planet known now as *Earth.*

Peace be with you, my lovely ones. I will see you in your dreams. Until then, au revoir, beloved of God.

I AM Mary.

21 February 2000

Kut Humi

I AM with you for but a short while. The one you are expecting is coming into your world within months in your time-frame. My message to the world is one of Peace and Love, as well as a commitment to one's brothers and sisters living on this planet known as Earth. The commitment, of which I speak, is one of brotherly and sisterly Love toward every other being on the planet. In this, I include the animals, mammals and all creatures that God created.

I cannot give a specific time for my arrival in a physical sense but, suffice to say, all is in readiness for this event. My time on Earth will herald in a new generation of loving beings on the planet and change will be inevitable and unstoppable. It will be a change for the better. It will be timely, because the planet and its people are going down a road to self-destruction again. To ones of Light in embodiment at present, this must seem an inevitable conclusion, but all is not lost. Your prayers have been answered and your love has moved mountains, as we knew always that it would.

My appearance at this time on Earth will herald the beginning of the end for those who have chosen, of their own free will, to force their will upon an unsuspecting population. They will begin to withdraw and begin to pursue seriously their options with regard to the promised time of accounting for past deeds. Those with misdeeds that are considered manageable will be able to negotiate a karmic path that will repay, to some degree, the damage that they have caused. These will be *the followers* – not their *leaders*. For the leaders, their fate is sealed, but panic will be upon them when they witness their followers of old making new arrangements that do not include them. They will find those whom they have relied on totally drawing away and not responding to negative suggestions and commands. It is a time of sorting and the sorting has begun.

There are many questions, which our beautiful Starseeds of Light have that are unanswered at present. Patience is needed as We, of the Light, begin the painstakingly-long task of re-aligning a planet that is totally out-of-alignment, due to the negativity of many of its inhabitants. The purpose of this Discourse is to bring hope to those who have prayed and pleaded for Love, Peace and Balance on Earth. Your prayers have been answered and it is time now to turn around this negative world and to bring Love back into the equation. We will do it together – and in the way that we have done it always. We will do it together – and in Love.

You have all spent such a long time in prayer, in meditation and in sending Love to Planet Earth and her inhabitants. This has assisted her greatly and has aided in our being able to move sooner rather than later to adjust the imbalances that are causing her to wobble so greatly on her axis. The loving members of the Space Brotherhood have done a *sterling job* in keeping her in her current orbit, despite the negativity and the interruptions to her energy flow caused by bombings and other man-made interference.

I cannot stress strongly enough the great contribution that the Starseeds of Light have made through their prayer and meditation sessions, either alone or in the company of others. Please keep up the great work. I know it is difficult in a busy schedule that most have, to find the time to tune into Spirit and to focus the Light and the Love of God upon Earth and her inhabitants, especially when most of your friends and family are off enjoying themselves in their *outer* world.

When you meet in groups of two or more, then the effect is stunning from our perspective. You may not be able to comprehend this while in physical form, but you do make a difference – a very great difference – to the vibratory rate of the planet in a positive sense. So, please, keep up this wonderful work, which I know is a labour of Love for all of our beautiful Starseeds who are working silently behind the scenes to achieve this very result. I congratulate you, one and all. Thank you.

We have all been together so many times before, in so many different lifetimes, as we traversed this path to spiritual enlightenment on a dark, dark planet whose Light and Love had been all but extinguished when the Starseeds arrived en masse oh-so-long ago. I AM here to tell you now that it has all been worthwhile and worth the effort that we gave so freely, along with our physical lives, in many, many incarnations. I cannot tell you how many times that this occurred to all of you and nor can I tell you of the pain and suffering that you have endured in the Name of God and God's Love on this planet. What I can tell you is that you have caused a great shift in consciousness to a Higher Consciousness and you have caused a vibratory shift that has been stunning to witness in Earth's final hours as a third dimensional planet.

Once again, our beautiful Starseeds, with little regard to their own needs and their own safety, have saved the day on Planet Earth; so, please, take a well-earned bow and pat yourselves on the back, because you have come through in the final moment, despite the pain that you are carrying deep within yourselves. Release, clear and heal the fear from the subconscious mind, so that you can rise in glory with the planet and the beautiful Starseeds of Light who have made such a remarkable breakthrough in this *NOW* moment on Earth.

Allow the negative ones on your planet to *burn themselves out,* as they are doing, as they fight amongst themselves to prove which religious establishment is the *true* one. If only they could see that that religious fervour, of which they are all so proud, could be better spent in helping one another in God's Love. They are all praying to the same God and killing God's other children in the most horrific ways imaginable – as they have done always – because there are some on this planet who never, ever learn any lessons at all. This is their choice, but they are all too willing to force their will upon others. In the religious supermarkets of Earth, there is but one path – the path of Love – but few recognise this Golden Thread of Love that has been woven through all the original teachings of all the religions of Earth. Much has been lost as men sought to control their followers by altering the original teachings here and there, thus changing the balance once again. This is the senseless way man operates on Earth – by changing the balance in everything.

Nature, the environment, family lifestyles and the consciousness of Earth have all been altered in a negative way, thus altering the planetary balance completely. Is it any wonder that the services of the wonderful brothers and sisters of the Space Brotherhood have been needed to keep the planet as stable as she has been up until now? It has been a mighty effort given the negativity and the stifling pollution that have suffocated her for thousands of years. Those horrific wars brought such pain and suffering to Mother Earth's emotional body – the lower Astral plane that has been clogged and clouded for aeons of time – that much damage has been done. This must be undone now and it cannot happen without Love and while wars continue unabated. It is the constant clearing of Earth at this level that has kept her as stable as she has been. It is the Space Brotherhood of Light that has achieved this remarkable feat while keeping the natural disasters to a minimum.

How is it that the population of Earth cannot see, to this day, the correlation between their negative behaviour and the planet's response to that behaviour, in the form of so-called *natural* disasters? This is beyond the comprehension of all who reside in the realms known as the *Planes of Light* above the level of the Astral plane. Truly, it is beyond belief. We owe a debt of great gratitude to those Beings-of-Light for their persistence and patience, not to mention their expertise in that particular field.

Our other great debt of gratitude is owed to the tremendous efforts of the Starseeds of Light who kept going against impossible odds when their family and friends, along with their own conscious minds and egos, were saying that *enough is enough* and that a return to the third dimensional vibration of Earth was the only solution. Earth could not have survived as a planet without that Love and devotion that was given freely by these beautiful Beings-of-Light in physical form on Earth at present and, in the immediate past Ages-of-Humanity, when darkness was the cloak that she wore constantly. This debt is acknowledged freely and, our tears are tears of Joy now, as we prepare for the New Age on Earth – The Golden Age of Light and Love!

So, let the negative ones play out their games to the bitter end, as they will do anyway with or without your intervention. These war games are all that they know, for Love is no longer a part of their thinking or of their vocabulary. When they utter the word, *love*, it is for selfish reasons. *Love* and *self* are opposing forces. One cancels out the other. Please remember that, dear children of the Light and Love of God.

Universal Love is a selfless love and it is the glue that binds *All* together. Love and war cannot exist together, no matter what the logical reason that is being given for that war. They are opposing forces. They have been always. They will be always. When these war games have played themselves out to their final conclusion on the plane of Earth, at a third dimensional level, then the Earth herself will be purged of their existence and memory. She will be cleansed and healed totally.

This will take many more Ages-of-Humanity to accomplish, for it did not accrue overnight, so it will not heal overnight. Those who have participated in perpetuating those wars and atrocities will be dealt with summarily and severely. Those who participated reluctantly – and, this includes most of the population – will be counselled thoroughly and advised to heal themselves. Those who managed, through an iron will and an unwavering devotion to the First Cause Who Is God, to raise their own vibration to a fourth dimensional frequency at least, will know so much Joy and so much Love that Peace will be the automatic flow-on effect. It has been worth it, dear ones. Truly, it has all been worth it!

Peace on Earth and Goodwill to all. Peace be with you. Adieu.

I AM Kut Humi,

Master of Light and Love serving The First Cause on Earth and elsewhere

1st March 2000

Onoraus

To be satisfied with one's *lot in life* is rare on Planet Earth. Finding a niche and settling into that particular place for the rest of one's life does tend to stop the flow of energies that are needed to keep everything in motion.

In times past, people did tend to remain in stable relationships and in a stable environment as far as their home life was concerned. Even intrepid explorers had stable homes, to which they could return when their adventures were at an end. In most cases, this is how it was.

In recent times, the energies have changed. Earth is being bombarded with new and lighter energies. These fine, etheric rays are penetrating deeply into everything that lives and breathes. From now onwards, change will be constant. Therefore, it will be necessary to shed many personal possessions, because the movement of heavy items from place to place will take its toll on the physical body eventually.

Old patterns and habits are being broken by these energies, also. Ones who are resistant to change are finding that it is impossible to stand still now. Movement – constant movement – is becoming the norm. These energies cannot be stopped. In fact, they are long overdue. As a new broom sweeps clean always, then so, too, will these new energies sweep all before them. The oceans are beginning to respond. Old boundaries are being wiped from maps and new ones are being drawn. Under the present conditions, is it possible for these boundaries to remain in place for long?

No, it is not, because these new energies are self-perpetuating and they can only increase from here, so more changes are inevitable. Those who are resistant totally to change can hold back this tide for only so long on the earth-plane and only as far as their own personal lives are concerned. Trying to use one's own free will to stem this tide of fresh energy would be comparable to attempting to prevent an avalanche from occurring on Mount Everest. The snow builds up; then, it becomes too heavy and it slides down the mountain-side.

So, too, it is with these new energies. These are feminine in character, so the balance of energies upon the planet will change markedly over the coming years. These energies on Planet Earth have been out-of-balance for far too long as the male energy has been the predominant one for many, many centuries. It is time to redress this situation; otherwise, science will outstrip Love and that can have only disastrous consequences for Earth and all of her people. It has occurred many times in the past, with disastrous results. It must not, cannot and will not be permitted to occur again. Divine Intervention has occurred already to allow this unprecedented flow of unstoppable feminine energy to flood the Earth to bring balance to an out-of-control planet and an out-of-control violent society that has little or no regard for the sanctity of God's Temples on Earth. By these *Temples*, I refer to the human bodies filled with the Spirit of God, Who walks the earth-plane night and day. I include, in these descriptions of *Temples*, the animals, plants, birds, mammals and all creatures great and small, that our Loving-Father-Mother-God has created for the enjoyment of the human species and for companionship. They were certainly not created solely to be slaughtered for fun or for food. This is a tragedy of mammoth proportions and it must be addressed and redressed very soon.

With the flow of new energies, this will occur. A timing for this, I cannot give, as ones of Earth know such a measurement. I can guarantee that it will cease as will the consuming of flesh of any kind. As abhorrent as cannibalism is regarded now, that is how the eating of fish and animal products will be regarded by ones who will be born into your world over the coming years. To feed animal products of any description will be sufficient to make a newly-arrived infant very sick and, by this, I refer to milk products, as well. How can it be thought that milk, produced by a cow to provide sustenance for her calf, could be suitable for a human baby who is new to your world?

The advent of what is termed *mad cow disease* has highlighted the folly of this practice of killing and consuming animal products of any description. Chickens produce eggs. These were never, ever intended for human consumption. They were merely a way of prolonging the life-span of that particular species. Can you not see how everything on your planet, without exception, has been tampered with, contaminated and *refined* in a way that was never intended by the Creator-of-All? This madness must cease and it must cease now, so that balance, harmony, joy, peace and Love can return sooner rather than later. It is a matter of grave concern in my world of Light and Unconditional Love.

I have no way of showing you my world, except in a deep, meditative state. But, my children, meditation is frowned upon by many in your world. Why would this be so? Do you think that it is because, through meditation, you may actually *get-in-touch* with your True Self and with True Reality? It may be so. What a frightening thought for many.

Let us play with this *what if* scenario for awhile. What if my world of Love and Light was all that existed and all that ever existed? And, what if at a time long past, a few spirit-beings decided to play a game – a make-believe game – in one, small corner of my world. No one took much notice to begin with, as everything was Love and Light and no one questioned anyone else's right to follow their own dream, shall we say. But, before long, others joined in the game in the corner. Let us liken it to a game of poker being played for fun by a few individuals while everyone else was enjoying a picnic. Then, one-by-one, others were drawn towards the poker game. At first, they were merely spectators. Then, a few more decided to join in this make-believe game. After awhile, others became distracted from their picnic and, out of curiosity at first, they became involved, also.

The original instigators of the game felt elation and ego was born. They decided to see just how far they could take this make-believe game and to gauge, for their own ego-elevation, just how far others would be prepared to follow.

The fabled Garden-of-Eden is my world, my children. You left it of your own free will to play an illusionary game in the corner of my garden. The game is being played still, in that corner, but there is no need for you to remain there. When sufficient Beings-of-Light realise how they have been hoodwinked and how trivial a pursuit that game really is, they will leave in droves. Then, the only ones remaining will be the ones of great darkness who, of their own free will, took that original, innocuous game from an innocent diversion to a gigantic nightmare of mammoth proportions for their own gain.

These are the ones who are controlling still the game in the corner of the garden. The purpose of the game is to bring as much trauma as possible into the make-believe lives of the players to see how much suffering and negativity can be endured at any given moment-in-time. Until now, the game has been permitted to continue in the hope that, one-by-one, the children of Light, would awaken to True Reality and would walk from that dark corner unaided. Alas, it does not seem to be possible for them to do so. The only way that we, of Light, can assist without violating the free will of others, is to pour as much Light and Love as is possible onto that corner, so that it can penetrate every fibre and every atom existing in that restricted area of darkness.

It began in innocence. It is innocent no longer. The instigators became the perpetrators and, what they have perpetrated is beyond the understanding of Ones-of-Light-and-of-Love. They know the time has come to face the music, so to speak, but they feel, because their egos are so large, that even now, at this final hour, they can defeat the Light once again. How can this be done?

As it has been done always, my children . . . create a diversion and one that is so traumatic that it will block out completely all the rays of new energy that are arriving at a great speed into that section of the garden. Do I paint a bleak enough picture, my little ones? And, what form would this diversion take, do you suppose? It will be a war that will make all other wars pale into insignificance. It will be a war that will pit every religion and every philosophy against one another. That, indeed, would be the *war-to-end-all-wars* then; would it not?

You see, my little ones, your games are at an end now. It is time to walk away from the nonsense and back into the Light and Love of our Creator's world. Anything else is illusion. It is the silent majority who make it possible for that other world to exist and to continue to function in its self-perpetuating negative state. If the silent majority turns its back – as one – and walks away, what is left? It is a dark corner where only the originators of the game can remain. They have to remain, because they have shut themselves off so completely from the Light and Love of our Creator that they cringe in fear when Light and Love come near them.

The new energies must be resisted from their perspective. They are at a loss to know how to block out the Light and Love of God. The scenario that I have depicted above is their only hope of survival, as they perceive it now. They are desperate. They have nowhere to turn so, once again, they must instil fear into the hearts of the silent majority, so that their final game can succeed. However, the silent majority cannot move, because of this ever-present fear and because no other way is being shown.

It is the children of Light, our precious Starseeds, who offered to go to that corner of the Garden to lead the majority of innocent ones out of the darkness to where they could see the path to the Light for themselves. Once they could see it, they would run from that corner as fast as they could, never turning a head to look back to the fear and negativity that had surrounded them for so, so long. My children of Light, my beautiful Starseeds, come home. It is time.

The energy of the male is the energy of the *doer,* the action-taker. The energy of the female is the intuitive, nurturing aspect of God – or, the Goddess energy, as some would term it. When there is perfect balance between the male and the female energies within one's physical body, for example, then there is perfection, because that is the God/Goddess Principle in perfect union, with the Light and Love of God flowing evenly and in perfect harmony throughout every atom within that particular body. Take a look at the great Masters who have come to that dark corner of the Garden to bring about positive change. They had that perfect balance of the God/Goddess Principle flowing within and around them. That is why they came under such sustained and ferocious attack in most cases. It was because their Light and their Love threatened those in darkness so much that it sent them into fear. Those in fear know no other way but attack.

So, what is to be done now by ones who are desirous of leaving the darkness of that corner of the Garden, which of course, has become known as Planet Earth?

Let us take another look at a piece of superfluous garbage, which all within that dark corner are carrying. It is called the sub-conscious mind. This is where the separation from God exists, because this is where fear exists. What is the source of that fear? The source is the sum total of all of the experiences suffered in that dark corner of the Garden. The sub-conscious mind is the storehouse – the sponge – that holds the memory locked in an iron-grip for future reference, so that old enemies can be recognised and their deeds remembered. The prefix, *sub*, means *under*. So, the mind that is *under* the surface, *under* the conscious mind, is the devil-in-the-piece for all Starseeds. Its memory is as long as it is deep. To walk unaided from the darkness in the corner means that the *sponge* under the surface needs to be cleansed, healed and then re-programmed. It has been created by each and every one of you. It cannot be discarded just yet, but it can be reprogrammed to think only kind, loving thoughts and to know to act only in Love, no matter how trying the circumstance.

This cannot be done by anyone else. You created it. You filled your own sponge with fear, resentment, anger, bitterness and regrets. You must be the one, the only one, to clear it, to heal it and then to re-programme it. It is a simple task. It is a simple solution to what seems to be – to ones in physical embodiment anyway – a complex and never-ending problem. To do this would mean one could walk away from that dark corner to the Light of the Garden. What is keeping you?

You did promise to bring at least one other with you. So, show another the way and then leave. Just walk away. Ask your disciple to show the way to at least one other. Hopefully, this will bring about a chain reaction. That was the original and beautifully thought-out plan in the beginning, was it not, my beautiful Starseeds of Light? What is keeping you?

Charging another for this service would be counter-productive and will keep you locked in as much negativity as those remaining in the darkness. And, what would you do with your reward? You cannot take it with you. The rest of the

Garden functions on Light and Love only. Your currency would be worthless.

So, let us all say: "enough is enough". It is time to end the nonsense. It was a nonsensical game to begin with and the ones who began it should have known better. They did, but they decided to test free will to its ultimate conclusion. There is no point in reliving old scenarios played out in that darkness. Let us begin again in Light and Love.

There is one final Discourse for this book and that, I shall leave to my beautiful Twin Flame, Constella, who commenced this work at the beginning of this millennium and who shall conclude it now, as the first Easter of the new millennium approaches. Who was the Master of Light and Love who left the darkness of that corner when he could have used free will to override all negativity? He was and still is a most perfect example of the balance of the Goddess/God Principle in motion. His sacrifice is commemorated during your Easter-time. He is waiting with arms outstretched to welcome all who walk, skip, run or crawl back to the Garden of Light and Love. Beside him are all of the other Masters of Light and Love who have ventured into the Garden to lead by example. If the Starseeds cannot follow their example, who will lead humanity out of the negativity, in which it is surrounded?

I will leave the Starseeds of Light and Love to ponder that question, but the answer to the question of how it can be done lies within the pages of these Discourses in this book.

To leave the darkness, one must return to the Light. To return to the Light, one must raise one's own vibration. To descend into darkness, one had to lower the vibration to begin with, so it cannot be too difficult a task; can it? So, ponder well, my beloved Starseeds of Light, but do not, I beg of you, procrastinate for too much longer. It could be disastrous for all concerned.

My Love surrounds you all now as my Light enfolds you. Leave all and turn your back on the darkness. With firm steps and a strong determination, face the Light and feel It drawing you towards the Love Essence of God That has been missing for too long from your consciousness.

Beloved of God, I salute you and your courage. Come on Home now. We await you eagerly and in Love. Adieu,

I Am Onoraus.

19 March 2000

Constella

Given the situation that exists upon Earth as it has been explained during these Discourses, it is necessary for ones of Light to gather strength from one another and to form bonds of friendship and Love that are unbreakable. While in spirit-form, between incarnations, these strong bonds do exist. It is only when one descends into physicality that one sees through different eyes as the ego-personality comes to the fore. The ego-personality exists, of course, during the sojourn one enjoys between incarnations, but it is kept in check by the strong and binding Love that all have for one another.

Unfortunately, this does tend to be lost upon Earth as the ego exerts itself in order to protect itself from further hurts, pain and trauma; but, as has been stated earlier, the ego was born of fear. Fear is what feeds it and what keeps it thriving in a state of active animation. It is the ego's fear of annihilation that will prevent it from accepting what is written here.

Know this, my little ones. Know this without a doubt. If there is nothing to fear and ALL is LOVE, what is the use of an ego? The ego-personality is the mask one puts on when taking on a new, fictitious identity in the dark corner of the Garden, as Onoraus has described. From my perspective, I prefer the analogy of the diving suit that one dons for another adventure in that dark, underwater world where Love has been all but wiped out, because fear has replaced Its Magnificent Light.

So, a glowing picture has been painted of my world of Light and Love within these pages. A very gloomy picture has been painted of your world. Does the description fit the reality of your world, as you see it? You have only to watch the violence and horror depicted in your movies and on your television screens to know that this is so. Your daily news reports mirror this violence and sickening horror as the make-believe of the screen becomes all too real in everyday physical life.

Children killing classmates at school is one example. Young boys and girls carrying weapons of destruction in their hands and being trained to use them from a young age, by sadistic and bitter adults, because of their fear of attack from another country, or from different factions within the country of their birth this time around. Perhaps, the Law of Karma may decree that they be born of parents from the other faction during their next venture into the darkness of negativity. Of course, free will exists, so they can choose whichever parents that they feel can help them in the best way spiritually. It seldom works out that way when the physical life begins in these strife-torn lands on Earth.

Surely now, at the beginning of this new millennium, there are ones who are sufficiently spiritually-aware and advanced, and who can suppress their own ego-personalities long enough to speak out and make a difference. How long will it be before the Starseeds wake up and take full responsibility for the turn-around that is so badly needed to change the consciousness of humanity? How long will it be, my little ones?

The time for procrastination is at an end. The time for frustration and planning is at an end. The time for dreaming has come to an end, also. I read over your shoulders the many thousands upon thousands of words that have been written over the past decade alone. I feel your frustration as the words concerning the *New Age that is to come* are repeated over and over again. They are the same words. The dates for predicted happenings have changed, but the words surrounding them have not. The writers of these words are genuine and sincere in the majority of cases, but nothing changes, does it? The wake-up calls of ten years ago went unheeded, except by a few brave individuals who stepped out in faith. Most were destroyed either emotionally and mentally, or financially. Perhaps, some suffered all three fates at the one time. They tried. That is the main factor. They tried. Their efforts, for the most part, were thwarted by other Starseeds whose egos were threatened, whose comfort-zones were shaken and whose livelihood, in some cases, came under scrutiny as questions were asked of the relevance of something that someone had studied and worked hard to achieve for many years. So, Starseed was pitted against Starseed. What a tragedy!

Is there an end to it? No, my little ones, there is not, because this scenario will be played out over and over again every time someone speaks out, or tries to change the status quo. Why? It is because the ego-personality goes into fear and as it knows no other way to survive, it attacks. So, the game in the corner of the garden, or in the underwater world, or whatever other analogy strikes-a-cord with the reader, will persist. Therefore, there is no point in continuing to try to change another person, or to alter their perceptions or their consciousness. To try to raise the consciousness of another, without changing yourself first, is fraught with danger. The danger is that you will come under attack, because you cannot prove that what you are saying is correct.

How can you prove it? It is by becoming so clear and so perfect an individual, while still remaining in physical form, that everyone can see your Light and your Love and, they can feel the vibration that surrounds you within your auric field. You can become the perfect balance of male and female energy. That is the ultimate goal. Why cannot this be achieved? It is because the ego exists to prevent it, yet it is the ego that wants it, because it craves the glory and the adulation that such a state-of-being provides. It is really a little like a dog chasing its tail; is it not?

To be in that state-of-being is to know only Light and Love on all levels. How is it achieved? This is by raising one's vibration to the frequency where the Higher Self can surround the physical body totally, as with a cloak and a hood. How does one raise one's own vibration? It is by asking the Higher Self to do it for you from within. It is oh! so simple, but quite impossible to achieve for ones in physical embodiment, it would seem. The problem stems from the ego-personality who is filled with fear. The fear cannot be released totally without the direct involvement of the Higher Self, despite what others say to the contrary as they charge high prices to relieve our trusting Starseeds of their past-life traumas and fears, not to mention their money. How much did Jesus charge for a similar service? He needed to eat and to clothe himself, as well as to provide shelter for his physical body nightly. How is it then that these New Age gurus have needs that are greater for their physical bodies than Jesus had, or any other Master of Light had, for that matter, when they were in embodiment upon Earth? It is all relevant, my dear ones. It is all relevant.

With every day that passes, another day is lost, because the opportunity is lost to clear, to heal and to re-programme. Is an hour per day too much to ask for every Starseed to spend in quiet communion with one's own Higher Self for the specific purpose of requesting of the Higher Self a favour? That favour being asked is for the clearing and the healing of all past-life and present-life trauma that has occurred and, dating back to – and including – the original trauma that commenced it all. All subsequent traumas, no matter how large or how small will mirror to some degree that original trauma when one very bravely took embodiment on Earth for the very first time.

Whether you – the reader of this Discourse – were a First Wave Starseed who offered to render assistance on the planet of Maldek; or, you were a Second Wave Starseed whose first mission was upon Planet Earth, the result is the same. You suffered an original trauma in one place or the other. Then, as a result, you lost faith in the Source-of-All-Love and you went into fear. To mask that fear, you invented the ego-personality, which you wear as your cloak and your mask to this day. In reality, your sojourns on Earth are similar to going to a masquerade party while wearing a costume that hides your real identity as you mask your True Self and play games for a time with a new, but temporary, identity.

It is time to discard the mask and the current identity and to join As-One with your own Higher and True Self. Come out of the closet and stop playing these childish games. Become the great Master Spirit of Light and Love who you are truly.

There are many who have difficulty with the concept of a Higher and lower self. One part of the whole is vibrating at a high frequency and, for reasons best known to itself, the other part is vibrating at a lower frequency. This lower frequency varies. Sometimes, it can be quite high, especially during deep meditation sessions. At other times, it can be very low due to stress and trauma, with the problem compounded by drugs and alcohol, which are used to alleviate the stress and trauma that have occurred.

Let us visualise these two parts as two horseshoe-shaped magnets that are attracting each other, but they are unable to link up to become the perfect circle, because there is a thick etheric film that keeps them separate and apart. The problem is, as always, the subconscious mind. The Higher Part can see the problem, but it is powerless to remove it, because the lower part possesses something called *free will*. This tree will is a gift from our loving Creator and, it is sacrosanct. Therefore, sadly, the Higher Self can wait only and hope that the lower self will realise the dilemma; then, it can ask for assistance before it is too late and another physical body is destroyed by this negative, etheric film. Does this present a clearer picture for the reader to study? All that needs to be done is to ask the Higher Self to cleanse and heal, so that the negative film can be removed. The second part of the requirement is for the lower self to override the ego-personality self, so that the time can be provided – merely one hour per day – to accomplish this task. However, the ego-personality is not anxious to lose control, so it finds many, many reasons for not allowing the physical body to sit still for this short amount of time per day. The reasons can range from chores to playful diversions in the company of friends. It is so very sad; is it not?

In light of these revelations, which are not new, it is highly recommended that the time be allocated for this specific task daily. As the clearing and healing takes place, the clarity-of-thought will come. With clarity of thought will come the reprogramming of the subconscious mind. The task is so simple and so easy that we of the Light have great difficulty in persuading our counterparts in physical form of the urgent need for this task to be completed in the *Now* moment. It will, in all probability, take many, many months to complete. There is nothing that is of more importance in your daily lives at present. There is nothing at all, believe me. Find the time to sit in meditation for one hour per day, for this specific purpose, everyday. Then, the Higher Self will pull-out-all-stops, as the saying goes, to make certain that everything else in your life runs smoothly for you. When you reach this stage, please do not allow the ego-personality to sabotage your combined efforts. This, I beg of you, dear ones.

There is little more to be said on the subject. These Discourses have covered most areas where understanding may have been lacking. If one hour per day is too long to meditate for you personally, perhaps spending some time in silent meditation and the rest of the time reading and re-reading these Discourses will help greatly.

Many ones-of-Light have gathered to bring these words and this understanding to our precious Starseeds-of-Light now. Please do not allow their efforts to have been in vain. Come Home to us, sweet children of the Light, and feel our Love surround you totally. Then, all fear will be washed away by our tears of joy at your triumphant Homecoming.

Blessed be the ones who are true to the Light no matter what comes. As your own vibrations rise, you will become the perfect Circle and all will marvel at the Glow-of-Love that surrounds you as, oblivious to all, you go about the business of your loving Mother-Father God on Earth while carrying out to perfection your pre-planned part in God's Divine Plan for Earth and all who reside upon her currently. No matter what befalls you, remember to repeat over and over to yourself the words:

"I AM in this world, but I AM not of it. I AM that I AM."

Peace be with you.

I AM Constella of the Light.

20th March 2000

Epilogue – Constella

It has been three and a half years since this series of writings began. The world has changed greatly in that period of time. The changes that will occur in the next three and a half years will be great, also, but whether these changes will be positive or negative remains to be seen, because this, as always, is in the hands of the population of Earth.

If the majority of Earth's population has learned not one lesson from the *wars to end all wars* that were a major part of history in the last century alone, then it will be more of the same – only on a greater scale. If *good* people do nothing, evil flourishes in all its forms. If the majority of the world's population – those with goodwill and love in their hearts – was to band together in peace and love – Universal Love – then, what weapons do those of evil intent – those with hatred and vengeance on their minds (because their hearts are closed and cold) – have that can defeat goodwill, compassion and Love for ALL of God's creation?

The usual catch-cry is that one individual alone is powerless. Did not your great seer, Gandhi, prove this to be an incorrect statement?

Rallies that are orchestrated to disrupt are not the way of Love. These are disrupted, no matter how great the goodwill and good intent of the leaders, by ones of evil intent. There cannot be conflict, large or small, without ones of evil intent planning and promoting dissension and inciting others to anger and to action. This was not Gandhi's way and nor is it God's way.

While ones of good intent sit back watching, waiting and feeling powerless, those of evil intent will draw their followers into another war that will make all previous wars pale into insignificance, because of its scale and its indescribable horror. There is a way to manoeuvre through on a central pathway. It is to gather in groups where those within the group are known to one another and are respected for their goodwill, compassion and Love.

These do not have to be great rallies where placard-carrying individuals march with anger in their hearts and showing on their faces while angry words are on their lips as they shout their demands outside government buildings. Are they any better than the ones who are inside the building and who have stopped listening to the voices of the people whom they claim to represent? Anger breeds anger. Violence breeds violence. Love brings forth peace.

There are public places that are designated places of safety where people can gather together to picnic and play. With ever-present cameras on hand to record events, will not the authorities baulk just a little at using violence if groups of families and friends are gathered in public parks while sitting in circles and praying to God for peace?

Sit on cushions and link arms if the night or day is chilly. Place a candle in the centre and draw down the Divine Love of God from above and see *It* going straight down into the centre or core of Mother Earth. Send Love to that beam from your own heart centre and into the heart centre of your Mother, the Earth, for she is the one who nurtures and nourishes you with food and water; is she not? Could you not send a little Love back to her in return?

It has been said many times that our Mother Earth has a grid system that encompasses her. This resembles a spider's web and at every intersecting point, there is an energy centre, or chakra, if you prefer that expression. To send Love to Mother Earth in this way, from all of the parks, beaches and mountain-tops around the world would be a wonderful sight to behold, for Earth would light up immediately to resemble a fully-lit Christmas tree. What a magnificent and brilliant spectacle!

There would be an added advantage to this situation. The Earth's vibration would rise remarkably and instantly, thus causing much annoyance within the ranks of those of evil intent. They may not understand at a conscious level why they are feeling annoyed and irritable and they may begin to take out their negative emotions on their subordinates who, in turn, may take their negative emotions out on those further down the chain of command. A *house* warring within itself cannot stand. It knows no barrier to Love, either.

The secret to the success of this mission – peace mission – is that on every energy centre throughout the world, there are Starseeds of Light living and working, so getting together a group of like-minded people should be relatively easy. However, caution is the way to proceed. Bear in mind that those of evil intent and with war uppermost in their minds will do all in their power to stop any dissent; but, who was it that designated man-made buildings as the only places where Earth's population can pray to God?

If candles are acceptable in churches, then why not use these in parks during prayer meetings? Do not flout the rules, for this will lead to upheaval and strife. Be within the law of the land at all times in order to cover one's back, so to speak. Have only those who are known to you personally in your group, so peace is assured. It may be advisable to avoid the use of crystals or any other apparatus that would cause dissent. After all, there are still in existence in some states and countries long-forgotten by-laws that could be enacted if the authorities of the day became desperate. Those relating to witch-craft spring to mind instantly.

Gandhi promoted peace, but change through civil disobedience. Promote peace and change, also, but do it through prayer in public areas designated for public use, without disrupting traffic flow. If there is not any violence, then these gatherings will not be newsworthy. Perhaps then, the media will become bored, pack up and go home. Or, better still, the individuals concerned may put down their cameras, recorders and pens while joining together to form prayer groups of their own. Anything is possible.

There are many, many thousands of people in towns and cities all around this world and these have peace, compassion and Love in their hearts. They may be happy and eager to form their own prayer groups, but they will never join rallies, because of the violence that erupts at many of these gatherings. Those who live by peace and Love do not wish to leave themselves open and vulnerable, because they witness on their television screens the anger on the faces of those involved, on both sides of these conflicts, and they cannot bear to be a part of such angry gatherings that achieve nothing but a hardening of attitudes on both sides.

It will be the Starseeds of Light who will need to stand up and be counted now. This is because most of the clergy, in all religious establishments, have failed to do so. These public prayer groups for peace could have been organised already by ones such as these and the question that needs to be asked is why they are not happening already. They were organised and carried out peacefully world-wide when the twin-towers were destroyed with great loss of life. Why can they not be arranged now, on a world-wide basis, to prevent a war that will make the twin-towers scenario a reality over and over again? Do men of ill-intent stop with one great *success*? Or, are they buoyed by that so-called success and then plan bigger and more spectacular scenarios for their own ego-elevation, regardless of what banner they are flying currently to justify such monstrous acts of barbarity and horror?

In the book, *UNDERCOVER STARSEEDS*, there are two great Masters whose writings are there for all to read; then, to accept or reject, as the case may be. One is known as

Zu Deus and the other is known as Selene. These ones are what you would term as a *Higher Self.* They are Masters of Love and Light. Each one has an offspring (lower self) in physical embodiment on Earth at present. In former times, these ones were on your Earth in different roles, as everyone reading this has been. They are in different guises now, but leadership is one of their greatest attributes. Love is the most obvious of all. One came as a great king who was renowned for his wisdom, intelligence and spiritual connection to the Source-of-All Light and Love. The other was a young girl who led a great army in a country known as France. She was greatly loved by many and was martyred for her cause.

When these two begin speaking out again in earnest, they will attract to themselves many followers who have been their devoted followers in many a lifetime. They will attract to themselves, also, the ones who were their enemies in other lifetimes and these ones of evil intent will plan and plot amongst themselves to find ways to firstly discredit these ones and, ultimately, to destroy their current physical encasements. But, that is as far as the power of these evil ones extends. As you say on your Earth – 'if someone is firing bullets at you, you must be doing something right'. In the public arena, no one fires bullets at fence-sitters. That is why there are so many of them on Earth.

The time for fence-sitting is at an end, because the negativity on the planet is growing stronger and darker. A line is being drawn in the sand and the fence-sitters will be required shortly to jump to one side or the other. Only prayer and the Light and Love of God can save the planet and rescue her loving inhabitants from this dilemma of their own making. Complacency is the reason that it is of their own making.

Public prayer vigils can make a difference. Worldwide public prayer vigils within one's own special prayer group, is the answer to all of this world's current problems. It matters not whether the number of your group is twenty, twelve, ten or two, as long as you can vouch for everyone in your group and, you know without doubt that violence and vengeance, fuelled by anger, is not their hidden agenda.

Be wary. Be ever watchful. Be free with your Love for ALL humanity, no matter which side of the fence they are sitting currently. There are people with peace, compassion and Love on both sides of that line in the sand and, you would not wish to have their blood on your conscience when you return to Spirit this time around, would you? I know the answer to that question, as you do.

Proceed with Love – God's Universal Love – for all. Do not allow fear to assail you. Draw to yourself the Divine Light of God. Draw to yourself the Divine Love of God. Put on the Armour of God, which is faith in our Creator's Love and Compassion. With a candle in your hand and Love in your heart, go change the world for the better.

This concludes my writings for the ones of Earth to whom I gave my promise and my commitment to bring forth knowledge, enlightenment and Love at the end of the Age. It is done. I bid all of my beautiful friends of Light a fond farewell and God Speed on your journey.

I AM Constella of the Light and Love of Almighty God.
20th March 2003

A promise was given to all Starseeds that this information would be released at this time on Earth.
That promise is fulfilled now.

I AM Constella

Transition

The Final Journey

Guidelines

To

Self-Healing

Introduction

There would appear to be three different groups of people on this planet. There are those who live a full physical life to the exclusion of all else. There are those who have a foot in each camp, shall we say, and these ones drift between these realities or belief-systems as they search somewhat intermittently for *Truth Everlasting*. This is because whatever is occurring now, in their current physical lives, is very important to them. This is not a criticism in any way whatsoever. It is simply how it is with these ones currently. However, the third group consists of ones who live in a totally-different reality when in embodiment on Earth. Their spiritual lives and their advancement in understanding come before anything else in their lives. These are the ones for whom the final books of this Series have been written. Whether the **Guidelines to Self-Healing** that are presented here are accepted is dependent on the current reality that one can countenance at this present moment. The following Discourse is the final one for this book, just as it was the final Discourse in *UNDERCOVER STARSEEDS.*

Jesus-Sananda of the Light

In the case of ones who wish to drink a beverage known in your world as coffee, then it is, for most, just a matter of going to the supermarket, taking a jar from the shelf, paying at the check-out, then going home to make an instant cup of steaming coffee. Not for one moment does anyone consider the effort that has gone into making this *instant* drink, not to mention the time and the money.

Let us consider a landholder somewhere in the world. This person has paid for the land, which would not be inexpensive, for coffee needs much space and a lush area, in which to grow. There are, of course, all of the government fees and charges, which are ongoing. Then, there is the purchase of the seed or trees, as the case may be. There is the labour needed to plant and then to tend the crop. It is an ongoing commitment and, for the most part, most of the profits would be required to pay for the next season's crop in this saga of planting and harvesting. Here, we have not even touched on the love aspect of the operation; nor have we mentioned the process that occurs after the harvesting in order that a jar of *instant* coffee can make its way to the supermarket shelf for the benefit of the ones who enjoy this beverage daily or hourly.

So, too, my children of Light, is the saga – the ongoing saga – of opening up the eyes of the Starseeds of the Light and Love of God and to pave the way for their Enlightenment.

It has not happened overnight and someone who is awakening at this late stage perhaps will pick up these Guidelines, be very excited by them, then they may feel that this is what they have been waiting for all of their lives. For most, this will be true, but it will be similar to picking up a jar of instant coffee from a supermarket shelf. There is not one thought given to the long, arduous process that has gone into the production. It was not done by one person any more than the jar of coffee was the result of one person's efforts. It was a combined effort on behalf of many Starseeds who listened to their own Higher Self when they could have been enjoying a full physical life. Not only that, but many, also, listened to the guidance coming from many Masters in my world of Spirit. In most cases, they have paid dearly for their pains in physical, emotional, mental and financial terms.

The newly-awakened Starseeds will take these Guidelines that are so freely given and try them for awhile; then, if there is not a noticeable difference within a few weeks, they will discard them. Others will see a way to change a few of the suggested methods a little; then, they will hang a shingle over their door and begin to draw in the unwary to relieve them of their money. Others will continue with the Guidelines and slowly, imperceptibly, they will begin to feel different. These are the ones for whom these Guidelines are written. These are our hope for the future of Planet Earth.

When the Guidelines are implemented by sufficient numbers, then a whole new wave of little children will flood the earth-plane. These ones are in Spirit now awaiting an opportunity to descend to Earth's atmosphere, but they will not do so until they are certain beyond any doubt that conditions upon Earth have changed for the better. They have been on the treadmill too many times before, as have the Starseeds who are in embodiment now. They cannot face any more disappointments and traumas. They wish to return to Earth to be a part of the Golden Age, the New Age of Love on Earth. They will be the cavalry arriving with fresh ideas, abundant energy and blossoming with the fullness and fragrance of the opening rose.

The will arrive *in the nick of time* for the Starseeds who are already in embodiment and who are struggling with their spiritual and personal lives while running out of energy fast. Before that happens, let us make one more concerted effort, as a team, to put all past differences behind us and to move forward in Love, armed with the Guidelines, to which we will adhere strictly. There is my fervent plea, my little ones, and it comes from my heart directly to your heart. Do not delay. Do not allow petty jealousies and past hurts to cloud your Love and to delay you any longer. Come Home to us now, in Love and in triumph.

Now, let us begin.

Guidelines – A Brief Outline

A full explanation of the Guidelines for Self-Healing was given in the book, *UNDERCOVER STARSEEDS*, which was published in 2000. Most of the Discourses from the Masters of Light that appear here in Book Four of this current publication were published originally in that book. As you begin this healing session, remember that – as with everything – it is the *intent* that counts. Ask your Higher Self to surround and protect you now. This will take approximately twenty minutes from when you begin this releasing, clearing and self-healing session. Allow approximately an hour's duration for the session for maximum benefit.

Step One

It is advisable to set the scene by making certain that distractions are kept to a minimum, especially with regard to telephone interruptions. The playing of soft music, especially meditation music, is helpful, also. Sit in a chair, on a cushion or wherever feels comfortable to you. Now, close your eyes and visualise someone whom you love deeply. It may be someone who is in the physical world; or, it may be someone who has passed over to the Astral Realm. It does not matter, as long as there is a powerful bond and a strong connection between the two of you.

Draw to yourself the Divine Love Essence of God. Feel it igniting your Heart chakra. Then, send this Love directly to the one whom you have drawn to you, in love. See a beam of Divine Love fly directly from your Heart chakra to the Heart centre of the one opposite you.

Visualise a bubble filled to overflowing with a pink mist of Love that is surrounding the two of you while sealing you together for this time. Then, see this bubble growing larger and the Love between the two of you becoming deeper. Speak to your friend now, if you wish. Divine Love knows no boundaries and its capabilities stretch far beyond healing.

Another attribute, which is not recognised often, is that Divine Love provides gravity. In other words, this Love that you are drawing to yourself, before sending out to another, is causing your vibrations to rise at a very steady pace. As your vibrations rise, the flow-on effect causes your Higher Part – your own Higher Self – to draw closer to you. It cannot be any other way. After approximately twenty minutes, your Higher Self will click around you. It may feel as though a cloak of Love has enveloped your whole being. This is when Oneness commences for you.

Hand over now to our loving Creator-of-All. If you wish, you can ask your friend to go on a small journey with you. It may be to a beach that is familiar to both of you; or perhaps, you may go to a garden, a forest, or to some place where you have shared some happy memories together. Alternatively, you may remain where you are and absorb the Love Energy of God. However, before you do so, draw to you now the Holy Spirit and ask for the Holy Spirit to infuse you.

Now, leave all else in the capable hands of your own Higher Self who will begin the releasing process. Please be aware that, as this releasing is taking place, memories are being stirred at a deep level within your subconscious mind; then, these are being released into your emotional and mental bodies, as well as into your auric field. These will be unpleasant sensations. You may feel them. You may not. There is no need to tune-in to these as they are being released. This could be counter-productive, as pictures may appear in your Third Eye, thus bringing old traumas to your conscious mind. Concentrate upon your friend and the Love that you are both sharing at this moment.

As with everything in life, it is the intent that is paramount in these sessions. Once the Higher Self has the permission of the lower self to release, clear and heal, not a moment will be lost in bringing about a swift and careful release. Once released, the dark clouds of negativity will pass quickly through all of the bodies and be cleared forever. These clouds will be transmuted into Divine Light instantly and these will pass from your auric field permanently. If you do not have conscious knowledge of the events that caused the releasing trauma, you are not likely to be able to relive the experience, as one tends to do now with traumatic events that have occurred in the current lifetime. By reliving these happenings, their imprint is being reinforced upon the subconscious mind, thus affecting negatively all other bodies including the Astral body. It is self-perpetuating.

If you are experiencing discomfort, or these sessions seem too long for you to endure, reach for a copy of the Discourses in this book and open it at whatever page you feel guided to read at this moment. It is advisable to have the book handy before commencing these sessions. Do not allow any session to proceed beyond the sixty-minute period, because this could be counter-productive. Perhaps, a timepiece that gives a soft, gentle chime or a piece of music that switches itself on when an hour session has concluded would be helpful.

There are one or two niceties to observe when concluding your session. Thank those whom you have called to you – your Creator, the Holy Spirit, your own Higher Self and, of course, the friend with whom you have shared your love during the session. It does not need to be the same person every time, but there does need to be someone to whom you can send Love and upon whom you can focus as you raise your vibrations to allow the releasing, clearing and, of course, the healing to take place.

Now, withdraw the Beam of Love. See this slide back into your Heart chakra. By opening your Heart chakra to receive Divine Love, you have opened wide automatically all of your chakras or energy centres. It is advisable, before venturing out into the world of the physical, to close these to their normal size. Otherwise, you may upset a few people who you chance to meet, especially if they are in negativity themselves at the moment of meeting. As an example, if you were to enter a large shopping complex where the auras of everyone under that roof are intermingling constantly, your high vibration might not be to the liking of others, shall we say.

To reduce your chakras, visualise every centre in turn while closing it to a tiny pinpoint of Light (or, a small lotus flower, if you prefer). Move to every chakra individually. The Crown chakra will reduce in size automatically and in its own time, as will the Core Centre. If you wish for added protection as you move from your sanctuary of Love to face the demands of the physical world of illusion, ask for an invisible shield to cover your chakras back and front. Many will say that this is unnecessary, and perhaps they are correct, but is a little extra insurance that is free of charge to be refused? I will leave you to decide.

That is all there is to your daily session. A few cue cards may assist your memory when you begin the process. After a few sessions, you will not need them in all probability. It will become second nature to you. If you wish, as you start your self-healing session, you can direct a beam of Divine Love into the heart centre of Mother Earth for she needs all of the love that she can receive now. However, do not forget to withdraw that beam before you close down all of your chakras.

Step Two

As has been stated in an earlier publication, it is the simplicity of these *Guidelines* that will draw much criticism, especially from ones who have a *better* way to release, clear and heal. Do not be misled. Re-read the Discourses and be guided by your heart at all times. Stay the distance and allow your Higher Self to lead you Home in Love. Practised daily, these sessions of one hour's duration can have one result only and that is to draw you closer to your Higher Self in every moment. A permanent state of Oneness will be the reward. What a prize!

A very advanced spiritual being and dear friend, who is a medium in her own right, read the words that related to *Divine Jade* in this book. She asked me what the words meant. It is a cryptic message, I know. However, I was surprised that she could not see the relevance and the hidden meaning at first glance. Perhaps, at a later reading, she may have come to the deeper understanding that is buried within its simple wording. What colour is our Heart chakra/centre? What colour is jade? If we could sit quietly in meditation for one hour per day, we would find the peace that we are seeking. Giving the ego-personality self full control for most, if not all, of our waking hours is not allowing our Spirit-self the time to find the peace and solace that our soul needs for survival while in physical form on Earth.

Mother Earth is in desperate need of this peace and solace, also, as she struggles to provide us with our daily needs in a world that is out-of-control, due to pollution, violence and hatred that abounds on her surface. Could we not block out the negativity of daily life for but one hour per day to sit in the *Silence That Is God Almighty?*

In this way, not only would we assist ourselves – our own special Spirit-Self – but also, we would assist our earthly mother at the same time. Would that not be a brilliant way to commence any day? Shall we try one such meditation? If it proves beneficial, could we not make this process a daily ritual for the remainder of life-on-Earth in this particular embodiment? Perhaps, on our return to our Astral home this time around, we may have risen a little higher in our quest.

What is our quest and ultimate goal, as the loving, caring and refreshingly-honest Spirit-Beings that we are – we *all* are – at our Core Centre?

It is en-*light*-enment, of course. We all wish to become lighter, because we are filled to overflowing with the Divine Light and Divine Love of God. We are exactly that at our Core Centre. Why can we not become so again, at an etheric/physical level? What is preventing us from achieving our ultimate goal of *Oneness* – complete *At-one-ment* with our God – The One?

It is trauma. It is a deep-seated fear that is within everyone who incarnates on Earth. What did Mary call this fear in the Discourse that was attributed to her in Book Four? It is given another name on Earth, especially within the current religions, as well as in the churches-of-old. Every person who was born on Earth was said to have incarnated while bringing with her or him an original *sin*. If *sin* and *fear* are one-and-the-same, as Mary has suggested, what is the fear that we bring with us in every incarnation? Could it be that when first we began incarnating on this planet, in order to help turn the tide in favour of *Love* – that being *Divine Love*– we suffered a severe traumatic event? What if, with every subsequent life experience, a similar situation arises for us and we go into fear immediately? Is such a happening possible? Is it possible that our sole intent and purpose in every incarnation is to clear our original trauma?

If we do not recall, at a conscious level, what that trauma was, it seems an impossible task. It is an impossible task unless, of course, we hand over to the one who knows and understands, at a personal level. This is our Higher/Spirit-Self. Therefore, this is Part Two, if you like, of our healing session. It is the second step for all. Step One is explained in these writings. This relates to the setting of the scene, so to speak. It is a quiet place, which is our own space where we will not be disturbed for our self-allocated one-hour session. It is the playing of meditation music softly in the background. It is making a determined effort to prevent interruptions, such as telephone calls and intrusions by animals and pets, as well as all other daily visitors during that time-frame. Once settled to this hourly routine of meditation in this manner, call upon one's Higher Self to draw close while placing a mantle of protection over the physical body. Asking for a pyramid of Divine Light to encompass the room may be helpful, also. Hand over to your own Higher/Spirit-Self, so that the two can become *one* for a time. Once your *Pure Intent* is known, all will follow in due course. From there, it is a matter of sending your Love directly from your Heart centre, along with Divine Light from your higher centre, into the Heart centre of Mother Earth, after you have directed your beam of Light and Love to your friend/loved one whom you have called to you.

In Conclusion

There is a Christ within all of us. At our Core Centre is our own special Christ Light. It is the Christ Light – that is Divine Love and Divine Light combined – that we are directing now into the Core Centre of our Earth Mother as our own Higher/Spirit-Self settles comfortably around us.

Ask for your etheric body to be cleared and healed now of all weapons and negativity from this and past lives. Once completed, the Higher Self can settle comfortably around your physical body. The usual time-frame for this to occur would be approximately twenty minutes. Then, for the next part of the exercise, which will last approximately forty minutes, ask your Higher/Spirit-Self to begin releasing, clearing and healing at this deep level – at your Core Centre – for the remainder of your daily session of one hour's duration (and no longer in any one session).This is what we all come down to do in every lifetime. By *we,* I refer to the children of

Light – the beautiful Starseeds – who have never turned away from their loving Father-Mother-God-Principle – our Source-of-All. We face such bitter disappointment when we return Home to the Astral level after every incarnation when we discover that, in most cases, we have not begun to do so by life's end. To avoid bitter disappointment and regret, start today. There is some sound advice. The Higher/Spirit-Self cannot begin this great task until the one who is in embodiment asks for help and requests this great service. Ask and you shall receive. Ask daily. What form could that request take?

"I command that my Higher/Spirit-Self releases, clears, cleanses and heals all of the debris, which relates to my *Original Trauma* when first I began this journey to Earth. Release, clear, cleanse and heal me at my deepest level and remove all memories and the aftermath of my *Original Trauma* from my *Core Centre* now. I give permission for my *Soul-Seat* to be released, cleared, cleansed and healed now, in God's Divine Light and God's Divine Love, as memories and the aftermath of my *Original Trauma* disappear forever."

Leave all else in the hands of one's Higher/Spirit-Self for the rest of the healing session and practice this great releasing and healing daily. It is not necessary for conscious recall of the *Original Trauma*, as this may be counter-productive. It has been stated in earlier times that one-hundred and forty-four thousand will rise up. As one lightens the load at the Core Centre and the Soul-Seat, a definite *lightness* will engulf this beautiful Being. Could this be the meaning of the statement regarding one-hundred and forty-four thousand rising up? Perhaps, it is so. Release, clear, cleanse and heal at the physical/etheric level first, so that the Higher Self can take over from there, with the full consent of the one in embodiment.

That is *Step One* of the process of en-*light*-enment for all children of Light. *Rising up* refers to our personal energy level. *Step Two*, of course, has been explained fully in this Discourse. *Step Two* is giving the Higher Self the full consent of the one-in-embodiment to release, clear, cleanse and heal at the level of the Core Centre and Soul-Seat. This is, without doubt, the complete removal of the aftermath and all memories relating to one's *Original Trauma*.

For many, the *Original Trauma* will have been a massive betrayal by ones who we loved deeply and trusted completely. The destruction of the loving community at Qumran is a prime example of one such betrayal. Patterns, once established in one lifetime, have an uncanny habit of re-appearing regularly in subsequent lifetimes. Such is the state-of-play on Earth at this time.

The children of Light have suffered greatly as a result of their own personal and *Original Trauma* being played out on Earth while in physical form and in many, many lifetimes. Mother Earth's emotional body in her etheric field bears testimony to all of the trauma that has been played out on her surface since long before time began and the calendar and the clock were invented. Is it not time now to bring all of these senseless and mindless games to an end permanently? These are self-perpetuating. Walk away from the senseless and mindless games-of-Earth now. Walk away and do not look back. How is this to be accomplished? The answer is simple and only you can do this service – this self-service:

We need to rid ourselves of the memories and aftermath of our Original Trauma as soon as possible if we wish to return to being the pure, loving Spirit-Essence that we were in our original state.

That is the secret.

Step One is to send Love from our Heart chakra to the Heart chakra of the loved one who we have drawn to ourselves in meditation. In so doing, we are raising our energy level/vibration, so that our Higher Self can draw close to us without any separation existing between us as two become one.

Step Two is our request that our Higher/Spirit-Self releases, clears, cleanses and heals us at the deepest level of all – at our Core Centre and our Soul-Seat where all of our bitter-sweet memories are stored. This is a clear, unequivocal request that all of the memories of the trauma associated with our original lifetime on Earth be erased completely and that the aftermath of the Original Trauma be removed totally from our Core Centre and Soul-Seat.

A way has been shown now. The decision from here is a personal choice. Perhaps, this was the real reason for the systematic removal of all passages relating to reincarnation from the Bible. If we have one-lifetime-only to *get it right*, so to speak, and if we arrive here to start that life while being encumbered with a so-called *original sin*, how is it possible to become *perfect* during our one-and-only-life? Great power is placed then in the hands of religious leaders who guide their faithful flock through this one-life-only experience on Earth.

At an earlier time on this planet, secret and sacred information was released to ones who were not ready to receive it. These ones passed that information onto others whom they trusted and the word spread rapidly. Can you imagine what Earth would be like now if ones such as Adolf Hitler or Napoleon Bonaparte had been in possession of the wisdom, knowledge and power that Jesus possessed?

The secret and sacred information was passed on indiscriminately at that earlier time and this unfortunate happening almost brought about the destruction of the planet. How do I know that this occurred? It came from a realisation and a deep-seated memory that was locked within. It relates to Knowingness. I cannot prove this statement. I am certain though that this event will never be permitted to occur again on Earth, as safeguards have been put in place to prevent such a happening. Once discovered, please use this information for personal healing only. Do not allow it to pass to another, for the old adage of: *sealed lips are worth a thousand words,* applies here. Those safeguards may include the premature return to Spirit, if the one who is in receipt of the information has obtained same by means other than their own efforts. That is a sobering thought.

My own personal trauma from my first lifetime appeared before my eyes after a deep meditation session. It involved a group of people who I have known in this lifetime. Most are unknown to one another this time around, but in that earlier timeframe, they banded together to bring about my downfall. This occurred while I was in meditation in a temple. It was planned and executed to perfection. Individually, I trusted them all back then and their betrayal came as a great shock.

During this current life, I have lived and worked in various cities and countries throughout the world. These have included London UK, Washington DC and Iceland, as well as Brisbane and Melbourne, in Australia. Some of those original traitors have been in positions of power in organisations where I have worked. Others were ones whom I loved during this life.

Several of them appeared to me to be *overshadowed* by a large dark cloud surrounding their physical bodies. This I could see clearly through physical eyes. Several caused a distinct shudder when they entered my auric field. In the Original Trauma, there was a gang-of-nine who attacked me while I was alone and meditating in a temple. There were two other males who I would describe as gate-keepers. One held the keys to the outer door of the temple and he allowed the group to enter late at night. Another was posted as the doorkeeper outside the room where I was meditating. The gang-of-nine that consisted of five women and four men, entered quickly, without warning, and the attack was over in a matter of moments. Their roles were well-rehearsed. They carried these out to perfection.

As a result, betrayal by ones whom I have trusted in this lifetime has been a constant theme. That, it would seem, was my Original Trauma and one that I am in the process of clearing and healing now. I was a high priestess at that earlier time. It was a long, long time ago and is lost way back in the mists of time when we all incarnated in our etheric bodies and before the creation of our flesh bodies became necessary. The weapons that were inserted were mostly crystal in essence and these were in the shape of small rocks and very thin rods. The rods were slid into strategic places in my astral body, thus forming a definite cross. The downward rod pierced my Crown chakra and lodged in the Solar Plexus chakra where a small rock had been placed. The second rod entered slightly below the right temple before intersecting the downward rod at the area of the nostril. From there, it exited through the left temple area of my head.

I reveal this ordeal simply to show that there has been a trauma that all children of Light have suffered. It is for everyone to come to terms with these revelations and to accept or reject them as one sees fit. If there was not an Original Trauma that needs clearing, why do we all keep reincarnating endlessly on Earth? Is that why the one-life-only theory and belief-system has gained such traction here? This information can be discarded easily by ones who are fearful of stepping onto the path of the determined spiritual warrior in this lifetime . . . as it will, in all probability.

In the writing of this Series of books, my role has been to throw up ideas into the air and to hope that these ideas land in a fertile place where they can germinate. It is an individual choice from here.

Allow ALPHA and DIVINE GRACE to lead you home by making this current lifetime your last one on Earth. Allow your personal quest to lead you along this spiritual pathway and on through this last leg of *the final journey* on the forever-long road back to your True Home.

I hope that the books of the *Stella McMillan Series* have provided enjoyment, entertainment, enlightenment and a greater understanding of the spiritual aspect of life. This is my final book of the Series. The next book to be published is entitled **Perception**. Quite simply, it will consist of some of my earlier books that were self-published between 1992 and 2000. The titles of these original books are listed below for the benefit of those who are interested. Details of the release of the book entitled **Perception** will appear on my website: stellamcmillan.com

Stella McMillan
20th July 2018

THE GOLDEN AGE– Published 1992
FAMILY OF MAN –Published 1992
THE REAL BOOK, REAL BEGINNING – Published 1999
UNDERCOVER STARSEEDS – Published 2000

Stella McMillan seven-book Series

FIRST TRILOGY – *ERA/ERROR of UNDERSTANDING*
Book One: *ERROR of UNDERSTANDING*

Watching from a safe distance in her present surreal world, Paula relived the lives of Louisa and Charles in nineteenth century Australia. The people and places all seemed very familiar to her, despite the fact that she had not visited this country previously and she had a busy life of her own back in Las Vegas in the USA. Following the car accident during her Gold Coast vacation, Paula remained riveted to the scenes that were playing vividly in her present consciousness. Soon, she would wake up from this dream-sequence and all would be well in her real world of the physical.

Victorian Victorians – a story within a story – brought Louisa Howard and Charles Lyndhurst together for the first time in that lifetime and their story progressed from there during the year of 1867. This was at a time when Prince Alfred, Duke of Edinburgh, was visiting Victoria on the first Royal Tour of the country and it depicted Louisa and Charles' involvement in many of the lavish festivities associated with the visit of Prince Alfred to Melbourne.

The title of the book refers to the consciousness of that particular era, especially where the error regarding the understanding of previous lives was concerned. Louisa was conditioned from birth to accept fully the doctrines and dogma of the Church of Rome.

Book Two – *ERROR PERPETUATED*

Paula continues her vigil while remaining transfixed as she studies the lives of Charles and Louisa in that long-ago timeframe.

Victorian Victorians continues the story and the next year saw this couple on a seesaw in their relationship as a third party entered their lives. This new arrival was determined to entice Louisa away from Charles. It was her religion, more so than her love for either Charles or Phillip, that weighed heavily on her conscience, thus causing her to make the choice that she did. Her absolute belief in the teachings of the Church of Rome and in the infallibility of the Pope was rock-solid, so the error of understanding was perpetuated.

Book Three – *ERA of UNDERSTANDING*

With Paula floating above her current physical form, she is puzzled by the scenes that flow in sequence before her stunned gaze.

Victorian Victorians follows the lives of Louisa and Charles to their ultimate conclusion in that century. The era of understanding did not arrive for this couple until each one passed beyond the veil of death at the end of that life experience. Then, all was revealed.

SECOND TRILOGY – *ERA/ERROR of DISCERNMENT*

Book One – AWAKENING TO AWARENESS

Here, Paula reviews an earlier period of her life when she was working as a croupier in a small, out-of-the-way casino in Las Vegas. When she met Lachlan Jefferson for the first time, her reaction to him was reminiscent of Louisa's initial reaction to Charles Lyndhurst in the previous century.

Together, Paula and Lachlan set about attempting to trap a confidence trickster who had Lachlan in his sights as his next victim. The place where most of the action takes place is the city called Surfers Paradise, on the Gold Coast in

Australia. The result of their endeavours has fatal consequences.

For Paula, her own AWAKENING TO AWARENESS brought with it a surprising revelation when she discovered that she was required to make a monumental decision.

From the detached reality in the hospital room where her physical body was fighting for survival, she was being guided to make a life-and-death decision regarding her current life as the twenty-first century made its appearance. Accepting that she had been Louisa in the nineteenth century lifetime was not possible for her at this point. Realising that this may not have been the only life that she had lived was beyond her comprehension. She had been conditioned from birth to believe that there was only one life, in which to become perfect. Everyone knew that as a fact-of-life!

The decision being asked of her was to name the reality that she wished to call Home at this point in her life. For Paula, this Awakening to True Reality reinforced a realisation of the impermanence of physical life.

Book Two – *ERROR PROFOUND*
ERROR PROFOUND saw Paula making a definite decision to change her life completely and, despite fierce opposition from Lachlan, she followed through with physical action. Because of his deep love for her, Lachlan went along with her somewhat *loopy* plans, but on the understanding that it was for a short period of time only. This upheaval in their lives was a profound decision on Paula's part as she sought to turn around the errors of the past.

Book Three: *ERA of DISCERNMENT*
ERA of DISCERNMENT brought more revelations and a greater understanding of the spiritual aspects of life.

Paula's discussions with her Spirit Guide, Gerard, continued as did her regression sessions to previous life situations that required a loving resolution in this life. Finally, she appeared to be succeeding in her efforts to coax the reluctant Lachlan along with her on her spiritual quest for enlightenment.

During this two-and-a-half-year period, her life had changed completely. This had taken massive courage and much determination on her part, in order to make the changes that she *felt, at a deeper level,* were vital for her, as well as for her immediate family. In this *Era* of greater understanding and awareness – this being the commencement of Aquarius – Paula's personal journey continued, as the errors that were accepted and perpetuated by previous generations were seen as the fallacies that they were. Paula came to the acceptance that reincarnation was an undeniable fact-of-life. All else was – and, always had been – *illusion!*

SUSPENSION – Between Two Realms – is the seventh book in the *Stella McMillan Series.*

This is a companion book to the earlier trilogies. As such, it can be enjoyed alone, or read in conjunction with the other books of the Series. The purpose of *SUSPENSION – Between Two Realms* – is to release the set of Discourses that was presented to Paula during and after her many sojourns into the spiritual realm of the Astral Plane where she met with her Spirit Guide, Gerard, on numerous occasions. Paula's visits there were interspersed with her time-travelling exploits and experiences, which seemed very real to her at the time. These challenging and life-changing experiences were described within the pages of the last two books of the second Trilogy, these books being *ERROR PROFOUND* and *ERA of DISCERNMENT.*

Transition – Book One –

This book is unrelated to the seven-book Series that preceded it. **Transition – Book One –** reveals what happened to Mary when she moved beyond the veil of physical death. Her ongoing spiritual life seemed real to her at this time. Watching her own funeral as her loving family members tried to come to terms with their loss was confronting for Mary. Accepting that her physical life as Mary was over became difficult for her before she moved onto greener pastures as her never-ending spirit life resumed. Recognising and being reunited with her loved ones who had passed beyond the veil of death before her, appeared surreal to her. Arriving at her home on the astral level, Mary accepted finally that she was home at last after her long, long journey had concluded.

Transition – *The Final Journey* –

This book is split into four sections, with a final section entitled ***Guidelines to Self-Healing.*** Included in its pages are many spiritual truths that the ones known as the *spiritual warriors* may find interesting. There is secret and sacred information contained within the book and, once discovered, it cannot be passed on to another. Book One describes the Transition of Mary while Book Two contains Discourses that may be of interest to those who are walking a spiritual path in this lifetimes. Book Three contains the ***Tenets of the Law of One*** while Book Four consists of Earlier Discourses that were published at an earlier time in *Stella McMillan* books. These earlier publications were entitled: ***UNDERCOVER STARSEEDS*** (2000) and **THE REAL BOOK, REAL BEGINNING** (1999)

Poems

In this Series, several poems were included and these appear to be quite profound. One such poem is *Eternal Call.* Other poems are entitled: *Lamb of Love, The Veil, Timelessness, God Speed, Gentle Starseeds,* and a twenty-one verse poem called *From The Rim.* These poems came from *nowhere* in the early hours of the morning and I reached for a pen while scribbling the words hurriedly.

Stella McMillan Series

For information regarding the *Stella McMillan seven-book Series* – both in print and digital formats – as well as the books listed above, visit the *Stella McMillan* website:

stellamcmillan.com.au

Follow the links to: **Amazon, Lulu Press, iTunes and Barnes and Noble**

stellamcmillan.com.au

Also: **stellamcmillan.com**

Stella McMillan Series

To purchase the books of the *Stella McMillan* Series – both in print and digital formats – visit the *Stella McMillan* website and follow the links to Amazon, Barnes & Noble, iTunes and Lulu: stellamcmillan.com.au
Also: stellamcmillan.com

First Trilogy – *ERA/ERROR of UNDERSTANDING*
Book One: *ERROR of UNDERSTANDING*
Book Two: *ERROR PERPETUATED*
Book Three: *ERA of UNDERSTANDING*

Second Trilogy –   *ERA/ERROR of DISCERNMENT*
Book One: *AWAKENING TO AWARENESS*
Book Two: *ERROR PROFOUND*
Book Three: *ERA of DISCERNMENT*
Companion Book to the *Stella McMillan Series:*
Book Seven: *SUSPENSION – Between Two Realms –*

Transition – Book One – (published March, 2018)
Transition – *The Final Journey* – (published 2019)
– included in this book: Tenets of the Law of One

Earlier Books by *Stella McMillan*:
UNDERCOVER STARSEEDS (2000)
THE REAL BOOK, REAL BEGINNING (1999)
Tenets of the Law of One (2002)

Books by Beverly Bree:
THE GOLDEN AGE (1992)
FAMILY OF MAN (1992)
Several of these earlier editions will be re-published shortly in the book entitled: ***Perception***